PENGUIN BOOKS
1166
THE LOTUS AND THE WIND
JOHN MASTERS

Leonard H. C. Lait.

JOHN MASTERS

THE LOTUS AND THE WIND

PENGUIN BOOKS
IN ASSOCIATION WITH
MICHAEL JOSEPH

Penguin Books Ltd, Harmondsworth, Middlesex
AUSTRALIA: Penguin Books Pty Ltd, 762 Whitehorse Road,
Mitcham, Victoria
SOUTH AFRICA: Penguin Books (S.A.) Pty Ltd, Gibraltar House,
Regent Road, Sea Point, Cape Town

—

First published 1953
Published in Penguin Books 1956

Made and printed in Great Britain
by Hazell Watson and Viney Ltd
Aylesbury and London

To the Lotus
To the Wind
To Barbara

CHAPTER ONE

*

THE girl leaned against the side of the carriage and looked down
the Indus. It was December, and in the dawn she had been cold.
Now the mid-morning Punjab sun warmed her and sparkled on
the river and made her screw up her eyes. She saw boats moored
in the stream, and an English engineer working over a plane table
on the far bank. That was where the bridge would go up.

From behind her, from the other side of the carriage, a sharp
voice cried, 'Anne! Anne! Where are you? We're waiting.' There
were soldiers around her, talking in many languages, and bullocks
grunting, but the girl picked out her mother's mood and rebelled,
staying silent where she was.

After a minute she said aloud, 'Oh dear, it's no good,' and
stood upright. 'I'm here, Mother.'

'Where have you been? What—? Your father's waiting. This
is not our carriage.'

'I know, Mother. I'm riding to-day. You said I could.'

'Oh yes. With—? Very well. Good morning, Major Hayling.
You're sure you don't mind Anne's company?'

'It's an honour, ma'am.'

Major Hayling was already mounted. The girl watched him
smiling down at her mother, and detected her mother's bridling
smirk. The major's good left eye, on Anne's side, twinkled
cynically. His voice was soft and his mouth hard; he was forty-
seven. His right hand ended in a stump and a steel hook.

The ungainly column was already on the move. The travellers
wound out in due order from the ferryhead, their faces to the
North West Frontier of India. The wheels, the hoofs, and the
boots pounded the Grand Trunk Road. Anne's groom helped
her to mount. She adjusted her hat and habit, took her crop from
the groom's hand, and was ready to go. Her father had been
posted to the garrison of Peshawar, and she and her mother were
going with him.

She looked at the river again, and at the savage rocks by Attock
Fort, and said, 'It's the grimmest place I've ever seen.'

'You'll see grimmer.'

'I don't want to. Look at that horrible slate cliff.'

'That's called Jalalia. And the one on the other side is called Kamalia. They're named after heretics whom the Emperor Akbar had thrown into the whirlpool. That has a name too.'

He was a strange thin man, with unexpected humours and odd enthusiasms. She watched the engineer at the plane table and listened with half an ear to her companion. The engineer was little more than a pin man in the distance, but she imagined his face and warmed towards him. He was building a bridge. The bridge would carry rails across the Indus. Then the rails would creep forward again and bring peace into this desolation. These travellers who pressed forward now about her were the fore-runners. They were not settlers, but they brought peace and law, with guns in their hands and pianos in their baggage. There were soldiers, Highlanders and Gurkhas, marching in step; there were officers' families, with wardrobes and chests and trunks full of curtain material, linen, and crockery. The families travelled in carriages or on horseback; their chattels filled a string of bullock carts. She watched the carts, and behind them saw Captain and Mrs Collett in a carriage, and waved shyly. Edith Collett wore a heavy veil to protect her complexion from the sun. Perhaps she had not seen the wave.

Major Hayling gestured, and the steel hook flashed. 'Alexander the Great crossed the river a few miles upstream . . .' It was funny how, as she grew older, she could tell by the sound of a man's voice whether he liked her, and in what way.

The land was trying to speak too, in the rustle of a dry wind over barren earth. It was a low, harsh voice, saying, 'Remember, before you forget.' She remembered the dawn, those few days back, where the rails ended. That was in the Punjab, where peace had already settled. In that dawn hoar frost made the grass white, and the Highland soldiers blew on their fingernails and chased each other between the rails like boys, yelling to keep warm; and the little Gurkhas swung their arms around and stood hunch-backed and stamped their feet. Back there in India men tilled the fields and women lit the cooking fires. This seventeenth day of December, 1879, she had crossed the Indus. India lay behind her. Central Asia ahead. Yesterday she had seen a shimmer of white suspended in the sky above the northern horizon, above the dust, above the clouds.

8

She touched her horse's flank with her heel and trotted up the road. Major Hayling fell into place beside her, and soon they caught up with her parents' carriage. Her mother looked up crossly, but Anne knew she would say nothing in Major Hayling's presence. The major was mature and a bachelor, so Anne had to be treated as a sensible, grown young woman of twenty-three, fully ready for the responsibilities of marriage. One day her mother would say so in as many words – then Anne would seize her opportunity.

Across the scrub-covered plain approached men with camels. The men had the faces of eagles and walked with a long, slow, lifting stride. One of them looked up as he passed by. Anne smiled at him, expecting the salaam and the answering smile of an ordinary Indian wayfarer. But this was not India. The man stared her down, from pale green kohl-rimmed eyes. He carried a long rifle slung across his shoulders; a woman, shapelessly swathed in red and black cotton, swayed on top of the camel that he led; a lad of fourteen walked behind the camel; the lad had no beard, but his stride was an exact imitation of his father's insolent lilt, and he too carried a rifle.

'Pathans—Aka Khel Afridis,' Major Hayling said. Anne stared after them, a little angry, a little frightened.

The dust of the Grand Trunk Road slid back eastward under her horse's hoofs. To the right, out of sight to-day, the ramparts of Central Asia rose up, tier upon tier, in her imagination, as clear in her mind's eye as they had been to her sight that day when she had seen them. To the left the Indus plunged into the Attock gorge, after that flowing on down between rocks and deserts to the sea. Behind her lay such peace and security as India knew. That was a good life back there. Simla was there, and Robin had been in Simla. Robin was out in front, to the west, now. In front the land was jagged and the people harsh and the sky unrelenting. Together they threw a challenge into her face. It was here that she had to live and make her home.

They were still riding near the carriage, and her mother raised her voice. 'That's Sunbeam that Anne's riding, Major. She won the Ladies' Jumping on him in Meerut last cold weather.'

'Well, congratulations!' The major turned to Anne in mock awe. 'You must be good.'

Anne smiled thinly. She might as well be a piece of prime meat

9

in a butcher's shop. Not that she disliked Major Hayling, really. He was infinitely better than most of the old men her mother seemed to approve of.

Mrs Hildreth trilled, 'It is *so* kind of you, Major, to ride with us, and tell Anne all about this.' She waved her hand at the bleak landscape. Her trill rose to a scream as she strove to make herself heard above the clop of hoofs and the creak of carriage springs.

Major Hayling said, 'Ah, Mrs Hildreth, you don't know what a pleasure it is to have such a charming listener.'

Anne tried to keep her face straight but she could not. The major's voice was just correctly unctuous, as if, from the bottom of his heart, he meant what he said. She caught his eye—it was on the side hidden from her mother – and it winked slowly.

Her father looked up from the week-old newspaper that bounced and fluttered in his hands as the carriage jolted onward. 'Seen this, Hayling? Bad news from Kabul. General Roberts was right all along. I wonder what the Russians will do, whether they'll try to push in, eh?'

'So do we all, Hildreth.'

'That's your job, isn't it?'

'What? Wondering?'

'No, no, finding out.'

'In a way.'

The two men began a desultory, shouted conversation. Mrs Hildreth eyed her daughter and made surreptitious gestures that Anne should smooth down her habit. Anne pretended not to see, and in turn watched her father. He was fat and had become hot, and his eyes bulged, but he was nice. She turned her head and looked out over the low hills on the left of the road.

The slopes were bare of trees, the rocks ochreous and black and green. Here and there a small bush sprouted in a patch of yellowing grass. She saw no people, no crops, no animals. The land was hostile to men. No – such men as the one with the eagle face and the green eyes would stride over it and enjoy its barrenness that matched their own. The land was hostile to women and all that women wanted.

She sighed. The sounds of the men and women moving down the road drowned the faint voice of the wind. They would all live in houses in this ferocious wilderness, but could they or she or anyone actually come to like it? Robin had said once that he knew he was going to like it; but when he said that he had never been up here. Where he was now, beyond the Khyber, it must be worse. There, over the passes, in the snowbound sloping deserts under the Hindu Kush, the land must be as cruel as the fanatic Afghan mullahs it bred. The mullahs who —

She heard a popping sound and looked around to see where it came from. Her father ploughed on with his diatribe about the Russians. Her mother made a pretence of listening to him. Major Hayling had turned his head to the south, and his face was strained; he looked like someone who is trying to hear two conversations at the same time.

Again – *pop! pop!* The sound came from the hills. She heard a louder, different *crack!* – emphatic as a snapping stick, then a long metallic whir overhead that was at last lost in the creak of the carts and carriages.

Major Hayling said brusquely, 'Listen, Hildreth – shooting. Don't be alarmed, ma'am. Sergeant!' He waved his hook at the sergeant marching beside a squad of Highlanders just in front of the carriage. Anne's heart beat faster. The popping had sounded so far away, the long whir so close. Her father put down his newspaper and stared with a comical mixture of rage and alarm at the empty hills. Mrs Hildreth screamed, 'Sit still, Edwin, don't you dare leave us! Oh, Major Hayling, what *is* happening? Why doesn't —?'

'I don't know, ma'am. A blood feud, probably, and nothing to do with us, or they'd have been much closer. Sergeant, there's some shooting going on over there.'

'Aye, sir, we heard ut.'

'Get your men ready for action, just in case. Jemadar-sahib!' A jemadar of Gurkhas had come running, and Major Hayling spoke to him briefly in Hindustani. The jemadar saluted, hitched up his sword, and ran back down the road.

The excitement communicated itself to the horses. Sunbeam skittered about on the road, and the coachman jumped down to hold the carriage-horses' heads. Breathless, Anne dismounted. The groom took the reins from her, and she stood in the middle of the road and stared at the hills, one hand to her throat. The N.C.O.s shouted orders, the bullock drivers screamed at their bullocks; the sounds echoed back, redoubled, from the rocky hillside.

The crest of the nearest low ridge ran parallel to the road and about three hundred yards away. Sunlight and shadow and outcroppings of rock broke up the surface of the ridge into a thousand patterns which seemed to move, dancing, as the air shimmered over it. Suddenly Anne saw a man running along the ridge. From somewhere out there – she couldn't place them exactly – more shots came in over the road. Near her a Highland soldier yelled and fell to his knees, his arm swinging limply and his face twisted. Hayling dismounted and ran up the road. A score of Gurkhas panted past, led by their jemadar. It must be a hold-up, such as they had in America – but who would be foolish enough to try and rob a convoy that included a hundred soldiers, all armed?

She wanted to run as the men were running, to shout and scream and join in their active excitement, but she did not know how to begin. She remembered the frightening whir of the bullets and slid down to sit in the shallow ditch beside the road. Her mother was in the carriage still, shouting furiously at her father. Her father swung cautiously to earth and lumbered forward to join the soldiers. Anne snapped, 'Be quiet, Mother, and come down here!' – but her mother did not move.

She had not seen a single 'enemy' except the one running man, and he had disappeared. One of those pictures in the *Illustrated London News* would have made it quite clear – tribesmen with knives rushing down *that* slope, soldiers standing *there* in a line – tongues of flame spouting from the rifles. But it wasn't like that. Some of the soldiers knelt, some stood. Bursts of vile language and – incredibly – laughter came from them. The shooting had stopped.

She saw the running man again, this time clearly, and she saw the long jezail in his hand. Her throat tightened so that the words she tried to scream came out as whispers. 'There! By that rock!'

Major Hayling had gone, her father had gone, her mother was blowing her nose. No one was listening. Anne caught up her habit in her hand and ran along the ditch towards the soldiers, scrambling over the uneven surface, stumbling as she turned her head to keep her eye on the running man. She saw him crouch and raise his jezail. The sun caught the brass bands around the long muzzle – but his aim was across the hill, away from them all on the road. Besides, he had dropped down to the left of a rock

12

for shelter; from the road anyone who knew where to look could see him clearly. Whoever his enemies were, they were farther over to the right. She stopped, panting, looked in the direction the lone man was pointing his jezail, and caught a glimpse of fluttering grey cloth and, for a moment, the jerk of a man's head.

She found two Gurkha riflemen beside her. They held her jacket, tugging at its hem gently and grinning shyly. They pointed back down the road and said together, '*Wapas, miss sahib, wapas jao.*' Their Hindustani sounded as angular and awkward as her own – well, it would be. Gurkhas came from Nepal, Robin had told her, and were not Indians at all.

She caught one's arm, pointed at the lone man on the hill, and yelled, '*Dekko! Admi!* Oh dear, that one – is he friend?' Then she pointed to the right, screaming, '*Badmash* there! Not here, *there!*'

The riflemen at once saw the lone man to the left of the rock. They lifted their rifles while Anne shook her head and screamed, 'No, no!' and looked around for someone who could interpret.

There was no one. She saw the Highlanders and the rest of the Gurkhas struggling up the right-hand part of the slope. If they went on in that direction they would come to where the lone man's enemies lay hidden. She saw her father's broad back up there, and on the hill close to him the bare bottom of a Highlander whose kilts had been pushed up over his body when he had stumbled on the rock. The Highlander got up, and the wind blew the laughter and the clattering of arms and the vile, incomprehensible words down to her. She heard Hayling's voice raised swearing, ordering, becoming fainter as the soldiers worked farther away across the hill. Out in front of them a shot was fired, then another. The firing grew to a fusillade. The soldiers stopped to fire, then ran forward behind her father, swung right, and puffed over the ridge and out of sight.

The lone man still crouched in full view on the hillside. On the road the bullock drivers hissed soothingly to their animals. A woman in green knelt in the ditch to tend the wounded Highland private's arm, and Anne saw with surprise that it was Edith Collett, whom her mother called 'fast'.

Then, from straight up the hill, four Pathans broke cover and ran down on the lone man with the jezail. He twisted around his rock, aimed, fired, and dropped down again. One of the running

13

men fell, the others came on, bounding from rock to rock with their robes flying and the sun in their hawk faces. The soldiers, over to the right, could not see them. The lone man rose, turned, and threw himself with desperate steps down the hill towards the road.

'He's looking for shelter, he wants help!' Anne screamed. The two Gurkha riflemen once more raised their rifles. One of the running trio of Pathans dropped to his knee, steadied, and fired. The lone man curled up like a shot rabbit and fell headlong. Where he fell, he crawled and writhed forward still, and still held to the long jezail in his right hand. Wriggling by jerks and spasms, he reached a cleft of the rock. Anne cried, 'Save him!' and found herself running up the hill. She forgot the bullets and the tightness in her throat. Her mind was empty of everything but the lone man's face. He had been so close to safety when the bullet from behind smashed him down; he was not young, but his face was the face of a man lost, a man far from mother or wife or daughter.

She stumbled up the hill. The running Pathans came on. The two Gurkhas began to shoot, hurrying a few paces, shooting, reloading, running again, yelling to her to come back. She understood the sense, although the words meant nothing. Her mother began to scream once more.

One of the three Pathans went down, shot in the head by the Gurkha to her right. She saw his bearded face melt, and he was gone. The other Pathans made to stop and shoot, but after a fractional hesitation they changed their minds and ran on. She and the Gurkhas could not reach the lone man before his enemies did. Her breath pumped in her lungs and her face grew scarlet. The lone man lay sprawled on his stomach. A red stream of his blood trickled down the stones. His right hand moved aimlessly across the bare face of the rock slab below his head. He had let go of the jezail. The Pathans reached him when Anne and the riflemen were still twenty yards away. Knives flashed, and the Pathans swooped. A long steel glitter ended in the lone man's back.

The Gurkhas' rifles exploded by her ear, but their hands were sweaty and unsteady, and both shots missed. The Pathans, without stopping their headlong pace, snatched up the lone man's jezail and swerved around and bounded like stags back up the

14

hill. They ran with tireless, irregular strides, jinking, separating, coming together again, their robes flying. The Gurkhas fired twice more each, but the Pathans ran on. Then they were gone.

Anne sank slowly to her kees beside the lone man. She did not feel the sharp stones beneath her. She caught hold of the knife-handle in his back and pulled. The blade grated on bone, blood bubbled under her fingers. If she had been told to do it she could not have, but it did not seem horrible now. He needed all she could give him. Anger against his enemies nearly suffocated her.

The blade grated free. For half a minute the blood oozed out through the lone man's robe, then it stopped. Anne lifted her head, the tears wet on her cheeks, and saw the two Gurkhas standing beside her. They looked down, their mouths hard; one of them stirred the wounded man with the toe of his boot. '*Wakhli, badmash*,' he said, and shook his head and wrinkled his nose.

Anne whispered, 'It doesn't matter. We've got to carry him down.' She made motions of lifting the man, who lay still on his stomach, his head turned to one side. She saw that his eyes were open and expressionless. His mouth hung open, but he could not move hand or foot. He had lost his turban, and the blood was clotting under his long hair.

Boots crunched closer along the hillside towards her. Major Hayling leaned, panting, at her side, his good left hand on his thigh, sweat pouring down behind the black patch on his right eye. Five or six Highlanders came, gathered round, and peered down at the wounded man and up at the hill. One of them said, 'Weel, ye kilt this yin, Johnny!' and clapped the Gurkhas on the back.

'No!' Anne cried. 'He's not dead. And he wasn't shooting at us. It was him the others were after!'

Hayling frowned and said curtly, 'Get a blanket. Hurry.' One of the Highlanders shambled away down the hill.

Hayling bent over the wounded man and spoke to him softly, insistently, in a harsh tongue. At last he stood up. 'He can't speak. I'm afraid he's paralysed. I wish I knew where he came from. He's not from around here. Nor are the others, the two dead up there. If they were, it would be easier.'

15

Still frowning, he stood there, his hook against the metal of his belt buckle. Anne sat down suddenly and put her head in her hands. Through her dizziness she heard Hayling ask, 'What was this man doing, Miss Hildreth, when you first saw him?'

His voice was alert, a little hard. He had taken off his helmet, and she saw the grey in his thick dark hair and noticed how hunched he was in the shoulders, how middle-aged now and tired. She liked him better than she had ever done.

She told him all that had happened. Hayling shook his head slowly, looking down always at the robed man on the rock, whose bleak eyes were fixed across the road towards the north. The man lay absolutely without motion or stir. Anne saw that he was still breathing.

Hayling said, 'They took his jezail? In every other way it seems like a blood feud. But why should they risk so much for his jezail? You're sure it wasn't a modern rifle?'

'It was one of those long old-fashioned guns with brass bands around it.'

'H'm. And they certainly weren't trying to rob the convoy. Those aren't quite ordinary Pathan clothes. He's from farther west somewhere, from over the passes. Here he ought to be a Khattak or a Jowaki or an Afridi or a Yusufzai – but he isn't.'

The Highlander returned, carrying a blanket, and with the help of three other soldiers began to lift the wounded man, not gently, on to it. Hayling snapped, 'Careful there! He's badly wounded. And he's not an enemy.'

When the soldiers raised the man Anne saw the blood on the rock where his body had lain, and she knew then that he could not live, and began to cry again. His blood formed patterns, lying in a pool in the centre, in streaks at the edges. The streaks looked like letters of the Arabic manuscripts she had seen pinned up in Indian bazaars, like the lettering in the stone of old mosques.

She said hesitantly, shaking her head to free her eyes from tears, 'Isn't that – writing?'

Hayling knelt quickly and peered at the face of the rock. It had been in the shade of the cleft where the man had lain; Anne remembered his hand had been there once, aimlessly moving. On the grey rock, in darkly shining outlines, she saw the signs:

'*Atlar*,' Hayling said slowly. 'Horses – in Turki or some Turkic language. Horses.' He stood a moment longer, then said, 'Come down the hill now, Miss Hildreth.'

She did not want to ask any questions. The two Gurkhas stood solicitously over her while she was sick. Then she was back on the road, and her father was there, scolding and puffing, and her mother was there, talking, talking. ... The lone man was there, stretched on the rough blanket on the floor of a bullock cart, his open eyes staring at the roof. Hayling was there in the bullock cart, sitting by his head.

Her father handed her into the carriage, and she felt the gruff admiration in his voice. 'Silly girl ... brave ... lie back, lie back.' She heard voices up and down the road, Major Hayling's among them. 'We must reach Nowshera to-night. Push on.' The carriage wheels creaked. She half fainted, half slept.

CHAPTER TWO

HER eyes closed, Anne knew that she was lying in a bed in one of the Nowshera dak-bungalow's three rooms. The door was ajar into the centre room, which was used as a living- and dining-room by the travellers who spent the night in the bungalow. Anne remembered waking once or twice on the journey, then dozing off again, then arriving here and refusing to be undressed by her mother. She had undressed by herself and got into bed. Now it was dark, and if she opened her eyes she would see that the oil lamp on the table in the centre room sent a vertical beam of light through the door and up the wall near her head.

She knew her father was in there, sprawled back in a wicker chair; and her mother, sitting upright near the table; and Major Hayling – he would be by the window because the lone man was there on a cot, still without the power of speech. In her mother's voice she had heard the desire to protest against such a misuse of dak-bungalows, which were reserved for European travellers. But the lone man lay there. His presence and the forms of death that sat at his head filled both rooms, so that Anne thought: If I let my hand drop over the edge of my bed it will touch his lined face. She almost called out that she was awake, then decided not to. She was tired, and frightened that the dying man might be left alone with death if they all came to her.

She heard her father say, 'I still don't understand quite, I must say. By the way, where's the wounded Highlander?'

'In the cantonment hospital,' Hayling said, and went on to answer indirectly the Hildreths' unspoken complaint. 'The surgeon said there was no hope for this poor fellow, so I thought it would be better to have him here where it's easier for me to be with him if he regains the power to speak. The surgeon said there was nothing more he could do, that even the bandages were as good as he could tie. Mrs Collett did a wonderfully neat job – where are the Colletts, by the way?'

'Ah, h'm yes, Mrs Collett. She and her husband are spending the night with friends in the cantonment.' Major Hildreth coughed nervously, as he always did when circumstances forced him to bring Edith Collett's name into a conversation. The first time, back in Meerut, he'd made the mistake of saying what a good-looking woman she was. Now Anne heard her mother sniff, and herself became angry. Mrs Collett was supposed to be fast. Perhaps she was. But she did her best to look attractive, and she laughed cheerfully with gentlemen and had a sort of tantalizing scorn for them, which they loved. Why, on account of that should her mother sneer even at Edith Collett's ability to tie a good bandage?

'The Colletts are going to be in Peshawar, are they not?' Major Hayling inquired suavely. Anne could image the queer, curved little smile on his face, a smile that his listeners could interpret any way they chose. Major Hayling too was said to be fast, but, because he was an eligible bachelor, her mother did not mind.

Mrs Hildreth said coldly, 'I believe *she* is. Captain Collett is going up to Afghanistan to his regiment. Why *she* could not stay behind in Simla or Meerut until he returns, instead of coming up to Peshawar, I am at a loss to understand.'

'Oh, come, Mrs Hildreth, perhaps she wishes to be near her husband, for when he gets leave.'

'Major Hayling, you are a man of the world. You know perfectly well that she is coming up here because in Peshawar there will be many gentlemen whose wives for one reason or another have not been able to accompany them that far.'

Major Hayling chuckled. It was peculiar to be lying here and listening to her mother's gossip, just as though they were all still in India proper, when they weren't in India, and a dying man lay on the floor. She imagined she could hear his breathing, slow, faint, unsteady, under the voices in that room and under the muttering of the servants in the compound and under the singing of the soldiers in their tents. Her mind ran back down the Grand Trunk Road to the whole rushed, muddled excitement. She crouched again in the ditch, the rocky hill in front of her, and wished Robin had been there. He would have been so carelessly brave. Then she heard Major Hayling speak, more softly than before.

'Anne is a very brave girl, Mrs Hildreth.'

A chair scraped. 'She's a very silly and wilful one sometimes, Major Hayling' – then hurriedly, 'not but what she couldn't learn – in the right hands, I mean.'

19

'She's a very beautiful girl too. Of course, she inherits it, so —'

'Now, Major Hayling!' – more chair creakings and scrapings, and a high laugh. Anne lay furious and stiff. He *knew* she was awake. How dare he pretend he didn't!

Hayling continued, 'I mean it – but have you noticed how exactly like Hogarth's shrimp girl she is?'

'Well, really, I don't think I have, I mean —'

'Surely, ma'am! The wide mouth, the laughing eyes, her air of health and normality. And, if I may say so, a sort of provocativeness which only the utterly innocent possess.'

'Well, now, Major Hayling, I don't know, it never struck me —'

Anne could tell that her mother did not know the 'Shrimp Girl' and had not at first been sure that the comparison was complimentary. She would be thinking that shrimp girls were not usually of aristocratic descent. Anne closed her eyes and felt a flush rising in her cheeks. Her mother would have been furious if it had been Robin who'd said that just now. But Robin never would. Did *he* think her provocative, or – awful thought – innocent, namby pamby? She loved him and would be everything, do anything, for him.

Imprinted on the darkness behind her eyelids she saw herself standing naked before a long mirror. Her skin was smooth and creamy white, and she was beautiful – provocative, not innocent. But, oh dear, she *was* innocent. She had never seen herself like that since she was fifteen, when she'd looked once out of curiosity and her mother had caught her and scolded her furiously and been breathlessly outraged. She must look better now. Behind her eyelids she certainly did; and Robin was there, looking over her shoulder, and she liked it. Then Robin dissolved, and Major Hayling was there, looking with his one eye, but her mother came and prevented her from covering her nakedness with her hands.

She opened her eyes. She knew for certain that as far as her mother was concerned Major Hayling could do no wrong. He was a gentleman by birth, a major, and well paid. He had lost an eye and a hand at Lucknow in the Mutiny. Her mother didn't know, or care, that he loved Anne – but Anne knew, because she was twenty-three, and it made her care. She did not want him to be hurt. She had only got to know him since Robin went away to the war. He was not so different from Robin in spite of the gap of years between them. Only, Robin's shyness made people want to walk around him at a distance, while Major Hayling's presented itself and invited you to break through it.

Her father said importantly, 'This war, Hayling, what do you make of it? Think it will last long?'

'That largely depends on the Czar of All the Russias, Hildreth. He and his advisers persuaded the Amir of Afghanistan to refuse to accept our mission last year, which caused *that* campaign. We have no evidence the Russians were behind the massacre of Cavagnari's party this September, but of course it's possible.'

'And if they were, you mean they've got something up their sleeves, eh? You mean the Russians must have foreseen that if our envoy to Afghanistan was murdered we'd have to go to war again, eh? And that would give them their chance to interfere?'

Hayling did not answer at once. Anne wondered whether these questions were closer to his work than he cared for. Her father had no tact at all. At length Hayling said, 'That's something we have to think about.'

'And find out about, eh?'

'If we can.'

'I hope you do, by George! Those dashed Russians have been gobbling up Asia like – like hyenas! Tashkent, Samarkand, Bukhara – what's the name of that place Burnaby rode to? – Khiva. If we don't put our foot down they'll be on the damned Khyber!'

'Edwin!'

'Sorry, sorry. I meant —'

A light knock on the outer door interrupted him, and Anne leaned up on her elbow, trying to see around the door of her bedroom. A new voice said, 'Major Hayling? I've got the maliks here.'

'Oh, thank you, Preston. They'd better come in first and have a look at him. Then we'll talk on the veranda.'

She heard the sounds of several pairs of bare feet crossing the centre room, and the swish of robes; a long silence; the feet returning to the outer door, the door opening and closing. Four or five men started talking on the veranda outside her bedroom

21

in the harsh, deep tones of the Pushtu language. Major Hayling spoke, the others answered. Then, after a quarter of an hour, in English – 'That's interesting.'

The man called Preston answered, 'Yes. But not very helpful.'

'Not to you. To me it may be very useful.'

'Of course. Can the maliks go now?'

'Yes. And thank you. Good night.'

When Hayling re-entered the centre room Anne's father said, 'Find out anything?'

'Only that the maliks disclaim any knowledge of the shooting. They'd heard about it long since, but they swear no local men were responsible. They don't know the two men who were shot, and they don't know *him*.'

'Damn liars! Trust a snake before a woman, and a woman before a Pathan, eh?'

'I don't think they're lying this time. I can often tell, and of course Preston knows them all personally.'

'Very strange.'

'Yes.'

Anne heard in Major Hayling's voice that he did not want to discuss the affair any more. It was time she got up. She was hungry. She called out, 'Mother, I'm awake. Can I have something to eat?'

When her mother came Anne said she would like her food brought in to the bedroom, but her mother answered, 'Nonsense, we'll wrap you up and you can come and lie on the couch. Major Hayling won't mind, I'm sure.'

The servants came in to set the table. The lone man lay on the floor, his eyes wide open. Anne said, 'How is he now?'

'The same. I'm afraid it's only a question of time.'

Mrs Hildreth said, 'He'll put me off my food, I'm sure. I couldn't eat a thing with him lying there and staring. He can't understand what we say, can he?'

'I doubt if the poor fellow can even hear, Mrs Hildreth, let alone understand.'

'Well, it's horrible, really – ah, chicken giblet soup!'

Anne pulled up her knees and, when she had finished her soup, said, 'I had such a lovely dream. I dreamed that Robin was in Peshawar to meet us.' That would teach her mother to try and sell her to Major Hayling in her sleep. It would warn Major

Hayling too. But the major only smiled and put up his hand to adjust the black patch on his right eye.

Her father grunted through his soup. Mrs Hildreth said, 'Robin? Do you mean Mr Savage? I hardly think you know him well enough to call him Robin.'

'I do, Mother. You know I do.'

She began to blush and became furious with herself. She only wanted to warn Major Hayling that she loved someone else. If she could do it lightly he'd believe her, yet he would not be hurt. But she had to blush and simper!

Her father grumbled, 'That boy's too thin, in my opinion. Thin in the face, too. Sometimes I thought I could see right through him. His father, now, there's a fine figure of a man.'

'Colonel Savage is indeed very striking,' Mrs Hildreth said. 'He somewhat overshadows Mrs Savage in that respect. She is in Peshawar already, I have heard.' She sniffed, but the sniff did not have the same import as the one for Edith Collett. This Mrs Savage was Robin's stepmother and a peer's niece, and some thought her stiff-mannered. Robin never talked about her or about his father.

Mrs Hildreth continued. 'The son, this Mr Robin Savage is – I don't know – he makes me feel uncomfortable. So reserved. It's not natural in a young man.'

'Not usually, ma'am. But I know the family a little. I suppose you are aware that the young man suffered some ghastly experiences as a young child? His mother was killed before his eyes, I believe. Then his father had to push him down a deep shaft to escape from the Rani of Kishanpur.'

'In the Mutiny?'

'Yes.'

'Why should that make any difference? That was twenty-two years ago.'

'Twenty-two years is not a long time for memories. I was twenty-five years old in the Mutiny, when I got these' – he touched the black eye-patch with the hook – 'and that was in fair fight too, in daylight. Yet the experience has altered my life. It made me something different from what I would have been – what I wanted to be.' He spoke seriously. Suddenly flippant, he finished, 'Instead I became a wicked and cynical old man.' He smiled at Anne, and she flushed but could not help smiling back.

Mrs Hildreth raised her voice, harking back to the subject of Robin Savage for reasons well understood by her daughter. 'Nevertheless Mr Savage is not quite normal. There was a time, you know, when her father and I seriously feared that Anne here was becoming – well, too fond of him. Anne doesn't mind me speaking about it, I know – do you dear? – because I'm sure it blew over. When are we going to get the next course served? *Koi hai!*'

Anne tightened the grip of her arms on her knees. She minded very much. It wasn't all over. She would not know how to tell any young man that she loved him, and Robin wasn't just any young man. His eyes were like the surface of a river that moved and shone and hid what was below. For herself, she knew. She loved him. She would never love anyone else. She had not been blind all those years while she was growing up. She knew he was strange, giving nothing, asking nothing. She knew it was love that made her want to give him presents and tell him stories that would bring a smile to his face. It was love that made her – who hated dependence – feel that there could be no life unless she and he came to depend upon each other. She did not know what he thought or felt, and had not been able to find out. He would talk quietly with her, say good-bye, and return to his company on Viceroy's Guard. Sometimes he seemed to come forward and open up his heart a little, until she really thought he would ask her father's permission to pay formal court. Then he would step back and close down, all with unfathomable politeness. He had once said, contrasting himself with another man they had been discussing, 'He likes people. He needs them.'

The servants brought on the next course. Anne took a few mouthfuls, wiped her lips, and said distinctly, 'It's not all over, Mother. When Robin comes back to Peshawar on leave, he will ask Father if he can pay me his attentions. And when he asks *me*, I shall say yes.'

'You've been writing to him! Behind my back!'

'I have, Mother, but not behind your back. You knew I was. Do we have to discuss this subject in front of Major Hayling?'

The major rose to his feet, came over, and bent down beside the couch to take her hand. 'Miss Hildreth,' he said throatily, 'we all wish only for your happiness.' He closed his eye slowly, while squeezing her hand. She stared up at his face. Forty-seven

24

years old, sometimes shy, sometimes sly – a secret-service man who loved her but didn't know how to show it any more than she knew how to show Robin. And he seemed to know something, to understand something, about Robin. She pulled her hand away gently.

The man on the cot breathed louder. Anne forgot everything else and heard only the grating of the air in his lungs. She watched Hayling as he knelt by the lone man's head.

Her mother began to speak. 'I think —' but Hayling hushed her curtly, and the four of them waited in silence, and the servants by the door froze where they stood. The lone man stared at the ceiling. The front of his robe lay open. Bandages made of shirts criss-crossed his chest, and there was a bandage around his head. His breath rasped more slowly, more loudly. Cautiously Mrs Hildreth began to eat again. The desperation of the man's effort struck out at Anne so that she gripped the couch and prayed that God would reach down with His fingers and touch the man to lend him back a part of the power he had once had, just a tiny part of the strength that had sent him racing down the hill. He only had to speak to be at rest.

But the breath rattled in his chest and died there, and was swallowed in the small, secret clatter of Mrs Hildreth's fork on her plate. From cantonments a bugle blew a peremptory call – the new discipline marching forward to order the wastes of Central Asia.

Major Hayling went out, and came back with a mirror and held it to the lone man's lips. 'He's dead.'

Major Hildreth said, 'Poor chap. Can't you cover his face, Hayling, or something? As a matter of fact, really, I think you might have him taken outside now.'

'I will. Here, bearer, *madad dena*.'

Anne had not been able to see the lone man's face before, even when she looked at it. Now that he had gone and lay wrapped like a mummy on his cot in the cold outside, she saw it clearly. It was strong, deeply-lined, black-bearded; it could be kind even when it was stern. She turned away, stared at the curtained windows, and began to cry.

The next day they had twenty-seven miles to cover to Peshawar. It was cold in the dawn, hot at noon. The dust lay thick in the road, and the carts raised it, and young Pathan gentlemen rode through it like wild princes on wild horses, hawks on their wrists; the marching soldiers swore at them. The bullock cart bearing the body of the lone man travelled in front of the Hildreths' carriage. Major Hayling rode nearby, for most of the day wrapped in silence, sometimes tempting Anne out of her sadness with his anecdotes of the places they passed through and the men who lived in them.

It was an uneventful journey, except for a confused little incident in Pabbi, eleven miles east of Peshawar. Major Hayling had just said to her, 'This is Pabbi we're coming into. It has the worst repuation for robbery and violence of any place in the district.' Then, as if the local inhabitants wanted to prove how right he was, five or six Pathans burst out of a shop on the left of the road and pushed through the travellers, shouting and shaking their fists. A couple of donkey boys joined in, and some more men, and a man on a horse. For a minute Anne was frightened. The quarrelling Pathans milled around the carriage and the bullock cart; a woman screamed from a housetop; Major Hayling shouted angrily in Pushtu. As suddenly as it had arisen, the storm subsided. 'And there's Pabbi for you,' Major Hayling said, wiping the sweat from his forehead.

Then, as the sun was setting, they came to Peshawar. The buildings closed in, and the road narrowed to a street. Guides came from the cantonments west of the town to lead the soldiers to their quarters. A man came for the Colletts, and their carriage left the column. The bullock carts ground to a halt in the western outskirts of the bazaar and waited. Major Hildreth muttered, 'Damn that fellow! He should have had someone here for us by now.' But no one came.

When a tall, stately Pathan and a young British officer came walking down the road, Anne thought they must be the expected guides from the commissariat depot, which her father had been posted here to command, but they were not. Major Hayling went forward and said, 'Hullo, Gluck, glad to see you. Ashraf Khan, *starrai mashe!*'

'*Khwar mashe, janab ali. Joriye?*'

The Pushtu greetings volleyed back and forth like tennis balls. Finally Hayling said, 'This is the man. You'd better take a look at him, both of you, before having him buried. Yes, I've searched him. Nothing.'

The officer and the Pathan stooped under the hood of the bullock cart. The officer stood up almost at once and exclaimed, 'When did he get this? Look, there's a stab mark through the bandages on his chest.'

Hayling started forward. 'My God, there is!' He stepped back, and the two men stared at each other. Hayling said, 'Pabbi. There was a scuffle there. Someone must have done it then.'

'Yes, sir. Why?'

'Been paid to, obviously. We could find out who, but not why. They wouldn't have been told. We'll have to do our best to get something out of them, though.'

'Sir, may it not have been done to prevent him talking? The people in Pabbi might have thought he was still alive - and whoever it was that hired them to do the job.'

'Yes, that would be their latest information, perhaps. Look here, Gluck, get Ashraf Khan to put the body on ice in our office somewhere. I don't want to talk here, but we *may* recognize him if we ask the right people.' His voice dropped so that Anne could not hear any more. After a minute the cart rolled away, with the young officer and the stately Pathan walking together behind it.

Anne cried, 'Major Hayling! Who is he? Please tell me! I do want to know. I tried to help him.'

The major had remounted his horse. He said, 'You deserve to know, Miss Hildreth, and I'll tell you when I can. Good-bye for the moment, ma'am. Good-bye, Hildreth. Good-bye, Miss Hildreth; it's been a pleasant trip for me – except for this – because of your company. May I hope I shall be allowed to see more of you when you are safely ensconced in this peaceful and happy cantonment?' He smiled suddenly and added, 'But I really would like to!' waved his hook, and was gone.

The commissariat guides came, full of apologies, and the carriage moved. A wide, unpaved road led westward past scattered shops towards the military cantonment. Anne sat next to her father, facing backwards, and huddled closer into her wrap. A bitter wind from the Khyber Pass chilled her neck and made the lamps flicker in the open shop fronts. The sun had set; the twilight fell greyer and darker every minute on the walls and the road and the leaves of the trees. Down-country the light had seemed almost blue to her eyes at this time of day. Here the iron of the mountains hardened it and took away its life. She looked over her right shoulder and saw a dim, flat plain, and beyond that, high up, the snowy cliffs of the Tirah, where the sun lingered.

Frontiersmen strode by with long, lifting steps. The trotting carriage horses drew the Hildreths slowly past a column of marching Highlanders. The young soldiers marched on the shoulder of the road, their tall khaki topis nodding in time to the slow swing of their kilts. They trod heavily, seeming to keep close to the ground; they joked in the ranks, yet moved with much majesty. Their individual bodies and the sense of their collective movement were slow and stolid against the litheness of the Pathans.

A young tribesman passed; he walked as though dancing in the road, and sang to himself, and had oiled, bobbed hair with a red flower in it. Camels sailed through the dust, riding in like ships to port from distant seas. It was Robin who had quoted that bit to her – 'a port belongs as much to the sea as to the land.' So it was. Peshawar belonged to India and also to the mountains and the steppes and the sand deserts beyond the Khyber.

The camel bells tinkled, growing fainter, down the road. They must have come from Afghanistan – right through the war zone, perhaps; from Russia even, across the Oxus and over the snowy Hindu Kush. Sighing, she snuggled up against her father. She saw that her mother had gone to sleep. Her father put a pudgy hand on her shoulder, and she was comforted. He was fat and old and hardly ever understood what she meant – but he understood now. This breath of Central Asia smelled as discomforting in his nostrils as in hers. It was exotic and exciting, but ordinary people had to band together against it. If they did that, she and her father – she and Robin – they could make a place for themselves in the midst of its hostility. Outside that place there would be these barren rocks, bullets, the law of the hawk, the dust, and the piercing, lonely wind.

Her father whispered, 'Do you really love him, miss?'

'Yes.'

'I'll see what I can do. Shhh!'

At the edge of cantonments an English sentry in a red coat challenged them. There was a strict curfew. Day and night sentries guarded the cantonment. From now on they were prisoners. But that was silly. This was not a prison but a place

28

where there could be homes and softness and affection.

Before she went to sleep the face of the lone man appeared to her. People had wanted to kill him. She tried to imagine someone wanting to kill her – not just any Englishwoman, because of race, but her, herself, Anne Hildreth. She could not do it. Instead Major Hayling came to her. He was not alone, but surely he was lonely. And at last, Robin.

Robin was silent and strange, but when he looked at her, her heart rose up to meet his eyes. He said he liked the wilderness and all lonely places. Surely he meant that they challenged him, that they aroused him to go out and conquer them? Or perhaps he meant that in such places he could think undisturbed and dream of what he would do with the world and the life before him? She must find out. Particularly she must find out what he felt about her.

That first – because unless he hated her she was going to marry him and be his woman. She did not know what would come after that; she only knew that a crumb of it, a smile in passing, would mean more than the love of a thousand Haylings.

So – that first. Then she would force her mother to accept what was already a fact that could not be altered. Daddy would help, bless him.

Was love, when your man shared it and returned it, like being in the shelter of your father's arm? Or like the mirror, and your skin taut and Robin's imagined eyes over your shoulder? Robin Savage. Anne Catherine Hildreth. She was twenty-three and, oh damn it, she was innocent. She'd have to watch Edith Collett and try to find out.

She went to sleep.

CHAPTER THREE

*

ABOUT a hundred miles west of Peshawar a young man in dark green walked slowly through a stream across his path. His head was bent, but he was not looking where to put his feet. The cold colour tones of the water interested him. Examining them closely he saw that they reflected the leaden sky above and absorbed the green smoothness of the pebbles below. In midstream he stopped for a few seconds, the better to observe the colours. The water ran through his boots and soaked the trousers under his black leather leggings. Then he hitched up his sword, tugged the pistol in its black leather holster farther around to the other side until it was again under his right hand, and walked on.

A Gurkha rifleman walked two paces behind him, stopped when he stopped, and, like him, had been looking into the water. But the Gurkha, who was even younger than the young officer, was looking for fish. His uniform too was dark green; on his head he wore a blocked-out pillbox hat of black cloth in place of the lieutenant's black topi.

Robin Savage, glancing up, saw that he had nearly walked into a camel's backside, and slowed his pace. He turned his head to check that all was well. His orderly, Jagbir, was there, two paces behind him; behind Jagbir, the groom leading the charger; behind the groom, ten Gurkhas, now splashing through the stream that crossed and recrossed the trail; a long column of camels; among the camels, Indian camel-drivers shambling along like so many scarecrows, each man so huddled into a blanket that only his nose showed out. Beyond again, the trail curved around a rock and out of sight, and jagged mountains climbed up to pierce the low clouds.

Facing the front once more, he could see more camels, more Gurkhas, more camel-drivers. The path threaded down a steep slope to the beginnings of a rocky plain. He could see no more because the sky hung like a grey carpet overhead and wisps of snow-filled cloud trailed across the foothills. It must be snowing back there in the pass they had crossed yesterday. It was December 23rd, 1879. Two days to Christmas.

30

The camels kept coming along the trail, around the rock corner, across the stream, down the slope. Their loads – flour and meal and meat and ammunition and tents and cooking pots – swayed with their long strides. On one camel the load was two stretcher-panniers, called *khajawas*. A man lay in one, his weight balanced by a couple of sacks of rice in the khajawa on the other side. Robin had spoken to him earlier in the day; he had a raging fever from pneumonia, and the camel's motion made him vomit every few minutes. They ought to put him in a hospital. But there was no hospital here, and the Afghans closed in behind the last man of the force as it passed by, and followed up to pick off the stragglers and the sick.

Robin turned again to look back at the mountains. They rose into the clouds, and in the clouds they rose up and up, perhaps to the sunlight. In the mountains the snow fell, and none saw it fall. He quoted aloud, ' "In the calm darkness of the moonless nights, in the lone glare of day, the snows descend upon that mountain; none beholds them there, nor when the flakes burn in the sinking sun, or the star-beams dart through them." ' He shivered with the intensity of his need to see the secret snow. But, if he saw, the snow would no longer be secret. His own presence and the fact that he saw would take the magic out of the snow and the lonely wind that drove it. If he saw, Jagbir would see, and Jagbir would blow on his fingernails and say, 'Snow, sahib,' as if neither of them had ever seen snow before, and start collecting wood for a fire; the fire would crackle, the mystery would fade, driven out by cosiness.

The camels were shying violently as they passed him, and the drivers reaching up, swearing, to grab the head-ropes. The air was full of the extraordinary but indescribable noise made by empty ghi cans when their sheet metal bends and straightens under pressure. None of the camels was loaded with empty cans, so Robin realized slowly that Jagbir was imitating that inimitable noise. He turned his head, 'Jagbir, stop that at once! Do you want one of these camels to break a leg?'

The young Gurkha grinned shyly. 'No, sahib.'

'All right. Now go back and tell Naik Dhanbahadur to come up to me, please.'

'*Huzoor?*'

Robin sighed. Jagbir could understand every shade of meaning in a dog's bark or a horse's neigh, but when a human being spoke to him his low forehead wrinkled and his smooth face became painfully creased. It was not stupidity, though it looked like it. Jagbir could understand anything, and quickly, as long as it was set before him in some medium other than words – if he saw it, for instance, or felt it. Robin repeated, 'Go back and tell Naik Dhanbahadur to come up to me, please.'

'*Hawas!*' The orderly's brow cleared. He unslung his rifle, gripped it correctly at the point of balance, swung on his heel, and darted back along the column. He ran as though his life depended on it. For a second Robin watched him, then smiled and marched forward again. A British soldier would have trotted a few paces, stopped at the trailside, and delivered his message when Dhanbahadur drew level. But Jagbir had been told to go back, and he was going. Robin rested his left hand on his sword hilt and thought of Anne Hildreth. He must be in love, to think of her so often. He dreamed of her at night. She was kind and open and affectionate. She was beautiful. But – but what? He could ask her. Yes, but —

He did not hear the horse clatter up beside him. The rider's hail jerked him out of his reverie, and he became puzzled even while he listened, because the last picture in his mind had been not of Anne, but of sunlit snow.

'Hullo, Savage! Your company on baggage escort to-day?'

That was a silly question. He wouldn't be here among the camels for any other reason, nor would his company be scattered in little groups up and down the unwieldy, vulnerable column. He said, 'Yes.' He had noticed that most people could answer these conversational gambits with a pleasant smile and a light phrase. He would have liked to possess that knack, but he did not. He just said 'Yes' flatly. He could often feel his brother officers reaching out for something about him to hold on to, a hand, a joke, a shared sentimentality, but he had nothing to offer and was sorry for it – well, not sorry, perhaps; he wasn't sure about that.

This was Alan McIain of the Highlanders, a tall brick-complexioned subaltern of Robin's own age, with fierce golden moustaches and bright blue eyes and the badge of the Mac-Donald Highlanders, a raven on a rock, on the left side of his

32

khaki topi. He slowed his pony to a walk beside Robin. 'Do you think we'll get to Kabul to-morrow?'

'I don't know.' After a pause Robin forced himself to add, 'What do you think?'

'Bad business if we don't, *I* think. Old Alma's so damned cautious. With General Bobs besieged we ought to be going hell for leather and devil take the hindmost. These barnshoots can't stop us.'

'No.'

'I suppose it was difficult for him when he had conflicting orders, but when he made up his mind to disobey General Bright and go to Kabul I should have thought he'd move faster. 'Tisn't as if we'd had any fighting to do, worse luck.'

'Worse luck,' Robin repeated mechanically. He had not seen action yet. Everyone else in the force seemed to be itching to shoot, shell, stab, kill. They oiled their rifles ceaselessly and stared hungrily at the empty countryside, hoping and longing, in much the same way that they longed for girls and dances. He didn't know what battle would be like. It would come. He wasn't afraid. This was the profession that he had been born to, even as he had been born to his masculinity, to love someone like Anne. It would be exciting, but – but ––

'But we will!' McIain went on cheerfully. 'We will!'

'Will what?'

'Have some fighting.' The young man raised his voice still higher. 'The Ghilzais are gathering, I hear. And of course there are forty thousand of them besieging Bobs. I hope the Russkis poke their noses in.'

Robin was silent. Outside the thin, straggling column, Afghanistan stretched away, as empty as the Antarctic. Yet Russians and Indians and Englishmen struggled and manœuvred for these barren rocks. He resented all of them – including the Afghans, including himself – and wished he were somewhere else, away from all their strife.

McIain yelled, 'I hear it was a Russian in disguise who actually murdered Cavagnari. Why don't they have the guts to come out and fight instead of this dirty underhand – What? What's that?'

Faintly from ahead Robin heard the crackling of intermittent small-arms fire. McIain shouted, 'There! What did I tell you?

I'm off ... a shame you ... stay ...' The words came indistinctly as the young Highlander settled down in the saddle, tucked in his kilts, and spurred the pony forward. 'It's a shame ...'

The pony sprang into a gallop, and stones flew past Robin's head. Robin raised his hand in a gesture of goodbye and settled down to the line of march. It might be nothing.

A voice at his left ear said, '*Huzoor, Naik Dhanbahadur ayo.*'

'Oh, yes, Dhanbahadur. Do you see that little rocky hill there? I want you to . . .'

When he had given his orders he drew off the track to watch the baggage column pass. The firing was louder now. Scattered shots sounded from a wide area to the front and left of the line of advance. He listened with part of his mind, the rest of him intently absorbed in watching the faces of the men who passed him. He tried to read something even in the noses of the camel-drivers, which showed out of the blankets they wore. He thought: Perhaps inside the blankets they don't hear the shooting. But he asked one, and the man mumbled, 'Yes, I hear.' They were so many pawns. They were unarmed. If the wild men swooped down from the hill and rushed among the camels, stabbing and shooting, the drivers would hide until it was over – or submit to death if it came to them.

The Gurkhas trotted by like squat hounds, heads lifted and wide nostrils sniffing the air. Robin's second-in-command, Subadar Maniraj, marched creakily at the tail of the baggage column. Somewhere behind, out of sight, there was a battalion of the Punjab Frontier Force, forming the brigade rearguard.

The subadar said, 'Shooting, sahib. Any news?'

'No, Subadar-sahib.'

Robin fell into step beside the old man. After half an hour, when it was mid-morning, a galloper came down the column. He stopped opposite Robin, wheeled his horse around, and leaned down with a note. Robin unfolded it and read. He said, 'We're wanted forward, Subadar-sahib.'

'The whole company?'

'Yes.'

'Who's going to take over baggage escort?'

'We're to go without relief.' He thought of the helpless camel-drivers and added, 'Some of these poor devils will be killed if the Ghilzais get in among them, I'm afraid.'

34

'We'll lose our tentage, and it's going to snow,' the old subadar said gloomily.

'Yes. *Sais!*' Robin struggled into the saddle of his charger. 'Collect the company and bring it forward, Subadar-sahib.'

He cantered up the trail, Jagbir and the groom running together behind him but slowly losing distance. As he rode he saw that the force had concertinaed to a halt among a tangle of low hills. Many camels of the baggage train had already squatted down to rest; most of the pack mules were searching for grass in the rocky soil. The men of the fighting arms scurried about and shouted to each other. He saw the giant mules of a screw-gun battery trot out from the column ahead of him, and heard the jingling crash of load and harness as they went into action. Even as he drew level with them they began to fire. A shell droned out over the valley and burst with an echoing *crrrump* on the hills to the left of the trail. A small mushroom of earth-laden smoke erupted on the hillside and hung there for a long time in the thick air.

He found his commanding officer, Lieutenant-Colonel Franklin, in a group gathered around the bulky figure of the brigadier-general, the man they nicknamed Old Alma. The rest of Robin's battalion, the 13th Gurkhas, were scattered like dark-green bushes on the hills flanking the trail ahead, and among the rocks in the valley. To-day, except for the company on baggage-escort duty, they had been the brigade advance guard. The MacDonald Highlanders stood at ease in solid ranks of four; nearly every one of them wore a heavy beard, and many were smoking pipes while leaning nonchalantly on their rifles.

Lieutenant-Colonel Franklin said, 'Ah, Savage, we have a job for you, an important one.' He smiled anxiously. Robin smiled back not because there was an important job but because he liked Colonel Franklin and had known him off and on since he himself was a baby. The lieutenant-colonel said, 'The general will explain it to you himself. Here, my groom will hold your horse until – Where's your company?'

'Coming up — Here, sir!' He broke off to answer the brigadier-general's summons.

'Mr Savage, how do you do?' Old Alma shook hands formally with him. 'We have not been introduced, I believe?'

'No, sir.'

The general stroked his thick, mutton-chop whiskers. 'I have had the honour of knowing your father very well for a number of years. You have every reason to be proud of your birth, young man. He is still on the staff of the Southern Force?'

'As far as I know, sir,' Robin answered coldly. Everyone knew his father and regarded him as a great hero. Perhaps he was, after all, but —

The general continued, frowning slightly at the tone of Robin's voice. 'Now, Savage, you are to have an opportunity to live up to him. You have been in action before?'

'No, sir.'

'Ah, h'm. Well, we all have to begin once. This is important, perhaps vital. We may safely rely on this young officer's breeding to overcome his inexperience, I think, don't you, Franklin?'

'Yes, sir, yes, sir,' Lieutenant-Colonel Franklin agreed hurriedly.

'Very well. Listen, Savage. Our scouts, supported by the word of an agent who came into the column this morning, inform me that ...'

Robin listened and watched the general's face. Old Alma had a small wart on his upper lip, near the nose, He was big and blustery and was said not to know what fear was. He had a Victoria Cross; but he seemed to relish the fact that a nice man like Colonel Franklin was afraid of him. There were a lot of V.C.s about among senior officers, mostly won in the Crimea or the Mutiny. His stepmother had told him once that they'd put his father in for a V.C. back in those days, but he hadn't got it in the end; he must have been disappointed.

The situation seemed quite clear. Several hundred Ghilzais had gathered with the object of blocking the brigade's advance to the relief of Kabul, where a still larger enemy army was besieging Sir Frederick Roberts and his men on the northern outskirts of the city. Old Alma intended to push an attack straight at the Ghilzais ahead of him, first sending Robin's company around the right flank to seize a hill which ought to overlook the Ghilzais' line of retreat; and another company, of Highlanders, still farther around on Robin's right. When the main attack began to drive home among the enemy, Robin's company and the Highland company were to move down and attack the Ghilzais in flank and rear.

'Very good, sir,' he said quietly when the general had finished.

'You don't seem excited? No, well, a cool head and hot blood— This is very important, Mr Savage. I rely on you. I would like to be able to send more men on that flank with you, but I fear I shall not dislodge the enemy from their positions on the hills directly in front unless I use all my remaining force. You may go as soon as you are ready. Wait! Major Brown will explain about your artillery support.'

Robin saluted and turned to talk with the gunner major, while Colonel Franklin fussed around him like an old hen over a favourite chick.

'You're sure you have it quite clear, Savage? We don't want anything to go wrong when we are acting in concert with the Highlanders.' He dropped his voice. 'I've heard some of them, officers too, doubting aloud whether native troops are to be relied on in a rough spot. It's the Mutiny, I suppose.'

'Yes, sir.' Robin had not heard much about the Great Mutiny of 1857, except what he'd been taught in school in England. The new Bengal Army of which he was an officer, was anxious to forget the tragic end of the old army. His father had fought all through the Mutiny but never menioned it. Only his father's bearer, old Lachman, would talk about it; and Lachman's tales were not of battles or loyalties but of the horrors in Bhowani the night the Mutiny began, of how the great Colonel Savage-sahib-bahadur saved his, Robin's, life – by putting him in a sack and throwing him down a well, or something. But the great colonel hadn't rescued his wife, Robin's mother. Robin carried a picture of her in a golden locket under his tunic. She had been really beautiful.

Lieutenant-Colonel Franklin rattled on. 'That hill there, the one with the ruins or something on top – what is it, an old grave-yard? Can't I see some prayer flags? It may be anything, an old mosque perhaps. The Highlanders – the captain's sick, and MacIain's got the company – are going on to the next hill on your right. *That* one. Then, when our attack here reaches its objectives, you are to advance, keeping close touch with McIain. You're sure you understand, Robin?'

'Yes, sir, I understand,' he repeated for the fifth time, and saluted and went to find his company.

Quietly he made his preparations. Tom Bolton, the adjutant,

came over and asked him soberly whether all was well, then went across to joke with McIain. The snub-nosed howitzers barked slowly, ranging in on their targets. Unseen enemy began a heavy sniping fire against the Gurkhas on the ridge in front. Overs smacked by among the general's staff. The general took no notice, though the horses tossed their heads and one or two officers began, out of the corners of their eyes, to search for cover.

At a shouted command from Subadar Maniraj, Robin's company shook out into open order. With the little green-clad men to right and left of him, and his scouts moving out through the rocks ahead, Robin waved to Colonel Franklin and set off.

For the first quarter of a mile nothing happened. The riflemen advanced in open order at the steady pace they had practised so often on the parade ground back in the regiment's home in Manali. Jagbir walked by Robin's left heel, his rifle at the trail. The company bugler, who was also the company wag, walked three paces to Robin's right rear, his bugle slung and his rifle at the trail. Robin glanced around, and the bugler grinned and said, 'Rum ration to-night, sahib!' Robin smiled and answered, 'Only half a tot for buglers.' He could smile more easily at the Gurkhas' little platitudes than at his fellow Englishmen's. That was because he felt that the Gurkhas were trying to put him at ease, while the English were trying to put themselves at ease. Also the Gurkhas did not try to pretend that he was really just like the other officers, because they knew that he was not. They acknowledged his difference but accepted him because his father had raised this regiment in 1858. There were men in it still who had come to it then as its first soldiers – Subadar Maniraj, for one.

A single shot rang out on the hill, still five hundred yards away, which was the company's objective. The Gurkhas' pace quickened perceptibly. The bullet split the air above Robin's head with a decisive clap. He looked up instinctively, trying to gauge how far off it had been. At five hundred yards it was good shooting, anyway.

Laconically the bugler said, 'Miss.' Robin knew that the enemy on the hill had picked him out because of his height and his sword and had tried to kill him. He wondered what the man looked like. He would have a beard and read the Koran – or, more probably, have it read to him. He would have courage and

38

faith in his God – but where would be his joy? Was it devotion that caused him to fight, or love of this country, or joy of fighting?

A small wind blew on his cheek, and a long, musical drone passed down the hill behind him. He walked on, trying to hold the pace steady. They'd all be tired when they got to the top if they kept going faster and faster like this. He was worried about Subadar Maniraj's heart. The old man ought to have been pensioned off years ago, but Colonel Franklin couldn't bring himself to do it.

Keeping his pace, he saw the company drawing away from him. He motioned to the bugler to come up to his side. He would have the 'Quick Time' blown. Subadar Maniraj forged ahead on the left flank. The enemy's fire increased. There were seven or eight men shooting now, all of them invisible on the hill crest. The bugler had his bugle ready and said, 'What call, sahib?'

He changed his mind. 'Nothing.' The enemy showed themselves for the first time. Five figures leaped up and danced grotesquely on the skyline, their ragged robes whirling out from their bodies. Individual Gurkhas paused in their advance, fired, moved on. Two of the dancing men pirouetted to the ground and out of sight. A Gurkha fell on the left, close to Maniraj. The subadar motioned economically with his drawn sword, and two men dropped back to stay with their wounded comrade. On and beyond the North West Frontier of India neither the wounded nor the dead were ever left alone.

All the time the pace quickened. Robin glanced to right and left and saw with astonishment that the Gurkhas' legs had taken control of their bodies and their brains. Naik Dhanbahadur there—he was trying to keep a steady parade-ground pace, but he couldn't. He'd walk, then his strong legs would drive him into a run; after a few steps he'd drop back to a walk; five seconds later he'd begin to run again. The intervals of walking grew shorter and less frequent. The enemy's fire kept on increasing.

Subadar Maniraj was yelling something to Robin from across the hill. With surprise he noted that he could not hear because of the noise of the battle. Howitzer shells rumbled overhead like lazy trains on an iron bridge, the bursts reverberating among the hills. Bullets clattered, and the Ghilzais screamed.

Suddenly there was silence. The company reached the shelter

39

of the last convexity of the hill's slope. Here the Ghilzais on the crest could not see them. This time Robin plainly heard the old subadar's yell. 'Fix bayonets and charge, sahib!'

The bugler did not wait. He whipped the bugle to his lips and blew the calls. The green men slammed their bayonets home on the bosses, lifted their rifles, and surged forward. '*Ayo Gurkhali!*'

The bayonets glittered on the crest, piercing the lowering snow clouds. Robin began to run. Battle was as exciting and as awful as he had expected; but he was only observing it. He had not committed any of his heart to it, and little of his mind.

A Ghilzai popped up like a jack-in-the-box from the ground fifteen feet off and ran forward with a yell. Robin stood still and watched the man coming on, his knife raised. In that fraction of a second he saw the passion in the dark eyes and then a flicker of something else. Doubt? Why? ... The man had a beard. Surely this was he who had fired at Robin down the hill. Then the eyes and the thing in the eyes faded, and the eyes dipped and the top of the head dipped. At Robin's elbow the smoke wisped from Jagbir's rifle. Standing motionless still, Robin watched Jagbir draw his kukri, grab the wounded Ghilzai's hair, tug his head back, and with a single sweeping stroke decapitate him. Then Jagbir, laughing, threw the head across at the bugler and said, 'Catch!'

Robin drew out his binoculars and searched the hillcrest and the barren terrain around it. Ahead, the hill bent down to a fairly wide, mist-wreathed valley. That was the valley which, according to the general, lay across the rear of the enemy facing the main body of the brigade. Close to his right was the hill which was McIain's first objective. Looking back, he could see the Highlanders fanning out at its base in preparation for the assault.

Subadar Maniraj was at his elbow, his face grey-green and the whites of his eyes red. Those red eyes – you read about them, but Gurkhas' eyes actually went watery red in battle. And with women?

The subadar said, 'We've got five of their bodies up here. The rest ran away. Riflemen Narbir and Tulbahadur killed, seven wounded, none seriously. And' – the old man's voice grew angry – 'why didn't you draw your sword, your pistol, sahib? You might have been killed. I saw. What would your father say to me?'

'I'm sorry, Subadar-sahib. I forgot.'

'Forgot! Shall I send the wounded back under escort?'

Robin fingered the cold butt of his pistol. Forgot? He hadn't even been in the battle; he still wasn't.

The wounded. ... The brigade would advance down the valley in front of him after its attack. His wounded men would have an easier trip going down there then than going all the way back now. He said, 'No, give them first-aid and keep them with us, sahib. And we'd better get ready to support the Highlanders on to their hill. And have "in position" signalled back, with the number of casualties.'

'*Hawas!*' The subadar saluted carefully and limped off, shouting orders and waving his sword. Jagbir opened his haversack, pulled out a cold chupatti, and began to stuff it into his mouth.

From the valley ahead and from the hills on the left, whence the enemy had seen that Robin's company was now on their flank, the Ghilzais opened up a sniping fire. Jagbir rolled over on his side behind a rock and went on eating. Subadar Maniraj chased the Gurkhas into covered firing positions. Perhaps there'll be a counter-attack, Robin thought.

Between drifting clouds he could see a long way towards the Hindu Kush in the north. Only the thickness of the air prevented him from seeing the whole world, surely. The heap of stones that Colonel Franklin had seen from below was a ruined building. Faded prayer flags fluttered in the icy breeze, their poles anchored among the sharp stones strewing the hilltop. Robin thought he saw a statue in the building. If so, it could not be a mosque. That was strange and interesting. He could see what was happening in the battle from there as well as from anywhere else. He walked over towards it.

CHAPTER FOUR

*

A SMALL eminence rose out of the hilltop, on the right. There the ruin and the statue stood. From below, the ground had looked flat, but actually it undulated and gave shelter in its folds to all who did not stand or walk about. Robin thought, as he went, that Jagbir had not seen him go. The orderly continued to stuff chupatti into his mouth and talk with the bugler; he ought to have kept one eye always on Robin – also Robin ought to have told him where he was going. But Robin did not want any-one with him now, not even Jagbir. He could not be alone on the hilltop, since there were a hundred soldiers here, but he could be by himself. The soldiers were here, but they were about their business of cleaning rifles, replenishing ammunition, preparing for the advance or the counter-attack. With Jagbir it was differ-ent; *he* was Jagbir's business.

The old temple was small and square. Probably it had never been very high, and now it stood almost level with the stones out of which it had been made and many times remade. Robin stopped ten paces from it, wondering who had built it in the beginning, and thinking of the conquerors and the invaders who had passed this way before him. From the time of Alexander many captains, leading many armies, had come this way, burst-ing out of the turbulent civilizations of Persia and Mesopotamia towards the India that was Golconda.

The outer walls were now one or two feet high. There had been an inner chamber, and the south wall of it was still three parts intact. The statue of the god sat on a little cracked stone dais in front of the wall. Robin paced slowly inside. Chips of sky-blue tile watered the dull stones of the inner chamber. Those would be relics of the Persians. The statue was descended from another civilization altogether; it represented the Lord Buddha, resting cross-legged in contemplation, looking out of empty sockets in the almond-shaped eyes, towards the empty north. The eyes must have been jewels, for they were gone.

Robin settled down near the statue, with his back against the inner wall, and looked across the narrow saddle separating

42

the hill from that other which was McIain's objective. He could look down on it, for it was appreciably lower than his. The Highlanders were moving up the slope. No enemy opposed their advance. Probably a few Ghilzais had been there earlier in the day, but they would have gone long since. Raising his head a little, Robin saw a line of Gurkhas stretched on their stomachs to his right, ready to give the Highlanders support if they needed it. But nothing happened. The Ghilzais had gone – to join their comrades of the main force, to go home – spirited away into the troubled gloom of the mountains. The steady sniping continued on the far flank, the left.

The Highlanders continued their climb. Robin picked up his glasses and saw that McIain carried a naked claymore in his right hand and a pistol in his left. Many of his soldiers smoked their pipes as they climbed. Their kilts were pale green and white, the ancient hunting tartan of MacDonald of the Isles. All the white spats moved together in a slow, pulling rhythm.

He watched until they reached the top, passed over, and began to move down the forward slope. In a minute the hill would hide them. He wondered idly why McIain was going over the crest when the general had ordered him to stay on top until the main attack developed. Well, those were his own orders, and the general had said McIain's were to be the same, but they might have been changed. It would have been a good idea for the general to speak to both of them at the same time, since they were to work in close co-operation. Confusion over orders was fairly common in this brigade. Some of the young staff officers in Simla had hinted that the powers thought Old Alma something less than intelligent.

Simla was a pleasant enough place, and his company had liked being on Viceroy's Guard. They had had plenty of time off, and so had he. From Jakko in the dawn you could see half the peaks of Kangra and Bashahr. Walk or ride fifteen miles out, and the wind blew away the febrile excitements of Simla, the hothouse flowers, the perpetual struggles for place and notice. There were struggles for love too, but there the wind only sharpened his doubts. He had liked going out with Anne. He might have liked it better still if her parents had allowed her to ride all day with him so that they could pass beyond the reach of Simla's atmosphere. If there was any girl in the world for him, it would be Anne. If ... He absentmindedly touched his breast-pocket, where her last letter lay. She should be in Peshawar by now.

At the back of the Highland company a soldier stopped on the crest, turned, and began to wave a short flag in Morse code. Robin read 'No casualties.' The signaller turned again and ran off to catch up with the still moving company. The message had not said 'In position' or 'Reached objective' or anything like that. So presumably McIain did have different orders. Robin put down his glasses and picked up one of the chips of blue tile lying on the ground about him. A bursting shell had made a small hole, blackening and scoring the earth around it and loosening the texture of the soil. He dug his fingers into it, crumbling the friable stuff against his hand.

He found a hard round thing in his fingers. Thinking it might be a shell splinter, he idly rubbed away the dirt clinging to it. Then he brushed it with the sleeve of his tunic. A small silver coin shone dimly in his hand. He bent his head, rubbed harder, and turned the coin this way and that, the better to catch the feeble light. Through the pitted, encrusted dirt of the years the shape of a head began to appear. The head was in profile, of a strong young man. His straight nose continued the line of his forehead, ending above a short upper lip and a curved, sensual but powerful mouth. The neck was strong as a young bull's, the head set imperiously upon it, and the eyes were deep sunk.

The coin lay flat in the palm of Robin's hand. Others had thought out and fought out the battle for this hill; he had merely watched himself take part in it. But the little coin jerked every chord of sensibility in him and set them all throbbing. That face – two thousand and more years ago this young man had marched out of the west, but the years had not passed away from him. His cities still stood and carried his name. Perhaps that was not surprising, because he had built the cities of stone. The astonishment was that Alexander still lived in men's hearts, though he was in his grave, and a hundred generations with him. In Asia peasants referred to him as if he had just passed their way last week and might come again next week. The more desolate the place, the more surely its people knew Alexander of Macedon. A mysterious pile of stones beside the road, a ruined tower on a hill – 'Who built that?' Robin had often asked. 'Allah knows!

44

Iskander, I expect.' The fact that the tower could not have been more than three hundred years old only added to the magic. Other conquerors, followed by great armies, had trampled through the hills and across these deserts, the latest of them in the memory of old men's grandfathers. But those had become – nothing; while hunters of the pamir knew every detail of their descent from Alexander. They might know nothing else; the traveller, searching back beyond living memory, might come upon twenty-two hundred years of oblivion – behind that, at the beginning, the shining young man Iskander, Alexander of Greece, Alexander the young god of the world's morning.

Robin closed his hand tightly on the coin. This he would never part with. It could not have been left here by Alexander himself, although he had passed this way. Perhaps he had sat on this hill and wondered why he was going where he was going. Robin rolled over on his side and looked more closely at the battered statue. It was Buddhist and it was old, but the face, for all the almond eyes, was Greek. It had been copied from one that had sat here before it, and that from another. The face had served different religions but always the same ideal of beauty. Sculptor after sculptor had moulded the statue into the conventions he knew, his hands trying to preserve the mysterious grace before him, each time losing something, always believing that the original had been a perfection suddenly waved into existence by the dazzling God.

There would be a sculptor's bones beneath this hill – dead by his own hand, his spirit wandering about among the stones, whispering, 'Where is Greece, where is Alexander? I tried.' Did the Ghilzais feel the magic here? Could it not, if it existed, bind the world together?

And what did Alexander seek in the desert? If it had been the mere glory of battle he would not be remembered. Surely he came into the empty places not to conquer, but to find.

> *The secret strength of things,*
> *Which governs thought, and to the infinite dome*
> *Of heaven is as a law, inhabits thee.*
> *And what wert thou and earth and stars and sea,*
> *If to the human mind's imaginings*
> *Silence and solitude were vacancy?*

He did not know how long he lay on his side in his reverie. Shots close by the temple, much louder than the irregular enemy sniping, brought him back to the hilltop. He picked up his binoculars. Someone twenty or so yards away was shooting down into the declivity between this and the hill the Highlanders had hurried over. He did not need the glasses to see two men half running through that saddle. Coloured ornaments, which the Ghilzais seldom wore, glinted on their clothes; otherwise they were dressed like Afghans or tribesmen. One of them carried two rifles, the other, one. They walked quickly, then ran, then walked, somehow giving the impression that the battle was none of their business.

As he watched, one of them fell. It was the man with two rifles. His comrade halted, darted half-way back to him, and came to an indecisive stop. As another shot kicked up the stones at his feet he turned again and ran on in his original direction. Now three or four more Ghurkas opened fire on him. He made no attempt to return the fire but ran faster, turning and jinking, until he was out of sight. A minute later Robin saw Jagbir bound down into the saddle where the man with the two rifles lay on his face among the stones.

It would be Jagbir – slow-witted, kindhearted, animally aggressive, seventeen and a half years old. Had he no remorse for killing, almost as a demonstration of marksmanship, a passing stranger? That was unfair; Jagbir burned with fierce loyalty and affection for his clan. The man with the two rifles had not belonged to the clan.

Jagbir trotted back up the hill, grinning widely, and brandishing one of the dead man's rifles. He came straight to Robin. 'For you, sahib. A present. There's a place for it on your wall in Manali.'

Robin took it from his hand and turned it over. 'Thank you, Jagbir. Look, it's engraved, chased. It's an old jezail and beautifully made.'

'I saw.' The orderly shifted his feet, mumbling, 'I knew you liked old things. The Afghans ought to practise with their rifles instead of writing on them. If they did, we—' He didn't finish the sentence. He had already spoken for an unusually long time.

Robin said, 'I suppose the man's dead?'

'Yes. There was another. Got away.'

'I saw.'

Jagbir held out his hand. 'I'll carry it.' Robin handed the rifle over.

Subadar Maniraj hurried up, puffing and holding his side, creases of anxiety deep between his bloodshot eyes. 'I've been looking for you everywhere, sahib.' He turned on Jagbir. 'Porcupine's prick! Little lump of owl shit! Why don't you —?'

Robin interrupted. 'It was my fault, Subadar-sahib. I've been sitting in this old temple. I found – this.' He pulled the coin from his pocket. Maniraj did not look at it but gave Robin a sharp, purse-lipped glance, mixed of vexation, despair, and love. That expression had become familiar to Robin since he got command of the company.

The old man said, 'The Highlanders went over their hill and right on down, out of sight. I think we ought to go too, or their left flank will be in the air. They're just like all British troops – never look where they're going, never listen, chatter-chatter in the ranks. We ought to have gone before this.'

Robin leaned back against the temple wall, noticing now for the first time that it gave him shelter from the bullets that continued to crack over the hill and smack short into the earth. The sniping blew up into one of its little flurries. The subadar knelt beside him. Jagbir stood in the open in the rigid position of attention he had assumed when the subadar started upbraiding him. Robin motioned him down and said to Maniraj, 'Our orders are to stay here until the main attack goes in. It hasn't yet, has it? There was to be artillery preparation. I haven't heard any.'

'I don't know. The guns have been shooting. It sounds as if they're still ranging. No messages on the flag. Can hardly see back there now. But we ought to go forward or those Highlanders will get into trouble.'

'We'll wait a bit,' Robin said, after thinking briefly. 'Until the main attack goes in, this hill is just as important as the valley down there. If we go there'll be nothing to stop the Ghilzais walking along here and retaking it. Then they'll be on the flank of the main attack and above our people when they get on down into the valley. Look.' He pointed.

The subadar shrugged his shoulders. 'Very good, sahib.' He rose, saluted, turned, and hurried off. Then he remembered that the riflemen could all see him and that he was being shot at. He straightened his back and slowed his pace to a stroll. Robin watched him go. If the old man were to talk to any other British officer of the regiment in the way he habitually spoke to Robin, he'd be under arrest in no time. But then the subadar knew that the other sahibs lived in the same world that he lived in, while Robin Savage was half the time somewhere else.

Robin heard the crunch of nailed boots on the stones, sighed, and put away his coin. A voice from just below the crest cried, 'Hey, Johnnie! Whaur's the sab? *Sahib kidder hi?*'

Jagbir answered the speaker. '*Sahib y'heen chha.*' Robin thought: There must have been a gesture – no, there was no need, because there was also the other thing he hadn't got, the mysterious sense of clan. He had seen Gurkhas and Highlanders lying side by side on the hills, holding eager conversation, each in his own language.

A private and a corporal of the MacDonalds burst over the low wall into the remains of the temple. In spite of the raw cold the sweat poured down their sunburned faces under the tall, conical topis. Robin sat up and said, 'Are you looking for me?'

The two bearded soldiers drew to attention, sloped arms, and at a muttered '*Hup!*' from the corporal saluted together by slapping the butts of their rifles with the extended palms of their right hands. Robin saw at once that the private's right hand, his saluting hand, was torn and bleeding. He said, 'You're wounded. Here, kneel down under cover. Let me look at it.'

'I am only slightly wounded, sir,' the private said in a sing-song voice. The corporal added, 'We couldna kneel doon, sir. Yeerr Johnnies maucht think we were afrightit.'

Well, aren't you? Robin thought. You look like it. He saw the corporal's lip twisted under his beard and believed for a moment that he was smiling at his own joke; then saw that he was not smiling but sneering, and knew at once why. Robin himself was well sheltered from the flying bullets by the inner wall. He could get up. Perhaps he ought to get up. But he was not afraid at all. As before, he was not even committed to this – this emotion, this violence.

He did not get up. He said quietly, 'What is it, then?'

'Mr McIain sent us, sir, for to tell ye to come quick. We're a' but in the bottom doon yonder, an' there's a lashin' of these paythans ever' which wa', shut'n' at us. Ten, twenty, maybe. Mr

48

McIain says, sir,' the corporal went on doggedly, 'an' ye'll excuse me, sir, he says ye shud've been doon there an 'oor sin', an' will ye for the Lord's sake hurry noo – sir!'

Robin wanted time to think it over. Someone had got his orders wrong probably. But who? It needed time to work out what was best to do. He could not think properly while the two soldiers stood there like ramrods, the mist droplets pearling their kilts. The guns began to fire steadily on the left. That sounded more like the beginning of something. They weren't ranging now. No one could see far. He couldn't get a message through in time. McIain might get into a little trouble – but he, Robin, had a job to do here, and clear orders.

He said, 'Tell Mr McIain that we'll come as soon as I'm sure that the main attack is being pressed home. Those are my orders, and I can't disobey them.'

'Ye're no comin' right awa' on the split double lak' Mr McIain askit, sir?'

'Not at once. I think it will be within half an hour, though.'

'Verra gud', sir. By the right, s'lut'!' The hands slapped on the rifle butts. The Highlanders turned with a swing of kilts and stumbled away down the hill. Robin stood up slowly.

The firing against his company's position was dying down. From the valley the guns gave out a continuous thunder. Rifle fire snapped and crackled like erratic lightning along the hilltops. He heard the rapid pop-pop-pop-pop of a gatling, then a hiccup and silence. The rolling clouds now damped the sounds of battle, now drifted apart to give them redoubling echoes.

He waited fifteen minutes. The guns stopped firing. He found Subadar Maniraj and said to him, 'We'll go on down now.'

'It's time,' the old man muttered and dashed away around the hilltop in a wide circle, waving his sword and shouting, 'Fall in! Extended order! By the centre! Hurry, hurry!' – mixed with streams of abuse and blows from the flat of his sword across the backs of the laggards. Robin called out, when they were ready, 'Bugler, *double bajao!*'

The bugler blew the 'Double', and the line of Gurkhas ran down the hill, packs and haversacks flapping, equipment creaking, boots scraping and striking sparks from the rock, bayonets flashing here and there with a livid glint under the darkening sky.

49

In the valley Robin could see little. He was not even sure they had reached it until he felt the ground rising again. At his elbow Maniraj said, 'We're there, sahib. We'd better wheel right and make contact with the Highlanders. I can hear shooting.'

'Not much. Sounds like a few snipers.'

The mist swirled momentarily away. The company stood in an empty valley, among gleaming sea-black rocks. Shots and a stifled scream sounded from the right, the direction in which the subadar thought McIain's Highlanders were. But there was more firing to the left, and some straight ahead. A pair of Ghilzais charged out of the mist from the left and were into the middle of the company before they recognized the enemies about them. The Gurkhas shot them down after a brief hunt – 'There! There!' '*Ayo!*' 'On your left, fool!' '*Ayo! Payo!*'

Robin said, 'We're going to lose ourselves in a minute, Subadar-sahib, if we're not careful. Wait.' He got out his compass. After the needle had steadied he pointed to the north – the right – and said, 'The Highlanders ought to be down there, very close. Our main body is coming from the opposite direction. They are! Hear the guns?'

'Yes. Heaven knows what they're firing at. But the Highlanders must be *there*.' The subadar swung his hand to the west. 'That's where we heard the shots from just now.'

'Which shots? There's shooting all over the place. It's no good chasing around in this, sahib. Mist makes sound seem to come from everywhere. We are in the right place, and the Highlanders, wherever they've got to, are in the wrong place. Any Ghilzais who retreat in front of the main attack will come along this valley, from that direction, and we've got to be ready for them. That's been the object of our whole operation. Form a defence here, facing south.'

'*Achchi bat, sahib.* But —'

'I'm afraid we must, sahib.' Robin did not want to argue any more, though he knew the old man's mind was obstinately set on heading for the firing, wherever it was.

The company settled down in their positions, some standing, some kneeling. Clouds drifted about the valley, and soon, through a long misty corridor, Robin saw the dull lustre of bayonets working down a hill. The drab-coloured uniforms told him the troops were men of the Frontier Force. The clouds closed down again. From the middle of his company he could not see the outer ranks, forty paces from him. Twice, running Ghilzais broke through the mist, dragging tendrils of it with them. Then the Gurkhas fired quickly, and the mist wrapped them all once more. Every minute it grew colder. A bitter wind began to blow the cloud in grey billows past him. More firing, in fits and starts. He walked to various points of his line and asked what had happened. 'Some Pathans, sahib. We missed them, they veered away,' or, 'We got one. There he is' – and a body lying crumpled at a rifleman's feet. But only ten or twelve Ghilzais in all had come this way. The sound of the bullets clacking overhead changed. They were Sniders now, not the muzzle-loaders that most Ghilzais had. The brigade was getting close. Wherever the main body of the Ghilzais had gone, it had not come down this valley. McIain hadn't stopped it either, or there would have been the roar of a big battle close by.

Soldiers loomed up like giants in the fraying mist. The Gurkhas of Robin's company shouted, '*Sathi, sathi!*' The Frontier Force sepoys stopped among them, lowered their rifles, and began to chat in low whispers. Soon horses appeared behind the sepoys.

The general rode through and approached Robin. 'Ha! So you got here, young man. Did you have good killing?'

'No, sir. Only a dozen of them have tried to pass.'

The general gazed down in surprise, absently stroking the drops of condensed mist off his whiskers. 'I didn't hear any firing, of course, but I thought you must be getting at 'em with the bayonet. The Frontier Force and the main body of the Mac-Donalds certainly chased four hundred Ghilzais off those ridges. Where in blazes have they got to? Where are McIain's lads?'

'Over there, I think, sir.' Robin began to tell the general what had happened but cut off his explanation with a cough. McIain might get into severe trouble. He'd better say as little as possible.

The general said sharply, 'You think! You lost touch with him then?'

'Yes, sir.'

'H'm. I hope it's all right. This is a bad country to lose touch in, even for a few minutes.' He turned to the Highlanders' commanding officer. 'Findlater, Savage here and your lad McIain

51

lost touch with each other. Savage thinks your people are over there somewhere. Perhaps they've had better luck. But you'd better send out a patrol to find them and bring them back into the column. We must get on, bivouac on the pass to-night.'

'Very good, sir. Which way did McIain go, Savage?' The Highland lieutenant-colonel turned on Robin with a frown. 'How did you lose touch? Why weren't you keeping contact by the inward flank? Why —?'

Robin began to answer, seeking his words carefully. The Frontier Force sepoys formed up to continue the advance. The horses of the general's staff stood with heads up and ears pricked, nervous in the moving mist, like islands in the stream of marching men. Two guns of the mountain battery went past, known long before their coming and remembered long after their going by the steady clank and crash of their loads in the harness. Then all sounds died down to the squink of boot-nails on the rock, the breathing of tired men, the scuff of the Frontier Force sandals. The cloud and mist dissolved, the wind dropped, and thin, gritty snow began to fall.

As the cloud lifted all those in the general's party saw a man in a kilt stumbling down the western hill towards them. The general had begun to move, but reined in his horse. They all heard the running man's gasps and sobs. First of all of them it was Robin who recognized the man as McIain. He had no helmet, and blood covered the side of his face and hung congealed in thick patches on the front of his tunic. While the watchers remained numb-struck the young officer fell the last twenty feet down the hill and struggled forward on hands and knees. He raised his bloody head. His once-bright blue eyes were blank as pits.

Then at last the officers and orderlies around the general ran forward to support McIain, and put their arms under his and lifted him up. His tunic hung in ribbons about him. His claymore was broken off six inches below the steel basketwork of the hilt. Robin saw every detail as he ran forward to help. But McIain clung now to his own colonel's knees and recognized no one else. He babbled ceaselessly, all the officer gone, and all the brave, moustachioed young gallant. In those seconds he seemed to speak from one of the other worlds in which Robin habitually lived, and Robin felt very close to him.

52

'They're dead, nearly all of them. All. I fought till – couldn't fight. They didn't kill me. Couldn't. McPherson's dead. Graham. Robertson. McIntosh and McKenzie. McLaughlan. All the MacDonalds. Laidlaw.' He dragged in breath between the names and wept so bitterly that the watchers and the men supporting him cast down their eyes in order not to see the young officer's utter loss of himself. But Robin watched every tear and heard every sob and recognized them all. He did not remember seeing and hearing this thing, but from his earliest years he had known it. This that he now experienced again, not this time as a half-memory from babyhood but as a fully felt reality, was the root from which he had grown and must continue to grow. McIain spoke from the pit where men are not men but so many grasping fingers of evil; where love and courage, hate and cowardice, are all equally vile because equally human, all equally far from the silence and solitude of God. McIain wept on the gaunt sides of Glencoe, Robin over the Mutiny – he knew it now. Perhaps for a time McIain would fear man as Robin did. These others, who could not bear to watch, had never known what McIain had just learned. They would never know the pit. Or silence.

'We got – right place —' Colonel Findlater tried to help McIain up, but he needed to kneel and had to speak. Embarrassment flooded the general's face, and the soldiers kept passing, shuffling on under the lacy snow.

'The Gurkhas wouldn't come. We got over the – down into the valley – a hundred, two hundred. With knives! They never – rifles. And we – not — Not time! They —'

His wandering, blank eyes passed over Robin's face. Robin stood still, limp from the welling flood of his understanding of the young man who had been thrown down into the same lonely place with him. He could not have borne for anyone to pass between them, cutting off the almost visible reaching-out of his spirit.

McIain said again, 'They – they – they —' He tore loose from those who held him. He hit Robin in the face with the back of his bloody left hand, and again with the palm. 'You – wouldn't come. Oh, coward. You were afraid. *Your* skin!' He began to scream, grasping Robin by the throat and feebly shaking him.

Robin felt the sting of blood on his bruised lips. One loose tooth grated against another. The snow fell like touches of an icy sword on his cheek. The Gurkhas of his company stood behind and around him, watching, their faces set in utter impassivity.

He said softly, 'I wasn't afraid, McIain.' He would not say any more now. He understood. If he did not explain it might still all blow over.

'Yes you were!' McIain had returned from Glencoe. If he remembered now that he had been there, he was ashamed of it. When he spoke he had regained a wavering control over his voice. 'You're a coward, like all your bloody Indians. My men saw you. My men saw him, sir' – he turned to Lieutenant-Colonel Findlater – 'two of them I sent up with a message, asking him to come. He was skulking behind a wall on the hill. There was just a little sniping. Oh, you – oh, God, you —'

'Have Mr McIain carried to the surgeon at once, Findlater, and well taken care of,' the general said harshly, raising his voice to cut into McIain's ugly, panting fury. 'The matter will be investigated. And about those men, your dead' – the general fumbled for words, then blurted out with awkward brusqueness – 'I can only hold up the advance for an hour.'

Findlater muttered, 'I understand, sir.'

The general swung his horse's head and turned down the valley, not acknowledging Robin's salute. Robin stood by the side of the track. Along the column the bugles blew 'Stand Fast!' McIain had gone, carried away, retching, on a stretcher. Colonel Findlater spoke briefly to a captain of his Highlanders; the soldiers ranked behind the captain stared at Robin or up the hill. The captain asked some question, Findlater answered, and a sergeant-major ran to halt two passing camels of the baggage train. The camels were loaded with picks and shovels. The captain gave an order, almost silently, and the Highlanders began to march, wheeling left and climbing slowly up the hill.

Robin watched the fall of the snow. And what *was* he, if to his mind silence and solitude were just – nothing? The answer was always the same: nothing. This that had come about to-day might make Anne understand without his having to hurt her.

The rest of the 13th would not be up for some time. He said, 'Maniraj-sahib, see that our wounded are taken care of by the field hospital.' Then he began walking up the hill with the Highlanders.

A lieutenant at the tail of the climbing column said curtly, 'There's no need for you to come, Savage.'

'I must.'

He walked up through the snow, knowing that he was alone, although Rifleman Jagbir Pun, carrying a service rifle and a long jezail, walked in his steps behind him.

CHAPTER FIVE

*

A NEW, light wind whirled the snow across the crest of the ridge
that separated the main valley from the shallow gorge into which
the MacDonalds had strayed. Thin snow dusted the rocks so
that the gorge knew neither life nor colour – only the whiteness,
and the blackness under the lee of the rocks and under the
hunched bodies.

The first they passed lay on his back, propped against the
steep hillside, his young face turned to the sky and the snow falling into his open mouth. A single, fierce, upward knife-stroke had
entered his belly and slashed up through belt and tunic and skin
so that his entrails hung out over his kilt. His rifle and ammunition pouches were gone. And another nearby, his kilt up,
displayed a mangled red mush at the base of his stomach to
show that he had been castrated. Another, sprawled forward, lay
separate by ten feet from his head and the glaring eyeballs in it.
Up and down the gorge floor and on the steep sides, the Highland
men lay in the isolation of death. The corporal who had brought
McIain's message lay here. They had taken his kilt, and the
richly woven fabric would be cut and shaped to cover a Ghilzai
woman's head against the next snow.

The Highlanders who had come to bury their dead stood
huddled together in the ravine. No one among them spoke, and
Robin felt the current of their emotion begin to rise striking
from one man into another, spreading outward, doubling and
redoubling in strength as it passed. The soldiers began to growl
together like animals in a pit.

The captain spoke, the sergeants shouted hoarsely, the men
ran to get picks and shovels from the camels. In the bed of the
ravine, the only place where their picks could break the iron soil,
half of them began to dig furiously. The other half spread in
threes on the hill, sought out the bodies and carried them down.
The lieutenant stood at the edge of the widening grave with a
notebook and a pencil, and wrote down the name and rank each
corpse had held. The colour-sergeant emptied the first pack to
be brought to him, and thereafter searched each body and put

the rings, the money, and the tobacco from it into the pack, while the lieutenant wrote.

Up and down the gorge sentries peered into the snow. The diggers and the searchers carried their rifles slung across their backs, though all knew that there was now no need. The Ghilzais had made their ambush and killed their enemies and gone. An instant of time, an opportunity seized, had wiped out the general's cautious combinations and sound manœuvrings. The Ghilzais would not return.

Robin sat down on a rock and groped back through time to the fight in the ravine. The men and their actions came easily before him – the eruptions in the mist, the bayonets and swords, a few startled shouts, the overwhelming silent storm of the knife men. He sought further, below the actions to the emotions, to the place where McIain had been. Only there could he gain full contact with any other human being.

It was no good. McIain had come back to his pride and did not know him any more. No one did. No one in the world. Certainly not his father, Colonel Rodney Savage, C.B. Nor his stepmother, Caroline, for all her strange insights, because she had long ago turned her spirit to face his father's. She hadn't liked his mother, either; she couldn't have, or she would not have married his father, not so soon.

It was no good, and it was better so. He had known people and trusted them once – his mother, for instance, and his father. No clear image of that time survived with him but sometimes he felt a glow like a distant fire and recognized it as the memory of childish love. He gathered snow in his hands and waited for the bite of it, watching the diggers and thinking – had he actually seen his mother suffer the pains of death, and greater pangs before dying? Had his father whispered of love while pressing him down into darkness? The snow was no colder than the sphere of glass within which those memories had for ever enclosed him. Worse, inside that diving bell he must have grown away from the human pattern, because to him men and women were scarcely more comprehensible than fish. They would come and open and shut their mouths outside the glass, threatening him or enticing him out to join them or begging him to let them in; but he'd die if he went out, and they'd die if they came in.

He sifted the snow through his fingers and put his hand in his pocket to find Alexander's coin. As a boy he had tried to forget all about them, the fish, and live only on what was inside his bell, which was just himself. Later he'd taken to watching them through the glass to find out whether he was indeed different from them or whether the difference lay only in his imagination. So to-day would be important all his life, because the events of to-day had proved to him that a difference in imagination separated man from man as surely as gills or wings separated species from species, fish from birds. He had interpreted people's actions as a man might interpret a shadow play, guessing what had to be done to cause a particular result or guessing on from the observed action to the emotion it would arouse. He saw that one man smiled and held out his hand on meeting another, and knew that they called it 'friendship'. He had no means of finding out whether what he felt on meeting Maniraj was that same emotion, although he too smiled and held out his hand. Love of women, avarice, ambition, hate – they used the words, and he had to, but the cold glass lay between him and them. Even fear was different; to-day's fight showed that. When you were about to be stabbed you felt fear – that might serve as a definition of fear; but whatever it was that he had felt in face of the Ghilzai on the hilltop, and it had been strongly felt, it was unlike what Jagbir or Maniraj or Bolton felt. To them it must have looked like curiosity, the way he had stood there without a pistol and peered into the eyes of the man seeking his death. Perhaps it was what they called fear that he felt when anyone came too close to his glass and looked in as though wanting to break it for love of him – such as his father, and Anne.

He held the coin tight. God, God, I don't want to be a freak.

At that moment the distant fire of remembered love warmed him. He could go out. All would be well. Anne loved him. From her he could learn what 'love' was, and so love her. But – if he went out to her the mysterious thing in him would die, and he and Anne would have murdered it.

He had sat here a long time, by the corporal's body. A sergeant and two privates came. The sergeant said roughly, 'Move over, sir, we have to take the corporal to the grave.' No respect for Robin's rank veiled the belligerence in his eyes. Robin moved away.

He heard steps behind him, turned, and saw Rifleman Jagbir,

carrying the two rifles. 'Why don't you leave me too, Jagbir?' he said with sudden bitterness. But if no man could be a part of him, if his spirit only sprang up to meet the wind's, why did tears well up in his eyes?

'Where shall I go, sahib?' Jagbir asked with no warmth in his voice, but no coldness either, just wanting to know. Robin muttered, 'Stay.'

Two more men had arrived on the gorge side. One wore a shapeless khaki uniform and a clerical collar, and kept wiping the snow off his thin-rimmed spectacles. The other was a tall private with a bagpipe under his arm. The captain saw them and called up. 'We're ready, padre.' The presbyter took out a book, and the soldiers stood with heads bowed and topis in their hands while the snow fell on the cropped stubble of their hair.

Robin turned when the prayers were over and climbed quickly up the hill. The snow muffled the clang of the flying shovels. Faintly from the crest he heard the Highland lament, 'Lochaber No More.' It had no weakness in it, nothing of tearful sentimentality. It came from that place of the spirit which he sought so hard to find – from a strong, lonely valley.

When he reached the track the 13th was just arriving, the head of the battalion drawing level with Robin's company where the men sprawled at rest at the foot of the hill. Maniraj gave the order to fall in, and Robin heard Major Whiteman, the second-in-command, ask, 'Where's Savage-sahib, Maniraj?'

Then he came up and saluted. 'I'm here, sir.' The groom held his horse's reins, he mounted, and rode up alongside the major.

'Oh, there you are. Where have you been? What's happened? What are all these rumours? Blood! Are you wounded? Did you have a good scrap?' The major's large, round face peered half anxiously, half exultantly into his. 'Bolton heard there's been a big battle. A brigade galloper said nothing's happened. Someone else said the MacDonalds are wiped out. The general's sent for the colonel. What casualties have you had? *Are* you wounded?'

'No, sir. We had two killed and seven wounded taking the hill. Nothing down here. The wounded are with the field hospital. McIain's company of the MacDonalds was ambushed over there and wiped out.'

'Phew! All their rifles taken?'

'Yes, sir.'

'Phee-ee-ew!'

Robin said, 'McIain escaped. He says my company didn't go to his help because I was frightened.'

The major swung heavily around in the saddle. 'What, what! Did you hit the cad?'

'No, sir.'

It was no use trying to explain to any of them how it had been, or how it had come about. He did not think that the muddle would ever be untangled. McIain had been in the wrong place at the right time. On this occasion Robin ought to have hurried to the sound of the firing. On another occasion he would have been wrong to do so. British troops were always half asleep. So was he. Major Whiteman mumbled angrily to himself about the honour of the regiment. How would he react when he heard the other version of the story – the true version? Except that the Gurkhas certainly had not been afraid.

Robin saluted, drew out of the column, and waited until his company came up, then edged his horse into the empty space at its head and rode on. He rode with head up, looking into the snow and hoping to see through it, in some God-sent break, a vista of Afghanistan's immense emptiness.

In the evening they came to the camp site on the wide plateau by the pass. The snow had stopped. Under the low clouds they saw the hills guarding Kabul, where an Afghan army surrounded General Roberts and his men. The time was sunset, but the steely light took on no colour, and they could not see the sun. Perhaps the sun shone for a minute over Kabul before it sank, because a single, long flash sprang out from the hills to the north of the city. It was a heliograph and it did not flash again. The darkness descended, and there was no more light to bring Roberts's message to them. Officers and soldiers in the camp paused as they worked and gazed out over the rough, new-built stone wall towards Kabul, then turned to look at the brigade signallers waiting beside their heliograph, ready to answer; but there was no more light.

At supper-time Colonel Franklin still had not come back. He will be having supper with the general in the brigade mess, Robin thought, and afterwards they will talk some more about me. His brother officers ate in silence. Looking at their faces as they bent over the bowls of watery soup, he knew they had already

60

heard the stories. He looked down at the table. He did not want them to think he was challenging them to meet his glance and announce by their expressions whether they were going to stand by him or desert him. The honour that meant so much to them was a strange thing. Up to a point it required them to uphold their friends, right or wrong; beyond that undefinable point it required them to find the offence unforgivable, to cut as cruelly as they could. Anyway, they were good fellows, and he did not want to embarrass them. It was possible that he and they had drawn closer now than ever before. For once they were all thinking about the same thing. It would not last for long, because already Shelley's lines were coming between him and this sad affair. Soon he'd be away, to leave them worrying about him and never, never understanding.

When Bolton, the good adjutant, began to talk about the shooting prospects in Manali for the next season the others took him up in eager relief. Robin finished his meal quickly. The colonel did not return. Robin pushed back his stool, formally said, 'Good night, sir,' to Major Whiteman, and left the dining tent. In the anteroom tent he gathered up his sword from the pile on a folding table and buckled it on. His pistol belt he wore all the time, like the other officers. He went out.

The battalion held the long, eastern perimeter of the camp. He walked slowly about among the rough shelters of his company. Most of the men were asleep. He stood at the sentry posts behind the walls and asked the sentries if all was well. They watched the darkness with unstraining Mongolian eyes and did not turn their heads to answer him. All was well. They stamped their feet against the cold. It was impossible to tell from their tone whether they had decided to judge him or not. Perhaps some of them were wondering whether he might not be a coward. His affection for them brought him back unwillingly to the incidents of the morning. Old Maniraj was so worried that at stand-to he could hardly speak properly.

The left flank of the company lay in the angle where the MacDonald's perimeter began. He heard angry voices raised there and walked over. Soon he could make out clearly what they were saying.

'Och, awa'! Git oot of oor lines, ye bluidy little mon. Ye're no better than the niggers, after a'!'

61

The brigade buglers had not yet blown 'Lights Out'. Dim lamps hung from the ridge-poles of officers' tents. Robin saw three big Highlanders, their rifles and fixed bayonets slung on their right shoulders, and a single Gurkha. For a second he could not understand. Normally the Highlanders were pleased to have the Gurkhas visit them in their lines. Other Indian troops they never pretended to like, but Gurkha riflemen were even allowed to enter those Wet Canteens religiously reserved for British troops, and to order their own rum and pay for it. Indian sepoys were 'niggers' or 'natives'; Gurkhas were 'Johnny'.

Then Robin understood and began to be angry. The Gurkha's back was to him. How could the poor devil know that he was to be held responsible for what one of his officers had done or failed to do?

Hurrying forward, he heard Jagbir's voice spitting in cold, furious Gurkhali. 'It wasn't our sahib's fault. It was yours! Why didn't he obey his orders?'

Jagbir did understand after all. No one in the brigade could be thinking of anything else. Jagbir did not know a word of English. It was touching beyond belief. Robin wanted to cry, but he could not interfere with this, and he stood back in the shadow of a tent. One of the Highlanders gave Jagbir a rough push with his hand and said, 'Get on awa'!' Jagbir clapped his hands to his right hip drew his kukri, and stood on guard, defying them to touch him again. The Highlanders unslung their rifles quickly.

Suddenly a change came over the quarrel. Through the mist blurring his eyes Robin saw the reason. Jagbir *did* look exactly like a bullpup about to take on three grown Saint Bernards. The biggest Highlander broke into a guffaw and shouted, '*Ye're* a braw yin. Ah apawlogize. It's onny yer officer we dinna like. On behaff of the MacDonald Highlanders, will ye honour us by takkin' a drap wi' us?'

They threw their arms around Jagbir, who put up his kukri, chuckled as suddenly as he had become fighting mad, and went with them. As he went he said earnestly in Gurkhali, 'Your sahib should have stayed on the hill.' The Highlanders said, 'Och, let's forget it, mon.' None of them had seen Robin. He turned and went back to pacing the perimeter.

Soon a bagpipe squealed and droned from the Highlanders' lines, then struck into the slow march 'Soldier, lay doon on your wee pickle strae.' All lights went out, one by one. For ten min-utes the piper marched in and out among the tents and shelters and jumbled piles of baggage. The tune died in a squeal of ex-pelled air, and the camp was silent.

At midnight it began to snow again. The snow fell faster than by day, and in big, soft flakes, sheeting the squatting camels and the mules in their lines, and the churned mud of the camp. Intermittently the air shook soundlessly to the vibration of distant guns, where Roberts fought for his life in Kabul.

An hour before dawn the infantry bugles blared and the artillery trumpets screamed 'Reveille'. Minutes afterwards, while the camp came bustling awake, the MacDonald pipers marched up and down to the relentless lift of 'Hey, Johnnie Cope, are ye wakin' yet?' Robin did not feel cold or tired or hungry and did not go to breakfast. Later an orderly came for him. Everywhere the tents were coming down, the shelters being packed away, the baggage loaded. Bubbling camels and shouting drivers sur-rounded the anteroom tent, which was still standing. Robin found Lieutenant-Colonel Franklin inside. There was no furni-ture left except a folding table and a Roorkee chair, in which the colonel sat. He was drumming his fingers on the table as Robin went in and saluted. Robin thought he was not angry, in spite of the grimness of his face, but only worried and battling with something he did not understand, perhaps did not even be-lieve.

The colonel said, 'The general's very perturbed about what happened yesterday, Robin. Look here, tell me in your own words what really happened. It's all so damn muddling.' He smiled nervously and continued to drum his fingers on the table.

Without hesitation Robin answered him. He did not want to fight – he was not fighting or blaming anyone now – but after what he had seen last night, of Jagbir and the Highlanders, he had to tell the truth.

When he finished, Colonel Franklin stopped drumming on the table and began to crack the joints of his fingers. 'That's better than I'd heard – than the general believes, unfortunately. Why didn't you say so? Perhaps you ought to have gone with McIain anyway. Or ought to have marched to the sound of firing – any firing. I don't know. It's a matter of opinion, unfortunately. Colonel Findlater is pressing for a court of inquiry. Court martial, he said, but there'd have to be a court of inquiry first, of course. Your father —'

'My father's got nothing to do with this, sir,' Robin snapped, suddenly sharp and bitterly angry. 'I'll stand on my own feet. I may have made a bad mistake. But I'm not a coward, nor is any man in my company.'

'No, no, Robin, of course not. Don't speak to me like that, boy! No one will ever know now who was in the proper valley, unfortunately.'

Colonel Franklin continued to crack his joints. Outside, the mess havildar bawled abuse at a rifleman for packing the sahib's crockery without due care.

'Did you confer with Maniraj? Did he urge you to do what you did, against your own judgement?'

'No, sir,' Robin said coldly. 'In fact, I disregarded Maniraj's advice.'

'Of course he wouldn't get into any trouble. It's your responsibility. But it might take out the sting – out of the talk. Just inexperience, they would say. And of course we in the regiment would know that it wasn't really Maniraj's fault. I mean, it wouldn't affect his chances for promotion to S.M., though you know as well as I that he hasn't got any.'

'Maniraj had nothing to do with my decisions, sir.'

'Well, I've talked to him. He says he held you back when you wanted to go forward. Of course it is still your responsibility, but the talk, the bitterness, will be much less —'

'Sir, Subadar Maniraj is lying.'

It was horrible that Maniraj should be brought to lying for him. That was the trap in all human relations. Out of sweetness there always grew corruption. In this case, from love, Maniraj had committed the first sin against God – lying. And so had he himself. Yesterday, on behalf of McIain.

'Well —' The colonel sat motionless for a minute. Then he said, 'I don't think you're a coward, Robin. But you're rather a prig sometimes. And extremely selfish.' He jumped up and jammed his topi on his head. 'The general's going to think about it. If it wasn't for your – well, I must be going.' He paused at the tent flap. 'Remember that it isn't just between you and McIain. It's between the British and Bengal Armies now. It couldn't be worse.'

'I know, sir.'

The colonel went out, and the tent flap dropped. For a minute Robin stood quietly in the gloom, then he too went out and walked to his company. They were fallen in and ready to move. On the trail the pace was fast. The wind blew strong from the west, driving wet snow into their teeth so that they gasped for breath on the occasional ascents. For the most part the trail led down. Signs of habitation increased. Dogs barked from nearby villages. They had come out of the waste and were approaching the city.

Near midday firing broke out close ahead. The column closed up and came to a fitful halt. Robin remembered that it was Christmas Eve. He rode slowly up to battalion headquarters to find the cause of the delay. The other company commanders were there already. The group of horses danced in the road, spattering the slush from under their hoofs. The officers talked loudly together to keep themselves warm. 'Who's firing?' ... 'They'll swamp him if we don't get on.' ... 'Why don't we attack *en masse*? Why don't ...?'. They peered into the snow as though they could see the four or five miles to Kabul. Visibility was two hundred yards, and the snow had swallowed up the houses, the mountains, and the plain.

A galloper came down the column, the same Sikh trooper who had come yesterday to Robin from brigade headquarters. Colonel Franklin looked up quickly when he had read the message. He said, 'Savage, report to the general at once. I'll have your company sent up to you at the double.' He took off his topi and wiped the sweat from his forehead. As Robin swung his horse the colonel followed him until they were out of the other officers' hearing. Then he said in a trembling voice, 'Robin, it's providential. And it's damned good of the general. Don't make any mistake this time, lad. We're with you, all the Thirteenth.' He waved his topi, and Robin settled down to the short ride, Jagbir and the groom running at his stirrups.

At headquarters the brigade pennon hung limp and wet from the orderly's lance. The general, mounted among his mounted staff, received Robin with a stiff smile. 'Mr Savage, I have a task for you. I take it that you will find it welcome?'

Robin said, 'Yes' flatly. The general thought that he was conferring a great favour by giving him this chance to retrieve himself. So did all the rest of them. And it was true; but some Gurkhas were going to be killed, and the purpose of their death would be to save Colonel Rodney Savage, C.B., from the embarrassment of having his son court-martialled for cowardice.

The general said, 'Good. That hill – you can just see the base of it through the snow – commands our road to Kabul. Frontier Force scouts have been up. There are about fifty ghazis behind a low wall on top. I am going to give them five minutes' shelling, then I want you to lead your company' – he emphasized the word 'lead' slightly – 'and take the hill at the point of the bayonet. Is that clear?'

'Yes, sir.'

'Good. Be quick, now. There go the guns. And – ah, h'm – good luck. You know —' He turned brusquely away, his heavy face flushed, apparently unable to finish his sentence. Somewhere nearby an unseen little dog was barking, setting the staff officers' horses to dancing and rearing up. Robin saluted the general's back and frowned at Jagbir. The dog stopped barking. The company had already arrived and was waiting by the side of the road, every man shaking with expressionless laughter. Six or seven other riflemen began to imitate dogs, and for a minute there was a noise like a dog-fight in the ranks. All the time the guns roared from behind, unseen, and sent their shells whistling through the snow overhead.

When Robin explained the orders to Maniraj, the subadar's old eyes glowed and the anxiety went out of his face. The rifle-men moved to their places, and the yapping died away They drew their bayonets and fixed them on their rifles. Robin saw the reddening of their eyes as they ran to get ready. Some of them were going to die or lose a limb for the sake of Colonel Savage's self-esteem, but they did not look at it that way. That was an anæmia of his own imagination – his priggish imagination? The Gurkhas were going to show the MacDonalds of the Isles and Old Alma and the fanatical ghazis that an order was an order. They were spread out now, and all was ready for the signal.

Robin took out his pistol to make sure that it was loaded. He did not think he would be able to kill anyone, but he had better look as if he meant to. The snow had caked into ice on the butt, and the pistol slipped from his hand. It fell, hammer down, against a jutting outcrop of rock and exploded. Robin heard the roar and felt the explosion as a slap in the face, but he did not know why he was sitting in the snow. He did not know how or why he had grabbed the pistol and now held it smoking in his hand. Light red blood ran out strongly from his right leg, staining the snow around him.

From their expressions as they came running to him he knew that no one had seen the pistol slip from his hand. No one in the world had seen it, though he had been standing among them. In that one second they had all been looking to something else – even Maniraj, even Jagbir.

With a gigantic effort he stopped himself from crying out. It was not physical pain, for as yet he suffered none. It was not even anger that they could believe he would inflict a wound on himself rather than face the ghazis. With gritted teeth and dry eyes, he held down a swelling melancholy greater than that which inspired the lament of 'Lochaber No More'. He had to live among people, being alive and human, and he was not equipped with the means for the task.

He tried to get up, but the bullet had torn the muscles of his leg. At last he managed it and hopped forward, leaning on Jagbir's shoulder. 'Advance, Subadar-sahib,' he cried. 'Advance! Quick! I'm all right.' The bugler blew, the subadar yelled the men into a run; but the general's curt voice was imperative.

'Go and stop him, Green. Let his subadar take the company up. Tell him to wait there beside the road until a surgeon arrives.'

The company disappeared into the driving snow. The last Robin saw of them was Maniraj's tearful face, before the subadar turned and stumbled away up the slope. The general and his staff moved a hundred yards farther along the road and out of sight.

His leg began to throb. Major Green had bandaged it with rough skill in a silence that showed that he did not trust himself to speak. Officers and orderlies came up from the rear and passed by on their way to headquarters. None of them had been here when it happened. How then, did they know what face to wear as they passed? Mostly they became absorbed in earnest talk as they drew near, or saw something interesting in the snow flurries on the other side of the road.

At Robin's side a hoarse voice said, 'Sahib, what's this written on the jezail?'

He turned and stared into Jagbir's eyes. 'Why aren't you with the company? Are you afraid? *Kaphar hunnu bhanda marnu ramro*, isn't it?' Bitterly he repeated the Gurkha proverb, 'It is better to die than be a coward.'

'I'm not afraid, sahib,' Jagbir answered quietly, his dark eyes sharpening minutely at the insult, then opening again. 'The jezail. There's writing on it.'

Robin clenched his fingers. He must push down the melancholy. He must not let anger replace it. That would be too easy. He said carefully, 'I know, Jagbir. You mean the chasing on the barrel? It's a few lines from the Koran, their holy book, written in Arabic.'

'Not that. Here. Look.'

Jagbir pointed to the underside of the stock, where a man about to fire the jezail would have gripped it. Robin took the weapon and wiped off the snowflakes with his finger. See the nice toy! He could pretend; he could do nearly anything now, not to hurt Jagbir. He said, 'Yes. You're right.' Indeed someone had scratched letters into the wood, using a nail or the point of a knife. 'I can read it, even. You see, my books and examinations have some use, don't they, Jagbir? Ha ha! It says "*Atlar shimal.*" *Atlar* means "horses", I think. *Shimal* means "north". Horses, north. That's all.'

'I wish I was an educated man,' said Jagbir suddenly. 'I want to be able to read and write.'

'What would you do if you could?' A furious battle began to range on the hidden hill behind them. He heard the concerted distant roar of the company. '*Ayo Gurkhali!*'

'I'd learn where all the animals came from,' Jagbir said breathlessly and shut his mouth with a click of teeth. Robin did not speak. For a minute more the shooting continued, then all was silent. The snow fell harder but made no sound. Soon a surgeon came with an orderly and a khajawa-camel, and re-dressed Robin's wound. He too had heard.

CHAPTER SIX

*

WITH her gloved right hand Anne patted the mare's neck, whispering, 'Come back, Beauty, wait, wait.' A couple of hundred yards ahead the master of the Peshawar Vale Hunt began to work his hounds along the bank of a scrubby draw. The plain stretched away to the south, in front the hills rose sharply, washed by the raw light of early morning. The dark trees and blue smoke-haze of Peshawar lay like a solid island in the east, binding together the empty plain and the thin, yellow sky.

Anne smoothed down the thick twill of her habit, touched her back hair under her topi, and adjusted the dark veil which annoyingly dimmed her view. Two young men were talking to her, one on each side, and Major Hayling was only a few yards off. She had got to know all the young bachelors in the station since her arrival here. These two were nicer than most, but she hardly listened to them, answering automatically – 'No?' and 'Yes' and 'Really, Mr Handy?' – as their vaguely heard intonations seemed to demand. Every day the necessity of getting out of the bungalow and away from her mother pressed more urgently upon her. Gerald Handy would take her out if she would let him. So would Rupert Hayling. Their attentions only sharpened her desire for Robin. He must come quickly for her sake – and for his own, to confront the rumourmongers and force them to eat their vile words.

Before she met Robin she used to feel warm when a man obviously admired her. It used to be like a radiance inside, and she would feel her skin tingling as though the sun shone on it and would know that she looked better than she had a minute before. Now she found only that she was sorry for them and sorry for herself that her own chosen man was not here instead of them. Well, the days were past when she could be forced to marry someone against her will, whatever her mother thought.

She saw Edith Collett on a great chestnut. A major of infantry was with her to-day. She sat her horse with superb grace, the major like a sack of potatoes. He looked flustered.

Anne frowned severely at her thoughts. The young man on her right backed away, saying plaintively, 'I say, Miss Hildreth, you look as if you want to kill us or something; and I don't believe you've been listening to a word I've been saying. I was telling you —'

She smiled suddenly. 'Oh, yes, I was. You were telling me about your part in the dramatics last November. It must have been very amusing — But look, I think they've found.'

A horseman on a distant mound lifted his arm silently and pointed west. The master waved his cap in acknowledgement. The whips broke out into a yelled volley of oaths. Anne remembered that she had once used one of those words at home, and her mother had sat down suddenly and called for smelling salts. The hounds streamed out across the plain, and the master's horn tootled. Anne set Beauty at once into a bounding gallop, taking the young men by surprise, so that in a second she was free of them. She settled down to ride. Without turning her head, she knew that Rupert Hayling rode at her side.

After a while he said, 'Bored with the young?'

'Not a bit, Major Hayling. At least, not as bored as I sometimes become with older gentlemen,' she said crossly. She had found that Major Hayling did not like to be treated with great respect. With him the directest remark was the least wounding. From the corner of her eye she saw his smile. He said, 'The ability to give a good insult is certainly one of the marks of sophistication, and I know how badly you want to be thought sophisticated. But I have my duty to do, remember?'

Anne had no answer to that. Sometimes her father came out with the hunt, but to-day he had not been able to, and her mother had told her she could not go without a chaperone. Anne had suggested Edith Collett, to be told angrily that that was worse than no chaperone. Then, when the matter seemed to have reached an impasse, Major Hayling came to visit and said smoothly that in view of his advanced age and undoubted respectability he might perhaps be trusted to – er — Her mother had accepted after a small, false hesitation. Major Hayling had added that as he possessed only one eye he was in less danger, by half perhaps, of being carried away by her daughter's beauty. Hateful, beastly, kindly, understanding man! This morning that lone, gleaming eye had scanned her from the top of her head to the soles of her feet, as if she had been a shapely vase. She had wanted to smack his face, except that – teasing or serious – his look had been admiring, so she had felt sorry for him. Besides, try as she would, she could not rank him with the rest. They only wanted her for themselves, while Hayling – well, she'd find out soon enough.

She lifted Beauty over a wide ditch. The mare scrabbled with her back legs against the far slope, got a hold, fought for balance, and at last heaved up on to the level. Hounds ran strongly to the right. The master blew a peremptory toot on his horn, and the whips cracked. The hounds gave tongue, and the shrill, strange music ran out ahead of them over the frosty plain. In front Anne saw Mrs Rodney Savage, Robin's stepmother. The slight figure in black and grey, topped by a small, hard, black hat, sat trimly upright on a big gelding. Anne watched the hat rise easily and sail, first of all the field, over another ditch. She would have liked to ride up alongside and talk about Robin. She wanted to tell Mrs Savage that she didn't believe the rumours, that Robin was – 'not a coward', she would have said, but she ought to say, 'My man, the man I'm going to marry, and I love him, and I don't care if he is a coward or not, although I know he isn't.' Most especially she ought to say all that – and soon, now that her mother was busy denying that there was or ever had been anything between her and Robin.

She had to talk to someone – Hayling, even, in spite of everything. Or because of it. She could talk to him more easily than to anyone else in Peshawar, anyone she'd ever met. She slowed the mare's pace and at last said, 'I think Beauty's got a stone.'

The hunt flashed by. The young men made to stop but she smiled at them and waved them on. Hayling swung down beside her and spent several minutes lifting up Beauty's hoofs one by one. When the last rider had passed he vaulted into the saddle and walked his horse at her right side. She touched Beauty's flank, and they trotted slowly after the others. The hunt remained in full view across the treeless plain.

She said, 'Did you find it?'

'You must not imagine, Miss Hildreth, that because I find you desirable I am feeble-minded. To do so would be to insult your own superbly-shaped charms. There was, of course, no stone. What is it, my dear?' he finished with a sudden, hard sympathy that cut down her anger. She did not want any sentimentality. He was a very difficult man to deal with.

71

After a minute she said, 'Robin. The rumours.'

'I've heard them. McIain, the MacDonald subaltern concerned, has been in hospital here for a couple of weeks.'

'They're not true! He's not like that. He's quiet, but he's as brave as anyone – braver.'

'Perhaps. Speak up, please, and tell me some more about him.'

'He's not tall,' she muttered. 'About five feet nine, I suppose, rather pale except for the sunburn – brown hair —'

'Curly?'

'No, it's – you don't have to be nasty about it. He has long eyelashes and long fingers. He's quite slight.'

'As you describe him he sounds a thought effeminate.'

She looked up quickly, but he did not seem to be teasing her. Of course Robin did not look at all effeminate, but it was difficult to describe him without giving that impression. The fact was that he was different from other men – that would account for it. She wanted to tell Hayling that his jaw became straight and hard when something hurt him, but she only said, 'He has a thin, high-bridged nose.'

'When did you meet him?'

'In Mrs Cornell's drawing-room in Simla, on Wednesday, the twenty-eighth of May.'

'By the door or by the window?'

'He was standing near the – you are a beast!' Hayling was leaning back in the saddle and laughing silently, and after a minute she had to laugh too. 'Forgive me,' he said, again serious, almost sad. 'Sometimes the choice is between laughing and crying. You and your mother were in Simla for the hot weather, weren't you, and Robin had a company of the Thirteenth down from Manali as the Viceroy's Guard?'

'Yes,' she said sulkily.

'And what exactly is the trouble? How can I help?'

She blurted out, 'I want to marry him, and I won't marry anyone else, but he hasn't asked me, and my mother won't agree even if he does. I'm sure he'd like to, but he's afraid, and —'

'Wait a minute. He's afraid. That's an extraordinary thing to say, isn't it? Do you mean he's afraid of you? Or of your mother?'

'Not my mother. Unless he thinks I might grow up like her,' Anne said bitterly. The truth was that Robin was afraid of himself. She knew it because she loved him, and for that reason couldn't explain it to anyone else. Sometimes she became a little afraid herself, contemplating what she knew and guessed of him. One night, lying in bed and thinking, she had suddenly seen Robin as the driver of a winged crystal chariot whose winged horses, of silver filigree, stamped and pawed the earth and looked up at the empty sky. Where would that flimsy, breakable thing take her? How long would it hold together?

Hayling said quietly, 'And you're worried that the gossip will affect him?'

'Yes.'

After a bit he said, 'I don't think I can give you an honest opinion, honest advice. You know that I love you, Anne.' In his voice there was the astringent melancholy that she liked best of all his moods.

She mumbled, 'Oh, I don't know what to say, but I'm afraid it's not – it won't —'

'I can see that. All I can say is that you won't find the answer to your problem in other people – nor much help, either. You've got to take the responsibility yourself.'

'I want to marry the man I love, and be loved by him, and that's Robin,' she said in a rush.

'You want comradeship, friendliness too, don't you, both from your husband and from other people? You don't want to live in a little circle of two?'

'No – but I'd prefer that with Robin to anything else with anybody else. But we'll have that too. Robin must want that. Everyone does, surely, or they wouldn't be people; they'd be cats or something. He wants it, but he's shy, and people are just beastly to him.'

They had fallen a long way behind the hunt. Major Hayling's face was lined, grey, and very old-seeming to her. He said, 'Since the rumours began, a lot of people who have met Robin Savage have been airing their views about him. I've listened. What most of them say is that he's too wrapped up in himself. Not healthy – now, now, wait. What they mean to imply is that he *is* a cat. You know, some men are cats, some dogs. No women are cats. I haven't met one who really, in herself, wants above everything else to walk by herself. But some men do. I've met one or two and I know the brand. It's in the eyes.'

'You are like that yourself,' she said, surprised, feeling that by his words he had suddenly chosen to reveal himself to her. Hayling looked at her and went on. 'And some men are thought to be cats, but they aren't. They want love, companionship, and all the rest, but for one reason or another they can't get it. They just have to make the best job they can of pretending to be cats.' He looked away from her, and she cast her eyes down in embarrassment as he continued, 'I haven't met your Robin yet. You're a dog – the liveliest, most affectionate, doggiest dog of a young woman I've ever known. Just make sure Robin isn't a cat – a real, genuine, born-to-walk-in-the-woods-alone cat. Come on, we'd better catch up the hunt.'

'No, wait, please.' For some minutes she had been watching a haze of dust that began over Jamrud, the fort at the mouth of the Khyber Pass, and spread in an ever-lengthening trail down the road towards Peshawar. She said, 'How will I ever know, if people's beastly rumours and lies drive him back inside himself? I won't have it! The next time I hear anything like that I'm going to slap their faces, and I don't care who it is! What is that?'

'A winter caravan from Kabul, probably. I doubt if it's come from any farther, because the passes from Turkestan will be closed. Do *you* like having your battles fought for you?'

'No, but Robin —'

'My dear Anne,' he said brusquely, 'I do not want to hear anything more about Mr Robin Savage. I am sorry, but I don't.'

She knew she had hurt him and was unwillingly pleased that she had been able to. It was a part of woman's power that she had lacked, the power that Edith Collett could exert over so many men with no effort and no hurt to herself. But the pleasure did not last, because she found that in her it did hurt. She said, 'I am sorry, Major Hayling. You know I like you, don't you?'

'When I choose to keep my place as a cynical but wise and kindly old one-eyed owl? Yes, I know. Come on.'

'No, I'm going home. You go on. I'll say you escorted me to the edge of cantonments.'

'This is the North West Frontier, miss. I will go with you. The road is over there; the shoulders will be easier on the horses than these stones.'

At his side she trotted towards the road. Away to their right the crawling caravan had dissolved out into separate figures of men and horses and pacing camels. The dust blew slowly away to the south as the wind caught it. Reining in, she scanned the scene and soon realized that it was not a caravan but a military convoy. She saw the commissariat carts and their straining mules. If Robin could only be with it – but he would not be, unless he was wounded or being sent back. Then, closer than the head of the convoy, she saw a horseman and a man on foot. Her fingers tightened; if she had not been wearing gloves Major Hayling must have seen the whiteness of her knuckles. Her lips were drawn together; that, surely, he must see. She relaxed, forcing her lips apart and holding herself more easily in the saddle, so that she was only looking down the road, not staring like a she-wolf ready to defend her cub.

She could not be sure. The distance was too great. The horse and the man came slowly, slowly on. She began to tremble. Please, Major Hayling, if you are kind, go away.

The walking man was a Gurkha, carrying two rifles – a modern Snider and an old jezail.

When Robin came to her he stopped his horse and saluted. He looked just the same as in Simla so long ago. He said, 'Hullo, Miss Hildreth.' He was contained, but his lips were tight as hers, and his jaw was set in the way that meant hurt or readiness to receive hurt.

'Robin.' She urged Beauty forward.

'Well, I will get back to the hunt.' That was Major Hayling's cool voice behind her. 'I will be seeing you again soon, no doubt. Good morning, Mr Savage, and – for the moment – good-bye.'

'Good-bye, sir. Who's he, Anne?'

'Oh – Major Hayling.'

'What regiment?'

'Bengal Lancers, seconded. Something to do with Intelligence. Robin, I'm glad to see you. Salaam, Jagbir.'

'Salaam, miss-sahib.'

'Of course, you saw Jagbir in Simla. How do you like Peshawar? I've only had one letter from you since you got here. That was about horses, dancing, and the man who was killed near Attock.' The horses stepped together down the Peshawar road, the very beginning of that Grand Trunk Road which led eighteen hundred miles south-east to end in the steaming stew of Calcutta.

'Heavens, yes! It's awful, but I'd forgotten about him. Major Hayling promised to tell me who he was if he could, but he never has.'

'My stepmother wrote and said everyone in Peshawar was talking about how brave you were. Congratulations.'

She spoke quickly, wanting to get away from the subject. 'That was nothing. His life was really saved – prolonged – by Edith Collett's bandages, I should think.'

'She's the wife of Captain Collett, Frontier Force?'

'Yes. My mother doesn't like her because she's supposed to be fast. Mind, Robin, you be careful with her, or I'll be jealous.'

Robin looked at her and said seriously, 'I don't think the situation will arise.'

She became angry with herself. She was no good at this tight-rope walking. She had become roguish and silly, like the Gillespie girl. How would Edith Collett herself have acted in this situation? Gone straight to the point probably, or somehow encouraged Robin to do so. But Robin was not an easy man to encourage.

While she hesitated he said, 'Is my stepmother out with hounds to-day?'

'Yes. Of course you'd like to see her. I'm not quite sure where they've got to by now —'

'I don't want to see her.'

She looked at him anxiously, for he had spoken with unexpected shortness. Surely he had not quarrelled with the only woman he could know as a mother? Surely Caroline Savage had not believed that dreadful McIain's stories against him, and written something in a letter to wound him? The thought made him seem more lonely, more gallant still. She stole a sideways glance at him. He had taken off his topi, and the wind ruffled his hair. He was a thin-faced, fragile Galahad, riding against the world's meanness, the fine lines of his profile set off by the merciless severity of the background hills. After a long silence he spoke again. He always managed to surprise her. She listened to him and tried to find the cord of thought which would have led him to say this, when so many other things must be more urgent in his mind. If she could not understand that, perhaps she would never understand him. He was saying, 'The P.V.H. is typical of all we are and all we are not. Most foreigners, and a lot of people

76

in England, would think that it was romantic and somehow exciting to hunt jackals through this barren wild. They'd get a sense of loneliness, feel almost they were explorers. They'd think they were adapting themselves to Central Asia.'

'Yes,' she said slowly. She had not joined him yet. As so often before, he was looking out of some secret window, and what he saw was not what she saw or what her father would see.

He went on. 'It's not true. They're adapting Central Asia to themselves. They ought to be hawking, at least.'

'That's cruel.'

'So are they. Or they ought to be buying camels and trading across the passes. They ought to be missionaries, streaming west and north like locusts.'

She was really astonished now. He caught her glance and fell silent, his expression closing almost imperceptibly against her. She said brightly, 'I almost forgot! There's a ball at the club on the sixth. To-day's the second, isn't it?'

'I don't know.'

'I'm sure it is. We're all going, and you must come in our party. You will won't you? Promise.'

'I don't go out much, Anne.'

'I know, but I do want you to come to this.' She gazed full at him and felt the tears welling up in her eyes. He would see them through the veil. That would give her away. He'd know how much she was worried about him, and why. But it might be a good thing. Anything would be good that brought him back from mooning at the window she could not find. She had thought more accurately than she relished when she saw him as Sir Galahad. She remembered now that she had never been able to understand what the Holy Grail really was. She remembered that she had loved Sir Lancelot, the hot fighter, and only admired Sir Galahad. She would be Robin's champion, but he was a man and must fight too, in a man's way, for his name and reputation. Soon she would be sharing them. If he saw her tears he might spring from his horse and drag her down, to kiss her fiercely and shout in her ear, 'Marry me! We'll go out against them!'

Robin held her eyes for a long time, leaving his horse to plod without guidance down the verge of the road. Then he said, 'All right, Anne. I'll come.'

She lifted her veil and with her handkerchief wiped her eyes.

77

Now he must know. She said in a choking voice, 'What was Afghanistan like?'

'It was wonderful.' She had to grip the reins in her astonishment. His voice was passionately eager. He couldn't have seen her tears or understood anything. He had been at his window all the time. He said, 'The wind blew from Siberia. There were tangled mountains. When we got out of them, if the air was clear, the view stretched for ever. Not a soul to see in it – though there were people, of course, hidden. I saw the Hindu Kush one day. Beyond that there's nothing for thousands of miles. I could feel it.'

She said, 'Isn't it lonely, unfriendly?'

'Lonely? I suppose so. I didn't find it unfriendly. "The everlasting universe of Things flows through the mind ..." I've been sent back for cowardice.'

Now that he had said it she could find no answer. He spoke so calmly that the hot anger she had nourished on his behalf froze within her. He ought to be fighting mad, furious over the misunderstanding. He ought to be grim. He ought to be scornfully offering her the opportunity to desert him – so that when she didn't take it both she and he would be lifted up by their choking love and loyalty for each other. Perhaps – oh, that must be it; he spoke of the joys of loneliness because he thought loneliness would be his fate now. Already he must have made up his mind that she would not stand by him.

She put out her hand and felt for his. 'We must fight them, Robin.'

She was practically proposing to him. Well, she wanted to, and it was leap year. Ordinary rules did not apply to Robin.

He said, 'I don't think I want to fight anyone, Anne. I used to be sure of that – but then I found that, because of me, other people were hurt: Maniraj, Jagbir. When I think of them and people like them, I do want to fight. But most of the time I just don't feel the same about anything as other people do, or think in the same way.'

She knew he was right, but this was the thing she had to fight in him. She rode over it, saying eagerly, 'It's not true. You are like other people, only better. What happened?' she finished lamely.

He told her, speaking in slow, short sentences, and ended, 'Then I shot myself.'

'Are you all right now? Does it hurt any more? How could they think you dropped the pistol on purpose?'

He looked along the road at the approaching city. 'Perhaps I'm not meant to kill anyone. The time before I didn't even draw my pistol. I intended to but I didn't. The next day, Christmas Day, the general came to see me in the field hospital. He told me he would like to court martial me. But he wasn't going to, because I was the son of the splendid Colonel Rodney Savage, C.B. He said I was to go to Peshawar. He said if I didn't send in my papers quickly he'd bring me back for court martial.'

'That's horrible! Don't do it, Robin. We'll get you a transfer to another regiment; then you can go back and show them. We've got friends. We know people. We can do it.'

'Perhaps, dear.' He smiled at her with so much warmth, and his eyes shone so affectionately on her, that she was ready to die of love. He went on, 'But I don't want to kill anyone. And I don't want to send in my papers because that would hurt so many people. They ought not to be hurt, but they would be. I don't know what to do.'

She was appalled. In her mind the words fell over themselves. It was not logical. How could he be an officer of Gurkhas and not kill the enemy? He meant killing someone himself, but he seemed not to mind giving orders which would help the Gurkhas to kill.

He was speaking again. 'I had to wait for a convoy down. By then the wound was almost healed. On the way I nearly got you a present.'

'Oh.' This was something she could understand again. She felt as if she had travelled too fast on a fairground merry-go-round.

'There was a man in Jellalabad. He came out to the staging camp, selling cloth and trinkets. When he saw that jezail Jagbir's carrying' – Robin turned and motioned with his hand – 'he asked to examine it. He said it was valuable, belonged to an important Ghilzai family, and offered me quite a lot of money for it. I'd just seen something he was selling that was very pretty. It was too much for my means. But if I'd sold the rifle and given half the money to Jagbir I could have bought it with the other half.'

'Why didn't you?' Her heart was pounding and her lips dry. He simply must not see her face now. She turned her head towards the hills. The hunters were miles away across the plain.

He said, 'It was a ring. I didn't want to hurt anyone.'

Again the tears burst from her. She faced him and saw through the blur the lights in his eyes and the sadness and the loneliness. She said, 'I love you, only you, no one but you.'

CHAPTER SEVEN

*

ANNE stepped into the third and last petticoat, pulled her dress down over her head, and walked in her stockinged feet along to her mother's room to have the laces tightened at her back. When she returned she sat down in front of the mirror and began, with her mouth full of hairpins, to build up her hair into the hill of tightly rolled curls that Eugénie, lately empress of the French, had apparently set as fashion for all time to come. The lamplight was too soft and flattering. It made her thick hair seem auburn, when really it was a lighter, tawnier red than that. Robin would laugh if he could see her now – well, he'd smile at least. She had not seen him since that day he came back, except once in the road, and then he'd hardly said a word except that he had to hurry to work. Monday – Tuesday, Wednesday, Thursday – and to-day was Friday.

Crossly she stuck another pin in place. Oh, for Edith Collett's assurance, just for a week or two, even at the cost of tight little crows' feet around her eyes; she opened them wide and saw they were green and large, and that, try as she might, she could not make them look soulful. Robin's note of this morning lay unfolded on the dressing-table: 'I shall not be able to come to dinner. Sorry ...' and a word or two about late work – after all the battling she had gone through to force her mother to invite him. But he'd be joining them after dinner, in time for the ball. And though she had beaten down her mother's will, recognizing with surprise its feebleness, she had had to compromise and allow her mother to ask Major Hayling as well – 'Because the party he was going with has fallen through, Anne. It would be rude not to ask him after all his kindness to you. You do not appear to realize ...'

The talk buzzed round and round Peshawar like swarming bees. About the war and General Roberts and Colonel This and Major That, and above all about the terrible affair at Tezin Kach, where the MacDonald Highlanders had suffered so bravely and the 13th Gurkhas had behaved so badly, especially Lieutenant Robin Savage. She mumbled angrily, working her lips in and out between her teeth, biting and bruising until the blood came to the surface to make them full and red. Perfume. She'd show her mother to-night, and Mrs Collett too. She touched liberal dashes behind each ear, and more down in the valley between her breasts – they were big, too big, her mother said. She pushed back her shoulders and thrust out her breasts. The aroma of perfume rose overpoweringly, and she began to giggle. There was a secret store of rouge in the back of the top left-hand drawer. The ayah had bought it for her in the bazaar at Simla. She slapped some on. It looked terrible, and she rubbed hard, trying to get it off, but it wouldn't all come. The pins were in place, her hair felt top-heavy, and her lip was nearly bleeding. She opened the door, lifted her head, and primped along the passage. The skirt clung so tightly around her thighs that she had to hobble. Most of the girls that she knew seemed to like the fashion, but she would have preferred being able to take a longer stride. In the drawing-room she lifted her bustle – exactly like a hen settling down over a clutch of eggs – and sat on the edge of a hard chair. She composed herself with some difficulty, crossed her hands in her lap, and waited.

When Major Hayling came her parents had still not finished dressing. She greeted the major carefully, and he went to stand in front of the fire. His mess-kit was grey and black with silver facings. He looked distinguished and deceitfully young this evening, in spite of his grey hairs. After a few moments her father and mother came to help her out.

As soon as they sat down to dinner her mind ran off, although she heard what the others were saying and tried to keep a place in their conversation. When she'd said to Robin – that last beautiful Monday morning on the plain – 'I love you,' the words had come from inside her of their own volition. She had not meant to speak then. But she had said those words and immediately afterwards found she had no more doubts. And Robin had answered, 'I must love you.' Meaning, I *must* love you, I've got to? Or, I must *love* you, because I think of you so much? Why 'must'? She frowned and grappled with her thoughts.

'I beg your pardon, Mother? Oh, dear, yes, of course.'

She dabbed her lips and got up. Major Hayling leaped attentively to pull back her chair. She followed her mother out of the dining-room, leaving Major Hayling and her father to their port. Even before the bearer closed the door behind them her mother began a rambling, nagging tirade about her company manners. A minute later, the doors of her mind firmly closed against the familiar, scratchy voice, Anne was away again. Sunlit clouds of content cushioned her. Then someone came to insult Robin, and she was haughty, bitingly cold, annihilating the faceless someone with a look. The someone grovelled to apologize. Another someone came. She wanted to scratch him with her nails. Robin stood by, too hurt to fight. She did all the fighting.

After dinner they all waited in the drawing-room for Robin. Half-past nine struck, and he had not come. Her mother fidgeted on the edge of a chair. Her father pulled out his watch, checked it twice against the grandfather clock in the corner, and muttered, 'Dash it, young Savage might attempt to be here at the time he's invited for. I don't know what these young men are coming to, do you, Hayling?'

'No, indeed. But I expect Savage will have some very good reason for his tardiness. We old fogies must be careful nowadays before we sit in judgement on those who already think we have both feet in the grave.'

'Ah, h'm. Fogies? Us? Well, I suppose we're not getting any younger.'

'Of course Robin will have a good reason,' Anne broke out sharply at Major Hayling; but she couldn't really touch him, because he was pretending to be on her side.

At ten o'clock Mrs Hildreth jerked to her feet. 'We can't wait a minute longer Edwin, or we'll lose our table. If Mr Savage is able to come to the ball he must meet us there.' At the door she turned to Major Hayling, and her voice became a coo. 'You are taking Anne in your trap, are you not, Major Hayling?'

'I did hope that I would be allowed that great privilege – oh !'

'I *am* sorry, Major Hayling.' Anne lifted her heel off his instep and looked him in the eye. She was not afraid of him any more, nor was she shy with him. In fact, he was fun when you learned to behave according to his scandalously incorrect rules. Now he was smiling and apologizing for getting his foot in her way. When her mother looked away he cast his eye up and down her in that manner he had, as though he could see through her clothes. There was a statue – 'The Slave Market', or some such title; he reminded her of that. She pulled her wrap tightly around her. It was bitter cold too.

83

'Wind from the north-east,' said Major Hayling, raising his head to sniff. 'Straight out of a thousand miles of mountain and two thousand miles of steppe beyond that.'

'May we go now, please? I am becoming chilled.'

Once the pony had started the light trap moving he shifted the reins to the crook of his right arm and with his left hand got out a cigar and lit it. She watched, fascinated but knowing she shouldn't help. The queer and warming thing was that she did not want to. He saw her watching and said, 'You learn. That's the easiest thing to get over.'

The idea sprang ready-clothed with words into her mind. She said breathlessly, 'Will you take me to Robin's bungalow? I'm sure there's something wrong.'

Hayling still had not answered her when he turned the pony into a side road, nor five minutes later when he said, 'Here.' The pony turned again and trotted up a short drive. The glimmering carriage lamps showed a camp bed in the middle of the tiny unkempt lawn. A canvas canopy sheltered the bed from the weather. Hayling whistled between his teeth. Anne gasped and choked down an exclamation. Two or three other bachelor officers shared the bungalow with Robin, but it must be he who slept out there in the cold of these February nights, in the blast of the winds. The other young officers must have ostracized him, that he did this thing to be away from them. Hayling answered her thoughts with a drawled, 'Perhaps he likes it.'

'Don't be ridiculous, Major Hayling.'

He looked at her thoughtfully. Jagbir ran out of the bungalow followed by an old Pathan in bearer's livery. Anne wondered what had happened to the bearer Robin had had in Simla. This was a new man. Why didn't he keep his servants for any length of time? It wasn't as though he was cruel or over-bearing.

Hayling called, 'Savage! Hayling here, with a friend of yours.'

Robin came out on to the veranda, dressed in his dark-green parade uniform, which was covered with dust. Hayling said, 'Aren't you coming to the ball?'

Robin looked at Anne and said, 'Ball? Oh, yes, I hadn't forgotten about it. We've had a robbery. We've been busy the last hour chasing the robbers and trying to get hold of Mr Johnson, the policeman.'

'May I have a look? Perhaps, in the circumstances, if nothing is said about it, Miss Hildreth could come too?'

'Yes, of course. Why not?'

She examined the barren little room with unconcealed interest. There were a table and two chairs, a stool, a long bookcase, two black japanned metal trunks, one on top of the other, a chest of drawers, and a wardrobe – no mirror. A hurricane lamp stood on top of the trunks, and another on the table. A door led off into the bathroom. No carpets covered the bare stone floor. There was no bed – that was out on the lawn – and she tightened her lips, feeling the unforgiving wind and the unforgiving cruelty. Two pictures hung on the wall, both oils – one of a mountain which she recognized as having seen from Simla on clear days; one of a flat, stony waste under an empty sky. She looked at them more closely while Robin muttered with Hayling. She could find no signatures on them. The light in them was peculiarly powerful and filled them with a radiance unnatural to the subjects. A long jezail hung over the mantelpiece. Presumably that was the gun he had nearly sold in Jellalabad to buy her a ring. The grate was black and empty.

Robin was saying, 'I don't think he can have been here more than a few seconds. I heard a noise, breathing, when I came in. I thought it might be Lascelles and Browning and their friends, come to wreck my room. But I grappled with someone, and it was only one man. Then Jagbir came in with a lamp, and I saw that the man had a knife. He was a Pathan.'

'What happened then?'

'I went up to hold him, and —'

'Were you armed?'

'No. I tried to make him drop the knife. He looked vicious but hungry. Then he kicked the lamp out of Jagbir's hands and dashed out. We searched all around and couldn't find him. The chowkidar's disappeared, too, so he must have been in league with this fellow. We haven't missed anything, nothing was opened or turned upside down. We found that someone had broken into Jagbir's quarters. It was just the same there as here – no signs of rummaging, nothing missing. We thought we saw a couple of men lurking around, but couldn't catch them. The bearer got Mr Johnson, and he's just gone. He took notes but didn't tell us if he had any ideas. It would be simple enough if

the man had been after the things they usually come for: money –
it's there on the table, but he didn't touch it – sheets off the bed
outside; clothes in those boxes – they're not locked.'

Hayling tapped his hook absentmindedly on the mantel. 'Yes,
that's strange. He may not have had time, as you say, but it
sounds as if he or they were looking for one definite thing, and
that too large to be kept in a box. You aren't secreting the Pea-
cock Throne in here, are you?'

'No, sir,' said Robin smiling.   'Look here, sir, and Anne – I've
got to change if I'm coming to this ball, and this is my only place,
so would you mind waiting outside?'

'All right.'

In the trap she huddled herself into her wrap and hoped she
would not cry. The horrible calm way in which Robin had talked
of Lascelles and Browning coming to wreck his room! He had
hardly met her eyes throughout her visit. It was the first time she
had ever been inside a bachelor's quarters – she did not count
going with her mother to see a rich old commissioner who had a
whole house. This place of Robin's was so bleak!

Hayling said quietly, 'Why isn't he staying with his mother?'

'Mrs Rodney Savage is his stepmother.'

'I know that. What of it? She has a huge bungalow. He's
allowed to live there. It isn't as if his regiment was here and he
had to live in mess.'

She did not know. She had not thought about it. There had
been more important problems on her mind. She thought about
it now and came suddenly on the answer. 'Because he won't
shelter behind her! He doesn't want these brutes, Lascelles and
everyone like him, to think he's running away from them.
Precious few of *them* have fought in Afghanistan, or ever will!'

'So you are wondering, even after this evening?'

'What do you mean? Do you mean I think Robin might be a
coward?'

'No. I hoped you were thinking about cats. Be calm now, miss,
here's your ewe lamb.'

At the club Anne knew better now than to expect trouble
over their late arrival, and, sure enough, her mother only raised
her eyebrows archly at Major Hayling. Then Robin, limping
slightly, followed them at a distance into the lounge, and her
mother frowned and said something behind her fan to her father

86

Anne rested her hand absently on the chair next to her until Robin came out of the cloakroom and sat down. Major Hayling began a conversation with her parents, and she took the opportunity to give Robin her programme and its little white pencil. She said, knowing that her eyes were brighter than they ought to have been, 'Write down your name on as many lines as you like. Oh, leave number sixteen at least; I've promised that one.'

'To him?' Robin inclined his head towards Hayling. She wrinkled her nose at him, and he wrote in the little pasteboard folder. When he handed it back she saw that he had taken only two dances, this number five that had already begun, and another much later in the evening. She was disappointed but she could feel the ends of her nerves tingling. To-night was important. People were already staring surreptitiously at her and at Robin. To-night she was going out against them. Robin ought to have taken more dances. She had said 'I love you', and it was like the final decision to embark on a voyage. With the words, she had stepped down out of her parents' ship into her own little boat. She was in harbour still, but preparing for the sea.

Whirling round in the waltz, cautiously so as not to split her dress, she glanced in the long mirror as she passed. The cream silk looked well against Robin's near-black green. A looping emerald sash hung down at her waist and kicked up behind over her bustle. A green stone sparkled at her throat. She wondered if there had been an emerald, a real one, in the ring that Robin did not buy.

There was only one officer of Highlanders on the floor, a tall young man with his right arm strapped to his side and a red scar, three-quarters healed, down the left side of his forehead and face. She said to Robin, 'Is that Mr McIain, in the kilt?' She knew it must be.

He turned his head, looked, and answered plainly, 'Yes. Alan McIain.'

She caught the young Highlander's bright blue eyes then, and lifted her head and looked away. 'He seems very pleased with himself,' she said '– the Wounded Hero.'

'Oh, no,' Robin answered quickly. 'Really he's modest and as straight as a die. Seeing me here has upset him – made him remember things, places, that he'd like to forget.'

She said softly with a touch of pique, 'Do you remember what you said the other day on the road?'

'Yes.'

'Is it true? Without the "must"? Do you really' – she put her head close for a moment of the whirling dance, whispered, and pulled away – 'love me?'

Robin said, 'I think so. We must talk. Not here. There are too many people.'

She was tall for a girl and did not have to look up much above the level of her own eyes. His eyelashes were long, and now the light from the hanging chandeliers shone on them. All the skirts rustled, hissing under the violins. She was alert, wary, and excited. She was waiting for some opportunity, but she did not know what it would look like or exactly where it would lead.

At the table a group had formed around an array of glasses of brandy and soda. Her mother nursed her usual glass of port. Anne was permitted to have one glass of port or sherry on these occasions, but Major Hayling signalled with his finger and on the instant a bearer trotted forward with a bottle of champagne. Mrs Hildreth made to protest when the waiter filled Anne's glass, but checked herself and instead glanced sharply at Anne. In this rather staid circle the breaching of a champagne bottle foreboded certain definite things. Anne wondered what the major was up to now, and saw that her mother was wondering too. Was he, who understood things, trying to give her a little extra courage?

Men kept appearing at her shoulder – young men, old men, fat men – to ask if they might have the honour of a dance. She would write their names in her programme, then listen and talk a little, then sweep out to dance on the arm of some gentleman coming to claim her, return after a while, thank her partner, sit down, listen, and talk – and begin all over again. The champagne sparkled in the glass and in the back of her head. She had only tasted it four or five times in her life. Major Hayling went away once or twice, but she never saw him on the floor. Her father circled sedately from time to time with duty-partners or with the youngest girls he could find. Robin never left his chair.

The fourth or fifth time that she came back the men were talking about Asia. She heard Hayling say, 'Asia has come to the crossroads. Perhaps the bottom of the hill is a better way to say it. For all practical purposes the continent is split up among three empires, and only one of those three – the Chinese – is truly Asiatic. And in large parts of the Chinese Empire one sort of Asiatic, the Chinese, is ruling other sorts who don't like it or him – Mongols, Turkis, Kirghiz, some Uzbegs, Tibetans. Now the three empires are beginning to jostle each other because they've used up all their room for manoeuvre – the Chinese did long ago.'

Her father said something about the rascality of the amirs of Afghanistan; then a partner was bowing at her side. Just as she left she heard Robin joining in the talk.

On her next return they'd got to Russia. It was Hayling again. '... It's fourteen years since the Russians moved against Tashkent, twelve since they took Bukhara and Samarkand. Seven years ago they gobbled up Khiva. Now they have a frontier with us on the Pamirs, where the Chinese Empire meets ours too. Farther west the Russians are down to the Oxus, so in that direction only Afghanistan lies between us and them. They're getting too close. If they get any closer India will never survive, whether it belongs to us or whether Macaulay's hope has come true by then and it's a separate empire.'

She listened perfunctorily, trying to catch Robin's attention. But, after rising briefly when she sat down, he had leaned forward to ask Hayling a question. 'But what do they want, sir? Do they want to put all that desert and steppe and pamir under the plough?'

'They say officially, Savage, that they don't want it at all, that they are being dragged forward by circumstances. It is a fact of history that no strong power has ever been able to prevent itself from fighting, taking over, and at last absorbing any unruly or turbulent areas or peoples on its borders. We did it in India – we just had to, though half the time the government at home was trying to force the Governor-General, the man on the spot, to go backwards, not forwards. The Americans did it in the West and in Texas. The Chinese did it in Mongolia and Inner Asia.'

Someone else said, 'Why haven't we taken over Afghanistan, then? Heaven knows it's unruly enough.'

'We nearly did – perhaps we should have – after the first war, in forty-two. Then the khanates, Samarkand and so on, would have been the buffer between us and the Russians, and we'd have been that much farther forward. Now it's too late because the Russians have reached Afghanistan's northern frontier. Afghanistan is therefore the buffer. You know, a buffer state is in a very enviable position. It can do just about anything. Neither great power dares interfere in its affairs, because the other will suspect an offensive move if it does. So Afghanistan, Persia, and Turkey are now the three buffer states between us and Russia. And ...'

Then another young man with long moustaches came for her, and she had to go. ... Back again soon, and they were talking about some other part of Asia. For her it was like a showing of lantern slides, lacking continuity. The group around the table had grown. A civilian and a captain were leaning over the backs of chairs and throwing in words of agreement or sage questions. Edith Collett was there. A resplendent major of Madras cavalry stood beside her. He had a royal-blue high-necked jacket with half a hundred gold buttons running up the edges, a crimson waistcoat, and long, tight blue trousers. Anne noticed his eyes; they hovered over Mrs Collett's body like hungry, fawning little dogs; his nostrils were pinched in, and his hands moved ceaselessly.

Then Edith Collett leaned over with a friendly smile and whispered behind her fan, 'Your Mr Savage is very *good* looking, Anne. Does your mother approve?'

'She won't,' Anne muttered. 'And he hasn't – well, I mean —'

'I see. If you want him, dear, get compromised. That's my advice.' She drew away, her deep violet eyes smiling still into Anne's. Then she rested her fingers momentarily on the cavalry major's arm and swept out of the circle. Anne watched the major hurry after her, stumbling over his precious dignity in his haste and not even noticing that he had left it behind him. Anne sighed and turned again to listen.

'The tribes who live astride this frontier were a problem to Alexander the Great and they've been a problem to everyone since then, including us.' That was the civilian, his thumbs in the lapels of his coat. She wondered when Robin would notice what dance it was.

'The tribes want to shoot each other. They do *not* want law and order. They want the blood feud. They want to guard their own idea of honour in their own way. Therefore' – the civilian wagged a forefinger at Hayling, who was seated across the table from him – 'are we guilty of oppression when we enforce peace, law, and order on them?'

90

Robin was on his feet, looking anxiously at his programme. He had noticed at last; but he had something to say. Standing now at the edge of the group, he broke in. 'But do you think any man, even a Pathan, is born wanting to die in a blood feud? Isn't it possible that circumstances – poverty, custom – force them to live by this code of killing and violence? I don't think anyone is actually born with a desire to hurt other people, to fight.'

'S-some people don't wanna fight, all right. Some people don't have the stomach to.'

Anne whipped around. It was McIain, drunk, his face flushed and his words running together. He was standing at Robin's shoulder.

A pimply young man of the commissariat, one of her father's juniors, said loudly from Robin's other side, 'No. Some don't want to fight at all, do they, Alan? *I* think dirty cowards like that ought to be tarred and feathered.' She heard another voice raised in agreement, like a yelp. Suddenly they were so many dogs, snarling and snapping at one who had lost his footing among them. She put down her fan and, trembling with a white and senseless rage, reached slowly out for a glass from the table, never taking her eyes off McIain.

Robin turned to McIain and said steadily, 'Hullo, McIain. I'm very glad to see that you're better.'

McIain raised his arm and smashed the back of his hand across Robin's face, then again. The skin of her body shivered, and she could hardly keep her seat, could hardly see. This was what McIain had done after the tragedy at Tezin Kach. Robin had told her. But then grief and pain had driven him mad; now he was just drunk. The glass shook in her hand.

'Again?' Robin said.

McIain raised his arm, and Anne threw the full champagne glass into his face with all her strength. It splintered above his eye, and the pieces fell tinkling to the floor. The wine ran down his nose and his scarred cheeks. He swung around and met her eyes and started back with a cry.

Major Hayling stood up abruptly. 'Mr McIain, you're drunk. Leave the club. Captain Golliatt, Mr Twombly, take him home.'

Anne sank back in her chair. A sickness of excitement rose in her throat. She felt strong, and when she saw her mother staring at her, open-mouthed, she stared her down.

McIain stood a moment, swaying on his heels, looking belligerently from Robin to Hayling but at all costs not at Anne. Then he bowed slightly and muttered, 'Very well, sir.'

Major Hayling said; 'Bearer! Sweep that up. Look here, we all need another bottle of champagne. This band is bad enough to …'

At her side Robin said, 'This is my dance, I think, Anne.' Her mother was signalling to her to remain seated, to make an excuse. Anne frowned angrily at her, walked to the floor on Robin's arm, and slid into the dance. His face was white, and all the skin stretched tautly over the fine bones beneath. His eyes flared and snapped, and his hand gripped hers firmly. It seemed to her that the other couples on the floor kept moving away from them, leaving them to dance alone in a widening circle of isolation.

He said, 'You'll do that for me?'

'Anything.'

'I didn't buy that ring because I thought, sooner or later, you would be hurt if you accepted. I can stand alone.'

'You don't have to.'

'That's it, Anne. Here, now, I don't want to. But – oh, don't you see? – *I might have to.*'

She did not understand exactly what he meant. He spoke from the depths, and she should try to understand. But she couldn't now. All that would come later when a year or two of time had proved to him that he could trust her. Then he would let her become a part of him and he would no longer know the meaning of aloneness. She whispered urgently, 'We've got to fight, Robin, or you'll be ruined. They'll make you hate everyone. They'll make you – kill yourself. It's happened before.'

Twice in a long circuit of the floor he opened his mouth to speak. Twice he said nothing. The third time he said, 'Anne, will you marry me?'

The opportunity for which she had been tensely waiting was upon her. In a few minutes, as this hypertension and ruthlessness faded in her, it would be gone. She whirled in his arms until they were in front of the band. There she stopped and, holding Robin's hand, beckoned to the bandmaster. Still playing his violin, he leaned over, and she whispered in his ear. He smiled, turned to his musicians, and raised his bow authoritatively. The music died in the middle of a phrase. Anne said to Robin, 'Tell them.'

The pianist struck a resounding chord. On the dais she gripped Robin's hand more tightly and faced the floor. The people's faces were like so many floating white balloons. None of them possessed any expression; they had not eyes or mouths or noses – except her mother. She saw her mother pushing forward through the dancers, her face pinched in horror.

Robin said in his high, clear voice, 'I would like to announce that Miss Hildreth has done me the honour of saying that she will become my wife. Thank you.'

The pianist struck a succession of chords and stopped to await the customary burst of handclapping and shouted applause and the rush across the floor. Of course it was also customary for the engaged girl's father to make the announcement – but what could the bandleader do? Anne knew there would be no applause and at Robin's side she stepped down to the floor. The only sound in the ballroom was a moaning shriek from her mother – 'Ooooooh!'

Major Hayling was there with her mother, half supporting her, when Anne arrived with Robin. She could not see her father anywhere. Major Hayling said to Robin, 'I don't suppose you'll ever know how lucky you are.' The sting in his voice robbed the words of their innocence.

Around them Anne heard the whispering, the hissed questions and answers. The whispering died, and there was silence. Everyone stood where he had been when the music stopped. At last the bandmaster caught the overpowering embarrassment and tapped his foot twice and began to fiddle furiously. Unsteadily, one by one, the band struck up 'The Blue Danube'.

CHAPTER EIGHT

*

As she tightened her chin-strap she yawned and had to wait till the yawn was finished. She felt discouraged this morning, and a little uneasy in her stomach. She turned up the watch pinned to the outside of her dress and saw that it was not yet quite six a.m. She was riding down the Grand Trunk Road towards Pabbi for a meet of the P.V.H. Hayling rode at her side. Above the clipclop of hoofs he said, 'And what time did you get to bed last night?'

'Four.'

'I thought so. Not without dust and heat?'

She mumbled, 'Mother was hysterical.'

Robin had returned to his bungalow almost at once. When they got off the dance floor her mother had started to call him names, so he had bowed, repeated that he intended to marry Anne, and gone away. At home her mother really began, and it would have been funny really, only Anne had been so taut with excitement that she could not see it at the time. After a while the storm had burst over her father – why hadn't she seen this coming? Why hadn't he stopped Robin making the announcement? Why hadn't he gone up immediately to the dais to deny that the engagement had parental sanction? Of course poor Daddy couldn't have done that. But her mother's crying and hysteria had been over what was done; she had not yet realized how easily it could be undone; she would, though, to-day or to-morrow. It wouldn't take her long to see that in the circumstances Anne needed her parents' approval even though she was of age.

Since she had awakened this morning, all the time the groom was saddling Beauty, all the time she waited in the drive for Hayling to come, she had been thinking what to do next. Her mother had never dreamed she would go out hunting, so she had not thought to forbid it. Daddy was the best hope. He wanted her to be happy and he'd promised to help her. He so seldom got what he wanted, unfortunately. Mother did not want her to be happy – or unhappy; she just wasn't taking happiness into account at all, although of course every few minutes she would

94

sob, 'It's only your happiness I'm thinking of.' Her mother was really, in one word, thinking of esteem. She was thinking of other people's opinions, of how the gossip would run, of money and rank and prospects.

Hayling said, 'I suppose you've worked out that you've got to have your parents' consent?'

'Why?' She knew the answer but wanted more time to think. Besides, Major Hayling might have an idea. Perhaps it wasn't fair or wise to trust him – but perhaps she had to. Anyway she could listen.

He said, 'Well, first of all you obviously want people to accept him, and a lot of them won't do it if he marries you without consent; it'll only reinforce, instead of removing, the reasons they already have for *not* accepting him. Then, unless some influential people – colonels, generals, and so on – pull strings on Robin's behalf, he's going to face a court martial very soon.'

'He's not a coward! They'll have to exonerate him.'

'They won't. They can't. Not enough evidence. They'll make a finding that will leave everything just about where it is.'

'But, wh-what c-can w-we do?' She bit her lip.

Hayling said, 'Oh, damn you, Anne! I may be able to help, but only if you get your parents' consent to the marriage. Now forget about it for a bit. We're nearly there.'

Five minutes later they came to the meet. A sprinkling of riders had already arrived. Hayling pressed forward, greeting his friends and acquaintances. 'Morning, Master. Morning, Featherstone; morning, Mrs Collett; glad to see you both out.' They milled around, twenty or thirty of them, men and women, for the most part mounted on rangy government chargers. They were dressed in khaki and grey and black, and the horses kicked up the dust around them while the riders exchanged shouted words of small talk. The whips were yelling. 'Gi-i-i-it up, Daisy. Ho, Crocus! Ho, Tulip! Lady, ho! Nancy' – *crrrack* – 'get your nose out of there, you bloody bitch. *Come* up, Violet, *come* up, I say!' *Crrrack!*

The field moved slowly off to the covert side. The young men greeted Anne with extreme self-consciousness. Mr Gerald Handy did not greet her at all and turned scarlet under her long stare. She felt a little better. The few women out congratulated her briefly on her engagement. She kept her face masked in a smile. Edith Collett whispered, 'Good for you! But remember what I said.' Mrs Savage was not out. Robin would soon be on his way to her big bungalow. He'd probably find her at the hospital where she spent most of her time helping to nurse the wounded soldiers. She'd know already what Robin was going to tell her. Word would have reached every part of Peshawar cantonment within an hour.

At the covert she drew apart and kept her eyes on the huntsmen while they threw hounds into the undergrowth. Hayling never left her side. As they waited he said, 'You've got to be quick. Apart from your mother, there's Robin.'

'What about him?'

'All right, I'll be cruel. You've got to understand. I don't think he's half so sure about this marriage as you seem to be. And since he's not afraid of physical things like pain – or death – he might bring himself to some harm. Accidentally, so as not to hurt you.'

'Oh, no! I couldn't bear it!' It was strange and rather terrible that she should have talked to Robin about this very thing last night. The weird part was that she and Major Hayling had come to that conclusion from opposite directions; she feared that the world would drive Robin to desperation, while, if Major Hayling's words meant anything, he thought that it was she, Anne, who would do the driving.

'Don't misunderstand me,' Hayling said. 'I don't think you forced Robin into asking you to marry him. If he loves anyone, it's you. He is being tortured, if ever I saw a man tortured, by some sort of conviction that he's not meant to find happiness that way – though he wants to, because of you.'

'I don't believe it.'

He shrugged wearily. 'All right, don't. That's my opinion. And I've already told you why it can't be unbiased. Believe what you want to believe. I don't pretend to know. A beautiful young woman in love can do just about anything. Certainly she can induce a middle-aged major of cavalry to make a fool of himself.'

'Gone *awaaaay!*'

Jamming her topi firmly on her head, she began to ride. For the next four hours she rode as she had never ridden before, galloping in straight lines, never deviating, recklessly hurling Beauty at every obstacle that came in the way. Hounds found twice and killed twice. Before the end, foam and sweat lathered Beauty's flanks, and she was so exhausted that she pecked at the lowest mud walls. Rivulets of sweat ran down Anne's face and neck, cutting muddy channels through the caked dust. Great black patches of sweat-soaked cloth stood out on her jacket among the green flecks of foam from Beauty's mouth. The master gave her the brush of the second jack killed. She did not know where to carry it on the long hack home and at last had to give it to Major Hayling, who stuffed it into a pocket.

He mopped his brow with a large, white handkerchief. 'I hope I never have to follow you again, Anne – at least not when you're upset. You've got too much courage for your own good.'

The rush of wind and the pounding of hoofs had dispelled her fears. Robin wanted to marry her, and she wanted to marry him. She would make it come about. She said, 'I've been worrying too much.'

'Well, now that you have recovered your nerve – though I've lost mine in the process – shall we go and visit Mr Savage? You don't look exactly fragile or pale, but I don't expect he'll mind. And I want to talk to him on a subject that concerns you both.'

'Go like this?' Her face was scarlet under the filth, but it might be better by the time they reached Peshawar. 'All right.'

On the way back she tried to get Hayling to tell her what he intended to discuss with Robin, but he only said, 'Wait. I don't want to have to go through it all twice.' Speculating in silence as the weary horses plodded onward, she weighed the various possibilities. It would not be anything to do with getting her parents' consent to the marriage; he'd already said that that was her responsibility. It might be about a transfer, some posting that would save Robin from being court-martialled – although what Hayling could achieve she had no idea. He must know that even he, with his contacts, could not persuade a regimental colonel to take Robin unless to send him straight out on some specially dangerous duty. And Robin had said he didn't want to kill anyone. She suppressed a groan. She didn't want him to take a delight in killing, but it might be his duty. He must realize that.

The little bungalow and its little patch of lawn basked in the motionless sunlight. Robin was sitting on the veranda, on the stool she had seen in his room. He rose, came forward to them, and helped her to dismount while his bearer held the horses' heads. As they walked up the verandah steps Robin said, 'Don't worry about the horses, sir. Bearer, tell the groom to loosen the girths and blanket them. I've seen my stepmother, Anne. She seems pleased. She'll be asking you to visit her later, I expect.'

They were standing on the veranda. Robin said, 'Would you care for a bottle of beer, sir? I have some carbonated water for you, Anne.'

'Robin, I can't stay long, really. I'd love some soda. Major Hayling wants to talk to us, dear.'

'Oh. Wait. I'll get the chairs out.'

'I'll lend you a hand. Literally one.'

Robin smiled at Hayling with one of his sudden, warm smiles. Anne smiled at the two of them and watched from the doorway while they went into the little whitewashed cell. Hayling glanced at the jezail over the mantelpiece. His hand grasped the back of a chair, ready to lift. He said, 'The chasing on the barrel there's unusually good. Where did you get it?'

'Off a Ghilzai who was killed at Tezin Kach. I'm not sure that he really was a Ghilzai, as a matter of fact. He and another man seemed to stray into the battle. Jagbir shot him. He had two rifles, a modern one and this.'

'This is fairly old. It's in good order though, as far as I can see. It's probably quite valuable.'

'I think it must be, sir. A man in Jellalabad tried to buy it off me on my way down.'

From the door Anne said, 'I wish you'd sold it.' But Robin did not smile at the reference, and she added, to cover herself, 'Perhaps that's what the robbers were after last night.'

Robin said, 'I'd never thought of that,' and took it down and handed it over for Hayling's inspection. 'D'you think it's all that valuable, sir? It's got some Arabic letters carved into the stock there, just under your hand. I made them out to mean "Horses, north". I suppose they're really part of the owner's name, or—'

Hayling shifted his hand along the butt and bent down to peer at the writing, resting the barrel on the back of a chair. Then he picked up the weapon and hurried out on to the veranda so quickly that Anne had to step aside hastily or he would have run into her. She moved automatically, thinking of something else; she had remembered the word the lone man had written in blood on a rock near Attock – *Atlar*. Horses.

Hayling said sharply, 'Have you or your orderly fired this? Did the man fire it before he was shot?'

'Not that I know of. We certainly haven't. I was watching when this man was killed, and I am sure he didn't fire it.' He related the story, which Anne had not heard before. He had an eerie, unfluent gift for words, and as he spoke she felt the mist of the Afghan hillside closing about her.

Major Hayling sat down slowly, the old jezail upright between his knees, the hook of his right hand resting lightly on it to keep it from falling forward. Anne sat down. Robin leaned against a pillar of the veranda in front of them. As Hayling began to speak Robin said, 'Wait, sir,' went back into the bungalow, and reappeared a minute later with beer, soda, and glasses. Hayling had lighted a cigar. Anne was pleased, because the smell of perspiration was very strong.

Hayling began. 'Late last November we got word that one of the government of India's secret agents in northern Afghanistan was on his way east to make an important report. None of us here knew the man by sight. He had served us for many years but used to make his reports through another man in Kabul. His message didn't say why he was coming to India, except that it was important.

'On December 17th a stranger was killed near Attock. Anne here saw him killed. His murderers, thinking they had *not* killed him, also hired rascals in Pabbi to stab him again and make sure. The people in Pabbi would not tell us much, and as they had committed no real crime we could not be very severe with them. However, the Pabbi incident was a mistake from the other side's point of view, because it made us think – and in due course we received descriptions that convinced us the dead man was the agent who had been on his way to us.'

Anne listened with parted lips and heart beating fast. This was exciting enough, but she knew from Hayling's manner that sooner or later the story would more directly affect Robin and herself.

The major blew out a cloud of blue tobacco smoke. 'The agent's name was Selim Beg. He lived in the Afghan frontier

99

town of Balkh, which is north of the Hindu Kush and faces Russian-controlled territory across the Oxus. When he was shot near Attock he had a jezail. His murderers risked their lives – unnecessarily, as we then thought – to get that jezail, and they did get it. In his last moments Selim Beg wrote the Turki word *Atlar* in his own blood on the rock where he lay. A little later, but enough later for a man to have covered the distance, and on the direct route from Attock to Kabul, and to Russia, your Jagbir shoots a man who appeared to have blundered into your battle. On him, as well as his own rifle, was this jezail. Its stock is marked with the words *Atlar, Shimal*. Horses, north.

'That, with the addition of the word "north", is the message Selim Beg gave us at Attock. So this is almost certainly Selim Beg's jezail. His murderers would have known or guessed that the key words of his report were on his jezail – the one thing that he would never allow to leave his hand, day or night. They hoped that if they got the jezail and prevented Selim Beg from talking to us we would not be able to guess what his report was about. Selim Beg, on the other hand, must have thought that the single words "horses" and "north" would be enough by themselves, if the worst came to the worst, to put us on the track. Now —'

He peered down the barrel of the jezail, and asked Robin if he could get a thin stick and some glue. Robin called Jagbir, who quickly found a stick. Robin himself went to borrow the glue from one of the other occupants of the bungalow – Anne heard the man's curt voice, but Robin got the glue.

Hayling rubbed glue liberally down one side of the stick, thrust it into the muzzle of the jezail and held it there. While they waited for the glue to harden he said, 'There's something here, all right. It's a favourite hiding-place, as long as you think you're not going to use the weapon.' As he slowly drew the stick out of the barrel a roll of thin paper came with it. With Robin's help he prised the gluey stick loose without tearing the inside paper. When he spread out the roll she saw that it was not one but four or five sheets of paper. 'A report,' Hayling muttered. 'But who from and who to, we'll have to find out.' He began to study the graceful, tightly-written, right-to-left script. 'H'm. Not, I think, to *our* address. That's interesting.' He rubbed his hand across his chin, his hook holding down the papers on his lap. The jezail lay on the veranda floor at his feet. 'I haven't got time to read them now. But tell me one thing, Anne. Did you see Selim Beg fire this, at Attock?'

She thought back carefully. He had been behind a rock, she saw him clearly; he'd turned, and – 'Yes, he did. I saw him.'

'Then he probably had no report in it. He might have decided to blow it out while shooting, but I doubt it. We'll work all that out later. This is not the place. All this is just an introduction to our talk – a timely one, but perhaps not altogether a coincidence. You see, we – representing certain branches of the government of India – have been looking for someone with an unusual set of qualities, the most important being an ability, a preference, for working in isolation.'

Anne sat forward on the edge of her chair. It was long past tiffin time. All the other riders would be back, and her mother would know it. Every minute she stayed would put her mother into a worse temper, make it more difficult to cajole her into the right mood for approving the engagement. But she had to stay.

Hayling said, 'Savage, I can offer you a post in Intelligence. More, I can give you a specific job. It will be dangerous, but you can make it as violent or as introspective as you wish.'

'I'll take it, sir,' Robin said at once. Anne clenched her left hand quietly. She'd have to do something quickly.

'Wait. You'll learn in a minute why I'm letting *you* hear all this, Anne. The task of the ordinary agent is to live in a place, travel about a bit, keep his eyes and ears open, and report. He does not deduce or infer, he just sees and tells. And he never sees much. No agent manages to hide under the table at Tsarskoe Selo. No agent gets the whole of a big plan, all at once. The key to Intelligence is this – the bigger the plan, the bigger the preparations. For example, if Russia intended to attack Afghanistan to-morrow the preparations would have been visible months or years ago – route reconnaissances, water surveys, road building, and, above all, the flow of Russian money, in bribes, payments for services rendered, for sweeteners, and so on. Now, half the agents in Asia work for both parties to any quarrel – and both the parties know it. What's more, each party knows just about every agent of the other party. Disguises, false beards, and stained faces are used all right, but almost as a matter of form –

it is not done to spy too openly. Agents are seldom arrested in time of peace. Once they are known, each side uses them to channel misleading information to the other side.'

Robin said, 'Why did they kill Selim Beg?'

'Ah. The charade ceases to be pretence when an agent gets hold of something really important. That very seldom happens. Important things are usually uncovered by the piecing together of innumerable unimportant ones.'

'Then if my job is going to be dangerous, as you said, I will be near something important?'

'Yes. The better you are at this work, the greater your danger. We have decided to find out what it was that Selim Beg had come to know. We have decided that none of our agents has enough learning for the job – except one Hindu who is now in Tibet, and he'd never do for Moslem countries. We have been waiting for the right man. We are in no great hurry. This is big and it will therefore develop slowly. You have the qualities needed for the work. We have the time to add to those qualities our specialized training. From the impersonal standpoint of duty, there is no further problem.'

Major Hayling got up and began to pace the veranda with long, slow strides. When opposite Robin on his third trip he wheeled curtly and snapped, 'Unfortunately, we are people. Do you want to leave Anne for months on end?'

Robin said, 'No, sir.' He didn't add, 'but I'll have to.' There was no need. She saw it in his face, in a kind of sadness that was not regret but something more remote.

Hayling said, 'You've just asked her to marry you. You realize that when you return – if you return – you may be a changed man?' Anne wanted to interrupt, challenging him. But it was Robin's place to answer that question. Also she thought there was an overtone to it; that it was not a simple question of whether Robin would still want to marry her, but something else that she did not quite comprehend.

Robin was white of face and sweating. 'I realize, sir. Whatever I do, someone will be hurt.'

Hayling said slowly, 'I fear so. But *I* am a person too, and I have to tell you that I love Anne. So – I will not be responsible for sending you away until you have married her.' With an effort he regained his usual hard self-control, but his hand still trembled slightly as he adjusted his eye-patch. 'I must go now. With your permission, I'll take the jezail. No, hand it up to me when I've mounted, please.'

When he was gone Anne said heavily, 'I've got to get back at once. Don't you want to marry me, Robin? You don't have to. I won't sue you for breach of promise.' After the hunt and the tension of Hayling's talk all her strings were unloosed and shuddering within her. She felt sick.

Robin said, 'I'll walk back to your bungalow with you. My sais can bring Beauty along.' She nodded dispiritedly. He said, as they set off down the drive together, 'Major Hayling is a good man. We've got to trust him.'

'We have? You mean *you* have. I don't trust him – oh dear, I suppose I do.' In the books men in Robin's position were always jealous. Jealousy was a terrible evil, but it was more human than this.

Robin stopped in the middle of the walk at the side of the road and faced her. He took her two hands in his. There were few people about at this time, but she knew the word would go around. In Peshawar nothing could be hidden. Her weariness began perceptibly to fall away, leaving her shoulders light and her head clear.

Robin spoke slowly, and his voice dropped a tone. 'Listen. Hayling seems to know exactly what I feel. Sometimes I think that what I want in life is outside me – you, love, friends. Sometimes I think it is inside me. And if that's true, then you and every other person would always be outside. The work Hayling has for me will give me the opportunity to find out which of the two is the truth.'

'But we can't wait,' she muttered. 'We have to get married before Major Hayling asks for you. And, Robin – I don't want to wait. I don't care how long you have to be away. Then I'll wait. I want you to know that *I* am here for you to come back to, whoever else changes, whatever else happens.'

He didn't pause long before answering. All this he seemed to have foreseen. He said, 'You deserve someone better than me. Someone different. Your eyes shine; your hair is so thick and beautiful in the sun. You are brave and kind. It's like being in the sun when you look at me.'

'That's because I love you,' she said. There *were* people about.

Someone's bearer was skirting carefully around them and listening, goggle-eyed.

'How can we get your mother's consent?'

She took a deep breath. 'Compromise me.'

He stared down at her, and she blushed a furious, welling crimson. 'Take me out riding to-morrow afternoon, say we'll be back by tea-time – they can't say no, and if they do I'll go, any-way – but let one of the horses lose a shoe, or we'll get lost and not come back till midnight.'

'It might not work,' he said calmly. 'They might guess the truth and take no notice.'

'Not my mother! She'll have the wedding arranged at once. That – that's all you have to do – to compromise me, isn't it? I mean, if – it has to be – something else, I – Robin – Robin!'

'That is all,' he said, and kissed her quickly on the mouth.

CHAPTER NINE

*

SOME people stationed in Nowshera – friends of the Hildreth family – had sworn they'd brighten up the dak-bungalow, but when Anne and Robin got there from Peshawar it looked as spiritless as on the last occasion she had seen it. Standing on the veranda, watching the hired carriage rattle away towards the Nowshera bazaar, she thought, They put Selim Beg to lie here in the cold, where my feet stand. Only travellers used the bungalow, and none of them for long, nor any with desire to impress their personalities upon it. But there should have been flowers for the traveller Selim Beg, if not for the travellers Robin and Anne Savage.

She'd have two days and three nights here with him, to remember as a honeymoon when he and she had parted. The carriage disappeared, and they turned together and entered the bungalow.

Robin went out again at once to find the watchman. For a minute she watched the Pathan bearer unpacking her dresses, then she sent him out. The old man knew nothing about women's clothes and seemed shocked and embarrassed at having to deal with them. She finished the job herself, working slowly and thoughtfully.

It had been a long day, and she had travelled far – from expectation to achievement, from Peshawar to Nowshera. On this, her wedding morning, she had seen the dawn. As she lay, mysteriously shivering, the fingers of light reached around the eastern horizon and spread behind the southern and northern mountains. A minute before, the night had held both the sky and the mountains wrapped together in the same blue darkness. Then the light came into the sky so that it slid farther and farther, infinitely far, away and left the mountains dark-blue, ragged-peaked, and alone. It was an ill joke to play on her – perhaps that was why she had shivered – that usually it was only on hunting mornings that she saw the dawn. All day the sun had shone. By noontime it had warmed the earth so that the air stirred and a breeze blew.

She closed the wardrobe doors, took off her shoes, eased her corset, and lay down wearily on the bed.

This was not just one day of journeying drawing to a close, but the last of twenty-two consecutive days. They counted from the stroke of that midnight when she and Robin had got back from their 'compromise' ride. The guards seemed to be expecting them; she found out later that that was Major Hayling's work. How had he guessed? She didn't have time to think much about it, still less to discuss it, though she had seen a lot of the major. She could not have got through those three weeks without him – him and Mrs Savage, Senior, Caroline. Rupert Hayling got most of the practical arrangements made, in the face of her mother's new dislike of him. She seemed to hold him responsible for the whole affair, presumably because he had not accepted the slave girl offered to him. Her mother could not know, and Anne did not tell her, that it was not his fault. So Anne had relied on him to do the things her father would forget to do. He had not failed her, and Robin was not jealous. Of course he had no reason to be, but – she set her mind to it and, after an effort, imagined Robin seeing as much of Edith Collett as she had of Rupert Hayling. She would have wanted to ask him questions about his visits – what did they talk about, why couldn't he get help from some other woman – herself, for instance – or from another man? Therefore she was a jealous woman, and not yet married twelve hours. It was a nice warm feeling. If Robin could experience that same little spurt in himself – why, he would come close to her and speak hotly, and then . . . Her heart kicked, and she got up quickly to wash her face in cold water.

From the centre room she watched Robin returning across the compound. He too was tired, and still dirty from the road. The watchman followed him in, salaamed to her, and drew a thin, dirty register out of the table drawer. He opened the book and brought out a pen and a bottle of gummy ink. He gave the pen to Robin and stood respectfully aside.

In the first column, under *Name*, Robin wrote 'Mr and Mrs R. Savage'. He did not turn and smile at her, though it was the first time he had ever written the words. Her right hand, rising to touch the fingers of his left, fell again to her side.

In the second column, under *Regiment*, he wrote '13th

106

Gurkhas.' At the third column, under *Nature of Duty*, he paused. Finally he wrote 'Honeymoon'.

Anne stammered, 'I have to change,' and returned to the bedroom. Most of the entries in the third column of the visitors' register read simply 'Duty' or 'Leave'. Some men she knew might write 'Honeymoon' as a joke. But to her, considering the way in which she and Robin had achieved their marriage, it wasn't a joke but a wound. Besides, Robin did not make jokes like that. He didn't make any jokes. She jerked off her dress and threw it down. Let the bearer learn how to put *that* away. Still it would have been as bad if he'd written 'Duty', and he couldn't write 'Leave' because officially he was travelling to Simla on orders. After that she didn't know. He would tell her if he could. She sat down in the zinc tub, scrubbed her back carefully with the loofah, and washed herself all over with soap and water. As she finished dressing, Robin knocked. She went out to the centre room, and he went into the bedroom.

She began to thumb over some tattered copies of the *Illustrated London News*, but they were old and she had read them. She heard Robin moving about; the walls were not thick, and there was a great space under the bedroom door. She looked at the backs of the books on a hanging shelf and pulled one out. She began to read. After two pages she found she could not understand what the writer was telling her. Also, fish insects had eaten pieces out of the paper. She put the book down and stared at the front door.

Robin came out of the bedroom, doing up the last button of his velvet smoking jacket. His thick hair was brushed down and shiny from the water on it. She leaned back in her chair, felt the brush of his lips on her forehead, and closed her eyes. When he spoke his voice came from far away. 'I expect we shall have barley soup, roast chicken, caramel custard, and Angels on Horseback.'

She sat up with a jerk. He couldn't be teasing her on purpose; he wasn't Rupert Hayling. It was lucky she loved him. She suppressed a giggle and said, 'I'm not going to argue with you, Robin. I've been in India nearly as long as you have, remember. But the chicken will be boily-roast.'

The bearer soon brought in the first course, taking the tepid dishes from the bungalow watchman on the veranda. The watchman, who was also the cook, had walked the better part of a hundred yards with them from his kitchen across the compound. She ate slowly. She wanted the meal to end, but she feared the actual moment when the bearer would say, 'Anything more to-night, sahib?' and Robin would answer, 'No,' and the bearer would put his hand to his forehead in his curt Pathan way and say, 'Salaam, sahib. Salaam, memsahiba,' and leave her to the lamp and the flickering fire and the strange man and the beds lying on the other side of the warped door.

She would be 'brought to bed of a fine boy'. It was a funny phrase, really, and of course she didn't mean that. What she meant was – she'd be brought to bed of twins, love and trust, and she knew that she would have to struggle to give them birth. Before her first talk with Caroline Savage, early in those three weeks, she had been in despair. She had hunted her love and brought him down, and when he lay at her feet and she saw the mysterious nature of him she did not know how she could prove to him, in life, that she was not really his huntress but his heart. Where was her strength, where would she find persuasion, when her man looked out of different windows, knew fear but no strife, and was encased in crystal armour? In her innocence she had not known, and she hated her mother for not telling her before and for making the secret out to be so tawdry when she did.

Her body could be proof and power and persuasion. There was no other way of showing Robin that not everyone who came close to him suffered hurt thereby. Mrs Savage had told her about the physical hurt, but that would be nothing. In her joy of possession, at the finding of this weapon of love, her body, she would notice no pain. That she knew.

She knew because . . .

'Salaam, sahib. Salaam, memsahiba.'

She was in one of the chairs. She must have eaten her way through the menu, and it must have been as forecast, except that there was a taste of curry in her mouth – chicken curry instead of roast chicken. And she must have been talking, because Robin was answering something she had said.

She knew because . . . Caroline Savage had greeted her in the big drawing-room of the big bungalow at the other end of Peshawar cantonment. In that room it was cool, almost cold, and yet the light flooded in cheerfully. Servants moved about all the time during her visit, and the door was open and the windows open.

Yet she was certain that no one would intrude or even overhear. More, she wouldn't care if they did. It was soon after the engagement, when every weapon she tried to use to prove her love melted in her hand.

Caroline Savage had white hair and a small face, young, and firmly boned. She said, 'I'm glad you helped make up Robin's mind for him. You are the best hope he'll ever know of happiness as you and I understand it. And he is your best hope of real happiness, greater than any other man can give you. You know that, I can see. I would never have forgiven you if you had faltered. Mind, I don't say he and you will be happy, I say it's his only chance and your best. He knows.'

Startled by the intensity of the words and the calmness of their delivery, Anne listened more attentively. She had come prepared for platitudes, or to be upbraided, and had deadened her mind in readiness. Mrs Savage continued. 'He doesn't like me very much, but that's neither here nor there. He is not an ordinary young man.'

'People don't understand him,' Anne murmured. 'He's a cat.'

'Who gave you that idea? Major Hayling? He's a wise man. But, my dear, you must not think that people are your enemies, that you have to fight them on Robin's behalf. I fear that your foe is in Robin, and I think you will need the help of people, not their enmity. If it is a sort of melancholia, you'll win. If it's – something else, you won't.'

'What "something else", Mrs Savage?'

'I don't know. The wind?' Mrs Savage faced her seriously. 'All the Savages are passionate, Anne. If it isn't for women, it's for something else – action, money, drink, even death, I've heard. Neither his father nor I can make out what Robin's passion is, though we have tried – tried too hard, perhaps. I hope and pray that it will be women – a woman – you! Do you know what passion is, Anne?' She looked her in the eye. 'Have you had sexual experience?'

Her mother's ugly, halting explanations that were no more than innuendoes made Anne begin to blush as she remembered them. Then she said humbly, 'No, Mrs Savage.'

Mrs Savage smiled quickly and leaned forward in her chair to kiss Anne gently on the cheek. 'I think that you know passion but have not had experience. I could wish that you had. I am

109

positive that Robin has not either, and ...' She got up, walked slowly to the window, looked out for a time, and sat down again. 'I am the only mother he has. I cannot have this chance for his happiness, and yours, risked by misunderstandings, shyness, ignorance. You know' – she smiled at Anne – 'the best person to tell you would be someone like Major Hayling. It would be less clinical, and he's a good man. But those days have not come yet ...

'Robin's mother was murdered in the Mutiny; he was only two and a half, and unconscious, but he says he saw it done. Really he remembers what Lachman has told him since, but it's real to him. Men he had trusted and loved all his short years picked him up by the heels and swung his head against a wall. His father carried him in a sack for hours, and later, with my help, dropped him down a sixty-foot shaft – to save his life, but he didn't know that. How could he? All he remembers is that we prised his fingers loose and pushed him down.

'Oh, there were many more cruelties. I am not going to have him saddled with another one, the idea that physical love is degrading to you and brutalizing to him. I am going to tell you that the body of the man you love, in you, *is* love. Haven't you ever felt that you wanted to wrap your love around Robin? God made us so that with our bodies we can physically do it. Haven't you ever felt that you were incomplete without him, that you were empty and aching for his love to fill you? That is love, Anne, and it comes about when passion – lust, I don't care what they call it – melts you together. You will never know anything more close to God's kindness, except bearing Robin's child. I am a nurse – but that's nothing. I am a mother, a wife, and' – she touched Anne's head with her fingers – 'a lover. My dear new daughter, listen while I tell you the wonderful way God made these things to come about.'

Anne had gone home at last, warm inside and crying happily into her handkerchief so that her mother asked what her high and mighty ladyship had said to hurt her. But Anne could only shake her head and run to her bedroom and lie down and remember. She dozed off, thinking of Caroline Savage's last words and final, brief smile. 'Now forget all the details, Anne. You are not going to take an examination for a degree – though some of our fallen sisters do exactly that, did you know?' Anne thought Mrs

Savage might have winked; certainly her eyes had crinkled up as she continued. 'You do not have to think physical love into existence, but only to take it – I know it is there between you and Robin – and grow it.'

The lamp on the table sputtered, and the wall at which she had been looking came into focus. She said, 'Shall we retire, Robin? We're both tired.'

In the bedroom she turned naturally, in front of the mirror, and asked him to undo her dress at the back. His fingers were slow and cool. 'There, it's undone.' She took off her petticoats and corset and sat down in her chemise in front of the mirror. Her husband stood a little behind her. She watched his face as she combed out her hair, bent her head, and began to brush the long, falling mass, stroking it hard.

Robin said, 'You have beautiful hair. The lights in it run in long bands as if it were made of something solid. It will be difficult to get that effect.'

She said, 'Painting? Do you—? Oh, Robin!' She put down the brush. 'Did you paint those pictures in your room in Peshawar?'

'Yes.'

'You never told me. I didn't know.'

'I'm going to paint you to-morrow. I've never tried to do a person before, but I must.'

'Thank you, Robin. I shall love it.' She took up the brush and after fifty strokes on each side of her head put it down. Slowly she took off her stockings. She sat down on the edge of the bed, wearing only the chemise and wide, split-legged drawers. Robin took off his coat.

She stood up and came half a step towards him and looked him in the eyes. His eyes were unchanged, like the moving browns and greens of a river, friendly, unreadable. She bent her head to kiss his hand. 'Robin, I love you.' The trust and the utter confidence swelled up inside her and passed through her lips. She did not know what shyness or lust or good or evil were.

He said, 'I know, Anne. I can feel it in my hand.' He lifted it up and looked at it, where she had kissed it. 'There. Now.' He kissed her hand as she had kissed his. It was only – a kiss, and she looked blankly at him because she knew he loved her, and where, oh God, where was the barrier?

He made her sit down again and sat beside her. Then he said, 'We have two days. After that we won't be together again until I come back from the training they are going to give me for my job – about five months. I have a lot to learn. When I do come back it may only be for a day or two. Then I'll have to go again, on the job itself.'

She could not prove anything important to him by sitting here half undressed and holding his hand. Mrs Savage was wonderful, but even she had supposed that there would be an opportunity. She had said nothing about making one. Anne took her night-dress and went into the bathroom. The nightdress was nothing but a plain white cotton gown with no lace and no frills. She looked at it doubtfully, put it on, and applied some perfume behind her ears. Were these, after all, woman's weapons and power, as they whispered in the ladies' rooms and behind the fans? These – line and shape, feel and smell – and not trust, affection, love? Or could not the outward designs serve the in-ward purpose? She waited, hearing the rustling movements of his undressing. Then there was stillness, and she came out.

He was standing near the light on the little occasional table in the middle of the room. She slipped into her bed, the one nearest the window. He turned down the lamp, and in the tiny glow she saw his face staring down at the wick as it died. Lying stiff as a bolt, she heard him kick his slippers off under the other bed. Then he walked barefoot across the matting floor. His breathing was close above her. His body moved, and she heard the small thump of his knees as he knelt beside her. She reached up tentatively. Above all, she must not seize him. He must forget that the huntress had ever existed; instead he must know that she was his heart and throbbed now in a perfect rhythmical ecstasy of trust, each beat reaching out farther, like a wave, than the one before.

He said, not whispering, so that the words beat very loudly against her ears in the darkness, 'Anne, I think I'm learning what love is. I couldn't bear to see you hurt yourself. Is that love?'

She said, 'Yes, but – Robin, with you I won't, I can't. Oh, darling, don't you see I'm hurt because I can't get close to you – only this way?'

After a long time he said, 'I can feel you crying. I shall feel

112

it all the time I'm away. It'll be worse, it will be impossible to bear, if you come to cry because there is nothing this way either.'

'There is, there must be.'

'Anne, I'm frightened. The closer I get to you the more frightened I become – for you. No, that's a bloody lie. For myself.'

She heard the nawar creak in the other bed. Half the night rats ran around on the ceiling cloth. Boards creaked suddenly in the centre room, and the waning fire crackled. She had not actually wept – Robin had felt those tears inside her – and, she clenched her teeth together, she would not cry now. She would not feel shame or outrage or disappointment – anything.

But it became difficult to order her feelings. In the early hours she saw Robin's love and trust as apples on top of a wall, beyond her reach. Caroline Savage's ladder wasn't long enough, or the ground wasn't firm enough to set it up – something was wrong. She did not feel the old misery of despair, because there must be a way to climb the wall that was Robin's nature. Somebody must know. Robin could not bear to hurt her, but because she loved him she would be hurt only if the wall proved to be unclimbable. Then her wound would be most desperate.

She was hunting again. Robin had not sought out her love or forced it from her. How could he know its depth and its power of perseverance? She was like nothing but a lioness, padding up and down, up and down, lashing her tail.

But, dear God, I only want to make him unafraid.

How do you expect him to believe that?

By getting close to him, and – oh, please, please!

Someone must know.

Two weeks later, on a Sunday morning, dressed in her best and having come back from church, she told her mother that she was going out calling. Her mother said, 'Upon whom?' She answered, 'Just calling, Mother,' smiled thinly, and left the bungalow. She was a bride now; in five months and two weeks she would be a matron.

Ten minutes later she turned into Edith Collett's drive. The bearer came in answer to her call, looked at her in some surprise, but ushered her into a sparsely furnished drawing-room and hurried out to announce her. 'Mrs Savage,' she had said her name was. She called after the man, 'Say, "Robin Savage Memsahib".' While she waited she examined the room with interest. The colours of the furnishings were much lighter than she had ever seen in a house before. Long curtains of light blue swept back in gentle, hanging curves from the windows. None of the wood was mahogany. It was not a cosy place, not particularly tidy, but it was striking. One would have to notice it.

Edith Collett swept in with a rustle of blue Madras muslin. She sank down on a pouffe as Anne rose, and pulled Anne down with a pleasant laugh. 'Our most beautiful bride. I am glad you have come. Would you like some tea?'

'No, thank you, Mrs Collett. I – just wanted to call.'

'Now that you're married you'd like to disassociate yourself from your mother's rudeness?' said Mrs Collett, suddenly ceasing to smile. Anne knew that her mother had never called. Mrs Collett went on. 'That's very kind of you. But I knew it wasn't your fault, Anne.'

Anne blurted out, 'I've always wanted to call, honestly I have. And now I'm married it's different.'

'I'm sure it is, Anne. Nicer too, if you're lucky.'

Anne took a deep breath. 'Mrs Collett, you see, you're alone here, and I wondered – I thought – would you possibly let me come and share it with you – I mean live here and learn about housekeeping and do the work if it wouldn't be a nuisance for you – if you'd help me, tell me what to do so that I could learn, and not be in your way?'

Somehow she had offended the other woman. Mrs Collett leaned forward sharply. 'You mean, not in the way of what your mother doubtless calls my amours? But the truth is that you can't bear living under the same roof with her any longer, isn't it? Any port in a storm?'

Anne jumped up, feeling miserable and muddled. 'No, no, Mrs Collett! I mean, I *can't* bear it at home but I do want to come and live with you. I haven't asked my mother, or mentioned it even. She'd have a fit.'

'Why?' said Mrs Collett, less angrily, and waited, half smiling, for Anne's answer. Anne could not speak because the answer was 'My mother thinks you are an unpaid harlot.'

Mrs Collett said, 'You needn't answer. I know quite well what your mother thinks of me. The point is, do you agree?'

Anne said, 'Of course not, Mrs Collett. But – well, I wouldn't

114

care if the worst she thought was true. You've always been kind to me. I admire you and – and I want to be like you. I don't want any more mothers, not even Mrs Savage. I could go there, and she would be wonderful. It's not what I want. I'm married – but I don't know anything. I don't mean about babies, I know that, I mean about being a lady, a woman – well, being something more than a girl, anyway.' She had stated the problem as accurately as she could, and in terms as personal as she cared to use at this stage. Later, if she could bring herself to talk about Robin, and if Mrs Collett was as understanding close to as she was at a distance, she might …

But Mrs Collett seemed to know already; she was saying '… sure of yourself, confident, as a girl, and now you're not sure of anything all of a sudden, is that it? My poor dear! Now, now, don't worry about it. It's good. Some of these modern young women are too hard or too stupid to realize that they lack something.'

Edith Collett rose quickly but smoothly from the pouffe and left the room. Her skirts were as tight as Anne's, but she did not hobble; she swept out, and how she did it was a mystery of locomotion. Anne waited quietly until she returned, carrying a silver tray with a decanter and two glasses. She did not pour out the wine but set the tray down and looked steadily at Anne. Then she said, 'Anne, before you come here you must know that sometimes I *am* an immoral woman. There is a reason. My husband happens not to like women. I suppose I should report him to the police, but he's a very kind man and I can't do it. I can't even divorce him, because it would take away his – oh, call it his protective coloration. He'll be discovered one day. Then he'll shoot himself. Meantime, as I can't be a good wife, I have to try and be a good woman. When men are lonely or frightened, that isn't what it sounds – at least not in my opinion. Why do you think I told you that?' she finished suddenly.

Anne did not understand all she had heard, but she knew that Mrs Collett was weary and sad and, like herself, fighting. She said, 'I don't know, Mrs Collett. I'm glad you did tell me, though.'

Mrs Collett said, 'Is Robin one too, like my husband? Is that the trouble? There's something the matter with you, Anne. Can't you trust me?'

Anne dropped her head. She couldn't bring herself to say, 'My husband won't give me my connubial rights' – Mrs Savage said it should be 'rites'. Besides, that was a result of the trouble, not the trouble itself. The trouble was her lack of *savoir-faire*. Women who had *savoir-faire* could make a man believe anything – why not, then, the truth? She said, 'I love Robin, Mrs Collett, but I don't think – well, I'm twenty-three and yet with him I feel as if I were seven or eight. Can you, will you —?'

She felt Mrs Collett's plump arms around her and her low, rather hoarse voice in her ear. 'Of course I will, Anne. It gets lonely here sometimes, but together we can have a good time and enjoy ourselves. And now we will have a glass of this wine.' The wine was the colour of pale straw.

'Oh, thank you, I couldn't, Mrs Collett. I'm not allowed to take wine until the evening, and then only —'

'Not allowed, *Mrs Savage?* Call me Edith. This is Manzanilla. Some very dry sherries are called Manzanillas, but that's wrong. It's different, it's a wine by itself, it's – well, taste it. Have you ever had anything like that before?'

'No. It's like water. No, it's like fire, only it's smooth.' She sipped again. 'There, I had it on my tongue, but it's gone, and there's no taste left in my mouth. Now there is again! It's bitter, Edith – not for long. It's sort of half sweet, just for a moment. Why, it's fascinating!'

'Exactly, Anne. You've been a good, straightforward, wholesome Madeira for much too long.'

CHAPTER TEN

*

As the ponies slid gingerly down the last scree slope of the last hill Robin glanced back over his shoulder. Jagbir, twenty yards behind him, looked out of place on horseback. It was the effect of his infantryman's uniform and had not been the case while he had been wearing the loose woollen robes and felt boots of a Hazara tribesman.

They were returning from their five months' training. Robin turned forward and with his eye swept the Peshawar plain. In the distance he saw the trees surrounding the city and the cantonment. In the foreground a goatherd piped on a sarnai, leaning back against a rock, his rifle between his knees. He stood up as they came closer and held his rifle loosely ready in his hand. Robin said, 'May you never be tired!' 'May *you* never be tired!' 'Are you well?' 'I am well.' 'Are you right well?' 'I am right well.' 'Are you in good health?' 'I am in right good health.'

The goatherd remained standing by the rock, watching them. The ponies wended on across the stony level among the scattered grazing goats. The sun of mid-July beat back from the gravelly surface, and heat poured out in waves from the oven-like hills.

In Peshawar cantonment the few passers-by gazed curiously at them as they walked the drooping horses towards the Hildreths' bungalow. There Robin dismounted. It was only just after noon, and the family should not be asleep yet. He called quietly, '*Koi hai!*' The bearer shambled out of the bungalow, recognized him with a surprised salaam, and hurried back inside. On Robin's order Jagbir led the ponies to the stable. Robin found that he still had difficulty with the Gurkhali tongue; it was only a week since they had reverted to speaking it to each other.

Major Hildreth came on to the veranda, a newspaper in his hand, and stared with screwed-up eyes into the shimmering noon. 'Well, I'm damned! Robin. I say, come in, boy.' In the dark hall he grasped Robin's hand and peered closely into his face. 'Why, boy, you're as black as the ace of spades! I mean the sun has burned you. Where have you been? Oh, suppose you're not allowed to tell me, h'm?'

'Afghanistan, sir. It's a big country. Where's Anne?'

'Anne? Didn't you know? Here, sit down a minute. Anne's been – ah, living with Mrs Collett since you went away. Much more convenient, you know – I mean, well, boy, two women in one house! Mrs Hildreth's got a notion about Edith Collett, but it isn't so. She's a fine woman.'

'I understand, sir,' said Robin, smiling. He remembered hearing some gossip about Mrs Collett while he was here last. Not much, because few people had been talking to him then. It was good of Anne, and typical, to go to her.

'Want a glass of beer, my boy?'

'Yes, please, sir.'

The bearer brought the beer and poured it out, stooping obsequiously beside Robin's chair. Major Hildreth's popping eyes ran cautiously over Robin's dusty uniform. 'You didn't get much beer in Afghanistan, I suppose?'

'No, sir.'

'See much action? I mean – h'rrm – how was it up there?'

His father-in-law's several chins quivered with embarrassment, and his eyes wandered away. Poor man, he really was kind, and as thin-skinned as a gazelle in spite of his appearance. Robin said, 'No, sir, I didn't see any action. I think, if you'll excuse me, I must move on.'

'Must you? Oh, well – Sultan! Tell the Gurkha to bring the horses round. H'm.'

'Give my affectionate regards to Mrs Hildreth, won't you, sir?'

'Of course, of course. She's in Kashmir – Srinagar. Went up in May. I'm a grass-widower. Hardly a woman left in the station, except Anne and Mrs Collett.'

They stood on the veranda, waiting for the horses. Major Hildreth hemmed and cleared his throat once or twice before getting out, 'Give Anne a kiss from her father, eh? She's been in often to see me since May. Goes out a lot. Makes me feel like a child now. She's a great lady now – and – ah – she loves you, boy.'

'Thank you, sir. Good-bye.'

'Good-bye. Well – good-bye.' Robin and Jagbir mounted, and Major Hildreth watched them till they turned out of the drive. From the road Robin saw him shake his head, pick up his paper, and return inside the bungalow.

Major Hayling greeted them without surprise. He said, 'Good. Right on time. Would you like a bottle of beer?'

'Not another, sir, or I'll go to sleep.'

'How did you get here?'

'Over the Shutagardan, then through the Tirah.'

'Ah. Very few of us have been through there. I'm surprised the Kurram Valley commander didn't forbid you – oh, you didn't ask him? And you were in uniform? Yes, I see. Jagbir must make a perfect Hazara in the proper clothes, but of course I agree that a Hazara would be an unusual sight in the Tirah.'

They had reached the major's office. The walls were bare of pictures or maps, and very few papers lay on the desk. A large, square safe stood in one corner. Hayling lit a cigar. 'Have you been to see your wife yet?'

'No, sir. She'll be resting. I'll go in the evening.'

'Good idea. It's hot as hell now. We're having a real brute of a hot weather.' He glanced out of the window at a thermometer hanging in the shade of the veranda. 'A hundred and eighteen. You must be fried to a cinder.' He drew on his cigar. 'How did you get on in Gharghara?'

'All right, I think. I can speak Hazara and Zaboli Persian well enough. Jagbir learned Hazara quickly. He doesn't have a big vocabulary, but as a peasant he wouldn't. I learned something about business when I went on a trading trip to Herat in the late spring with Faiz Ali. I think I'm ready.'

'Good.' Hayling surveyed him through the cigar smoke. 'We're ready, too. You remember that report in the barrel of the jezail? It was from an agent in Jellalabad, to the Russians.'

'How is that known, sir?'

'Because the fellow works for both sides, and we know his handwriting. It was routine stuff, about our troop movements in Afghanistan. Our reconstruction of the whole story goes something like this. First, our man Selim Beg discovers something. He dares not trust even a word to paper. He scratches "Horses, north" on the butt of his gun and comes east, meaning to report to us well beyond the places where the Russians would expect him to come in. He was probably heading for Rawalpindi – even Simla. However, they get him and take his jezail because they suspect that he has his report rolled up in the barrel, or because they know he's scratched those two words on the butt.

'On the way back to their base – which was probably Balkh – they'd have to pass through Jellalabad, where the two-sided agent lives. He says, "Here, save me a trip, take this with you," and gives them his monthly routine report. They roll it up in the jezail. That's important, in spite of the report's actually being valueless, because it proves that the men who murdered Selim Beg and took his jezail *are* connected with Russian espionage, which in turn proves that Selim Beg had something big to tell us. Well then, these two stumble into your battle, and so – you get married and live happily ever after. Damn it, I'm sorry, Robin.'

Robin's head kept nodding forward. The major's spurt of bitterness could not penetrate his weariness.

Hayling said, 'Keep awake another minute. We – by which I mean the Viceroy and the government at home – have come to the conclusion, on other grounds of course, that the Russians mean business. Events may change the Czar's mind, but at this moment his generals are planning further large advances southward. Our agents will remain at their posts. As they are local men they cannot readily move. Independently of them, you will enter Russian-controlled Asia and find out what the Russians' specific plan is. We know their general intention – an advance on India. What we don't know is the methods by which they hope to achieve it. You and I leave by dak to-morrow morning for railhead, then train and dak to Simla. In Simla you will receive full information, but no more instructions. There aren't any.'

'Will I be coming back here afterwards?'

'I doubt it.' Hayling pushed back his chair quickly. 'That is not my doing. Here.' He pushed open the door of a small room off his study. It contained a narrow camp bed and a single camp chair. 'Sleep here until you're ready to go to your wife's. Come back at seven to-morrow morning. By the way, where are your desi clothes, and Jagbir's?'

'In the Nau Jabbar Khan serai in Kabul.'

'With Dost Khan?'

'Yes, sir.'

'Good. Now get some sleep. I'll tell that little man of yours.'

Robin awoke and knew without looking at his watch that it was five o'clock. The sun still shone, but the glare had died out of it, and a slight, hot breeze ruffled the trees. He dressed and whistled quietly outside the servants' quarters. Jagbir appeared immediately, wearing only white cotton drawers. Robin said, 'I'm going to my memsahib. There's nothing for you until seven to-morrow morning, here. We're going to Simla.' He walked across the compound to the stables and began to resaddle Bahram, the shaggy pony he'd bought during his schooling period in Gharghara.

Behind him Jagbir cleared his throat cautiously; then again. Robin said, 'What is it, son?'

'Got no money. Want five rupees. Loan. Till pay-day.'

Robin smiled, found a ten-rupee note in his pocket and handed it over. 'The government owes you a lot more than this by now. Remember these people here are not Hazaras but Pathans. Pathan husbands have long knives and short tempers.'

'And fleas.' Jagbir smiled shyly, a warm, quiet grin that just showed his regular white teeth, and said, 'Perhaps I won't even need any money.'

Robin watched his back as he returned to the quarters. Jagbir knew all animals and knew himself as an animal, and women in their animal nature. He was never unhappy.

Robin rode out of the compound and across the cantonment to the Colletts' bungalow. He found Edith Collett in the garden, wearing a dark-blue dress and a large straw hat. She was walking slowly along behind a gardener and telling him which flowers to cut among the roses and the cannas. She looked up as he came in, and floated easily across the dry grass to him, her hand outstretched. By the time he dismounted a groom had appeared, running, to lead his horse away. She was well served.

She held out her hand. 'Why, Mr Savage! Oh, I'm going to call you Robin, whatever Anne thinks. Why didn't you warn us you were coming?'

'I couldn't, ma'am. Is Anne in?'

'Yes. Now don't go rushing in, dear boy. You'll frighten her into a fit. Wait in the drawing-room, first on the right inside, and I'll tell her you're here.'

She slipped into the house ahead of him and entered a door farther along the passage. Robin sat down in the drawing-room, leaned back, and waited. He wanted to see Anne but also he was afraid. In some ways he felt more confident than ever before in his life. He knew that he would face the work ahead of him with a kind of hard-edged competence. Here he was – lean, sunburned, fit, and ready. He could stand away from that able young man, appraise him, and admire. That man, Lieutenant Savage of the Intelligence, was like a razor. But Robin felt fear because he thought Anne might like the young fellow – she must have come here to Edith Collett's to cultivate competence – while he himself was not at all sure that he could bear to live with him.

For he – Robin, the doubtful searcher – was in no better case than when he had left for Gharghara. He still lacked something – a sign, a vision, what the chemists called a catalyst. The job, perhaps? Or Anne? He'd have to see what the months had done to her; she'd have had time to think. ... Asia was always waiting to see, waiting for travellers to come or to depart, waiting for camels, for horses, for the rain-storm to begin, the dust-storm to end.

He noticed that the language of his thoughts was Zaboli Persian. That Lieutenant Savage would surely go far. Mrs Collett walked with great poise, but perhaps she was not altogether happy. It would be sad if Anne had caught from her other unhappiness besides her own. Jagbir would be on his way to the bazaar to drink strong spirits and fall upon someone's wife. Jagbir was a lover but not a Lothario. He seemed able, just by looking shyly at her, to soften the fibres of any woman in Asia. In Gharghara the only people who had loved him better than the women were the women's husbands. He outdrank them, outclimbed them on the mountain, seldom spoke, heard a song once and sang it perfectly a week later, and ate great hunks of raw flesh with them as if he had been a Tartar of the Horde. He could not read and he could not write.

Robin had not moved hand or foot and he had been waiting a long time. She must be making a careful toilette. Five months ago she would have rushed in to him, flushed from afternoon sleep, dress awry, hair undone, face gleaming with sweat.

She came in almost silently, but he heard the thin shimmer of her dress. He guessed that she wanted to surprise him, so he did not move. She closed the door secretly behind her and slipped around until suddenly she was in front of him. He had been examining men and women for five months, learning to remember in one glance every detail of their faces, dress, and manner. Anne was very beautiful. Her red-gold hair was cut into a short fringe in front, highly curled on top, and coiled at the back.

Her dark-green dress curved up under her breasts, pushing them higher. The dress had a high neck and mutton-chop sleeves. Her waist was three inches smaller than it had been, and her bustle six inches bigger. He heard a low muttering in the passage and recognized the voices of Edith Collett and a servant.

Anne said, 'Robin, my darling husband!' She held out her hands, leaning back a little. He stood up, took her hands, and kissed them. They were white and smooth as alabaster, the nails manicured. Her eyelids fluttered down over her eyes, and she leaned forward to him, her lips parted. He pressed his lips, closed, against hers and turned his cheek gently to caress her face with his. Slowly she opened her eyes, carefully she disentangled her hands. 'Dearest! Oh, you're sunburned, but handsome!' Her eyes were bright, then the lids sank half over them again in a kind of drowsy abandon.

Her voice sounded strangely deep and throbbing. He said, 'Have you got a cold, Anne?'

She sat down. Leaning back in the chair, she said, 'No, silly! I'm feeling wonderful,' but her voice went uncertainly higher, and some of the words were almost as clear as of old. She said, 'Robin dear, I don't know where Edith's got to. Do go and call her.'

He went out into the passage and heard Mrs Collett's voice at the back of the house. Surely Anne must have asked her to stay away for a few minutes, until these first greetings were over. Why then did she pretend that Mrs Collett had disappeared?

Mrs Collett heard his footsteps and came along the passage to him. Her bearer followed with a bottle of wine and three glasses on a silver tray. In the drawing-room Edith said, 'Please pour for me, Robin.' He decanted a little into his own glass, sipped, and poured out for all three, filling his own glass last. He noticed Anne looking at him approvingly. She drawled, 'This is a Manzanilla, Robin.'

'Oh.'

'Whom shall we drink to, Edith?'

'To the bride and bridegroom! Then you can drink to each other and I to both of you!'

Robin lifted his glass and drank. It was a bitter-sweet, sophisticated wine, and he did not think Anne could really like it. The women chatted idly about people and events of Peshawar.

123

Anne used her hoarse new voice with a pleasant assurance. She made witty interjections, leaning back in her chair and holding her glass as if she had been born with it. Edith asked him to smoke, as neither of them minded tobacco. He drew cautiously on the first Egyptian cigarette he had seen for five months. After a hookah it tasted like hay. Anne had cut herself down so that she fitted perfectly into this environment; but she thought she had grown up to it. She sat in beauty and ease among the furniture, like a piece of it gifted with the power of speech.

In Afghanistan, above the Helmand River, the plains swept free to the mountain wall, and the wind blew cold across them. Men and women alike wore sheepskin coats and high felt boots. The black tents dotted the plain, and in them the women made a world and came to resemble their goats as Anne resembled the Chippendale. In the tents there was a cosy, familial smoke and the smells of fat and women and fecundity. Outside, the barren wind blew from pole to pole.

'Wouldn't you like to go and change now, Robin?' Anne asked at last. 'We'll have a late dinner. Your clothes will be laid out for you by now.'

The bearer was waiting for him at the door of the bedroom. This had been Anne's room alone for – what? – four months? It was new-pin tidy and smelled of eau de cologne and perfume. The red-gold curtains and bedspread would exactly match her hair. He turned back the cover curiously; the pillow-cases and sheets had been changed since she got up from her nap. The portrait he had painted of her hung above the bed. Looking at it, he saw that it contained nothing of her. The technique was good.

He told the bearer to leave him, and climbed into the tub. He had never liked servants hovering around him, and in the past months had got used to doing everything for himself. He hoped Anne would come and talk to him while he changed. The Anne he had left would have. That girl would have been running anxiously in and out to see if he needed anything, to assure herself that what she had arranged was right. However, everything *was* right, and this woman Anne knew that it was, so she wouldn't come.

It was strange, but he had not felt lonely in Gharghara. That had come only when his time was up and he had to return to

India. Every night of the journey increased his eagerness to see her and talk to her. He would keep berating himself for a fool that he had ever had a doubt about her. He would tell himself that her lively, radiant innocence was like the sun that he had once compared her to, shining into the dark corners of his mind. She could be a companion on the mountains to him, if he would teach her, he had said. He and she would share together whatever wonders they found in life, he had said.

Now it had all changed again. This place was not his place. Surely it was not hers either – but was she not altering herself to fit into it? At seven o'clock to-morrow morning he would be gone.

In the drawing-room he found Anne alone. He said, 'Where's Mrs Collett?'

'Do call her Edith. She had to go out to dinner.'

That was another lie. Colonel Franklin had properly called him a prig because such little deceptions hurt him. Of course Edith had gone out so that he and Anne could have this evening to themselves. He said, 'I won't have the chance to call her anything for a long time. I have to leave to-morrow.'

Anne's carefully arranged roguishness dissolved. He watched real sorrow and near-panic sweep across her face. Then she got control of herself. '*Robin*, what a shame! But I suppose it can't be helped. I did so want to hear all about what you've been doing, but we won't have time, will we? Have another glass of Manzanilla. Sit there and just let me look at you. You're thin, but so – strong-looking. You're not angry or anything, are you?' Her last words were uncertain and on them her voice wavered out of its low pitch.

'No. Why?'

'Your mouth.'

'I was born with it, Anne. I can't help it.'

'I love it.' When she poured out his wine she leaned across him, pressing her breast against his arm. Her perfume was the same as that which subtly permeated the bedroom. Before, she used to apply a simple flower perfume to herself in large quantities and smell wonderfully young and happy in consequence. This was heavier, tangier stuff, and it reminded him more of animals than of flowers.

She began to tell him of the efforts she had made not to feel

125

lonely while he was away. She was enthusiastic over the kindness and hospitality of the numerous grass-widowers in the station, who had been as lonely as she. She had seen a lot of Rupert, nearly as much of Tom, and quite a bit of Harry. Rupert was Major Hayling; she did mention the surnames of the others, but he forgot them by the time she'd finished the sentence. He nodded and agreed that they were good men to be so kind to her. Her manner changed. She became more hesitant and began almost to pout. After a time she changed the subject with a queer mixture of pique and relief. Soon after that the bearer announced that dinner was served. She stood near the door, smiling at him, until he held out his arm. Then, her hand light on his elbow, she glided at his side into the dining-room.

A single four-branched candelabra stood on the small rosewood dining-table. The light fell on the glowing wood and on the bank of white roses at each side. More roses in a wheel-vase ringed the base of the candelabra. Two silver-staved oak buckets stood on the sideboard, and from each protruded the neck of a bottle of champagne. The gold-foil labels glinted against the background of sparkling ice and rosy wood. The bearer pulled back Anne's chair, and Robin handed her into it. The double damask napkins were folded into patterns of rings, hers plain his spreading out at one side into a signet. The bearer served them ice-cold *consommé*.

She had changed, indeed. She drank two glasses of champagne for every one of his. He liked champagne but did not need much of it, and she kept urging him to take more. It had no evil effect on her; only her eyes sparkled and her tongue ran more easily, always smooth, always witty, sometimes warm. She dominated the little banquet without effort and without a word to the servants. She lifted her eyes off his for a fraction of a second, and a course was cleared away. She moved two fingers of her hand, and the glasses were refilled. Robin recognized with a pang that she had become expert in the mechanics of living, and that she thought the achievement was of the first importance. She showed the depth of her new competence when the main course came, and it was roast lamb. Robin said, 'I'm sorry, I don't eat meat any more.'

She took it in her stride, answering easily, 'Oh, really? I should have asked you,' and then for the first time spoke to the bearer. Five minutes later a plate of toasted cheese reached the table.

Afterwards she did comment on the incident. She said, 'You used to eat meat?'

'Yes, I gave it up.' He could not tell her why he had, because he wasn't sure that he could isolate the true reason. Perhaps it was just that he had been training himself to live on the simplest foods – the cheese, milk, curds, whey, and yoghurt of Gharghara. Perhaps it was something else – but Jagbir loved animals more than he did, yet would happily eat any meat except cow.

Ever since his arrival in Peshawar the weariness that followed him had been drawing closer. His sleep in Hayling's bungalow had hardly checked it. The champagne had slowed its advance, but here at Edith Collett's sadness and frustration had compounded it, and soon it would catch him and bear him down. Then after dinner Anne suggested going to bed, and in the invitation he heard the hour toll for his second trial. He was a young man and knew that he was loved. He knew, from the messages of many starlit, lonely nights, what joy she held for him and only for him. A part of him pressed eagerly forward because he was sure that the act of sexual union must contain a mystery, and he was seeking a mystery, a solution and appeasement of the mysterious isolation of his spirit, and this might be it. But he had no clue to the nature of it, and those men and women to whom it meant most were least able and least willing to explain it. Besides, if physical love contained – possibly – a mystic core, the act of it assuredly flung out tentacles which bound the man and the woman together even when they both had come to desire only separation. That he had seen and thought about many long nights, but found no explanation for. Some people said that the children born of the union became the bonds which held it together, but he thought they might be only physical reminders of unseen, always-felt moral ties. So to-night, if he could master his wilful body – which, to help him, was tired – and his hungry spirit, Anne would remain free and unbound until he *knew* what it was that he sought. It might be her. With a sudden foretaste of loneliness he prayed it would be. But it might be something else, and in that case, if he failed to-night, Anne would never be whole again. A part of her, wrenched out by the trailing fingers of to-night's union, would always follow him, wondering, searching,

127

trying to see what he saw, experience what he experienced.

The big bed was ready. While he undressed, Anne slipped out and returned in a minute with an opened split of champagne and two glasses. She went into the bathroom and came out a quarter of an hour later, wearing a muslin and silk nightdress with a low front and short puffed sleeves. The lights danced across her body as she moved, and the shadows swung closer together to shape her, like a woman seen through a misty waterfall. She raised her glass and drank to him, smiling over the rim.

She saw him staring at her and said, 'From Paris. Do you like it?' He nodded. She sat down in front of the mirror and began to brush her hair. He saw that her eyes watched him in the glass and that she was frightened.

His weariness, the only ally of his compassion, had deserted him. It was raised aloft, poised above his head ready to smother him, but on the field of battle were only two enormous strengths fighting their way up inside him – the strength to do and the strength not to do. Reaching out for help, his mind brought him visions of dogs that strove, with their tongues out, in the streets and of the bitches crying in pain afterwards because they could not escape from what they had achieved. He saw the young Hazara man and the Hazara woman whom he had surprised together on the hillside; he knew them, and each was married; unseen, he had watched the greetings, the play, the whole course of the love that became violence and, at last, despair.

Anne sank slowly back on the bed, never taking her eyes off him. Her slippers slid from her feet, her hair spread out in an aureole around her face. When she drew up her legs the night-dress fell back above her knees, wrinkling in transparent folds about her thighs. She raised her arms to him.

He held still, away from her, and knew that she would see the shape of his hurt in the lines of his chin and mouth.

The unnatural champagne-sparkle died in her green eyes. Her voice was like a frightened girl's, who sees death for the first time. He watched the tears spring out in the eyes that she could not seem to shut against him. She wept with wide eyes and, while weeping, slipped awkwardly under the sheet and pulled it up around her neck. No beauty remained in her face, only the ugliness of slack mouth and swelling eyelids and streaming cheeks. Robin's frantically rising lust sank away.

He had won. Perhaps a little, she had helped, because while he had been away she had made herself, to perfection, the woman that all men desire, and he was not 'all men'. He was himself, and it was easier for him to deny that woman than the simple, loving girl of his honeymoon.

As he had won, he saw that she had lost. She had failed to chain herself with the bonds that she desired and he feared. Everything she knew, he doubted.

For the first time he had come to grips with her beneath the layers of competence or shyness or ignorance. He was no longer aloof, fenced inside himself, but struggling face to face and eye to eye against her. She had broken his glass and come too close, and he was afraid. Hers was the same love, but stronger, that once long ago had suddenly vanished and become a long fall in a black well. She had been pushing him to the edge of a longer fall, a blacker well. But he had won and he hated her for loving him, with a crawling hate that flew up his spine and crinkled the short hairs at the back of his head. There was no escape from such love.

Her eyes changed as she saw his face. She knew. He ripped off the sheet and heard the fearful ecstasy in her cry – 'Robin!' He sprang on her, fierce as a hunter at her shriek. She struggled with him all night, with teeth and nails and flesh, until in the first light she fell back, open-mouthed, bleeding, insensible, and triumphant.

CHAPTER ELEVEN

*

ON August 14th, 1880, Robin and Jagbir came late in the afternoon to the city of Balkh. Here, forty-five miles south of the river, the Oxus valley was like an airless oven. The trail ran across flat loess soil to the grey walls of the dilapidated city. Small patches of orchard and market garden, listless and still in the heat, dotted the flat. Close on their right, where a string of camels showed that another road converged here on Balkh, humps and hillocks of older cities rose above the plain and the gardens. The walls of Balkh were in utter disrepair. She that had been called The Mother City of all earth had fallen on sad days. Robin wrapped the end of his robe more tightly around his mouth and stretched his legs in the wooden stirrups. The path widened, and Jagbir – who was not Jagbir, but Turfan – came up to ride at his side.

Jagbir wore a heavy black sheepskin cap, a doublet of dirty coarse-woven grey wool with tight, long sleeves, trousers of the same material ending under ragged puttees, and high, cross-laced boots of untanned hide. A grey blanket, carefully rolled to show its red and black border, hid the front arch of his saddle. He had a long rifle slung diagonally across his back, the muzzle pointing upwards and to the left behind his left shoulder. A curved sword hung from his leather belt on the left side, and a thin-bladed twelve-inch knife on the right side. Robin wore a grey astrakhan cap, a long white robe of fine linen, and red Persian slippers. He carried as weapons only a rifle and a jewelled knife in a jewelled sheath. They were, respectively, a Hazara peasant who had temporarily become a body servant, and his master, an Afghan trader of Persian descent.

A third horse, heavily loaded, walked at the end of a short rope behind Jagbir's pony. It carried bulging saddlebags, a goatskin full of water, several small sacks of food and fodder, a rattling miscellany of pots and pans, and bundles of blankets and spare clothes. Slung on Robin's and Jagbir's ponies were two or three more small skins full of water.

Robin coughed to clear the dust from his throat; some always

130

filtered through. The taste was as familiar as if he had never left Gharghara. The fleeting visit to India had never taken place; he had never worn that tight green uniform, never rushed in a train across the Punjab, never sat across a table under the Simla deodars, against a bank of rhododendrons, and talked in the cool midday with the heads of the government of India. But he had taken possession of his wife, and she of him. That was real; this scouring heat and harsh emptiness of Asia were real; three weeks' hard travel from the Indian frontier to here were real; Bahram's habit of biting his arm when being saddled was real. The rest was a dream.

He said, 'Nearly there now, Turfan.'

The language was comfortable in his mouth, and as right as Jagbir's gutturally mangled Turki. 'Yes, master. Where do we sleep the night?'

'We shall see. We'll refresh ourselves in the first tea-house we come to.'

Seen from outside, Balkh appeared to have died six hundred years before. Inside, the streets throbbed with life. It was still a caravan city. The black tents of Powindahs dotted the plain to the west, and the men were here in the town bargaining in Pushtu at the shops. The dust was here, brought in from the plain, deposited by generations of travellers, stirred up by hoofs and feet. The houses were drab, the stalls bright with cloth and fruit. Veiled Afghan women passed silently among unveiled, yelling Turki women.

After the silence of the road the noise beat at their ears. They slid down from their ponies in front of a small, open-fronted shop, tethered the ponies to the posts supporting the shop roof, and went in. The proprietor sat cross-legged at the back. Robin said, 'Iced sherbet for me and my servant.'

'Can't have it iced.' The proprietor grunted, remaining seated. 'No ice till next week.'

Robin shrugged. 'Some of your tea, then, if you have *that*.' Being of Persian blood, he was expected to be superciliously aware of the three thousand years of Persian culture behind him.

The proprietor brought them tea in tiny cups of delicate porcelain, but chipped and unwashed. When serving Jagbir he wrinkled his nose with great distaste. Robin sympathized with him. Jagbir was living his part completely and reeked of goat

131

and grease and sweaty wool. Robin lifted his cup between his palms, for it had no handle, and sipped noisily. 'These cups are filthy.'

'I do my best, lord,' the proprietor whined. Robin tossed down a coin. The man surreptitiously rang it on a stone and made to return to his carpet in the corner. Robin said, 'Wait. Do you know Selim Beg, the Learned One?'

'I know *every*body. He never was much of a customer here, and he's been away for some months now, I hear. Why, what do you —?'

Robin stared coldly at the man, who looked from him to the morosely glowering Jagbir and fell silent. Robin said, 'Has he moved his house recently, by any chance?'

'No, lord. Same house, at the corner of Tartar Street.'

Robin nodded and tossed him another small coin.

'Blessings on you, lord, the blessings of …'

Robin put his lips to his tea. Since leaving Simla he had been thinking whether or not he should publicly avow any connexion between himself and the dead Selim Beg. If he did avow it – as he just had – his unseen enemies would know that he was looking for Selim Beg; if they guessed the reason they could act at once, either to kill him or to dog his footsteps and hinder his investigations. On the other hand, Selim Beg must have had contacts. At his level, Asia being Asia, many of the people he talked to must have known the purpose of his questions and guessed whom he worked for. It was very possible that Selim Beg paid a few pence to his poorer confidants for their gossip. So, by making public that there was a connexion between himself and Selim Beg, he would announce himself to Selim Beg's friends. They might come to him with their news and their suspicions. He had to start somewhere, and had decided to take the risk.

When they had finished their tea they remounted and forced slowly on down the crowded street, one behind the other, the led packhorse last. Where Tartar Street bent sharply to the left the roadway widened. There was a well in the middle of the road there, and, set back on the right, a house behind a high wall. Its gates hung open on torn hinges. A fountain had once played in the courtyard, but it played no longer. Three mulberry trees drooped against a wall of cracked mud. Since the outer gates could no longer be closed, dogs and men used the courtyard

132

for a latrine. Robin pulled his pony to a halt and called, 'Ho, within! A friend of Selim Beg wishes to speak with him.'

A frowzy, black-costumed girl opened a door in the lower storey and shuffled out to stare at them. On the upper storey, behind a balcony just above the level of Robin's head, the dim, large face of a woman came to peer at him from the shadows of a room. Lastly, a pockmarked man joined the girl in the court-yard and said with no welcoming manner, 'Who are you? What do you want? The serai is outside the town, to the north-east.'

'I am Khussro of Gharghara, a horse trader. The benisons of Allah, of Mohammed, and of Ali his chosen successor be upon you!'

The man spat. 'We are Sunnis here.'

'So I guessed. That makes no need to deride the name of God. I would wish to talk with Selim Beg – a matter of business. Is he, by chance, within reach?'

Movements of a heavy body shook the upper storey. Sandalled feet thumped and clacked down an inside stairway. A fat hand came around the door and tugged the man's sleeve. He bent back his head and listened to a shrill whisper from inside the doorway. The servant girl stared numbly at Jagbir.

The pockmarked man turned to Robin. 'Come in, then. I am the brother of Selim Beg's wife. She is here.'

Robin followed the man into the house. Jagbir said a word to the servant girl, who burst out giggling but came to help him with the ponies. Selim Beg's wife was big and fat and encased in black robes with red patterns. A heavy black veil hung across her face just below the eyes and kept slipping down. Every minute she adjusted it; every other minute it fell down. She led the way into a small room. Light entered through a square hole in the wall. It was breathlessly hot.

She said, 'What news? You have seen him?'

Robin caught the brother's suspicious, pockmarked frown. He said, not speaking directly to either of the others, 'It was here that I hoped to receive news of him. There is this little matter of business that has remained unsettled for over a year. I found myself in Balkh, so —'

'We don't know anything about his debts,' the brother broke in roughly. 'We are not responsible for them.'

'I have not, I think, suggested that you are,' Robin said coldly.

133

'I hoped only to see Selim Beg himself, who is my friend. If he is not here, I am asking your hospitality under false pretences and will remove myself. Good day.'

'No. Stay!' the woman said abruptly. 'How long will your business keep you in Balkh? A few days? We can manage. Don't argue, man! If your brother-in-law owes this gentleman money, what less can we do?'

'He hasn't said yet that —'

'*Chut!* Show him the chamber at the end there. Food is ready, guest. We were just about to eat.'

The smells of hot bread, curry, and spice filled the house. The men sat down, and Jagbir joined them. The woman muttered at the servant girl, and the two of them brought on the food. Its quality did not live up to the savoury smell. It was poor stuff, and there was little of it. After the meal Robin soon went to his room. If the woman had anything to say she would come to him. He lay awake a long time on the threadbare rug in the middle of the floor. The moon shone in through a Persian grille, and the sounds of the town died slowly under the stifling heat.

He awoke silently and sat up. She was squatting beside his knees. She put her face so close to his that he could see the enlarged pores of her pale, yellow, shiny skin. 'What news? The truth.'

He took both her arms, above the elbows, and held them tight, his fingers sinking into the fat. 'Be brave. Do not make a sound. The man of your house is dead.'

She rocked to and fro on her heels. In spite of his warning her mouth opened, and she moaned, a long, low sound like wind in the streets at night. After a minute she whispered, 'He was my sun, and I his moon. Our children are long gone from our house. Are you one of his, like him?'

'Yes.'

'So much I felt in my bones, even through this fat. I was like a young doe.'

'Our enemies killed him near Attock on the borders of Ind, where he went with an important message. He died. He was true to his salt. What can you tell me that he – now – is no longer able to?'

'Little. He was afraid when he went, so he talked to me. He could not say much. What would I understand? But he did say

134

that much money, in gold, was reaching certain people here, from the west.'

'From the *west*? Are you sure?'

'Yes. From Herat and Meshed. He didn't tell me why; I think he did not know. That was all. I must go. My brother will kill me if he finds me here.'

'Listen. I'll stay a week or so. We'll get a chance to talk again. I have gold for you, for one thing, a pension from my government.'

'Ah, gold. He deserved it. But he is dead. *That* I won't show to my brother.' She rose creakingly upright.

He said, 'Wait. Whom used he to meet and talk with most?'

'Zarfaraz the banker and Gol Mohamed the trader in the Narrow Street.'

'I'll remember.'

She slipped out. He fell asleep at once.

Late the following afternoon, leaving Jagbir behind in the gloomy house, he strolled into the town. In return for a penny a crippled beggar answered his languid question – 'Where, O beloved of Allah, might one expect to find Gol Mohamed the trader at this hour?' Robin found the teashop indicated, squatted down, and ordered tea. Only one other customer was there. After a suitable time Robin said that this was a bigger town than Gharghara, in Hazarajat, where he came from. There followed between long intervals of tea-sipping silence, various polite questions from the other customer, among them one which would have exposed Robin's ignorance of Gharghara – if he had not indeed lived there for a considerable time. Robin became more alert. After another hour, as the sun was setting, he said, 'I must be going. Oh, yes, there is one small matter which had all but escaped me in my pleasure at conversing with you. Do you happen to know where Selim Beg is now, Selim Beg the Learned One?'

The other chewed on a cardamom seed, spat it out, and popped another into his mouth. 'No.'

Robin shrugged. 'He owes me a few rupees. Not enough to inconvenience him.'

A long pause. Still gazing out into the street, Gol Mohamed said, 'I used to see him once or twice. He was a discreet man.

135

He left town some months ago, I hear. I don't know where he went. Why should I?' Three minutes' silence. 'Some men from the west had business with him. Also a matter of debt, strangely. They were looking for him a day or two after he left.' Silence again. 'He seems to have had more debts than one suspected.'

Robin folded his robe about him and returned slowly to Tartar Street leaving the other drinking tea and chewing cardamom seeds exactly as when they had met two hours earlier.

The following evening at the same hour Robin went to the shop of Zarfaraz the banker. The banker sat on a carpet on a low wooden dais at the far end of his shop. His turban was pushed to the back of his head, displaying his stubbly grey hair. His grey beard wagged as he muttered to himself, and the beads of an abacus between his knees clicked like shuttles under his fingers. An Uzbeg in loose robes and a sheepskin hat, sweating profusely, squatted with a blunderbuss in the front of the shop.

From the step Robin said, 'Peace be with you, friend. Can you spare time for a little business?'

The banker looked at him over the tops of his spectacles, and after a time nodded imperceptibly. As Robin squatted near him, the old man said, 'You are Khussro, to whom Selim Beg owes a few rupees?'

Robin said, 'Yes. But I have come to ask if you will lend me some money.'

'How much and what for?' The banker continued working on the abacus, his fingers flicking the beads with such speed that the whole contraption rattled.

'Two thousand. For horse-trading. Until the end of the season. At any reasonable rate of usury.'

The banker leaned forward and wrote in a ledger that lay open on the mat in front of him. 'Where are you going to trade?'

Robin paused to emphasize his answer. 'North.'

'What security?'

'Note of hand.'

The old man shook his head and glanced up for the first time in some minutes. 'Not a hope.' He added as an afterthought, 'Horses are risky unless you know the ropes.' He turned the ledger accidentally with his foot, and Robin saw the word 'west' written, the ink still wet on it. The old man picked up the book.

'I'm getting old, can't add now.' He crossed out the word so that it was illegible and wrote a set of figures under it.

Robin said, 'I know my business, Zarfaraz. One other thing – do *you* happen to know where Selim Beg is? The money he owes me might be enough to finance my trip if I am careful.'

The banker said, 'I don't know. And if I did I wouldn't put his creditors on his trail. He doesn't owe me anything. I was his friend – like Gol Mohamed the trader and Yakub the jeweller.'

Robin rose, saying carelessly, 'He was a friend of mine too. Not all debts can be paid in rupees.' He strolled back down the street, looking at the shopmen's wares as he went. It did not take him long to find the shop of Yakub the jeweller. He paused there and began to examine the cheap scarabs, trinkets, and semi-precious stones on a tray near the front of the shop. He picked one up at random and said, 'How much is this?'

The wizened jeweller leaned forward and peered myopically at the stone, his head close to Robin's. 'Midnight. Here,' he mumbled.

Robin held the stone between the forefinger and thumb of his right hand, turning it this way and that to catch its feeble lights. '*That!* For this trash?'

The passers-by pressed close but saw only the familiar scene, a bargain being struck. The jeweller shook his head mournfully and said, 'The back door. Blue.'

Robin said, 'Half that, and I might think about it.' Yakub gesticulated and whined but when Robin put down a coin he took it, bit it, and hid it away in his belt. Robin moved on, the glass bauble in his hand. He circled around the bazaar until he found the alley behind the shops and in it noted Yakub's blue-painted back door. When he reached the house he called for Jagbir and warned him to be ready at a quarter to twelve.

They slipped out of the house a few minutes before midnight and walked purposefully, like men on their way to an assignation, through the bazaar. The voices of singing harlots sounded muffled and nasal from the boarded upper storeys. When they came to the blue door Jagbir scratched it with his nails, and it was opened at once from inside. The shadowy figure of Yakub started back in the passageway, whining fearfully, 'Who are you? Spare me!' Jagbir stood aside, and Robin entered, closing the door behind

137

him. To Yakub he whispered, 'Don't bolt it. My man stays outside.'

'Oh, is that who it is? I was afraid —'

'Well, hurry up, what have you got to tell me?'

'I know something, sahib-bahadur.'

'I am Khussro of Gharghara.'

'Sahib, I was a jeweller for ten years in Delhi, in the Chandni Chowk. You know it?'

'No.'

'I was there during the Great Mutiny. Many English sahibs had to pretend at that time that they were something else. I can tell an English sahib day or night, deaf and blindfolded.'

'You talk too much. What do you have to say?'

'Don't be afraid, though. None of these oafs would know you in a thousand years for what you are. Selim Beg went east. He was pursued, from the west.'

'Why? Who by?'

'A week before he left a traveller happened to tell me that the Russians were building a new town in the Akkal oasis on the edge of the Kara Kum, north of the mountains from Meshed. I asked myself why. I told Selim Beg. Perhaps he was taking that news east.'

'Perhaps.' The government of India had knowledge of the new town. It was not north of Balkh, but west, and it could not have anything to do with horses. It would probably turn out to be a station or depot of some kind on the railway that the Russians had just started building south-eastward from the Caspian Sea at Krasnovodsk. Robin said, 'Do you know of anything to do with horses that Selim Beg was interested in?'

'Horses? No, sahib. There would be a lot of camels around the new town, but horses ...' Robin felt his shrug.

'The north, then? All this talk is of the west. Did Selim Beg mention the north? Did he go north before that last trip?'

Again the shrug. 'The north? No.'

Robin paid him, slipped out, and returned to the house. He spent two more days in the same fashion, asking after Selim Beg, listening, inquiring, but found nothing further. The next evening at supper Selim Beg's widow began to upbraid Jagbir over his behaviour with the servant girl. The girl was squatting in the women's corner beside her but took no notice of what was being said. Neither did Jagbir. At last the widow directed her grumbling at Robin. 'Lord, please beat that little Tartar savage of yours. Or tell him to keep away from the girl. When he's here she does no work.'

Robin said, 'Have you tried telling the girl to keep away from him?'

'Tried?' She was grumbling but laughing too. She had given up all pretence of keeping herself veiled in their presence. Glancing over his shoulder at her, Robin saw by the light of the smoky wick that her eyes were twinkling. It was the first time since she'd heard of Selim Beg's death that she had shaken off, even for a minute, her pressing melancholy. Whatever Jagbir did, someone seemed to benefit. She went on shrilly. 'Tried! I've beaten her until her little bottom is black and blue. She doesn't mind as long as that – that young ram bruises the other side for her. Then she sleeps until midday, sleeps on her feet while she's supposed to be working! Working!'

Jagbir ate, said nothing, and maintained intact the round emptiness of his expression. The girl giggled foolishly.

After the meal Robin wondered whether he should speak to Jagbir but decided not to. To-morrow or the next day they must leave Balkh. Jagbir took no more thought for the morrow than a young stag. He stole with one hand and gave back double value with the other. He had an instinct for life, which everyone understood. If Robin himself possessed it, his life with Anne would be happy, whatever the ... But he must put young Savage to work on the imperial problems confronting him.

It was not often that the two parts of himself interfered with each other. When they did it always came about in the same way – that Robin broke into the deliberations or actions of Savage, as though to say, 'Let me help. I am more concerned in this than you realize. I alone can lead you to a solution.' It was not wholly a fanciful idea. In the train Hayling had asked him if he knew why he, particularly, had been chosen for this work. He had not known. He had thought once that Hayling might have got the job for him on Anne's behalf – so that he, Robin, could erase the stigma of cowardice from his reputation and so make Anne's life more comfortable. But he had soon realized that Hayling could not afford to indulge in such gestures, so he was glad when, there in the train, Hayling answered his own question. Hayling had spoken carefully, keeping his good eye fixed on Robin. 'You have a feel, an affinity, for emptiness. If I am not mistaken, you are looking for something in emptiness – in other words, in nothing. You are unhappy because you think you might not find it, and unhappy – for other people's sakes – because you think you might. The part of Asia where the solution of our problem lies consists of emptiness. Therefore I feel that the intrusion of the world there, however secret, however carefully concealed, will be more apparent to you than to others. Any Russian plans will involve the intrusion of the world. The desert and the mountains will look different, feel different – to you, not to me.'

Robin had nodded. Hayling's single eye saw a long way, and his single hand had a firm grasp. What Hayling did not say, but what he must also know, was that his reasoning held good in reverse. Because the work lay in the wilderness, Robin must enter the wilderness. In finding a solution to the public problem he might find a solution to his personal mystery.

Soon after supper Robin went to his room, lay down on the rug, folded his hands on his chest, and closed his eyes. The time had come to move.

Where?

In Asia, England and Russia faced each other across land that was like a broad, long, rough-hewn table. The prize was India, the great diamond in England's grasp at the eastern end of the table. The land was the deserts of Afghanistan, Persia, and Turkestan. For the most part there were no metalled roads, no rivers, and few people. Mountain ranges rose from the deserts, and the ruins of ancient civilizations dotted the oases. Geological chance had built a protective mountain barrier – the Karakorams, the Pamirs, the Hindu Kush – around the northern and western faces of India. England had no desire to advance from India against Russia, because whatever she took would be beyond the range of her sea power to hold. Already the landlocked Amir of Bukhara had asked Queen Victoria's permission to join the British Empire and had been regretfully refused.

Russia did desire to advance, and what she took she could, since the advent of railways, hold and expand.

From her position Russia had three lines of attack available to her. Firstly, she could move straight forward; on this line she

140

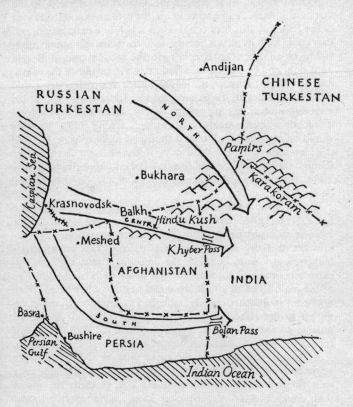

Sketch illustrating Robin's speculations on possible
Russian invasion routes

would pass through Balkh, climb the Hindu Kush, and advance
again through Kabul on Peshawar. Secondly, she could move
right; on this route she would keep south of all the mountains
and come in on India's left. Thirdly, she could go left; athwart
this route lay the immensely difficult passes of the Pamirs and the
Karakorams.

141

Against each of these attacks India could be defended. In the first case, if Russia came straight on, the defenders could advance to the Hindu Kush; they could reach it before Russia could, and they could hold its passes because their rearward communications would be shorter than Russia's. In the second case, if Russia went right and by-passed the Hindu Kush in favour of the southern deserts of Persia and Afghanistan, the defenders could receive the attack in the passes guarding India itself – the Bolan Pass and others, less important, nearby; there again their communication lines would be short and strong while Russia's would be stretched back over a thousand miles of waterless and trackless desert. In the third case, if Russia went left over the Pamirs, the defenders could forestall her on the passes and, once more, their rearward communications would be shorter and better.

In all this India would be taking advantage of what the general in Simla had called 'interior lines'. But there was a severe danger. Neither side possessed good lateral communications. For the attacker this did not matter very much. Once an attack is launched, it is launched. For the defender, India, the lack was extremely serious, because if she was deceived as to the direction of the main Russian attack she could not move her troops from one front to another quickly enough. For instance, troops committed to the Hindu Kush in the centre could not be moved quickly to the Bolan Pass in the south if the Russians' plans turned out to have been misinterpreted.

At Balkh, Robin lay in the direct line of a direct Russian advance over the Hindu Kush. All the rumours urging him west pointed along that same direct line, towards the towns that could become the Russian bases, advance bases, and staging areas – Meshed, Herat, the new town in the Akkal oasis, Krasnovodsk. When he looked west he was gazing down the barrel of a cannon aimed at India. But was it loaded? Would it ever be loaded? And Selim Beg had written 'north' in the wood of his jezail. There could be more than one cannon. West was the land of camels, north and farther north the land of horses.

North meant Bukhara, Samarkand, Khiva perhaps, Tashkent, Andijan, the Farghana. Russian activity there, as anywhere else, could mean one of two things – an attack, or the appearance of an attack.

Anyone knew that much. He was here to isolate the single truth, not to enumerate the multiple possibilities. He'd better classify exactly what the Russians could do, then deduce the clues that would be visible in each case, and then decide which clues to look for first.

Very well. Working backwards from that future day in eighteen-eighty-something when the Russians arrived in India – they would be coming along the northern, the central, or the southern route, or on a combination of those. Whatever this true plan of theirs is, let me call it the lowest level, the level of truth. Note One: They are unlikely to use all three routes because they would be too scattered. Note Two: For the same reason they will not use the northern and southern routes together. Note Three: They will not use the northern route by itself, because the country there is too difficult to enable them to deploy more than a small part of their available forces.

On their route or routes of invasion they will hope to meet no opposition. They will have made plans to achieve that end – that is, to hide the level of truth under a layer or level of deception. Because we are meant to find it and act on it, this level of deception will be closer to the surface than the level of truth, and easier to find and easier to work along. But it will be deep enough and difficult enough to convince us that it *is* the level of truth. And it must be – tactically, strategically, and administratively – as sound as the level of truth. If it isn't, we might find it but we wouldn't believe in it.

I am looking for work in progress. When I find it I must also find clues or facts that will help the government of India to decide whether it is the level of truth or the level of deception that I have uncovered. What such clues or facts might look like, I don't know. But I think I will know when I see them or feel them. No, that's what Hayling hopes will happen. I don't know.

Robin twisted uneasily on his rug. The floor was hard and comfortless. Which way? Not south, now. He'd have to look in that direction later. North? West? Which first? He might not live to cover both.

In this crisis he recalled the thoughts that had been holding his mind after supper. West of Balkh there were certainly deserts, but the land was not as empty as in the north. The farther west

143

he went the more he would move in civilization and among people. In the north were a few towns of ancient, long-departed glory; in between them and all around them, nothing – the Black Desert, the Hungry Steppe, the inexhaustible silence of the Pamirs. 'What went ye out for to seek?' The hands of men pointed west. He would go north.

CHAPTER TWELVE

*

BUKHARA was the capital city of an amir who had once been the chief among many independent princes of Turkestan. Now all the principalities lay under the hand of Russia, and though the khans and the amirs still reigned they did not rule. In Bukhara, Robin and Jagbir stayed in that one of the city's several caravanserais which lay closest to the eastern wall. From the first day they worked separately but on the same plan. They went out and strolled through the huge bazaars that contained seven intricate miles of streets. Their story, to be told only when asked, in the main to be left for the hearers to infer, was the truthful one that they were interested in horses. There was plenty to see and plenty to hear.

On that first day, within the first hour, Robin sensed that the stifling city reeked of intrigue. The Russians had been here twelve years. There were few overt signs of them – a hurrying officer seen in the bazaar, rumours of emissaries who wrote the Amir's letters for him, stories of barracks that were shortly to be put up outside the town to house Russian soldiers. That last would have been interesting, except that the government of India already knew it, and that taken alone it meant little.

Robin listened to talk of horses, asked people's opinions, gave his own, and heard a great deal. He could not tell yet whether any of it had value for him. In Bukhara everyone talked behind his hand, in undertones. In every tea-house and coffee shop there were three or four men perpetually whispering together. Once he placed himself so that he could, unknown to such a group, hear their talk. It was about a sacred text that had recently come up for sale in the book mart. In Bukhara secrecy had become a habit.

The bazaars were roofed over, every street separately, with roofs of beaten clay on undressed timber. They formed a many-branched endless tunnel where every noise echoed and redoubled itself, every smell stayed at the place of its birth to be increased by subsequent smells. And behind all, the whispering. On the third day Robin sought refuge in the quiet under the high brick dome of the book mart. Studying the famous text he had heard discussed, he saw that the man on his right, who had come to admire the same treasure, was a Powindah horse-trader. He had met and talked with the man the previous evening. He thought it might not be a coincidence that they met again here, so he said, 'May you never be tired!'

When the Pushtu greetings were at last out of the way the Powindah said, 'Let us retire to a corner. It is a happy chance to see you here. I have heard of a piece of business that may interest you.' Robin agreed politely that their meeting had been an opportune coincidence. It was obvious that the Powindah had come looking for him. When they were settled the Powindah said, 'I have been offered good money to take a couple of Russians, a man and a woman, south into Afghanistan.'

'Indeed? I hope you will get your money in advance.' Robin was not thinking of what the Powindah had said but of his motives in saying it.

'I'm not accepting. My business lies here, and north. I'll be going back south, of course, in a few weeks, but not the way these people want to go. If I recommend you to them, now, could we work out something?'

'I think so,' Robin said slowly. It was no good trying to assess the Powindah's motives until he knew what the Russians wanted. He'd have to take the offer – but not sound too enthusiastic about it – and in the meantime just note that the Powindah had guided him to it. This was not a trail that he had discovered by himself. He said again, 'I think so – a percentage perhaps? And I'll buy from you whatever animals I need for the trip? Something like that?'

Buyers moved slowly about the mart. Close by an old man droned aloud to himself from the Koran, his voice never changing pitch or tone.

The Powindah said, 'Twenty per cent.'

'Ten.'

'Fifteen.'

Robin shrugged, and the other said, 'Someone will come to you in the serai to-morrow morning.'

The following morning, while Robin and Jagbir were squatting over the little cooking fire in their serai cell, a Turki entered the main gate and asked a question of the keeper. The latter

146

pointed at Robin, and the Turki picked his way forward between the kneeling camels and the littered piles of dung. He wore ordinary Turki clothes, with the addition of a red waistcoat, which gave them the appearance of a livery. He stopped in front of Robin and asked, 'Are you Khussro the horse-trader?'

'Some say so.'

'My master wishes to speak to you. He is a foreigner, a Russian. Muralev is his name. Come at once.'

Robin answered coldly, 'I'll come when I am ready. Wait there.'

He ate his meal with deliberation while the servant stamped and fumed in the yard. At the end, after belching, Robin said to Jagbir, 'I'm going with this fellow now.' Jagbir grunted. Last night they had arranged that he would follow at a distance and watch the house until Robin came out.

The Turki led the way through the streets for over half a mile, to a house off Bukhara's great square, the Registan. Robin kicked off his slippers and followed the Turki up a narrow flight of wooden steps. The upper chamber was nearly dark. He paused inside the hanging curtain at the head of the stair and stood still until his eyes became accustomed to the gloom. Then he saw two people sitting on cushions at the far end of the room. He could not tell how tall the man was, but he seemed to be of medium height. He was about forty-five years old, and streaks of grey marked his thin, fair hair. He had a long nose, a big, tired face, and narrowish rather stooped shoulders. He wore European clothes, not too clean – white trousers, sandals, a white shirt. His coat lay in a careless heap on the rugs. He wore rimless spectacles.

The woman was a little younger, forty perhaps. She had thick blonde hair, a wide mouth, a good, short nose, and pale grey eyes set wide apart in a square face. Her high-necked Russian blouse looked extraordinarily incongruous above a pair of red silk harem trousers and big bare feet. Robin stared at her, forgetting his Persian manners. He knew in that instant that she was a Russian agent, and he was trying to work out why he knew. But it was no good. He dropped his eyes and stood in impassive silence until the man spoke.

'Greetings! Do you drink tea, Khussro? Ho, out there, bring tea, please! Take a place.' He had a thin, rasping voice, nasal but

147

not unpleasant. He spoke classical Persian with an accent.

Robin folded his feet under him on a cushion and still did not speak. He wanted to look at the woman again. She had not said a word and had hardly moved, but she exuded a dominant vitality. Now she spoke, also in Persian. 'You come from Afghanistan? Where?'

'My home is Gharghara.' He must not look directly at her. His first stare could have been excused on the grounds of surprise and curiosity.

'You know the route between here and Balkh and the roads east and south from there?' Her voice was full and strong.

'Well enough.' He did not know any routes beyond Balkh except the one he had taken from Kabul. He would have to cross that bridge when he came to it. A few questions in any serai would tell him all he'd need to know.

'Our friend the Powindah tells us you are interested in helping us.'

Robin said, 'I might be,' addressing the man. 'I want to hear more details.'

It was still the woman who took up the tale. She spoke directly at him, her voice like a tenor bell, her personality wholly feminine, yet very strong, demanding his attention. He would not look at her. He stared at the man, and the man, quietly absorbed, stared at him, studying him from head to toe.

The woman said, 'We, my husband and I, are – there's no word for it – we're birdcatchers. We catch birds and animals, skin them, and send the skins back to our friends in Russia, who put them in a big house and give them all names.'

Robin shrugged. Khussro would not know what a naturalist was, nor would he believe there were such people when the word was explained to him. He would be insulted that anyone should expect him to believe such a rigmarole. He said coldly, 'As the lady says.'

After a few words in Russian to her husband, the woman went on. 'We have enemies at home. They are jealous of us because our success puts us in greater favour than they with His Majesty the Czar. These enemies, who are also birdcatchers, are always trying to prevent us from reaching the places where the rare birds and animals are to be found. You see, there are honours to be earned for this work, from the Czar's hand. If we do not get

148

the honours, these others will. They are all learned men, but even learned men can be jealous. They say that we will cause trouble for Russia if we go where we want to, but their real reason is jealousy.'

Robin held his face immobile. He knew to what lengths the collector's passion will carry men, however learned and civilized. Khussro the trader, however, would not know, or at least would never be able to think of dead birds as reasonable objects of such a passion. His proper course now, and it would be a part of the Persian good manners expected of him, was to extend the appearance of credence to this nonsense, while indicating that in due time he would prefer to have the truth. He said therefore, 'There are indeed people in all countries who say one thing and mean another.'

The woman said, 'We want to go into Afghanistan – to Balkh first, thence probably east, we are not sure. We hear there are rare birds in the upper valley of the Oxus.'

'How did the lady hear?' said Robin quickly, addressing the man.

'We hear. We pay such men as you for news. We have been in these parts for some years, off and on. Well, we want to go, but the Amir will not let us. You realize that a Russian official advises him on many matters? That Russian is the brother of our greatest enemy. On his suggestion the Amir forbids us and has given orders that no one is to provide us with transport. Will you get ponies for us, arrange a small caravan, and take us? In secret, you understand.'

Robin stroked his chin. This latest information, if true, made it just possible that self-preservation was the Powindah's only motive in steering him here. Better a percentage than the bastinado. He said, 'My business brings me frequently to Bukhara – like the Powindah. Next year or the year after, when I return, the Amir will bastinado me or cause my ears to be cropped. Or perhaps he will have me thrown from the tower.' There was a tower two hundred feet high near the Kok Lumbez mosque. Nearly every day a criminal was cast screaming from the summit.

Muralev rasped softly. 'We don't think so. The Amir's adviser will shortly be replaced by a political agent, and we know who he will be – a friend of ours. Besides, we will pay you so well that you can afford to miss Bukhara for two or three years.'

Khussro would now want to know the truth behind the nonsense about catching birds, that they should be willing to spend so much money. But Robin did not want to press the Muralevs on that point yet. While he hesitated Muralev suddenly said, 'You are a good man. I would like to go with you.'

In the context it was a strange remark. Robin noticed that Muralev had shadowed blue eyes and poor teeth. There was something familiar about him – an air, a manner, a breath of aloofness or loneliness, something. Muralev said, 'If we have to have someone with us in the deserts and the mountains let it be you.'

Robin's nerves, taut till then, relaxed. He smiled and said easily, 'I will come.'

The Muralevs began to talk together in Russian, which Robin did not understand. He did not listen and did not look at them. There were three possibilities. Firstly, they might really be naturalists. If so, he'd be wasting his time with them, except that Muralev was an interesting man. Secondly, they might be Russian agents who had picked on him by chance to help them. That would be an amazing piece of luck. What was the Powindah's part in this? Thirdly, they might be Russian agents who knew that he was a British agent. Then what was their object? It could not be to kill him because that they could arrange in Bukhara at any time for a few coppers. It must be that they wanted to put him on a false scent – either right off the track or on to a level of deception.

The woman's whole personality shouted to him that she was not a naturalist. That left the other two possibilities, in both of which the Muralevs were Russian agents. Either suited him well enough. Even a false scent, if recognized as such, would be nearly as valuable as a true scent.

The Russians finished their discussion, and the woman turned to him. 'Attend! We want a riding horse, properly saddled, for our servant. We don't need horses for ourselves, because we have them. We want four or five ponies or donkeys to carry our tent, bedding, food, and the equipment we need to skin the birds and animals properly. Later, as we eat down our food, we will load the skins on the ponies. Can you get all that for us? Except the skinning things, of course, which we have here.' She pointed to two leather-bound boxes on the floor against the wall behind him.

'I want to take my violin,' the man said. The woman gestured with a helpless, affectionate smile and answered in Russian. She turned to Robin again. 'How soon can you arrange it?'

Robin thought before answering. 'Two days. On the second night I or my man will lead a donkey by here and stop for a minute in the courtyard, as though peddling. The donkey will have as load two empty boxes, like yours. While it is in the yard, change the boxes.'

'Good! Excellent!' the woman cried.

'On the third morning I will set out at dawn on the road to Balkh – the one that goes by way of Karshi. You go out shooting, on horseback but without baggage of any kind, some time that morning. Go north. Circle around the town till you meet the Balkh road, then go down it. I'll be waiting for you. We'll have to set off again at once as soon as you come, so nurse your horses. You cannot take your servant. He must stay here. He can say he does not know why you haven't returned from your shooting, if he's asked. Or he can say you're both ill of fever, smallpox. It depends how much he values his neck.'

'You seem to have much experience of these matters, Khussro,' Muralev said with his quiet harshness.

'No. But I live in Afghanistan.'

They both laughed, Muralev naturally, the woman with a full, slightly artificial trill.

Robin said, 'The second night and the third morning, then. I'll want two hundred roubles now for buying the animals, and fifteen a day – weekly, in advance – as long as you're with me. All in gold.' He noticed that it was the woman who gave him the money.

Later that day Robin completed his arrangements with the Powindah. All went well, and in the dawn of the third day he and Jagbir left Bukhara. The pack-pony's head-rope was attached to Robin's saddle, and Jagbir herded the five trotting donkeys as he rode. At nightfall the Muralevs joined them in the desert, and the whole party then moved on for another fifteen miles before pitching camp.

The next day the Muralevs cantered out ahead of the little caravan. He carried a collector's haversack slung on his back.

She wore baggy Russian trousers and top-boots, and she rode astride. Most of the time Robin could see them as little dots in the clear, dry atmosphere. Occasionally a trick of light made them very large ahead of him and raised them twenty feet or so, so that they seemed to be trotting on air well above the surface of the desert. They stopped frequently and Robin noted the places, and when he reached them looked carefully around to see what had interested the Muralevs. Sometimes he could detect nothing; sometimes they were places where the grass of the desert was slightly greener than elsewhere.

Towards the end of the day he caught up with them. Muralev turned over the page of the notebook on which he had been writing and beckoned him. When he came close Muralev showed him the book. The top page now carried a drawing of a small animal like a squirrel. Robin had seen many of them near this road when he had travelled it in the opposite direction. They were cheeky little things that sat up and chattered at travellers from a distance.

'This is a suslik,' Muralev said. 'There are many varieties to be recorded. Have you seen any?' He peered at Robin through his spectacles.

Robin shaded his eyes with his hand and glanced around. 'There.' He pointed.

Muralev took off his spectacles, stared, and said, '*Spermophilopsis*. Not a true suslik, but we'd like him.'

'There'll be plenty around our camp to-night. We can't stop here. We must get on. Come up!' Robin jerked the pack-horse's lead rope.

'Are they easy to catch?' the woman asked.

'I've never seen anyone try. They are unclean, not to be eaten by believers.'

'Of course. Well, let's move on.'

Jagbir had already passed them. He could not afford to stop or the donkeys would scatter and begin to graze. The Muralevs fell in on either side of Robin, they all talked pleasantly enough together and in due course came to the staging site.

The following afternoon the Muralevs left camp as soon as it was pitched, and headed off on foot to the north-east. In that direction a man on horseback, or from a desert hillock, could see the broken green lines of vegetation marking the courses of the

Karshi River, which here consisted of many channels that wandered through the desert like travellers lost and searching for water.

Jagbir freed the donkeys to graze. Robin saw that one of them was wandering off. As an excuse, it would do. He said, 'One of the donkeys has strayed, fool. Can't you keep an eye on them?'

Jagbir looked at the donkey, which was still in full view, and said, 'Do you want me to go and find it, lord?'

'No. Guard the camp.'

Robin mounted Bahram and set off on a circling course that would bring him through rolling dunes to the Muralevs. When he could get no closer without showing himself on the ridge tops, he dismounted, left the pony nibbling the grass, and climbed slowly up the dune. He dared not lie down; that would look suspicious if they were watching him, and he did not know exactly where they had got to. He stopped a few yards short of the crest so that, as he stood upright, only his head showed. For a minute he could not see them. Then he found them. They were on the near bank of a branch of the Karshi River. It did not seem to contain any water. They had their backs to him. The man was sitting, with something spread out on his knees – the notebook perhaps, or a larger volume. The woman was standing beside him, her rifle in her hand, moving her head slowly, looking around the grey and brown and green waste. Robin watched for ten minutes.

The susliks ran about and chattered at him from a safe distance. A hawk hung on racing wings above the desert. There was a hillock there, perhaps half a mile across this nearest branch of the Karshi. The hill looked familiar, and he stared at it for a long time. There was a ruin on top, a heap of scattered stones, no more. He put his hand to his belt where Alexander's coin lay. That was it. The hillock over there, though smaller, was the same shape as the hill by Tezin Kach. Well, Alexander had passed by this way too.

He shook his head, trying to dispel the warm haze of speculation that filled it. There was nothing more to see here. The Muralevs would soon go back to camp, and he had better be there before them. Whatever they were doing, they were not collecting specimens.

He walked down the dune, mounted, found the strayed

donkey, and urged it back to camp. Soon afterwards a rifle banged from the direction where the Muralevs had been. Half an hour later they straggled into camp, the man dusty and tired, the woman looking as clean and strong as ever. Robin saw her take her husband's hand as he sat down, and rub it gently and whisper something to him. The first time he had seen her he'd been sure that she was a Russian agent. Now he had another certainty, that she was a wife. She loved Muralev all right, but there was more to it than that. She was an agent and she was a wife. She must have had a great effect on him, on his personality, his spirit. He seemed too weakly fibred to match her. Anything, any person that she loved, she would overpower.

Later, when the fires were lit and she was cooking food, she looked up and spoke in Russian, wheedlingly. Muralev got out his violin, blew the sand from the battered surface, and began to play. He played a lilting gypsy air, and after the first statement the woman began to sing as she cooked. It was a desert darkness around them, grey-blue, cold, and a half-moon hung in the east. Orange leaves of flame grew in the fire and withered and grew again. The woman sang softly at first, but soon the rich contralto voice swelled and embraced the whole desert. Each note hung a time in the air, then vanished, without blur and without echo.

And there was a counterpoint. Jagbir was singing. Softly, level with the woman, far below the violin, he sang a Gurkha dancing song. '*Jaun, jaun, pareli, ankhen ma gazeli samajaunchhu Dehra Dun.*' His rhythm was different, his tune difficult and full of chromatic slides, his voice a nasal tenor. But it made a perfect counterpoint, and the meaning, the view of life, could not be far removed from that expressed in the woman's gypsy melody. Jagbir's song ran, 'When you see mascara'd eyes winking, you know you're near Dehra Dun.'

Robin thought drowsily that it was dangerous. But Jagbir would have guessed that the Muralevs could not recognize Gurkhali when they heard it. For his own part, dangerous or not Robin was glad. He would always remember this night.

Muralev drew the bow across the strings in a violent discord. In Turki he said, 'Enough!' and put the instrument away. He turned to Robin. 'We got a suslik, *Citellus fulvus oxianus*, a new species, I think. Perhaps it will become *Citellus fulvus oxianus Muralevi*. That means it will be named after her.' He nodded

154

towards his wife. 'The suslik has too many enemies. Every animal in the desert likes to eat him, and all the birds of prey. After supper I shall have to work on the skin. I would rather have left him to live in the desert all his life.'

From the fire the woman said, 'Don't be silly, Peter. If we didn't kill him, something else would. You've just said so.'

Robin thought: His fibres are not weaker than hers, but different. They run on another plane – like wings, perhaps – and she can't understand. She is his wife and she will keep his feet on the ground by the sheer strength of her love.

The woman said cheerfully, 'Food's ready,' and the group broke up.

CHAPTER THIRTEEN

*

LYING rolled in his robes, under blazing stars and the moon dark yellow in the west, Robin thought of the hill and the ruin he had seen a mile away. It was a beautiful night. But the work, the imperial problem, he had to think about that.

The Muralevs *were* naturalists after all. It was not only the technical talk and the Latin names, but the genuineness of Muralev's manner. Well, they could easily enough be both naturalists and agents. They were taking him south when he wanted to go north, and they seemed to be reconnoitring for water, or forage, or both. The growth and decay of towns had altered the water plan of this area; rivers which used to reach the Oxus or the Sea of Aral now died in the desert. A water survey would certainly be necessary if large bodies of troops were to use this route, which had once been more important than it was now. The Muralevs would probably continue their survey south of the Afghan border. He ought not to waste much time with them. Once he had established what they were doing and in what area they were working, he should leave them and return north.

All that was Lieutenant Savage's common sense. Robin the uncertain, wanted to stay with Muralev – and had not Hayling said that the two natures complemented each other?

He thought: It does not matter what Muralev does or does not do; he *is* something. I've got to find out what he is. I'll stay with them. If they plunge into some city and begin intriguing there, it will be different. But Muralev won't. He'd hate it, he'd be no good.

Anne would think the night cold if she were here. She would find harshness in the smell of the desert and crudeness in the sour daytime smells of sweat, hot wool, and dust. There was a little pang in his breast to-night, but whether it was for what Anne would not know, or for what he lacked by her absence and because her glowing hair was not spread under his hand on the desert, he did not know.

He got up silently. Jagbir did not stir. Jagbir swam like a

duck in the perilous waters of secret service, except that when he slept he sank fathoms deep in sleep, a log, an inert, stertorously heaving chunk of granite. He had a Gurkha's single vision and unshakable faith in himself. The Muralevs were in their place, lying close to each other but not touching.

Robin slipped away to the north-east. As soon as the faint aromatic tang of the roots smouldering on the fire faded in his nostrils he quickened his pace. After half an hour he crossed the branch of the Karshi River where he had seen the hawk. Only the wind was awake, sighing over the desert, and an owl far to the west.

He came to the hill and climbed slowly. Coarse desert grass held the soil together; otherwise the edifice on the summit could not have stood for even five years. The hillock's summit stood about forty feet above the dry bed of the river. He saw water to the west, short, motionless bars of dull green-yellow light. The moon, a week off the full, was lower and had taken on an orange tint. He walked to the ruins and found them nothing but a few square-cut stones, the chiselled edges softened by time and sand. He searched the hill carefully, but there was no statue. He thought the stones were sandstone, rose red and 'half as old as time'. It was difficult to define the colour when the moon bathed them and his hands in orange.

He knelt then and searched among the stones. A coin here, another one? There might be. Did the conqueror pass by here? Yes. What did he see, what conquer? Not men – susliks, the bends and folds of the sand, this light on the Karshi streams. He rose from his knees. There was no coin here, and the moon lay athwart the horizon, a half-moon halved. He walked across the hill, lay down, and closed his eyes.

He heard breathing, the creak of dry leather, and the hiss of sand stirred by some effort more convulsive than the long fetch of wind. He saw Muralev breast the far slope. Feeling rather than seeing, without fear or excitement, he recorded Muralev's wanderings about the hilltop. Muralev sat down among the stones. As the moon sank Muralev turned his face to the west and watched it. In the light of the stars he sat there alone and motionless. After half an hour he got up and walked across the flat hilltop, this time towards Robin.

Robin stood up. Muralev stepped back in an instinctive

shuffling movement, and Robin thought the starlight flashed kindly on his eyes, but he was wearing spectacles, and no one could interpret light seen through a glass. It was not fright, whatever it was.

Muralev said quietly, 'Khussro. I am glad to see you.'

Glad? It was a strange direction to take, a strange plane to choose for whatever talk they must hold with each other. Robin would have liked to meet him on that same calm, unreckoning level, but an efficient bell was clanging and made him say sharply, 'What are you doing here? Don't you realize the desert is dangerous at night? You might get lost, and then they will accuse me of murdering you.'

Muralev brushed aside this calculation, saying, 'I came here to savour the ruin by night. I saw it by day but – I wanted to come at night.'

Robin thought, he means alone. She would have accompanied him if he had told her. She would be sure that whatever he saw she could see, whatever he sensed she could sense. But Muralev the agent ought to have some more convincing story than this.

Muralev said, 'Places like this that are lonely and peaceful draw thoughts up from inside you, as the builders here drew up stones to form a shrine.' He looked out to the west. 'Did you see the moon set? Why do you come here?'

Twice Robin tried to answer according to the laws of common sense – that was to say, on the level of deception. He wasn't sure enough of himself to go direct to the truth. Muralev was. Muralev was that much older, that much farther along the road to certainty. No wonder, he thought, he had experienced so strong a feeling of recognition when they met in the darkened upper room in Bukhara. He could take courage now from Muralev's example. Between them there could exist nothing but truth, even if part of it, that of their service to rival empires, must remain unspoken.

Robin found his coin and held it out on his palm to Muralev, turning his hand slightly so that the starlight showed the silver circle in it. He said, 'Once, in another place, there was a hill like this and a ruin on it. I found this coin there. It is of Alexander the Great.'

Muralev's irregular teeth glinted in a smile, and from the inside pocket of his coat he brought out a feather. Peering down,

158

Robin thought that it was a pale sandy brown, barred at the tip with black. Muralev said, 'There is my coin.'

'What is it?'

'It is a pin-feather of an inaccessible bird.'

'What bird?'

'I don't know for certain. One of the bustard family, but a new species, I think, if I could only find it. I saw this one on a winter day near the Caspian ten years ago. It flew over, and a little later, while I was still watching it and it had become just a pinpoint in the east, this feather dropped down, spiralling down, round and round, to the ground at my feet.'

It would be foolish and unnecessary to ask whether Muralev hoped to find the bird here by the Karshi River in the middle of a chill September night. Robin himself was not expecting to find another coin. But the coin had brought him here, and the feather had brought Muralev.

Robin said, 'I'm going back to camp now.'

'I'll stay here a little longer.'

Robin went down and returned the way he had come. By staying on the hill, so that they would not arrive in camp together, Muralev was forming a conspiracy with him. Its badges were the coin and the feather, and Lenya and Jagbir were outside it. There was no sense to be made of it, because it did not belong in the world where sense reigned.

Jagbir had awakened while he was away. Perhaps the cold had got in through his robes. As soon as he lay down Jagbir muttered, 'I thought those two had murdered you.' Anger and readiness for violence charged his low voice.

When Muralev returned, Jagbir had fallen asleep again, but Robin was still awake and he heard over there the woman's voice, a whisper, as Muralev rolled into his blanket. He could guess the words and translate them into English or Gurkhali, because they were spoken in the same *lingua franca* of emotion, of mixed love and hate. 'I thought those two had murdered you.'

The next morning the Muralevs rode out ahead as usual. About ten o'clock, when Robin and Jagbir and the donkeys and the led pack-pony reached a small oasis where the party was supposed to gather for a rest, there was no sign of the Muralevs. Visibility was bad and getting worse. A burning wind from the south whipped sand into their faces and lifted loose soil and hurled it at them, mixed with gravel and small stones. The air became dry as the inside of a bone.

After a brief pause at the deserted oasis they pushed on. Half an hour later they heard a shot some distance in front, a pause, another shot, two more. The rattle of a little fusillade, deadened and intermittently distorted, blew down to them in the howling wind. It could not be the Muralevs collecting specimens; there had been too many rifles firing. Jagbir unslung his rifle and held it ready across his saddle.

Through the grey-black, whirling pall two horsemen came at them, riding fast. Jagbir shouted, 'The Muralevs'. There were four or five others behind the Muralevs, to judge from the shooting, but the storm hid them. The Muralevs galloped up and wheeled the little ponies around.

She cried, 'Bandits!' – shrieking into the storm. 'Get off the trail, to the east.' Her horse curvetted and bucked, but with her strong legs she held firm in the heaving saddle. She carried her rifle like a standard, the butt on her thigh. Muralev's nose seemed longer than ever. A flying pebble cracked the glass of his spectacles, and he took them off and peered at them with half-shut eyes. The dust lay deep in the corners of his mouth and nose, smoothing out the angles of his face. To Robin he said, 'I'm sorry.' The woman yelled, 'Go east for a bit! We will draw them off west. We can outdistance them. Meet us in Karshi.'

Jagbir cried, 'No. We fight together. We have four rifles.'

'No, no ... save our specimens ... equipment ... Karshi!'

She plunged away, and Muralev's pony bolted after her. Jagbir cursed the donkeys into motion to the east. The wind howled and volleyed sand into their right ears. Robin thought, Jagbir's right, we ought to have stayed together. Turki bandits were reputed to be cowards who never pressed an attack if resisted. But the Muralevs had gone. The woman just wanted a gallop and some excitement. He could have a look in their boxes before he reached Karshi. There might be something of importance in them.

In the lee of a low rock ridge Jagbir halted the donkeys. They all lowered their heads, men and animals alike, turned their backs on the storm, and stood still. No bandits appeared out of the murk, and after ten minutes they moved on. Robin rode a hundred yards ahead, searching the blackness downwind through smarting eyes. Once a horseman passed three hundred yards away, a rifle in his hand, and vanished. Still farther away someone fired a rifle. Another horseman appeared; at the shot he dug his heels into his horse, turned, and galloped towards the sound, the dust bowling around him. That must have been the Muralevs who fired. The woman was clever.

For another hour they expected every minute to see horsemen come lunging at them out of the dust. Robin rode with his nerves tightened to the limit. Last night he had decided to stay with Peter Muralev, whatever common sense thought of it, and now Muralev had gone. Plenty of things could happen before they all met together again in Karshi.

A brassy sky appeared above the dust. The dancing clouds boiled away down the wind. The desert spread slowly farther and farther to their sight, and it was twenty degrees cooler. Robin called a halt and looked all around but saw no one. He said anxiously, 'Come on. We've got to get to Karshi to-night.'

As they waited in the crowded caravanserai in Karshi, and the hours passed, his nervousness increased. That night the Muralevs did not come, nor on the next day nor the next night nor the third day. The third evening a small caravan arrived from Bukhara. The camelmen had seen neither bandits nor strangers. In the night Robin lay awake, thinking. He must go out with Jagbir and search the southern deserts for Muralev's body. He had forgotten in his worry to look into the boxes. He must do that.

In the morning he did and found nothing – a couple of skins, three books containing drawings of birds and animals, several knives, a few bottles of chemicals. They had had their notebooks with them. He closed the boxes and explained to Jagbir what must be done.

Above him a strange voice interrupted. 'Khussro?'

'Yes.' He jumped up. It was an Uzbeg mounted on a big camel. The man said, 'I have a message from your employers.'

'Yes, yes, where are they, are they all right?'

'They are at Keikchi.'

'Keikchi!' Keikchi lay on the north bank of the Oxus and sixty miles due south of Karshi. He could not understand why they had had to go that far south.

'At Keikchi. They are going on along the southern road to Balkh. They want you to meet them there, in Balkh.'

Jagbir cut in shortly. 'What have *you* got to do with them?'

'I was guarding my flock in the desert near Keikchi when they came. They paid me to deliver the message. I am an honest man.' The Uzbeg glowered at Jagbir, turned his camel, and left the serai.

Robin sat down on a box. The society of the coin and the feather had been dissolved by Muralev, the Russian agent. He had something in common with the man, but – it wasn't good enough, he couldn't afford to be hoodwinked, led about by the nose. Firstly, then, the bandits could not possibly have forced them as far south as Keikchi. So the truth was that when the bandits came the woman saw her opportunity to be rid of him, Robin, at least for a time. Why did she want to be rid of him when she had hired him in the first place? He couldn't answer that yet. Perhaps there was no answer beyond the already established fact that she had got rid of him. She had, so to speak, launched him on his own – but she had pointed him in a certain direction, south, before releasing him.

He shook his head. He thought he knew what Muralev would do, but it was the woman who had the power. He looked up. 'Turfan, what will that woman do now? What's she thinking?'

Jagbir answered, when he had taken time to understand the question, 'She thinks you will go on to Balkh.'

'Do you believe she will go there herself?'

'No. That bandit attack was false. She arranged it all to get rid of us.'

Robin did not know. He could not be sure. He was positive that Muralev would not want to return to Bukhara; but the woman had the power. Jagbir was probably right about the bandits. It had been exciting and convincing enough at the time, but now, in his memory, it did not ring true. Nothing about the whole expedition rang true. He would do well to assume that, from the time he arrived in Balkh asking after Selim Beg, word had gone ahead to Bukhara describing him and Jagbir and giving their probable profession – British agents. Then the Muralevs had picked them up with the express purpose of getting rid of them by the most effective means, which was by sending them off with a good clue in the wrong direction. So much for that –

except that Peter Muralev himself was a clue and a much more important one than notebooks or maps.

He thought again of Selim Beg's last message. 'Horses, north.' Sooner or later Muralev would go north, where the empty plains were.

He said, 'Turfan, saddle up. We'll go back to Bukhara.'

CHAPTER FOURTEEN

*

THEY re-entered Bukhara late in the evening, lodged in a different serai, and for two days did not venture out before dark. They had sold the donkeys in Karshi and burned the Muralevs' boxes on the trailside.

If Jagbir was right the Muralevs would also return to Bukhara, there, presumably, to pick up the threads of whatever they had been doing before they decided to deal with the British agents. Robin kept watch on their house, but they did not return, and after five days he became so worried that he determined to ask the servant directly what had happened. He had to know where the Muralevs were. They might easily have gone north – to Samarkand or Tashkent – without coming through Bukhara at all.

In the house a light shone upstairs. Robin called and called again, and at last the pompous Turki servant came to the door. His eyes and the filthy disorder of his dress told Robin that the Muralevs were not here. The servant, tormented by the dying fumes of hashish, snapped, 'Well?'

'Where are your masters? We were attacked by bandits and had to split up. Afterwards I could not find them again, so returned here.'

'They're not back.' The man glared at him with large eyes and held the doorjamb to support himself. 'You're lying! You've murdered them!'

'Shut up, fool! Would I come here if I had? The donkey with their boxes was lost in the sandstorm. I wish to explain to them. Come to me in the serai by the Mir-Arab mosque when they return.'

He left the house and went back to Jagbir, suppressing a desire to run. Surely the servant would suspect something? The fellow would not be an agent himself, probably, but he might have orders to report to the chief Russian official here if anything untoward happened to the Muralevs. Then the Amir's soldiers would come out hunting.

At the serai he said to Jagbir, 'We've got to go. You stocked up the food, didn't you?'

164

'Yesterday. Where are we going?'
'Samarkand.'

They set off on the Golden Road to Samarkand, a hundred and twenty miles away. Now, towards the end of September, the air at night carried a breath of the hard winter lying in wait on the steppes. The fevers that had hidden themselves during the summer crept out, and Jagbir's teeth rattled, and at night he lay sweating, wearing all his clothes and some of Robin's. In the morning the travellers at the camp sites coughed much and were taken by unusual stiffness and thought aloud that they were getting old.

Every day Robin watched the road ahead for the Muralevs, but he did not see them. On the fifth evening he came with Jagbir to Samarkand. The routine began again – of talking, drinking tea, listening. Here the air was fresher than in Bukhara and the city incomparably more beautiful. The turquoise cupola of Tamerlane's tomb hung like a vision above Robin's fretful comings and goings. In the evenings he said his prayers in a street where he could see it. A cold wind blew off the Zarafshan at night, and in the daytime, from a minaret, he could see the mountains. Here Alexander had murdered his special companion, Cleitus. Where was Peter Muralev?

He devised the plan of mentioning in his conversations that two Russians had bilked him of his dues farther south – a man and a woman. He described them angrily. Had any one seen them? He would like to find them and force them to pay what they, kafirs, owed him, a believer. It was in vain. Neither in Samarkand by the Zarafshan nor in the desert caravanserais had anyone seen or heard of the Muralevs. There was news of other Russians. They were moving up and down this road in increasing numbers, soldiers and civilians, but there was never mention of a woman. No one could ever mistake Lenya Muralev for a man, whatever clothes she wore.

Still searching north-eastwards, he came to Jizak in a bitter rain. The wind blew drops like spears into his face. A rock defile funnelled it as it screamed in from the Hungry Steppe and whistled through the desolation of what had once been a great city. Here Alexander had stood and made his final decision – to go on or to go back. Bombastic petty conquerors, passing this

165

way, had carved their fame in the rock and were forgotten. *He* had written nothing, and had retreated, but was remembered. The steppe stretched away, as black and empty as dreams of death, beyond the town.

Alexander died at last, without finding what he was looking for. If here, at Jizak, he had gone on, what would he have found in the north? This road led to Andijan, to the enclosed Farghana, which Baber had loved. There were horses there, the best in the world. But the season was far advanced, the horse-traders were winging south like swallows, and Peter Muralev had not passed this way. Slowly Robin blinked his eyes, turned his back, and went to find shelter for the night.

He hurried back to Bukhara. If the Muralevs had not continued south after the affair with the bandits, and if he had not been able to find any trace of them in the north-east, they must have gone north-west, to Khiva. Khiva was the third of the world's three forbidden cities – Lhasa, Mecca, Khiva. He would inquire again in Bukhara before setting out.

When he saw the towers and minarets of Bukhara rise out of the surrounding orchards, the sun was high. When he came close to the walls the sun was low, and a furious red sky hung above the city. Citizens strolled, talking, on top of the thirty-foot walls. Soldiers stood guard at the gates. A string of camels and horses marched out of one gate as they approached it, and at once turned right on to the Karshi road. Robin recognized the Powindah who had sent him to the Muralevs, riding a short-barrelled grey stallion. It would soon be dark, but sometimes the caravans left at this hour to march through the night, if they knew the road. The Powindah was a link; perhaps he was an enemy too, but that didn't matter now. Robin raised his hand and shouted across the hundred yards of intervening wasteland, '*Starrai mashe!*'

The Powindah looked, swung the little stallion, and galloped across to him. When he was close he muttered, 'Join me at once. Do not argue. Perhaps the guards at the gate have not yet noticed you.'

Robin gestured to Jagbir, and they turned left, joined the Powindah's party, and began to move away from the city. Robin said quietly, 'What's the matter?'

166

'The Amir's jackals are after you for helping those Russians travel in forbidden territory. Of course there was always that risk, you knew that when you took the —'

Robin said absently, 'Yes, of course. Are those two in Bukhara?'

'No. They came in not long ago, then left again. Deported, it was said, but of course they weren't really. Anyway, they've gone.'

'Which way?'

'I didn't hear – but if you didn't meet them on the road from Samarkand they must have gone to Khiva.'

'Thank you. I've got to get into the city. I need food and fodder.'

'For the sake of Allah, don't go! I'll give you a few sacks.'

A mile farther on the Powindah halted the caravan and handed over the food, brusquely refusing payment. When all was again reloaded and they were ready to part, Robin said, 'Again, thank you, and may God guide your footsteps.'

He watched until the caravan disappeared in the gathering twilight. He did not know what the Powindah's role was, if he had one, but the man certainly arrived at the most opportune moments and with the most useful information.

It was dark. Until dawn Robin and Jagbir stumbled westward through the gardens surrounding the city. In the earliest light they found a hiding-place among a wilderness of tamarisk scrub and settled down to pass the day. There was no water nearby, so they set out again as soon in the evening as they dared, ate and drank beside a branch of the Zarafshan, and once more faced the road to Khiva, two hundred and fifty miles away.

The road ran for most of the distance beside the Oxus, and the horses found good grazing. In the silence between the river and the desert Robin was content, and on the tenth day, early in November, they reached Khiva.

In these heartlands of civilizations each city had grown a spirit distinctly its own. The greatest tides of history had rolled over them, from the China Sea to the gates of Vienna, from Xanadu to the Nile. The cities had faced history and been moulded by it into different forms. Bukhara was secretive, Samarkand gracious, Balkh a desiccated and squalid resentment. Now Khiva confronted them, and Robin saw a dark, cruel, closed city. The walls were high and thick, the gates tall and narrow. In the streets the citizens scowled narrowly at each other.

The familiar routine began. Horses? Two, three days in succession he asked his questions. Nothing. The Muralevs? He began to feel the presence of a rumour, and behind that a fact. The town contained more Russians than Bukhara, so the Muralevs ought, by logic, to have been less remarked. But he became sure that they had been seen here. It was the woman the Khivans had noticed. The Russians were not allowed to bring their families here, yet everyone knew that Russian women did come to Khiva. The Russians smuggled them in occasionally, and the Khivans' expressions showed what sort of women they were. Among all this there was talk of a different woman. If she existed, she had been here ten days ago. The gossipers thought she had gone. They were not sure. She might still be living somewhere in the gloomy recesses of the city. They did not know, because she was different and because the Russians did not make a trail to her door every night.

The fourth morning, as he and Jagbir passed down one of Khiva's sunless alleys, a roughly-dressed Turki pressed past them from behind. As he drew abreast of Robin he said quietly, 'The Khan's men are coming for you to-night. What's that worth?' He had his hand out, palm up, at his side. Robin heard, said, 'A lot,' and began to fumble for money. Before he could get at it the man drew away ahead, Jagbir pushing hard on his heels. Thirty yards on, the stranger and Jagbir turned into a side lane that was no more than a slit between neighbouring houses. Robin followed them and saw that Jagbir held a knife concealed against his body, pressed to the stranger's ribs.

Jagbir said, 'Ask him, why does he tell us?'

Robin realized then that he had to know the answer to that question. If this had been the first case of the sort he might have accepted it as good fortune. But now Jagbir had awakened old nagging suspicions about the other times. Why had the Powindah sought him out in the beginning? Why had not the Muralevs been more careful before engaging him? Why had the Powindah been there at the gate of Bukhara, ready to warn him and deflect him from danger? Singly, each incident was nothing. Together – he felt a bit in his mouth and the pressure of reins on his neck. Jagbir, the animal, had felt them earlier.

168

The Turki was angry and not frightened. He said, 'That's a grateful bastard of a Persian horse-trader for you! We're all enemies of the Russians, aren't we? I overhear something, I'm a ditc h-digger in the Khan's gardens, why *shouldn't* I earn some money by telling you, in the name of Allah? A patrol of the Amir of Bukhara's cavalry came in yesterday to take you back.'

'Why should the Khan of Khiva obey the orders of the Amir of Bukhara?'

'They both have to do what the Russians tell them, don't they? By God, *I* don't think your life's worth a snap of the fingers, but I thought you would.'

'Put up your knife, Turfan,' Robin said slowly. He gave the Turki ten roubles, and the man went away, scowling and muttering. His story made sense in every particular; standing by itself, it could not be faulted – only it came on top of all the others. But they had no choice now. They had to get out. Jagbir had long since restocked with food and fodder.

In the serai Robin said, 'How are we going to pass through the gates? They're closely guarded.'

'Only one sentry on each. He's asleep on his feet from two till four – all the ones I've seen. We ought to go separately. They'll be looking for two of us together if they're looking at all. I don't think they will be.'

'Why?'

'If that Turki's lying, they want us to escape. So they won't try and stop us. If he's not, they still won't warn all the soldiers in town. Only the troop who are going to arrest us will be told. Half these people would give us the news at once, for money.'

In the drowsy afternoon they passed through the south gate, Robin half an hour before Jagbir. The sentry dozed against the wall, his eyes hardly open. It was impossible to tell which of Jagbir's suspicions was correct. Having met again, a mile outside the walls, they moved on until nightfall, stopped, and built a fire. The fire crackled, and they huddled close over it. The dry, biting cold of the deserts to north south, east, and west crept in as far as the edge of the fire and touched their backs to make them shiver, while their faces glowed in the heat. They had ten days' food for themselves, and perhaps six for the horses, not including whatever grazing they could find.

Robin knew where he was going. He could not go back to Bukhara, south-east down the Oxus. Northward lay Russia proper; Khussro the Persian and Turfan the Hazara would be conspicuous there, and the advancing season would shortly bind the land in snow. But southward across the Kara Kum – which meant 'Black Desert' – lay the Akkal oasis and the new town the jeweller of Balkh had talked of. From there he might go up and down the Russian centre route of invasion, or he might go on south and look at the southern route. The Akkal would be about two hundred and seventy miles away, and the direction south by west.

Before light they loaded up the patient horses. The black wind hissed steadily from hidden horizon to hidden stars. No road existed. Travellers marched by the wind, by the stars when they shone, by the sun and the tattered prayer flags on the graves of those who had died. They steered by the arched bones of dead camels, by the green brilliance of grass at a waterhole, by the very hostility of the desert, which closed in more fiercely about them, and so made known their mistake, as soon as they left the right path.

The hours drew past, one behind the other. The ponies plodded ever more slowly, pace by pace. The sun swung across the sky in front of them but seemed not to move until the evening came, when it dropped down into the earth like a monstrous ball. Before dark they halted in the shelter of a horseshoe dune and off-saddled. Nothing marked the place but the dune, one among a thousand like it, and a single leather sandal, corroded with sand, desiccated and brittle as a cracker. They gave the ponies water from the skins and drank a little themselves, and set out to collect fuel. Stunted saxaul and calligonium grew on the dune, trying vainly to bind it to the earth against the thrust and drag of the wind. The wind blew without cease from north-west to south-east.

So went the next day, when they came to a waterhole, a grey depression in the dark soil, its water so muddy and saline that the ponies would not drink.

And the next, when they found no water and camped again in the lee of a dune.

They rode on broad reaches of baked clay, across ridge after ridge of grey-black sand, over walking dunes that moved with the

170

wind. There were sand waves seventy feet high and four hundred feet apart that rolled ahead for as far as they could see. There were tamarisk and artemisia and the withered leaves of spring tulips – and, for miles on end, there was nothing.

On the third evening two men mounted on camels came rolling up out of the south, like ships under bare masts. They were desert nomads and as they came close they stopped, but at a wary distance. Robin shouted the Turki greeting and discharged his rifle in the air. Jagbir did the same; then the nomads. So when the four rifles were empty and the four-sharply watching pairs of eyes had seen no one attempt to reload, they all came together.

'Where to?' asked one of the strangers, perched on the rear hump of a hairy, thick-set Bactrian.

'The Akkal. Is the water on the road good?'

'Bad enough. But passable unless the two Franks and their train in front have emptied the wells.'

'Franks?' Robin asked. 'Are they men of peace? Is it safe to close with them? We travel fast.'

'They seem harmless. They are mad – birdcatchers – one a woman, as bold-faced as her they call the Well, in Khiva. With bigger breasts too, but no harlot for all that. They are a day ahead.'

A day ahead. Jagbir would suggest catching up with them and shooting them. That wouldn't do any good. Besides, Jagbir must not be allowed to shoot Muralev. Robin thought slowly, his lips burning, his eyes swollen and red-rimmed. He could continue to follow, as he was doing. But if the Muralevs increased their pace he might lose them. Or if the Muralevs slowed down he'd run into them unawares. He said carefully, 'Those two Franks – I fear we know them. We had a little difficulty with them in Bukhara. They say we stole some trash of theirs. Is there another way to the Akkal?'

'There is and there isn't. A couple of miles on from here you come on a flat place of clay. There is a flag where Uiuz my uncle died of fever, may he rest in peace. The true road goes straight across the flat, but if you bear left at the flag and cross the high sand ridge, there you come to a wide plain. Sometimes we go that way with camels. There are four oases, a long way apart, and then you reach Bezmein in the Akkal oasis.'

'Is it shorter than the other way?'

'By twenty miles. But at this season not a soul lives in any of those oases. Our people have gone south. There may be water at some, there may be no water. The stages are forty and fifty miles each.'

When the nomads had gone, floating north over the sand sea, Robin said to Jagbir, 'We must take this other road. We may die of thirst and exhaustion.'

He wanted to explain the risks to his servant and friend and ask him whether he wished to turn back. Like a dog, Jagbir felt his need before he could express it in words. The Gurkha carefully scanned the empty desert, assured himself that the nomads were indeed a mile away and receding fast, then muttered, '*Hawas, huzoor!*' – the Gurkhali phrase that accepts an order. A minute later he added, '*Natra, kya garun?*' – What else can we do?

The ponies were already exhausted, and after an hour Robin and Jagbir had to dismount and drag them the last eight miles. Whenever they slackened the strain on the reins the ponies faltered to a stop. Worse, they tried the whole time to circle to the left. It was full dark. Time and again the North Star, which should now have been directly behind them, appeared over their left shoulders. Then they swore and wrenched the ponies' mouths and turned again south.

At last Jagbir said, 'I smell water.' In the utter dryness of the desert even that slight dampness blew like a sea breeze on Robin's cheek. The ponies raised their heads and, instead of pulling left, swung right and broke into a trot. Two hundred yards up-wind they came to the water, a muddy pool, and flung themselves into it.

In the morning it took an hour to fill the skins, so shallow and soupy was the water. It lay like a green-black stain in the hollow, and Robin knew that if he had been able to see it the night before he could not have drunk it. That day the ponies marched for six hours, were dragged by the reins for three more, and then lay down. They would not move until Jagbir emptied the noisome water from a skin down their throats. Before the day ended they had emptied two more skins. From midday on recurrent attacks of diarrhoea twisted Robin's and Jagbir's bowels and spent their strength. At the next oasis, which they reached about two in the

172

morning after a forty-mile stage, twenty hours on the road, they found a prayer flag and a shallow, unlined well. The well contained no water.

Near the well and the flag, the moon shone on a discarded saddle. It was of a strange pattern and might have belonged to one of Tamerlane's riders. The aseptic desert had bleached, dried, and preserved it, to remind them that here was the point of no return. With the remaining skins they could either reach the next oasis ahead or go back to the last behind, but only with great hardship in either case. Behind they knew there was water – that filthy puddle. Ahead there might be no water.

A bowel spasm gripped Robin, and with it a similar knot of angry doubt. He found himself here not of his own decision but because someone had sent him, in this case a nomad on a Bactrian camel. Was he too an agent of Lenya Muralev? If so, she intended him to die of thirst in a place where no one would even know that he had died. He might be on the wrong road, but assuredly not on the wrong track. He would go forward.

There was no reason to wait, because they were too tired to sleep. It was best not to break the deadly rhythm of movement. They gave the animals half a skin between them, wetted their own tongues, and moved on.

Late in the afternoon, from the summit of a mountainous dune, Jagbir pointed. A dark-green band of colour, absorbing the light, lay like a blot against the shimmering horizon.

Ten more miles reeled back behind them. With infinite caution the green band separated out and in the moonlight became the dappled shadow of bushes. Jagbir first saw the hollow that held the well; then the horses sensed it and gathered their strength. Robin held Jagbir's elbow. Together they all ran down the last dune, across the flat, over the moon-washed, sun-dried patterns of trampling hoofs and camel pads and human feet. The ponies won the race by several yards, and each sucked in a long draught. The water was deep and clear.

Even as the first drop passed over Robin's lips its bitterness, like a serrated knife, ripped his tongue. He rubbed sand in his mouth and shrieked. The poison burned into his gums. He ran to a skin and rinsed and rinsed until he could breathe again. One horse was dead, the others lying sprawled on their sides at the edge of the water, their necks flat along the ground, the lips

173

drawn back over their teeth. Those two lived still but had no strength left to struggle against the poison in them. Soon they would die, as the first had died and as Robin was ready to die, of disappointment and despair.

Robin lay down, collapsing slowly from the knees. When he opened his eyes he saw that all the ponies were dead. There was plenty of food, but it was all dry. The water had been poisoned. Lenya Muralev had lured them into the desert and they could not turn back. Once, on the road to Karshi, Bahram had playfully bitten her. Now she'd killed him too. He had been a good horse.

Jagbir said, 'We've had to pull the ponies sixty miles. We're better off without them.' He moved about slowly but unhesitatingly, collecting the things they must carry – the last waterskin, three parts empty, a bag of raisins, some dates, a dozen discs of unleavened bread. 'The gold,' he said. 'Let me carry your belt.'

Robin said, 'It's not heavy. Can you manage the water? I don't think I can carry my rifle any more.'

'We'll leave it. I have mine.'

Being beyond hope, they could sleep. In the freezing dawn they faced the last stage but one. If there was no water at the end of it, it would be, for them, the very last. Robin's fingers were so numb he could not tie his load on his shoulders, and Jagbir had to do it for him.

Robin thought he must have marched unconscious for half the day, because next the sun was glaring down, and the wind stung his neck. The effort to march became a physical pain, increased to agony, was surmounted, and became an effort to live. That in turn increased as the other had, but it would be the last. Only death or water could surmount this. The words of the song Jagbir had sung in that camp near Karshi thrummed and drummed and rumbled in his head – *jaun, jaun, pareli*, in time with his steps, stumbling when he stumbled. Jagbir gave him water, and he cried because he could have no more. *Ankhen ma gazeli*, and McIain came running down from the slaughter at Tezin Kach, and here were the faces of all the men who had not seen him shoot himself, and the snow whistled past his ears. *Samajaunchhu Dehra Dun*, and Anne Savage, who ought to have been Anne Hildreth or even Anne Hayling, loved him and

174

believed she could lift him by force of love out of the deserts to a place of water and shade and no wind.

He only wanted water.

'It is finished,' Jagbir answered.

Jagbir's feet kept on and on, left, right, left right, just in fron t of him. There was a length of rein reaching back from Jagbir's waist, connected at the other end to – well, his own hand, towing him along.

When he found it was black and hot and he had sand in his mouth, Jagbir picked him up.

So when he found it was black and cold and he had sand in his mouth, but no firm hand lifted him, he rolled over on his back and prepared to die while he yet had the strength. He must not be carried helpless and feeble past those gates. He must walk in wide-eyed and strong, looking about him.

Jagbir had gone. According to his pompous father, Colonel Rodney Savage, C.B., Jagbir had deserted him, spat on the glorious tradition of the regiment, and behaved like no true Gurkha. Nonsense. But it was strange that Jagbir, who did not fear death in battle, should run away from death in the desert. And foolish, because in the desert death would only follow him the more relentlessly. He would be lonely when he died.

He was not lonely himself. All the people had gone away. *Jaun, jaun, pareli* had gone away. The imperial danger had gone away, and the Czar, and Lenya Muralev, and Jagbir of course, and at last even Peter Muralev. Being undisturbed, he was able to concentrate on the immediately pressing problem – what was God's purpose in giving man awareness of God?

The water in his mouth caused his arms and legs to twitch, then the cold to bite and the wind to blow and his stomach to bind in a spasm of cramp. A quarter of a mouthful, and his throat swelled so that he could not swallow. The water that was in his mouth trickled down his face to the sand. He rolled over and licked at it, but it became grit.

'Slowly, sahib, there is enough.'

Soon he found strength to take another sip. After an hour he went to sleep.

In daylight he saw that Jagbir, asleep beside him, nursed a half-full goatskin in his arms. His face had filled out, and he opened his eyes when Robin moved.

Robin said, 'What happened?'

'I was not tired, not very. The moon was up, and I could go faster by myself. You were resting.'

'Dying.'

'I went on, though I became a little more tired.'

O master of the matter-of-fact, Jagbir. You were lonely and dying.

'I knew we must be near the oasis. After a mile – three, perhaps – I saw a camel. When I went down to it I saw a man asleep. The sand deadened the sound of my feet.'

'And he gave us water? It was a – miracle. It was the work of —' He paused. He did not like to use the name of God aloud when he did not know whether God was like a man or like a thought or like a pamir.

Jagbir did not answer directly but said, 'Let us go forward to the water now.'

Robin found he could not walk by himself, but Jagbir helped him. Soon he saw the camel, ridiculously close and large and alive, squatting by the waterhole and chewing cud. He saw its saddle and load neatly stacked beside it. He saw the man lying curled up ten yards off, still asleep.

Jagbir said, 'It was not the work of God, sahib. It was the work of the Russian woman.' Robin thought, Not the woman, surely? She wouldn't help us. Peter Muralev, you mean? But Jagbir pointed to a glass jar full of blue powder that stood in full sight near the sleeping man. Jagbir said, 'All this way I prayed for this. I know that woman. We were travelling fast. This man, her servant, thought he was still a day ahead of us. He was going to poison the well in the morning before he went on. Until then he needed the water for himself and his camel.'

Robin looked again at the man and said, 'Then – he is not sleeping?'

'No.'

Robin put his head in his hands. After a while he said, 'We will rest all day here. To-morrow we will take the camel and go to the Akkal. But I did not hear a shot.'

'I did not fire. I gave him a drink of water.'

CHAPTER FIFTEEN

*

So they came, both riding the camel, to the end of the desert. The mountains rose ahead in a pale wall from eastern to western horizon. The Akkal oasis stretched for many miles under the mountains. It was not a single well but an area where melting winter snows formed pools that did not dry up all year, and where the pressure along the hill faults expressed water in a hundred widely scattered springs. The black tents of the nomads dotted the plain. There were clumps of trees and bushes. There were small villages and herds grazing and tiny patches of cultivation.

Had the Muralevs already arrived? It depended whether they had hurried all the way or had gone slowly and spent time collecting specimens to reinforce their role of naturalists. In any case they would soon expect the owner of the camel, the man with the poison bottle, to come and report to them. After a couple of days they would cause the whole of the route to be searched.

Robin felt strength returning to his body, but his mind fretted, and he was sick. He could not believe that Muralev would pollute the desert with man-made poison. If he had, he'd lost the mysterious quality which united him to Robin and to the secrets of the open places. It could have been the woman alone. He would have to believe so or he would not want to continue. Only one thing was sure, that someone had earnestly tried to kill him and Jagbir. 'The charade ceases to be pretence when an agent gets hold of something really important.' He never forgot Hayling's words. Yet – yet he was here, and alive. So many other methods could have been devised to kill him in the Black Desert, methods that could not have failed.

Jagbir said, 'We have to get fodder and more food.' They had already eaten largely at a nomad encampment.

'What about this camel?'

'It depends where we're going next, lord. Either buy another or sell this and buy two horses.'

'I don't know where we'll be going. We'd better get horses and ask about the Muralevs.'

Jagbir considered and said, 'Isn't that dangerous, lord?'

'A little. But we can't hide the fact that we've arrived. They'll find that out as soon as they begin to inquire. All these nomads have seen us. We must get some information and then disappear again.'

Bearing a little to the east, they came to a small hamlet. Its principal tradesman knew nothing of the Muralevs, but he knew where Robin could certainly get hold of them. If they were Russians, he said, they would be heading for an encampment outside the village of Bezmein. He took Robin up to the flat roof of his house and pointed west. 'There, that's Bezmein. It's over ten miles away. It's no larger than this, but a lot of the caravans stop there because they have women and liquor and we don't. A party of Russians arrived several weeks ago and camped outside it, on the far side. Nobody knows what they are doing. They walk about with big boards and tall things on three wooden legs. They won't let us go near them. But they go into Bezmein, some of them, and get drunk like all kafirs and yell and sing and womanize.' He spat over the parapet.

Robin said, 'Thank you. But you misunderstand the purpose of my questions. I do *not* want to meet these Russians. They say I owe them money. So if they should happen to ask after us, perhaps you will ...?' He handed over a couple of silver coins. The merchant nodded and spat again. 'To hell with all unbelievers!'

'Amen.'

When they had bought two horses, sold the camel, and transacted their other business, Robin and Jagbir headed eastward out of the village. Bezmein was to the west.

The wind blew all night and hid their tracks as they circled round until in the dawn they camped in a fold of ground at the limit of the hills. It was like a little eyrie. The Bezmein oasis lay among thin trees half a mile in front of them and fifty feet lower, so that they overlooked it. They could see the village and, about a quarter of a mile to its left, a grove of trees. They saw in the grove at least five tents. There was as yet no need to go closer. The party there could only be surveyors. Later, if they could, they must try and find out what the Russians were surveying for, but first they had to be sure that the Muralevs were coming here.

In the middle of the day the Muralevs came. From the ridge

178

that sheltered their little valley, Robin and Jagbir saw the dust of the caravan miles out in the Black Desert. The Muralevs were riding ahead as usual, on little ponies. A mile behind them followed half a dozen loaded camels, two more horses, and six armed men. Even from that distance the weariness of all of them showed in their paces and in the hunched, rolling way the men sat their animals. Some of the surveyors came out of the camp to greet them, then they all disappeared.

Robin sent Jagbir to search the hillside for water – where they could take the ponies after dark – and a sheltered place where they could light a small fire and cook their food. Then he settled down to watch the camp. He saw men working under the trees, and soon another tent rose. He saw Muralev and a stranger come to the edge of the scrub and stand a while with their backs to him, staring out to the north. In that directon he and Jagbir were supposed to be lying dead. A little later another man rode out on a camel. Robin hoped he would go north into the Black Desert, because then he could not return with news in less than three days. But the rider went first into Bezmein village, came out again after an hour, and headed east for the hamlet where Robin had talked with the merchant on the rooftop. He would learn something there, all right. He would be back later in the evening or early the following morning.

In the twilight Jagbir returned. 'I've found a good place. A little dell two miles up this valley.'

'Good. We'll not be able to get close to that camp except at night. And one of us will have to stay with the ponies.'

'We ought to work together, lord. The ponies will be all right. They're not frightened. The wolves aren't hungry yet.'

Robin agreed. Jagbir knew. They hurried to the dell, ate quickly, tethered the ponies with strong cord, and returned to the eyrie. Jagbir said, 'Lord, when it's dark I stay here with the rifle. You go forward and find a good place, where you can lie up even by day. You will try to get into the camp to-night, perhaps? You lie in the hiding-place all to-morrow too. Then to-morrow evening we change over.'

'How are we going to eat, cook, feed the horses?'

'The one who is here with the rifle can do all that at night. It is only by day that he must be here, in the eyrie, all the time. With the rifle, by day, he can make the enemy go slowly if they

179

discover the one who's lying out. By night he can do nothing.'

'All right.'

They settled down to the new routine. Robin went the first night and found that Uzbeg sentries guarded the camp. Lying on the desert, he saw their black sheepskin caps and their slung rifles against the dim lamps in the tents behind. There was no hope of entering the grove under these conditions. Before dawn he found a trio of bushes two hundred yards from the eastern edge of the camp, and with his hands burrowed in the sand until it nearly covered him. Then he put down his head, placed a pebble in his mouth to suck, and lay still as the sun came up. He lay still until the sun went down. No visitors came this day to the camp. The nomads grazing their their flocks kept away in the distance to the north. Villagers came out from Bezmein but did not approach the camp. The surveyors did not leave, nor did the Muralevs. The messenger on the camel returned early, and Robin heard angry voices. Later Lenya Muralev came to the edge of the grove and stared suspiciously around the horizon, searching the hills with particular care.

The following night Jagbir took over. By day Robin saw from the eyrie that five visitors came to the oasis. They came from the south, where a track emerged from the mountains a mile or two east of Bezmein. At the change-over that evening Jagbir said, 'Those men who came, they're still there. They're not white unless they're in disguise. They don't seem to be Uzbegs, Afghans, Turkis, or Persians – at least not the kind of Persians we saw in Balkh and Kabul. They seemed to be speaking a sort of Persian, not Zaboli like ours.'

The next day, lying in hiding behind the three bushes, Robin saw the visitors depart. They returned the way they had come, one by one, at long intervals, passing close by him. He thought they might be tribal chieftains from South Persia, Qashqai perhaps. One other thing of interest he saw – a Russian who left camp at dusk and returned, very drunk, at midnight. The sentries took no notice of him and did not even challenge him but stood aside and let him find his own stumbling way into the encampment.

At the change-over Jagbir said hesitantly, 'I don't think I should go out now, lord.'

Robin said quickly, 'Of course not, son, we'll leave it for a

180

day.' He thought: It is not really strange that Jagbir should be frightened; he does not like being alone. Jagbir went on. 'No. I feel sure that woman will have the ground about the camp most carefully searched to-morrow.'

Jagbir was right. In the middle of the morning the whole surveying party and all the guards came out of the camp and walked in circles, at intervals of a few paces, around the grove. One stopped by the three bushes where Robin had lain, and stirred the sand with his foot. Then others came to him. The woman walked out from the camp to look, and shortly afterwards they all seemed to give up the search, returning into the trees. At noon the surveying party set out with horses and plane tables and theodolites, and during the afternoon the watchers saw them working along an east-west line a mile or so from the foot of the mountains.

'Now they've found our hiding place,' Robin said slowly. 'We can't go back.'

'By night we can, lord, as long as we don't go to those three bushes. They'll never catch us if we're careful. But we must go together. Out at dusk, back before dawn.'

'How much food have we got left?'

'Four, five days for us and the horses. It'll take us a day to reach a place where we can buy some more.'

On the second night under the new arrangement the same Russian that Robin had seen before left the camp just as they crept into position. He almost walked into them. He hurried on towards Bezmein, jingling money in his pocket and smoking a foul cheroot.

When he had gone Jagbir whispered, 'We can get him on his way back. Nearer the village.' Robin nodded. The Russian might have nothing of interest on him, but time was running out.

After half an hour they walked silently closer to the village. Most of the villagers had gone to bed, and only a few lights shone out from the meagre, mud-built hovels. Later someone began to sing. Much later still, when the chill of the desert had frozen them to the sand, they heard the Russian come out on his return journey.

Jagbir muttered, 'Do you want me to kill him?'

'No.'

181

The Russian staggered past them. Lying down as they were they could see his head nodding against the stars. Twice he fell down and lay a while, breathing heavily and muttering to himself. When he was half-way to the camp they ran up silently, one on each side. Robin pushed him gently from behind. He ran forward to catch up with his falling body and ran into the ground, his legs still working. Jagbir jumped on to his back, cupped one hand over his mouth, and punched him hard on the side of the head.

Robin whispered, 'I can't see. Search him. Has he got any matches?'

After a pause – 'Yes.'

Jagbir emptied the Russian's pockets. Soon Robin held a little pile of papers in his hand, besides a small knife, a dirty handkerchief, a slide rule, two cheroots, and some small change. Then he crouched down and held out his robe like a tent over the Russian's head. Jagbir lit a match under its shelter. A trickle of blood from above the unconscious man's eye ran down the side of his face. His shirt was torn, and there was no sunburn line around the base of his neck. The brown continued down evenly. His face was almost darker than ordinary sunburn could have made it, for, like all Russians, he wore a hat even at night. Yet Russian was his native tongue. Robin did not know that language but he knew enough to recognize the sound of it. The match burned out, and he carefully put the dead stick in his turban. Jagbir lit another, and Robin began to examine the loot from the Russian's pockets.

There were two official-looking printed documents. He'd have to take them. There was a booklet of logarithm tables. No sense in taking that. Another booklet, thin and paper-bound. As Jagbir kept striking matches Robin turned over the pages; this was a phrase book – Russian on one side of each page, and, on the other, Persian. From a quick glance he thought it was not classical Persian but a dialect of some kind – and not the eastern dialect, Zaboli Persian, which he himself had learned. In the back of the book he found an outline map of Persia. Someone, presumably the owner, had underlined Bushire in pencil. Bushire was a town and seaport on Persia's southern coast on the Persian Gulf.

Robin kept the documents and the phrase book. Then, in

an effort to show that the robbery had been the work of common thieves, they scattered the rest of the Russian's belongings carelessly around, kept his small change, and took the ring off his finger. It was worth trying, because the Russian might want to keep quiet about the affair anyway, for fear of trouble over being drunk. On the way to the dell Robin took the matchsticks from his turban and buried them in the sand.

As soon as it was light Jagbir went to the eyrie and stood sentry there. Robin remained in the dell with the papers.

The party to which the drunken man belonged was certainly surveying the course of the railway which, as the government of India already knew, the Russians were in process of building south-eastward from Krasnovodsk. But the drunken surveyor had some interest in South Persia, as evidenced by the map and the phrase book. The dialect would be a South Persian one of some kind. Did this all mean, then, that the Russians intended to push the railway south into Persia and across Persia to the gulf, near Bushire? It might – but he'd better not cast his surmises too far ahead of his facts. Let him take the situation at its face value only.

The facts of geography were unalterable. Here on the edge of the Akkal oasis he was near the beginning of that direct, central invasion route which ran from the Caspian through Balkh and Kabul to Peshawar. The drunken surveyor's map, and the language in which someone had decided he should be instructed, and the appearance of the visitors to the camp, pointed not straight ahead but to the right, the south.

Very well. If the Russians were going to use the southern route in force, there would be some signs to show the fact. He would have to go south and find them.

He went down to the eyrie and told Jagbir. Before they left, Robin stared once more at the grove that hid the Muralevs, and across the Black Desert, which the poison had befouled. Selim Beg had written 'Horses, north'. Every clue since then had pointed west, and now south. The trail would take him from here towards great cities and into the steaming bustle of the Persian Gulf. He wanted to know where Muralev would go now. Muralev wouldn't find his bustard on the shores of the Gulf, that was certain. He'd be unhappy down there. It would be like the poisoning and the subterfuges – a level of deception

183

forced on him by his wife's love for him and his own love for his country.

At last he said wearily, '*Lo bhayo, nani! Jaunu parchha,*' and they returned to the dell, saddled up, and worked southward through the mountains until they came to the Meshed road.

CHAPTER SIXTEEN

*

His appointment with the Sheikh Abu Daabi was for half an hour after dusk, in the sheikh's house. He had tried to make it earlier but without success; the sheikh was insistent. Robin paced the long upstairs room of the lodgings, his head bent under the low roof, and reviewed his plans. A British steamer lay alongside the quay not a hundred yards away. She was due to sail for India two hours after dusk with her cargo of dates. Yesterday he had slipped on board and made his arrangements with the master who obviously had not believed what little of his story he could reveal. He would have liked to be on board now, but Abu Daabi said he had something important to disclose. Besides, the shipmaster didn't want them to embark during the loading.

It was three o'clock in the afternoon of April 30th, 1881, the sun had inclined to the west, and the streets of Basra were deserted. From the window he could see the masts of the steamer and an empty reach of the river. The Shatt-al-Arab, the joined Tigris and Euphrates, flowed silently at high flood level past the foot of the street. The melting snows of Ararat and a hundred other mountains had filled and overfilled its bed. Above the city the floods covered the Mesopotamian plain.

Jagbir slept. Each time Robin reached that end of the room he paused and stooped down to brush the flies from his companion's face. They had seen much together and travelled far since they left the Akkal oasis five months before. They had visited Bushire but they had not gone by the shortest route. The Russians could not fly over the intervening country between Turkestan and the Persian Gulf. If they had any intentions in that direction there ought to be a continuous line, traceable on the land, connecting the one with the other. So Robin and Jagbir had journeyed south and west and south again, hunting like dogs for the scent. They did not know exactly what they were looking for, but they knew what the clues would be.

Firstly, there was gossip. When strangers travelled the roads and asked questions there was gossip. Sharp eyes would note, idle tongues relate – a man in such-and-such clothes passed here

185

in such-and-such a month; he asked the way to Hamadan; he asked where Qasim lived; he looked for a long time at the stream.

Secondly, there was gold. When a great power interested itself in a country where the people were generally poor, it had to use money. The larger its interest, the larger would be the outlay of money. In certain areas more money would flow than had flowed before, and, most revealing, it would flow in new channels. The gold must go to the people whom Russia regarded as helpers, allies, or potential allies. It was not always hard to surmise who these might be, because an invader's natural friends are those who, like him, wish to upset the existing order. In Asia this did not mean the people, the peasantry, for they did not count. It meant not the chief khan but the second, who would like to be first; not the feudal rulers but the elder sons waiting impatiently for power and restive under the suspicions and hard restraints of Mohammedan fathers.

Thirdly, there was the knowledge they had already garnered. It was possible for them to pretend to more than they knew. Of suspects Robin could ask questions a shade more pressing than he would otherwise have been able to. At times he could, by mentioning a name or a fact, lead a man to believe that he was himself a Russian agent, and so get another name, follow that up, and, like a rolling snowball, gather still more names, more information.

As they passed through Teheran they had, by circuitous means, contacted the British Embassy, got more gold, made a report, and handed over the papers taken from the surveyor at Bezmein. As Robin had suspected, the printed documents were of no importance. The dialect of the phrase book was that used around Bushire. That first report would have reached India long ago. He wondered what Hayling would think of it. He had made another and final report two days ago and handed it to the ship-master here in Basra for safe custody until he could board the ship himself. Looking back at his work, he could see that there had been mistakes, false trails, some danger. But, in the large, there had been no doubt. A direct line of Russian interest and Russian preparation led from the southern border of Turkestan to the Persian Gulf. There was no need at the moment to follow it farther on land by turning east and traversing the deserts to the

Indian frontier at the Bolan Pass. It *must* go in that direction – unless the Russians proposed to attack the Turkish Empire here in Mesopotamia, instead of the British Empire. Agents working out of India could unearth the plan in more detail.

When he returned to India he could say that his evidence had ed him to two conclusions: that the Russians intended to use two routes of invasion, the central and the southern; and that the principal weight of the attack would be in the south. Further, he could say that the centre was the level of deception, where the clues were comparatively easy to find, and that the south was the level of truth. That poison bottle had been no prop in a charade. Therefore, the Russians will feint a single, central attack through Balkh and Kabul; once we move our troops to counter this, the real Russian attack will come in along the southern route, directed on the Bolan Pass.

It was all very neat, neater than he had the right to expect after only nine months' work. Only the original impulse which had launched this quest now seemed strangely misdirected. Perhaps no one would ever find out what Selim Beg had meant, or what he had discovered. Perhaps he had meant just what he said, for his clues, having been meticulously followed, had led to Basra. Robin had gone north from Balkh, asking about horses. By way of Bukhara, Khiva, the Akkal oasis, Meshed, Gurgan, Teheran, Hamadan, Isfahan, and Bushire, he had come to Basra.

He had not been happy these last five months. There were too many people, perhaps, too many cities, too much intrigue. He had wondered often whether he would meet Muralev and, if he did, whether such a meeting would make this work in the south seem less or more important. He thought it would depend what happened – if the woman tried to kill him, for instance, that would be one thing; if she did not, it would be another. It would depend on what Muralev did too, how he looked, how he spoke.

Also Robin was a little unhappy because he knew he had failed to see much that another, more experienced agent might have seen. Hayling had picked the wrong man after all. The trail ended in the squalid gutters of Basra.

He looked out. The sun was low and the streets beginning to stir with noise and movement. A breeze ruffled the river, and a few dhows crept out from the bank and heeled into the racing current. He awakened Jagbir.

187

The Sheikh Abu Daabi's house lay on the south-western extremity of Basra. The road thither led away from the Shatt-al-Arab and across a vile-smelling creek which bisected the town. A dozen narrow bridges spanned the creek. The crowd was thick on the bridge that Robin and Jagbir chose to use. When they reached the mid-point, where a press of people and donkeys pushed them on, they saw the Muralevs. Robin sighed in sudden relief; this had to happen, everything would have been wrong without it. Then he thought that the Muralevs, Lenya at least, had seen them first. There might have been a plan. He felt very tired. There would be struggles and manœuvrings, lies, threats. The Arabs edged away and stared insultingly at the unveiled woman as though she had been a harlot dancing naked on the bridge. Beyond the bridge the narrow street ran on south-westward. There was a coffee shop on the right-hand side near the end of the bridge, and a stunted tree. A Turkish policeman in a red fez stood under the tree, his rifle slung on his shoulder.

Robin looked straight ahead. Jagbir dropped his hand to the handle of his knife. The Muralevs stopped in front of them, blocking the bridge. Peter Muralev said in his accurate Persian, 'Khussro, it is a pleasure to see you again.' He tugged at his ear and smiled shyly.

Robin turned. He saw with a shock that Muralev looked ill. His skin was pale grey and shiny with sweat, and his eyes deep-sunk behind the spectacles. They were a new pair, with thin steel rims. The woman would have a pistol and she meant to kill him. He read it in her sparkling eyes and parted lips. The lust of battle was in her.

But he had to get back to Anne. The whole search, which should have been like a scouring, cleansing wind in his mind, was turning to a foul breath. He had found the secret they had sent him out to find, but he had found nothing else. Peter Muralev was as ill and as wretched as he, and still had not found the home of the bird that had dropped a brown feather at his feet.

It was Jagbir who spoke, a short, wonderful sentence of warning and triumph. 'Greeting! We have done our task and are returning to my lord's place.' Robin saw that he had told Lenya Muralev it was no good killing them, because their report to India had already been made.

188

'Oh, yes?' said Muralev absently. 'That is good. I hope you will like it at home.'

The woman cut in. 'It was a profitable journey? Are you sure that you have as yet paid the full price for your goods?' Looking at her, Robin knew that she would kill him with her own hands if all else failed. It was not personal spite. She had some sound reason, on the imperial plane.

Muralev said, 'Will you come and have a cup of coffee with us?'

'No,' answered Jagbir and tried to push past them but the woman turned with him, and he could not get rid of her. She walked at his side, talking animatedly; Peter Muralev followed with Robin. At the coffee shop Jagbir seemed to change his tactics. He said, 'This will do,' and squatted down in the very front of the shop, directly under the policeman's eye. Lenya Muralev hesitated, then joined him, and Robin and Peter followed suit. The woman ordered black Arab coffee and a dish of sweetmeats.

To Robin, Muralev said, 'I suppose you couldn't keep those books of birds that were in my box?'

'No. I'm sorry. We burned them all. It took a long time.'

Muralev nodded and was silent. At length he said, 'I apologize about the poison.' Robin felt the old sympathy rising in him. Muralev might have put the blame on his wife, where it certainly belonged, but he had not.

Jagbir said, 'She did it.'

The woman smiled widely. 'I did. I thought it was necessary, and I was right. It wasn't enough, even. After all, here you are, safe and well. Besides, there are no rules, are there? You think it was not – cricket?' She said the word in English.

'We're not playing cricket,' Robin said. 'I'm not playing any game.' To her it was like polo or pigsticking, but more exciting.

Muralev shook his head slowly. 'Nor am I. It was wrong, the poison. It did not fit in. It was wrong, untrue.'

'My husband is a dreamer,' the woman said, 'but also a genius.' She looked at Peter with a sort of warm, uncertain pride. Robin saw her with a new and newly painful understanding. She was a good woman and she loved her husband. The thing that Muralev felt for her could not properly be called love because it had none of the attributes of love. Can a bark love the

189

rope that ties it to the wharfside? And in the end what would happen? He must be near when that time came, to find out. Would the strong, brave rope be left trailing forlorn in the water, broken, while the ship heeled to the wind in the open sea? Would there be a tidy unfastening and casting off? Would – could the ship stay for ever by the pier while the wind blew, and wild, mysterious birds flew overhead in the night?

Lenya Muralev caught his scrutiny and the expression behind it, and said, 'Do you have a wife?' When Robin nodded she said, 'She will not be happy that you are here. You dream and are happy sometimes, I think. Perhaps it will be better for her the way things will have to be. She will be happy thinking that you *would* have come back eagerly to her, that she and you *could* have lived happily ever after. Only you didn't come back.'

Robin looked her steadily in the eye. He was not afraid of her. She was afraid of him, and not because of what he knew. She must be afraid all the time of Peter. Was Anne afraid? To Muralev he said, 'Did you find the bird?'

Muralev took off his spectacles, fumbled in his pocket, and drew out the crumpled feather. 'No.'

Robin wanted to say: You won't find it here. But there was no need. Muralev knew that.

Muralev began to talk, the feather in his palm, while the woman fidgeted impatiently and Jagbir, next to her, kept his hand on his knife. Muralev talked of the Takla Makan desert, where he had never been. He would go there one day. Robin noticed Jagbir's glance at the sky. Their ship would sail in less than three hours now. If they delayed their escape much longer her thugs would have time to arrive. Basra had the worst reputation of any city in the Middle East. He had not seen her make a signal, but a servant could have been following them on the bridge and gone off unnoticed to gather the cut-throats.

Muralev tried to explain why he must go to the Takla Makan, and Robin forgot about the ship and about the murderous gang already perhaps collecting in back alleys around the café. It was not easy to understand what Muralev meant. They spoke in Persian, and the ideas were abstract, while their vocabularies were limited to concrete things. Muralev talked of the monastic ideal which, in the West, men now laughed at; but in the East they did not laugh at it. He asked what made a Hindu mystic

190

climb a tall mountain and stay on its summit in contemplation all his life. Why was such a man called a mystic?

Robin said, 'Why, then? You've asked the questions. Do you have no answer?'

Muralev looked at him with sad eyes, his spectacles in one hand, the barred feather in the other. The shopkeeper lit a lamp in the back of the shop. Muralev said, 'I have an answer. Desire. The mystic has desire – desire for God, if you like. What I have not solved is whether that desire is evil and selfish, or good and the true gift of God.'

Robin nodded. Muralev would never find the answer to that question because it was in its nature unanswerable. That meant – From the corner of his eye he noticed that the Turkish policeman was watching Jagbir's back with bent brows. Suddenly Jagbir reached across the table, seized Muralev's coffee cup, and dashed the dregs into his own face. After a second's motionless pause he sprang to his feet, the coffee dripping from his cheeks, and cried, 'You.. ! To Gehenna with foreigners and unbelievers! Let us depart in peace. Cease from pestering us!'

The policeman started forward. Robin jumped up, shocked out of his preoccupation. A scene here, the policeman leading them to the jail, questioning, delays, imprisonment perhaps – Jagbir must have been mad. But the policeman shouldered past and began to shout at the Muralevs. Jagbir tugged impatiently at Robin's sleeve. They ran into the street, turned away from the bridge, and plunged down an alley. 'Where now?' Robin muttered.

'Our house, down this lane, over the second bridge. Hurry, lord!'

They dropped to a quick walk. The evening crowds closed in behind them. Robin said, 'How did that happen?'

'I was holding two gold medjidiyes behind my back.'

They reached the house and ran up the narrow stairs. Jagbir said, 'Have we got everything now? Out of the back window! Hurry, lord. That damned woman was already producing money, more than mine, before we'd got into the street.'

'Do you think she realizes we are going out on the steamer? Does she know we live in this house?'

'I don't know. I think the meeting on the bridge was by accident. I don't like it. Can they stop us getting on the ship?'

Robin considered. There was a way. If the Muralevs had laid a suit for civil debt against them or accused them of complicity in some crime, the Turkish authorities would arrest them on the ship. But it would take time to make the complaint and produce some proofs. They would find out when they reached the docks. Meantime, hurry! They dropped from the back window into an enclosed yard, climbed over a low wall, and turned towards the Shatt-al-Arab. They walked quickly, one behind the other, their hands on their knives. They had no rifle now; in Basra it would have made them look suspicious.

Almost at once they saw the tracery of the ship's yards above the warehouses. Lights on the hidden dockside shone up on the masts and lit the black smoke billowing away downstream on the wind. Crouched behind a crate, they saw five Turkish policemen patrolling the quay. A minute later a fat officer with a tasselled fez waddled down the gangplank, a large document in his hand, and took his place there. They saw the English captain's bearded face, picked out by the binnacle light on the bridge.

They turned away. These arrangements had taken time. The Muralevs must have known for days that they were here, and had made their plans in good season. The next step was a Turkish prison, and in the prison a sudden illness, or an accident or a shot in the back while 'attempting to escape'.

They crept back to the house the way they had come, over the wall, up through the window. Robin crouched down in a corner and covered his face with his hands. In the early days it had been exciting, but now, here in the stinking city, it had become horrible. Every night black rats ran over their bodies. By day the wind blew the smell of garbage down the noisome lanes. The task had become like that – rats, a foul smell, and above all, hopeless exhaustion. His nerves were overstrung to the point of snapping. For days on end his stomach would not hold the food he forced himself to swallow.

It was time to give up. A brave man would not have, but he would. He had had enough. Whatever it was that God had made him for, it was not this. That terrible woman looked more beautiful, more intensely alive, than when he first saw her in the dark room in Bukhara. Was it sheer lust of action that drove her to try and kill him now when his work was done and she knew that it was? Was his work so vitally dangerous to Russia that she would kill just to prevent him expanding his written report with his personal explanations? There must be a reason, but he could not grapple with the problem now.

They would have to go to the British consul, make him believe the situation, and then – what? The consul could not prevent their being arrested on whatever charge the Muralevs had laid against them. He could not explain why he was especially interested in them. They would still be dealt with as Khussro, the Afghan of Persian descent, and Turfan, the Hazara peasant, neither of them British subjects, neither deserving of any special privileges. The case would never come to trial. In truth the only man in Basra who could help them now was the Turkish governor of the Basra Vilayet. But there would be guards at the gates of his palace who would allow no one to enter without a pass. If the consul could arrange a private audience with the governor – on what grounds? Also, Lenya Muralev's thugs would be all around the consul's house by now. They'd never reach it.

There was nothing left to do, no path, no way open. It was true. But he couldn't say just to himself, 'All right,' and die. He had to ...

Jagbir said, 'We'll be late for our appointment with the Sheikh Abu Daabi.'

Robin burst out in near-hysterical laughter. It was something. Perhaps the Muralevs did not know about the sheikh. Thrown like that into his contemplation of nothingness, the sheikh became very large and important. He said to Jagbir, 'Let's hurry, then.'

They left the house by the same back way and hurried across the city. In the streets Robin heard feet behind him and could not be sure whether the sounds were real or existed only in his head. The streets were crowded. He heard so many feet, and some of them must be on a murderous errand because they pitter-pattered as fast as his own, no faster, no slower. Jagbir gripped his elbow, and he found he had been on the edge of running – yet his feet dragged, and he seemed to cover no distance, hurrying always in the same place. Of the other feet, behind, some were bare, some in sandals, some made slippers go clack-clack. A ship's siren boomed mournfully over the housetops. They began to run. So the feet were real; otherwise Jagbir would not have allowed him to run. He led, Jagbir followed, hissing encouragement in his ear. That was wise. If Robin had been at the back he would have stopped and given up, standing against the wall quietly, tired, until the feet arrived. He knew Sheikh Abu Daabi's house and ran in without calling or knocking. The gates were open, there were two soldiers in the yard and an officer by the door. He saw them and recognized them for what they were, but the man standing by a curtain-hung arch was the sheikh, with whom he had an appointment. The sheikh held the curtain aside, they entered, and he followed them. Robin stopped in the room, turned, and said heavily, 'I am here. Khussro. I had an appointment with you.'

In the silence, listening for the feet, he did not hear them. They must be outside, waiting. There was a fourth man in the room, a portly man in a long Arab robe. He held the end of it loosely over his face below the eyes. His eyes were dark and sunk in fat, his forehead was wrinkled, and he wore a fez. Glistening top-boots and the end of a gold scabbard poked out under his robe. Robin stared at him for a second, then dropped his eyes. He was like a king incognito, a personage whom everyone recognizes but pretends for the sake of formality not to recognize. The fat man's inefficient disguise was like Queen Victoria's calling herself Mrs Windsor-Balmoral.

The sheikh said, speaking in slow French, 'These are the persons I spoke of, sir. Khussro, this is Osman.'

Robin made a low salaam. The fat man was the Turkish governor of the Basra Vilayet, whose name was not Osman. There was an etiquette in these affairs and Robin said, 'Osman, I am honoured to know you.'

The fat man said, 'Good.' he had a squeaky voice, the robe muffled his mouth, and his French was bad, but he could be understood. 'We have not time to waste. Khussro, I want you to tell your master that we are interested in your business, and for the same reason. You will have realized that if our neighbours should seek to trade in the south – with headquarters in, say, Bushire or Shiraz – neither of us will learn until too late whether they intend to open further markets to the east, in India perhaps, or to the west. Their western market would be —'

'Here,' said Robin.

'Precisely. I do not think that would suit you?'

'No.' He could not speak for the British or Indian governments, but it was impossible that either of them could allow the Russians to install themselves on the Persian Gulf at the expense of Turkey.

The fat man continued, 'Very well. Our masters will doubtless be discussing these matters in other places. I have no official position, you understand.' The dark eyes flashed warningly, and Robin nodded. It was clear now why Abu Daabi had insisted that the appointment be for after dark. The fat man went on. 'So I cannot speak officially, but there will be advantages if, like our masters, we smaller fry keep each other informed. The sheikh here will always know where to reach me. You will tell your master?'

Robin bowed. The fat man insisted. 'The top one you will tell? The Lāt?'

Robin said, 'The Lāt.'

'Good.' The fat man got up. 'Now I have to go. Farewell. And remember!' He bustled to the curtain, pushed it aside, and clanked down the passage. Robin hurried after him. 'Excell – Osman, sir, we are in trouble. The neighbours of whom you spoke – some of them have prevented us from boarding our ship. They —'

'Do you think I didn't know that?' The fat man chuckled delightedly and clapped Robin heavily on the back. 'Of course I was going to take you down to the dock. I have to have my little joke sometimes.'

Unaware of Jagbir's contemptuous stare fixed on his back, and still chuckling, he climbed into the waiting carriage. Jagbir and Robin followed, then a lieutenant aide-de-camp squeezed apologetically in, two mounted outriders took their places behind the two before, and His Excellency set off incognito for the dockside. If he had not been incognito there would have been two full troops of cavalry and a trumpeter.

Robin sank back in the seat between Jagbir and the aide-de-camp. Opposite, Osman sat alone, saying nothing, his dark eyes darting restlessly from side to side.

It was finished, and the ship waited on the tide to carry him home. Lenya Muralev had tried hard to kill him because he had found the truth. The resources and cunning of the Turkish Empire had been secretly at work and had confirmed that truth. Next year, or the year after, the Russians were coming, centre and south, their main weight south. That was the level of truth. It must be.

Even as the carriage jolted in a deep pothole and he smelled the rotting sewage in the river, he knew it could not be. *The* plan, on the level of truth, would be Muralev's plan. But every line of Muralev's body, every look from his shadowed blue eyes, denied that this was his place. Here he was living a deception foreign to his nature. Robin could read the message because in his own body and in his own eyes was the same warning. No god left his coin here for you to interpret, no flying bird its feather.

Hayling would understand, even if he did not agree. But how could the Lāt, the Viceroy, be told of these things? In only one way. By finding and placing before him some of those mutable things called facts. Robin thought again of Alexander; the true proof of his power was his legend, yet some men – most men perhaps – would take one of his coins to be more positive evidence. It was not so. Coins could be coined; legends and mysteries, never.

He was on his way back. Almost at once, whether Hayling sent him or refused to send him, he'd have to go again. There was Anne waiting for him, but he'd have to go. He had found no solution to the private mystery or to the public problem. Somewhere coin and feather, Peter Muralev and Robin Savage, truth and deception, legend and fact, would come together.

At the docks the aide-de-camp scrambled down and whispered to the police lieutenant at the foot of the gangway. Robin and Jagbir went on board, the police lieutenant saluted, the aide-de-camp returned to the carriage, 'Osman' clattered away. A last tremendous blast from the siren, and the lascars ran the gang-plank inboard. The lascars called out, and on the quayside men cast loose the hawsers. The ship drew away, her engines pounding and her single screw thudding heavily in the deep, fast tide.

CHAPTER SEVENTEEN

*

W HEN some of the excitement had died down Anne left the tent, the telegram held tightly in her hand, and walked to the edge of the lake. The tents were spread in orderly confusion under the trees behind her. A belt of chenars and pines and deodars ringed the lake except on the far side, where a high wall enclosed a Kashmiri leper colony.

From the dining tent Caroline Savage's quiet, penetrating voice called, 'Tiffin time. Come along.' Two banjos twanged to a stop as Robin's stepsisters, two half-grown girls, answered the summons. The smooth voice of Shivsingh Rawan, Robin's foster brother, the young Rajah of Kishanpur, called, 'We're coming, mother.'

She was not hungry. To-morrow Robin would be here. Here – the family encampment of Hildreths and Savages by the little lake outside Srinagar in the Vale of Kashmir. Robin. She stared at the lake but could not avoid seeing the wall, so she closed her eyes.

She turned to find Colonel Rodney Savage at her side. He took both her hands in his own, and she looked inquiringly up at him. He was tall and now, in his middle age, resembled a greying eagle. He had retained the sidewhiskers that used to be fashionable in his youth. They curled around on his thin sun-burned cheeks and gave him an air of strangeness, as if he had stepped down from a portrait gallery. His eyes were deep-set and icy-blue under undisciplined eyebrows. Black hairs sprouted from beneath the sleeves of his jacket, and grey bands streaked his thick jet hair. She had never met him until he and her father had arranged to take this leave together in Kashmir. They had done it so that when she had her babies both sides of the family would be present.

He was Robin's father, and Robin did not like him. But she had found him, from the first minute, everything she expected a man to be. He shot wild birds, yet he loved them. He risked his life to kill ibex and markhor on the mountains, yet he spent more time talking of their wonderful ways than of how he had shot them. He drank steadily and had a fine port-and-leather complexion, but she had never seen him even remotely near drunkenness. He smoked strong black cigars and smelled entirely male, and his flesh was hard.

He said, 'So your husband and my son are coming back to us to-morrow.'

She smiled uncertainly. '*Are?* They're the same person.'

Colonel Savage said, 'Are they? For your sake I had hoped not.'

She said, 'Do you know what he's been doing? I don't want to know secret things, but I would like to find out what sort of life he's been leading. It will make it easier these first few days if I know.'

'I know a little, Anne. Hayling came down to the southern front specially to tell me. Robin's work has taken him through some of the loneliest, wildest parts of Asia. He's done the work brilliantly. What the work has done for him' – he gripped her hands tightly – 'we'll find out soon.'

She said slowly, 'I wonder whether he felt the loneliness. Whether he thought of us sometimes.'

Her father-in-law hesitated, then said, 'Not often, I'm afraid. We'd be deceiving ourselves if we imagined that he kept longing to be back with us, or even thinking much about us, any of us. A man in his position, on work like that, can think only of his circumstances from hour to hour, and of his task. We have to be content to be a sort of floor beneath his feet. Then at the end he may realize that the floor has been there all the time, supporting him. Then – he may wonder whether we're a good floor or a poor one, wonder even whether he needs a floor at all.'

'I see.' She nodded her head vaguely. She was prepared to fight. She wished the enemy could be a concrete reality, preferably human – another woman, for instance. Edith Collett's example had shown her exactly how to deal with that. Or slandering, doubting, so-called friends; them she could beat down or persuade.

Colonel Savage said quietly, 'My son does not love me, Anne. You know that, of course. But I love him. It's only that I do not understand him. I never will, and the fault is not in him. Robin extends beyond my limits. Don't tell him I love him, that never does any good.' He paused and looked meaningly at her before continuing. 'Don't tell him, but – if you can – let him know somehow. I'll be happier. I think he will be too.'

She did not know what to say, so said nothing. He nodded brusquely, dropped her hands, and walked with quick steps to his tent.

Anne went to lie down beside her sleeping babies. Her breasts ached, but the twins were asleep in their cots under the single mosquito net, and she would not awaken them. Robin might have changed so much after what he had been through. And what was that? What lives had he lived, what had he seen, what done? Whatever they were, she could never share in them, however hard her love drove her to try, as he could never share in the actual experience of giving birth.

Her mother came in. 'Oh, I didn't know you were asleep. The darlings! Aren't they hungry yet?' The babies woke up and yelled together. Anne fed them and watched her mother's quiet face. The babies were wonderful, but they were not her mother's. How could they do this, then? How could they, just by existing unstring the muscles controlling that face, so that it lost its familiar angularity and was possessed instead by a kind of voluptuous calm?

After that she went to sleep. Then she ate, fed the babies, ate, slept. She could not tell one day from another, or yesterday from to-morrow, they were so much the same, except that suddenly it was *the* day. After lunch she moved aimlessly about in her tent for a while, shifting a hanging there and a rug here. She fed the babies. Soon after, she had to lie down because she was so tired. Lying there, thinking of Robin a bit, then of Colonel Savage, then of the babies, her eyelids dropped more heavily down, and her thoughts revolved more slowly in that darkness, and she awoke in a sweat to see Robin standing in the doorway of the tent.

It must be Robin. He was dark, dark fierce brown, and in the dim light his face had the same angles as his father's. He did not look like an eagle, though, but like some hungry, weaker bird. He came into the tent and stood beside her bed. 'There's no one about except your father's bearer. He told me which was your tent.'

'Darling, darling! I went to sleep. Shivsingh went in to Srinagar to meet you; he must have missed you on the road.

199

Everyone's in their tents, waiting. I went to sleep – oh, I fell asleep.' She began to cry from mixed joy, tension, and exasperation.

He knelt on the mat beside her bed and kissed her face and brow and cheeks. She felt his lips, which were cracked and baked, absorbing her salt tears. She stopped crying and lay still, unable to find the strength to get up. He rose from his knees and walked over to the babies. After lifting the mosquito net, he stood beside the cots without speaking for five minutes, while she lay with her head turned on the pillow and watched his face for a sign.

He said, 'They're ugly. They're mine?'

He spoke wonderingly, and she knew he meant no insult.

'Pink and blue. A boy and a girl. Hayling told me in Simla.'

He lowered the mosquito net, sat down suddenly in a chair, and said again, 'They're mine,' this time not as a question. It was worse, though, because his voice went flat and expressionless. She sprang out of bed and rummaged through the chest of drawers, throwing on her clothes. 'Oh dear, what time is it? The sun's down.'

'A few minutes after six.'

'I'll never forgive myself for sleeping. I had so much to do and I never did it.'

He looked at her and said, 'I prefer this to last time. That was too much arranged.'

She smiled, feeling happier. The old Robin and the old Anne could not have discussed the interlude at Edith Collett's, because their communion with each other lay at a shallower level. They had now reached deeper waters together and could see each other more clearly. She said, 'I was silly. But don't blame Edith.'

'Where is she now?'

'Up here in Kashmir somewhere. I don't see much of her.'

'You ought to. She's a good woman.'

'I think so, darling, but—' She did not finish the sentence. She did not see much of Edith because in the months of pregnancy she had had time to discover that Edith's solutions did not answer her own problems.

The evening passed. No one came to disturb them. The bearer brought dinner to them. She could not eat, but Robin ate well. When he had finished he sat back in an armchair, his face like a mahogany dummy's, much darker than Shivsingh's, against the cretonne cover. She said hesitantly, 'Robin, wouldn't you like to see your father for a minute? Just to say hullo.'

He looked down at his slippered feet, stretched his legs in a curious, tentative way, and stood up. 'Yes.' He kissed her suddenly as he went out. She joined her hands behind her head and waited quietly. He had changed all right. Every minute the waters ran deeper and faster. Where to?

By the time he came back she had undressed and got into bed. He sat on the stool by her dressing-table and began to take off his boots. 'I've got a pair of corns from wearing these things,' he said, and twisted his foot to look at the sole. After a while he said, 'I had a talk with my father.' He took off his shirt. 'I went over because I thought it was my duty. I used to dislike him. On the road, whenever I thought about him, which wasn't often, I still did. Now I don't. He must have changed.'

'Or you have.'

He stood in the middle of the rug, under the high ridge-pole, and she saw that the skin of his torso was stained brown. His body was paler than his face. He saw the direction of her glances and said, 'That won't come off for months unless I have the special lotion brewed up.'

'You must do that to-morrow, Robin. I'd rather have a white husband.'

'Why?' He didn't wait for an answer but went on at once, almost as if evading some further query on her part. 'I have changed. I used to try not to dislike anyone, but I did, really. Now I don't. I can't. The feeling doesn't come.' He kept his head turned away from her.

To his back she said, 'Or love anyone?'

'I don't know. I thought I'd find out, but I haven't. Jagbir. You. Them.' He stared at the babies. 'They're very quiet aren't they?'

'I fed them while you were out. They do nothing but eat and sleep. You'll hear them in the morning, though.'

'Yes. I did not think much about people unless they were connected with the work. Everything else I only felt. I was in mountains and deserts a long time. In some places I heard nothing but the wind – not the howl of a wolf or the sound of a bird or a tree branch creaking. Just the wind. I realize now it made a sort of backdrop, a curtain behind everything else.'

201

'A curtain, or a floor?'

He stood in his trousers in the middle of the tent and turned to look at her. 'A floor? Yes. Jagbir saved me from trouble more than once because his floor is so much more substantial – people and things he loves, food, memories, hopes. He's here – or in a brothel in Srinagar. What happened to my painting kit? It was in that long canvas bag.'

'It's over there.'

'I'm going to do some painting while I'm here.' Then, without change of emphasis or tone, he went on. 'We are all very small, and nothing about us is smaller than our fear.' He pulled on his nightshirt, took off his trousers, and came over to her. He blew out the lamp and lay down beside her, and she felt the warmth of his body, and, inside it, the cold of empty space. He did not seek warmth, he did not seek cold. Only because he was shaped in the form of a man did she imagine these things. He should have been born deformed, to make it easier for him. Or God should have sent his spirit to inhabit winds and mountain-tops, instead of putting it into a sheltering, enclosing body so that it became Robin Savage.

This was ridiculous. He was not like other men, but she had known that when she married him. He was hers, and she his. She curled closer to him in the big bed and warily put her arm over his chest. She said, 'What *is* the matter, darling? Can't you tell me?' It was on her tongue to say, I love you, but she remembered Rodney Savage's warning look and did not say it.

His chest rose and fell slowly under her arm. He lay flat on his back, and she knew that his eyes were open and that he was staring at the tent roof. His attitude was stiff, but his muscles were relaxed. After a while he said, 'I want something which I don't seem to be able to find among people. I think I've only met one man who could help me, and he is an enemy. I don't know why he's so important to me, because I only spoke to him three or four times. But things happened that made me sure he is like me, only farther on, closer to finding what he's looking for. His wife loves him, too.'

'But he doesn't love her?' Anne asked quietly, her arm stiffening.

'Yes, he does, as far as he can. How can I make you understand, when I hardly understand myself? What's the good of

202

talking about ships, ropes, birds – or coins?' But he knew the purport of her question well enough and continued his answer in a more direct fashion. 'You think it's something lacking in you, I think it's something lacking in me. I believe I do not have the capacity for love as you and Jagbir and Lenya Muralev have it. I may have been born this way, I may have grown into it. Whatever the cause, the effect is the same – that I'm afraid of people. Even of you.'

'Oh, my darling, no!'

'Yes, I'm afraid of your love. When I try to explain to myself why that is so I say that every good human quality is balanced – usually overbalanced – by an opposing evil. I say that there is no humility without pride, no love without hate, no courage without cowardice. Don't you see that each word, each idea, has no meaning without its opposite? But in the end I think there is no explanation.'

In the dark, lying in a tent under the Kashmir stars, in that vale of plenty ringed about by silent lakes and mountains, he was slipping away from her, borne by the irresistible power of a glacier. He breathed quietly under her arm, and she must not let him go from her. In the early days she had struggled against the world for him, and she had fought a good fight and in the end won it, but it was the wrong fight. She and the world – the peopled world – should have fought side by side to rescue Robin from a power that was little known and much feared. She had learned that this strange power – let her call it the wind, as Robin did – moved in men but not in women. It was far more mysterious than the so-called 'mystery' of sexual love, which was no mystery. The wind set even the most humdrum of men to dreaming of escape and free movement, footloose athwart bare landscapes. Another power, the motionless calm of the lotus, existed in all women and bred in the most untamed, the most ethereal of them, longings for a place of her own, children, a hearth, human love.

She thought: It's my tragedy that I'm nearly all lotus and I had to give my love to the wind. Of course a man would not be a man without some trace of it – what woman could be stirred by a spirit as exactly feminine as her own? But in Robin there was nothing else.

There must be. And it was silly to talk grandly of tragedy. She

203

did have to give her love to Robin – she couldn't help that – but it wasn't tragic. Not to have this, her own love, burning inside her, that would be tragedy. Tragedy! She was not a cabbage to sit rooted to the earth while her lover flew away. She was not a lotus, even, but a woman with legs to move and a brain to think and a spirit to search. She could fly up and find the wind, as much of it as God gave her power to find. Robin should be held by the love of the lotus, and step down a little from the bitter, inaccessible peaks he saw and tore his fingers to scale.

The babies cried, first one, then the other, an impotent, importunate wail. She smiled to herself and slipped out of bed, whispering to him, 'I'll just lift them and pat them.' She had beautiful, wonderful children to help her.

Later, but she could not be sure whether it was a week or a day, she was alone with him in a shikara on the Dal Lake. It was after a picnic at Shalimar, and all the rest of them had gone on ahead. Thin streamers of mist lightened the dusk over the lotus. The water showed only in small and scattered patches. A temple stood on a jagged peak within her sight. Beyond, the mountains leaned back, lifting higher and higher to the snow. Arms of cloud caressed the peaks. She lay back on the cushions in the narrow boat, rested her head against Robin's knees, and watched the lotus drift by. The bows cut like a slow knife through the floating carpet of them. Their mauve and white flowers and flat, green leaves spread as far as she could see. She trailed her fingers over the side, willing that he should not speak, for the water was calm, and silent mountains looked down on them.

She plucked a lotus flower and carefully tied it into her hair. She would not speak because the day had spoken her words for her and showed on her behalf everything that she had to show. There were these:

Shalimar, that was old yet not stern, whose thick grass and shaded arbours were good and beautiful only because people existed to enjoy them. Every experience shared was thereby doubled. (Yet Robin quoted – 'The snows fall and none beholds them there.')

Her mother dozing in a camp chair, snoring rhythmically, a low grrmph-grrmph, her parasol collapsed across her face that had become almost lovely, her hand resting on the cradle.

The girls, Mary and Ada Savage, bright red ribbons in their hair, white skirts, white shirtwaists, playing rounders with her father and Shivsingh and Colonel Rodney – and Robin, who laughed with the rest of them.

The twins, whom she had been feeding behind a high wall of the emperor's garden when, in the fullness of content, her husband surprised her. (Yet he had passed from brooding to decision. He wanted to speak to her but could not or dared not. It was fantastic that he, who sounded in her every note of awe and love, should fear her. But he did.)

Robin paddled slowly. She wondered whether she was asleep, so like a dream was their soundless passage among the lotus. After a long time she moved her head and stroked it against his knees. It was dark. She said, 'We must have the babies christened. We can't go on calling them The Boy and The Girl. What do you want to name them?'

'I haven't thought.'

'Robin! And godparents?'

Robin said, 'I have thought about that. The Girl should have two godmothers and one godfather, The Boy two godfathers and one godmother, shouldn't they?'

'Yes.'

'I would like Shivu to be The Girl's godfather. What about Edith Collett for one godmother?'

'We-e-ell.' She ought to have expected this but she hadn't. She was taken by surprise and a little shocked. An Indian, even though he was a rajah, as her daughter's godfather? Why, a real godfather might help to bathe her as a baby, and could certainly give her clothes, even underclothes, when she grew up. She felt that she was a beast, a cruel and unkind woman, to think like this. But she could not help it. After all, there *had* been a Mutiny.

Robin said, 'I think they'd both like it.' Trails of phosphorescent water ran out at every stroke from the end of his paddle.

That was true. Shivsingh and Edith Collett would feel they were loved, and she knew how much both of them needed that. Her niggling, unpleasant doubts remained, but pride and admiration began to push them deeper down inside her. She thought: No one else in the whole world would think as Robin thinks. Whom have I married? What place will I reach if he lifts me, by the strings of my love for him?

Robin said, 'The other godmother, I have no ideas. I would like The Boy's godfathers to be my father and Jagbir.'

'Jagbir!' In spite of the tenor of her recent thoughts the exclamation was forced out of her on a rising note of incredulity.

'Yes, Jagbir.' He laughed softly. 'Jagbir will never be able to do much for him, except perhaps teach him to be a good officer. Then only if he wants to be a soldier and joins the regiment. Jagbir will never be an officer himself. He'll finish as a havildar.'

'Robin, it's —' She fumbled cautiously for words. 'It's so unusual. I'm afraid people might laugh at him when he grows up and they hear his godfather is a rifleman, a Gurkha. My mother was hoping the commander-in-chief would accept. Your father knows him, and he could be so useful. And don't you think godfathers have to be Christians, at least?'

'That would apply to Shivu too. I don't know. I want The Boy to grow up as good and happy a man as Jagbir. I don't care what name the godfathers call God by.'

She did not want to argue with him to-night. She said nothing more about the godparents but instead mentioned the names she had long ago decided she wanted her children to be called by. Robin answered at once. 'Catharine's a good name, but not Robin. Peter. Catharine and Peter.'

She had not expected him to agree to his son's being named after him, so she did not protest. She said, 'All right, then. Peter and Catharine. Can't you push the shikara into the reeds there and rest a minute? I'm getting a crick in my neck talking up at you like this.'

With a single stroke of the paddle Robin nosed the bow of the shikara into a reedy island that loomed darker ahead above the glistening flowers and the starlit water. The lights of Srinagar shone on their left hand, lending ghostly form to the trees along the edge of the lake. He slipped down to the cushions beside her, and she wanted love to be made, literally. She wanted to create love out of the warm air and the lotus and the water, and lap him in it. She opened her arms to him.

Her body floated down and she saw it in the shikara as she rose, borne on lotus balm, and embraced him in the windless air above the lake. How far could she rise, how far lift him with her?

The strain on her arms and at the back of her closed eyes grew intolerable. She had to let go. She opened her eyes and stared silently a long while into Robin's. His head was a dark shape on the sky; his eyes held no answer to her question, nor would he say where he had been, how high, how near, how far.

She said, 'What are you going to do when your leave's over? Does Major Hayling want you to stay in the Intelligence? Did your father talk to you about returning to your regiment? You know he's been able to fix something with Old Alma and Colonel Franklin so that – I mean, they aren't going to —'

Robin leaned away from her with a gentle movement. He laughed quietly, not bitterly. 'Good heavens, yes, I'd forgotten I was a coward. They were right, though. I am.'

'Robin, please!'

'The question won't arise for a bit. I've got to go.'

Got to go where? What do you mean, go? The rising tide of alarm filled her throat so that she could not say the words. She knew now that this was what he had been trying to tell her ever since he came to Srinagar.

'Why do you have to go? Have you been ordered to?'

She forced herself to speak in a business-like tone – although she felt the wind rushing about her in the calm of the lake, tugging at her because she loved Robin, and tugging at him to tear him apart from her. The lotus was in her hair, and the wind was jerking at it to cast it out and away – but the water was calm, and the flowers on the lake did not stir petal or stem.

Robin was speaking. 'I haven't been ordered to go. I've been ordered not to go.' He began to explain to her about central routes and southern routes and railways and mountains and deserts and rivers, and the Russian whose wife was like an anchor – or was it a rope he compared her to? At length he said, 'I'm waiting to get my strength again, then I'll go.'

'How long will that be, before you're fit?'

After a short hesitation he said, 'I'm lying, even to myself. It isn't physical strength I'm waiting for, but moral courage – and it hasn't really got much to do with the secret-service work. That's just the – the arena in which I'm struggling. I'm waiting for a sign that says "Go", and gives me the strength to do what I ought to do – leave you alone.'

'For ever, not to come back?' She spoke very calmly.

'I don't know. Will I find another coin and be able to interpret it?' Then, suddenly forceful, 'Anne, I'm sinking.'

'*What!* Is the boat leaking?' She sat up hurriedly and peered over the side.

He laughed hard, a fresh laugh that blew away some of the phantasms his words and his manner had conjured from the lake to frighten her. He said, 'Not the shikara, Anne. Only me.' Then, seriously but not tragically, he said, 'I've told you. More love is being heaped on me than God gave me capacity to bear.'

'Oh no, Robin, no! We're not asking you to give anything back, none of us. We only want you to be yourself, to be happy.'

He said flatly, 'Love is a load, and I don't think I can carry it without its breaking me. If it did break me I'd become a better husband, a better son, a better father. But – I can't *willingly allow myself* to be broken, Anne! I can't. You couldn't! Nobody can!'

She thought he might mean the excess of domesticity that had surrounded him since he came back. She thought he might imagine that with the babies he would be tied all his life to paved roads and padded comfort. She thought a hundred things – while the wind whistled in her ears.

She said, 'Let's get away from our people for a bit. Let's go up the Sind Valley. Your father says it is beautiful and wild. We can shift camp as often as you like. Peter and Catharine will have to come, but they can be carried in doolies. I'm not very strong yet, but when we get into camp you can go out and fish and shoot and climb. You can paint.' She kneaded his right hand between both her own. A hardness and dryness in her mouth prevented her from swallowing while she waited for him to answer.

He said, 'Yes. All right. That will do.'

'Then we'll start to-morrow!'

'It'll have to be the day after. We can't arrange it in time for to-morrow. I'll warn Jagbir to-night.'

She bit her lip, then determined to say it. 'Please don't bring Jagbir, darling. I think he reminds you of everything you've been through. He's not part of this – this thing, this horrible thing which makes you believe you can't love people. He doesn't know the answer, he can't tell you anything.' She finished, breathing deeply, and as soon as the last word was out of her mouth she wished she could recall it.

It was the old mistake, of fighting the wrong fight. She was a

208

fool to set Jagbir up as an enemy in her mind, as someone who competed against her for Robin. Jagbir was on her side and he was a friend. Jealousy, in connexion with Robin, was the last fatuity. Robin feared all who came close to him. He had just explained to her that he feared they would break into him to exorcise the comfortless presence reigning over his spirit. But the presence, however forbidding, was the gift of God, and he had to fight to prevent man substituting for it any lesser gift. Anne realized now that anyone was her ally who could help her show Robin that human love did not have to be demanding. If a woman of the streets could for a moment persuade him of the reality of any kind of love, that woman was her ally and to be loved by her. If Jagbir could show him the reality of faithful, un-asking, all-giving devotion, Jagbir was her ally and her friend. But the words had been spoken, and Robin took them up quickly. 'Very well. I'll leave Jagbir behind.'

The enemy blew down from the mountains, and she jerked her head against it, knowing it was not real, just a wild wind of her imagination. But the lotus blossom fell out of her hair and dropped to the surface of the lake, where it lay motionless, its petals extended.

CHAPTER EIGHTEEN

*

SITTING in front of the tent, she watched Robin move down the face of the mountain. He had gone off from the previous camp at five in the morning, to explore a side valley for flowers and rejoin the rest of them here.

She heard the bearer tell her that tiffin was ready, and acknowledged the message with a nod but did not turn her head. They had been five days on the trail by now, and the business of pitching camp had settled into an easy routine. She had to crane her neck to see the cliffs beneath the hidden summit of the mountain. Below the cliffs a grassy alp hung to the face of the rock. Below that the slope bent steeply down through thin, insecurely anchored pines. A lammergeier circled, a tiny dot, across the face of the cliffs, the wind carrying his dark, rushing shadow over the marmot in its hole and the hare in its form. She saw Robin run down across the alp and drop into the pines. Twenty minutes later he came out on the last slope, walking now with a long, easy stride. He did not stop at the stream but came straight on across it, leaping from stone to stone and, when the boulders failed, stepping down to wade through the boiling, icy water. Then he ran up the slope to her and reached the grass. His light-grey tweed trousers were wet from the waist down, and the breeze could not stir his perspiration-wet, dishevelled hair. He held a bunch of flowers loosely in his right hand.

He extended his arm. 'I found these up there on the cliff.'

'Above the alp? It looks terribly steep.'

'It is. Look, isn't this one like edelweiss? And this is a blue poppy.'

'Darling, it's beautiful!' She leaned over the flowers in his hand and sniffed them carefully. There were white and pink and scarlet and blue. The poppy was like a flower carved of veined blue ice, so cold and fragile it seemed in Robin's brown hand. Beside it the red button of an anemone winked gaudily from the protection of a frieze of spear-like grey-green leaves.

He said, 'Take them, put them on the table. They don't last long in captivity but while they do they're worth the getting.'

She took the flowers and got up from her chair. 'Tiffin's been ready for half an hour. You're soaked. You must go and change or you'll catch pneumonia.'

'Not a hope.' He looked down at his shirt. 'But I've been sweating. I'll change.' He glanced up at the sun and around at the rocks and the shadows of the trees with a curious, all-embracing sweep of the eyes. 'It's just after one. I'm hungry.'

At tiffin she remembered that she was going to persuade him to stay here at least an extra day. She said, 'What shall we do this afternoon? Let's fish. Then to-morrow you can take me up there.'

His eyes were hollow and blue-rimmed, and the brown and green flecks in them did not move with the light as they used to. A transparent pallor was visible under his sunburn, like a ghost seen through a dark veil, and in the evenings she imagined sometimes that his skin shone like phosphorus. She knew that he hardly slept at night. Twice she had awakened to find him gone from the camp bed beside hers. She had heard nothing until he came in from outside, when by the dim lantern she saw that he wore only his nightshirt and that his feet were bare. He had become impervious to cold and heat.

He said, 'Fishing?'

'Yes, Robin.' She laughed lightly. 'Trout fishing. That's what we came up the Sind to do. Remember?'

He said, 'I must go up the mountain the other side.' He waved his hand behind him. The tent door faced the stream, but she had examined the other side of the valley while waiting for him to come, and she remembered what she had seen. The pines climbed up from the camp site until, after several thousand feet, they died away, and the eye, climbing on, passed over a desolate square mile of scree where cloud shadows moved in procession across tumbled rocks. Above again, wisps of cloud wandered along the distant, set-back crestline. She thought, Above the trees there will be small mosses pushing through between the stones; alpine flowers stippling a wilderness of grey and black with pinpoints of colour; the mist will embrace the climber in dank arms, then release him suddenly and set him on a platform where the view stretches for ever; the sun will shine a minute, then an icy breath will bring the cloud, and the sun will hide. She must go up and experience all these things for herself. She

211

said, 'I'll be strong enough to come with you to-morrow, I hope. Won't you fish to-day?'

'I must go up. I'm going to paint. I'm sorry. We'll go together to-morrow, though.'

He wiped his mouth, left the table, and went to collect his painting kit. Two minutes later he came back to say he was off. Canvases and miniature palette were slung across his back. In a hollow metal cylinder at his side he carried paints, brushes, and charcoal. He kissed her hand, looked carefully at the nails in his boot soles, and began to climb up through the pines. Soon she could not see him.

She fed the twins and after that took her rod and walked slowly down to the stream. She began listlessly to cast the pool a hundred yards above the camp. One of the coolies followed her, appointing himself the carrier of her creel and gaff, but she could not talk to him. What could he answer if she said to him, 'There is a Russian woman, beyond those mountains somewhere, who is my ally. How can I tell her that I am her friend, that I pray for her and for myself?' She had not managed even to tell Jagbir, before leaving Srinagar, that she was on his side.

She had not been fishing for half an hour when, looking around, she saw movement on the trail beyond the camp. There was a little pass where she had stood and watched the men putting up the tents. She peered under her hand, thinking for a moment it might be Robin, but of course it wasn't. It was a horseman whom she saw breasting the slope, and behind him another. Other horsemen followed the first two. She did not count them but watched while they passed above the camp, disappeared into a re-entrant, and reappeared higher up the hill. At last the pines and the convolutions of the valley hid them, and she turned again to her fishing. She must remember to tell Robin about them and ask him who they could be. One or two of them had guns on their backs, which had made her think for a moment that they must be a detachment of Kashmir Cavalry, but she had dismissed that idea at once because they weren't wearing uniform and because, apart from the men with the guns, the riders were slung about with sacks and baskets, as were most of the horses. Besides, there were women among them. They had made an odd, silent little procession as they passed north. She would like to know who they were and where they were going.

212

She was glad when ayah brought the twins down to the river and squatted at her side. She did not protest when ayah brought out an old stub of one of Robin's cheroots and began to suck noisily on it, though she had told her often enough not to smoke near the babies. Ayah said, '*Baba log* like noise of water, sleep well, memsahib.' Anne nodded and tried to concentrate on the fishing, but found herself glancing continually at the hill behind her.

The sun sank below the mountain crest, and suddenly it was cold. She packed up the rod and returned to the camp.

The dusk came, and the small sounds of day faded – the sounds that are not heard individually but by their mass nevertheless deaden other noises. So when it was dark the river roared louder, and the wind droned in the pines, and the men spoke more softly. She held up dinner for an hour, but then she had to eat because she was hungry and the babies were crying. When she was alone at last her mind leaped back to something Rupert Hayling had said on one of those hunting mornings – 'He's not so sure as you are. ... He might bring himself to some harm.' Robin hadn't taken a gun with him up the mountains. But on the mountain were crags and cliffs and precipices. The terrors of doubt might drive him to the edge. She saw pictures that were darkly lighted but chillingly exact. He lay dead at the base of a cliff. Blood ran from his head. It was dark and steep, and the searchers could not see him, so he lay there for ever. It began to snow.

She jumped up, shouting, 'Alif! Alif!' – and when he came, 'The sahib – we must go and find him.'

The bearer clucked soothingly. 'It is a steep hill, but the sahib is a good man on the mountains, almost as good as a Pathan. Do not fear. I will collect the coolies, and if he is not back in half an hour we will go with lanterns and look for him.'

She heard the mutter and bustle of their preparations and tried to sit still until the half-hour was up. With five minutes to go she heard shouts, and Robin came in. His hollow eyes shone in his dark, gleaming-wet face. The green lichen that clings to high rocks stained his clothes. He stood upright and did not sway on his feet, but she had never received so strong an impression of exhaustion. He was empty of physical strength, even enough to hold the flesh to his bones and the skin to his flesh. In a minute he would disintegrate before her eyes. She unstrapped his gear

213

and led him to his bed. There he folded at the waist like a jack-knife, sat down, and lay back. She lifted his legs to the bed and called Alif. Without a word the bearer took off Robin's boots and socks and began to massage his feet.

Robin's eyes were open. He said in a low voice, 'Did you see some horsemen passing up the valley?'

'Horsemen? Oh, yes, twenty or so, but don't worry about them now. You need —'

'They are real, then. I didn't imagine them?' Alif slipped out and returned with whisky, tea, and a steaming bowl of lentils. Robin sat up in a single hurried movement, as though he must move fast or not at all. He said, 'I saw the horsemen, on top.'

'On top! That's – miles up.'

'Five thousand feet from here.'

Five up and five down, and at least four this morning – fourteen thousand feet in a single day. He'd kill himself.

'On the way out I gathered some more flowers for you. They're in there.' He gestured towards his satchel. 'I came down to a col on the crestline. I was going to paint there. A steep trail leads over it from this valley into the next one to the east. I was moving along the mountainside towards the col. I sat down to rest in shelter a little below the col and a quarter of a mile from it. Then the horsemen came.'

He groped for the glass, swallowed the whisky in one gulp, and began to cough. His eyes, on hers, swelled out with his coughing until they seemed to fill his face.

'I saw them coming. When they were below me, climbing up, they were little men on horses. There was mist about, and some cloud. Anne, Anne, as they went over the col they grew huge, they towered up on the skyline in the drifting cloud like giants, monsters on monstrous horses. The hill didn't alter, it stayed the same – so the horsemen towered over me, but the ground under their horses' hoofs was a quarter of a mile away. I couldn't count them, I had to stop because nothing in my brain worked. On the path they'd been twenty-two. I'd counted them. They kept coming, looming up, going over the pass – scores and hundreds and thousands of them in the smoke and the cloud, and long rifles on their backs.'

'Only two had rifles, Robin.' He had seen a mountain mirage but his frenzy strained at her common sense until she could not be sure whether it was for his sake or for her own that she held his arm so tightly. She said, 'It was a trick of the light. It does happen in mountains. I've read about it.'

'I know. I know the horsemen were not all armed. I know they were Baltis. I know there were only twenty-two of them. I know they were crossing from this valley to the next on a short cut back to Skardu. But – now I've got to go.'

In the end it came suddenly, like a pistol fired in her face. She started back as though he had indeed shot a bullet between her eyes. Her head hurt, and she stammered, 'D-darling, not now. You're so tired you can't think. *Please* lie down, let me give you a sedative.'

He did not speak.

'You can't go in those clothes. You had disguise before, don't you remember?' She had not thought of it until this moment, but of course he must have had. Without the proper clothes he'd have to go back at least to Srinagar, perhaps farther. Once in Srinagar, she would secretly send a telegram to Major Hayling, who would order him not to go – but Major Hayling had already done that. If she could only get him back to Srinagar she'd have time to think of something.

'I have my clothes here.'

'Money,' she said. 'You'll need money. We've only got a few rupees in camp. You can't use them over the passes. They'll give you away. We'll have to go back to get some money.'

'I have money here, in gold bars. I bought them in Lahore with my back pay.'

'What'll happen to us here, to me and the babies, miles up this horrible, lonely valley?' she cried. 'You can't leave us here!' Anger began to flood into her as soon as she thought of the twins. She longed to hit him, to strike him down and hold him so that he could not escape, because she loved him and he was impossible.

'I'm sorry. Alif can get you back to Srinagar without any trouble. It's June the seventeenth today. I will sleep for a few hours because I'm tired. I told you a sign would be given to me. I will go before dawn.'

'It wasn't a sign, it was a mirage you – you lunatic! Or a notion about your secret service.'

'Mirages are outside the head, signs are inside. I suppose if I

215

was willing to lie to myself I could call it a message from some sixth sense, about the job. But, Anne my dearest, I've got to go, to find Muralev. I'm sure I'll come upon the truth this time.'

All the strength had surged back into him. He got up and walked lightly out of the tent, and she heard his soft call in the dark. His voice vibrated with energy now. The hurricane lantern burned on the table, but she could not see through her tears and fumbled her way into bed and lay down engulfed in misery. If this was her load of love it would break her too.

In the morning she awoke, and it was late, and he had gone. The sun shone in through a crack in the tent flap and set a golden fire behind the babies' mosquito net. They began to mutter and wail, and the biting mountain air penetrated the warmth under her bedclothes. She remembered; but she was not so altogether cast down as she had expected to be. The morning crackled in Himalayan splendour, and Robin had been with her, and he would come back.

CHAPTER NINETEEN

*

'Horses, north'. The giant horses walking through cloud over
the pass and blowing long jets of vapour from their nostrils ...
Ahead on the trail Robin saw with his eyes the last village in
India and beyond it the ramparts of the frontier, but his mind
saw the horses on the pass. Selim Beg had pointed the way, and
he, Robin, had not persevered in following. Lenya Muralev had
led him in the wrong direction across Asia, among smoky
bazaars and the smells of lamp oil and greasy candy and hot
dung. He had made his mistake at Jizak that day when the sleet
from the Hungry Steppe slashed his face and Jagbir shivered with
fever at his side. East and north of Jizak the land lifted higher
and higher to plains of swirling grass, to the mountains, to the
misty roof-trees of the world. Not too far from Jizak, if he had
gone on, lay the Farghana.

There were horses in the Farghana. It had been famous for
them since the beginning of history. Hundreds of years ago a
Chinese emperor had decided he needed better horses if his
armies were to beat off the Mongolian hordes that stormed over
and through his Great Wall. He had sent men to the Farghana,
two thousand miles from his capital at Pekin, to bring back
stallions and brood mares.

Like that dead emperor, Robin would go to the Farghana,
and Muralev would be there. He was sure of that – or the horsemen on the pass would not have loomed so gigantically among
the cloud wraiths. But why had he left Anne lying asleep in bed
with dark rings under her eyes and her hair a lifeless dull red
mass in the first dawn light? Couldn't he even have kissed her
and told her he loved her more than any other person in the
world? Then he'd have had to explain again what love meant to
him, and tell her that he could see the messages of love she sent
him from her eyes and mouth and with her hands, but he could
not read them. It was like communication by helio. There had
to be two, each focused on the other. However vital the message,
however brilliant the flashes, one could not understand unless the
other was in the same focus. Muralev, without effort, flashed a

message straight into Robin's eyes so that he could not avoid reading. Did he then 'love' Muralev more than he loved Anne or his father or his children or Jagbir? Muralev's message wasn't about love. It was about God and the loneliness of God. He could read it, and it began to make sense as he thought of it, but not yet enough sense. He had to find Muralev.

Few travellers used this route that arched over the roof of the world to link India with Chinese Sinkiang. Most of those who did accompanied the infrequent caravans of Central Asian merchants. The farther he went the more conspicuous he would become by travelling alone; nor was it easy to carry enough food; but he could do it. He forced the little pony over double stages every day. It had started from the Sind Valley in excellent condition, but now it flagged and failed, and many times on the long ascents he had to walk, leading it behind him.

He came to the last village and spent a day and some of his money in buying food, equipment, and information. He wandered around the tiny bazaar until he found out what he wanted to know about the Chinese frontier guards. The frontier lay on the Mintaka Pass, the Pass of a Thousand Ibex. He learned that the Chinese maintained a small detachment of soldiers nine miles beyond the pass, where the valley widened out. Twenty miles beyond that post, at Paik, there was a larger post with an officer. He did not know how he would get past them; he'd have to wait and see what the ground looked like.

He set out again, and on the second day began the ascent to the Mintaka. From a deep gorge the trail scrambled up to the side of a cliff, climbed on trestles over dizzy gorges, where through the rotting planks the eye could follow the four-thousand-foot fall of the precipice, and climbed again. He moved up slowly with the trail, every minute his breath coming thinner into his lungs. The lammergeiers coasted level with him along the cliff. He heard the whir of the wind under their wings until as he ascended they fell away below him and he looked down on them, and the sun touched the white marks on top of their wings as they glided across the screes and corries and the black gulfs. The mountains rose with him, the greater forcing above the lesser until near the pass they stood around him like the jagged towers of a city.

At last, his lungs tight and his head aching with sudden, bitter twinges, he stood on the rock-strewn pass. He sat down slowly, and the pony hung its head. The near mountains thrust up in white pyramids, in cathedrals of ice and rock supported by flying buttress-ridges ten miles long. Beyond them the peaks and glaciers of the Karakoram spread like a frozen army to the horizon.

Men came. The cries of the caravaneers sounded far and faint in the thin air, then the wind took the sounds and whipped them away over the void. He huddled into his sheepskin coat, got up, stamped his feet, and prepared to move on. Already the wind, made of something thinner than air, had penetrated coat and clothes and skin and flesh, into the marrow of his bones. He waited, swinging his arms, for the caravan to come up out of China. The leaders struggled abreast of him. The first man picked up a stone, threw it on a cairn beside the trail, and struggled on with a word muttered in surprised, cautious greeting to the lonely figure on the pass. Others came on behind him, the loaded horses stopping every third pace, but coming on. The men drove long nails fixed on sticks into the horses' muzzles so that the animals could drag more of the icy air into their bursting lungs. The blood frothed and bubbled out through their nostrils. One after another the men came, looked sideways at him from under the heavy hoods of their coats, did not pause, and went on down into India.

Robin took his pony's bridle and tugged. The pony would not budge. A stone rolled noisily down the path on the Indian side, behind him, and he turned his head. There was a man, leading a horse.

Jagbir halted, facing him. He was fine-drawn but otherwise as he had always been – a short, bulky figure in the trappings of a Hazara hillman. Robin saw in his face that he wanted more than anything in the world to stand to attention and give his number, rank, and name, and the information that he was reporting himself fit for duty – *Ursath bais, Ruffaman Jagbir Pun, hazir ayo ra kam ko laik chha.*

Robin said angrily, 'Who told you to follow me? I didn't say I wanted you with me, did I?'

Jagbir did not answer, nor did his eyes show any sign of hurt. Robin stared at him for a minute, then said, 'All right. We've got to get on.'

'Yes, Lord Khussro.'

Half-way down the long descent, while the horses stepped delicately and stretched down their necks to sniff the blood spattering the rocks, Robin said fretfully, 'I'm sorry, my friend. You know I can't give you anything but disappointment.' Jagbir shrugged his shoulders and asked, 'How far is the post?'

When he judged they were perhaps a couple of miles from the first Chinese frontier guards Robin led the way into a narrow cut between huge boulders at the right of the trail. They dismounted, fed the horses, tied them to big stones, and sat down together. Robin said, 'How are we going to get past them?'

'Why don't we go out that way?' Jagbir lifted his head and pointed with his chin to the west. There, over intervening ridges, they saw a rolling plain. The sun shone into their eyes as they looked, and made the short grass of the plain a mottled golden yellow.

'The Russian Empire,' Robin said. 'Here – the Chinese Empire. The other side of the Mintaka – the British Empire. I know the Russians keep quite a large detachment of Cossacks over there.'

Jagbir thought, his brow wrinkling painfully. At length he said, 'We must go on then. The Chinese soldiers will be inside their hut before midnight. I do not expect they will have any discipline.'

They ate some hard cheese and curds compressed in a muslin bag, scraping them out with their fingers and washing them down with water burning cold from the stream beside the trail. No travellers passed in either direction. The dark came, the stars burst out, the North Star flared over the empty pamirs. They waited beside the drooping ponies. At eleven o'clock they mounted and urged the ponies at a walk down the trail. They trusted to a light wind to blow away the click and clatter of hoofs on the stones. At last the path turned sharply right, the dim silhouettes of the flanking hills stood back, bowing lower, sweeping in a bow to the earth, and ushered them on to the high plain. Close at hand a hut crouched beneath the ridge. A chink of light shone under its door. The acrid smell of burning yak dung drifted to them from an invisible chimney.

In the hut a horse suddenly whinnied. While Robin stared

breathlessly into the darkness Jagbir leaned forward and seized the muzzles of both ponies, Robin's and his own, pressing his fingers in fiercely. The ponies whickered but did not neigh or whinny. No one came out of the hut.

The Taghdumbash Pamir spread ahead of them, a dim expanse of blue shadow and flat blue-green highlights under the stars. They passed the post, bore left, and walked the horses steadily out on to the pamir. After twenty miles they would come to Paik and the larger Chinese post there. When they had ridden for two hours Jagbir said, 'We will not reach Paik to-night. We might get near it, but we have to get around too. They will want to see our passes?'

'Yes.'

'We had better ride till first light, then lie up. Move again before dark, so we can have a look at Paik.'

In the first pale green light of dawn they turned right and headed towards the mountains. The ponies walked among yellow and white and red flowers. The land rose, tilting up at first in a straight, smooth line like an inclined table, featureless and shelterless under the grass and the flowers, then in transverse ridge and furrow to the foot of the mountain wall. In one such fold they slid to the ground and picketed the horses. Jagbir slept while Robin stood guard. Early in the afternoon when the sun had warmed them and they had both slept and were hungry, they ate together. Then, leaving the horses, they walked slowly to the brow of the ridge, a hundred feet off, whence they could see a wide stretch of the plain. They lay down side by side, and Jagbir said, 'There are many flocks on the pamir, but the nearest is five or six miles off – there. It has one herder, a boy with a rifle. A Kirghiz, I suppose. Where are we going, lord?'

'The Farghana. Six hundred miles.'

Robin noticed that Jagbir was lying on an ant's nest. While he spoke the rifleman had been slowly digging his hand into the nest. The ants rushed about, and he let them crawl on to his palm and up his arm. They did not bite him, and he took no further notice of them as they scurried in hundreds all over him.

Robin said, 'After we've done our business we've got to get back to India again. It will be late September at the earliest. They would have made you a naik when you got back to the regiment, for what you've done already. Now, they'll be angry,

221

court martial you perhaps. And I' – he watched the ants in Jagbir's hand – 'I don't care the way you care.'

'I am your *sathi*, your *choro*,' Jagbir said, using the Gurkhali words that mean 'comrade', and 'son'. 'The heart is small without *sathi* and *choro* and women.'

Robin said, 'Cannot a woman also be a *sathi*?'

'No.'

'Why?'

'They are different. One can leave a *sathi* for a woman's sake, but a woman cannot be a *sathi*. They do not understand, and we do not understand.'

'Very well. There are many who would not agree with you. But *I* do not understand either woman or comrade or son. Listen. Part of the Farghana, which is like a province, the Russians hold, and part the Chinese hold. The big town, which is in the Russian part, is called Andijan. They grow good horses in the Farghana. We are going to see the horses and find out if they are in any way connected with the Russian plans to invade India.'

'Will those two, the man and the woman, be there?'

Robin hesitated before answering. 'I think he will be. The woman – yes, I suppose so. I don't know.'

'If we see them,' Jagbir said, 'we should kill her at once. Otherwise we will never return from this country to our own.'

'And the man? Should we kill him?'

Jagbir shook his body carefully, then his arm alone. The ants dropped to the ground and scurried back to their disturbed nest. Jagbir said, 'Yes,' backed down until his head was below the crest, and walked alone to the horses.

Robin scanned the silent vastness of the pamir, then the flower that was in his hand, then the ants, and began to sob, his chest heaving in soundless spasms.

CHAPTER TWENTY

*

THE man Robin was talking to, a middle-aged prosperous-seeming merchant of Andijan in the Farghana, said curiously, 'We haven't seen many of your kind up here this year, or last year for that matter. There used to be twenty for each one there is now. Have our horses deteriorated?'

Robin shrugged. 'Trading's easier in other places, that's all. The Russians are making it difficult for a man to move about. It's examinatons, questions, octroi, browbeating, all the way from Balkh northward.'

'Ah!' the other agreed. 'Our new masters are a funny lot. Suspicious.'

'Your horses are as good as ever,' Robin continued earnestly, knowing the intense pride of every Andijani in his country and its horses. 'They're better. But they're not easy to buy even when we get here.'

He knew that was true because he had tried. He and Jagbir had ridden out two and three days' march in every direction from Andijan, making inquiries about horses. The horses were there, roaming the rich plain in herds, each herd under a pair of herdsmen, but, except for a few old screws, they were not for sale. The herdsmen always said they were already sold but were to be kept here until wanted. They knew no more. They were only paid employees of others.

So now, back in Andijan, Robin tried to find out who was buying the horses and why, having bought, they were not taking possession. That meant they must be paying a monthly retainer to cover the cost of looking after the horses. This Andijani merchant was the sort of man who might easily own horses as a sideline – but he was not giving any information away. To Robin's remark he replied only, 'No, it's not easy. Someone's buying them up. It might be the Russians, except that they are importing Mongolian ponies here, as if our Farghana mares needed any but the weight of a Farghana stallion on their backs!'

'Those Mongolian ponies are good doers and hard goers,' Robin said, sipping his tea.

'Yes,' the merchant admitted grudgingly. He eyed Robin cautiously. 'Of course it might be the Russians all the same. They're up to something here. But they act through so many intermediaries even in the simplest business that it's difficult to know for certain. What if a brother of the Khan of Khokand buys my horses? – "If", I said. Can *I* ask what he wants them for? Can *I* cross-examine him if he buys the whole lot and says he'll pay my price next spring, but I'm to look after them until then? Why, if the Russians want to buy a sack of rice in this town, first they send the police to spy out the land, then they get someone's brother's wife's uncle's sister's son to make an offer for a dozen silkworms.'

Robin was satisfied. The Andijani dared not talk freely, but he had given a good hint. The next step was more difficult. The horses were here, but where were the Russians? Where was Muralev? Unless he came across something more exact in the next few days he'd have to go on to Tashkent, where there was a Russian political agent, and see what he could find out.

He and the Andijani were still talking desultorily an hour later, drinking their tenth cups of tea, when Robin heard shots from the west. The eating-house where they sat lay on the outskirts of town. The shooting came closer. A cloud of dust rose over the dry fields, and soon he saw animals under the dust. Five minutes more and they took shape as small men on galloping horses. The men were wrapped in sheepskin coats and wore big sheepskin hats with ear-flaps, though it was a hot, sunny day. They carried short carbines, which they fired into the air as they came. The shaggy ponies galloped with ridiculously short strides through the crops, while the riders whooped and waved their carbines above their heads.

'*Ai-ai-ai-ai-yeee!*' The riders swirled into the street, fired a couple more shots apiece into the air, and flung themselves to the ground. After a shouted argument they tethered the ten ponies and came towards the eating-house. Robin glanced quickly around to see if Jagbir had come back. The rifleman had gone off on his own in the morning and would report here before dark. But he was nowhere in sight. The strangers rolled on like small, square-built ships. If they had come to arrest him there was little that he could do about it.

Sweat and grease shone on the men's flat faces. Their heavy

felt boots padded on the steps of the eating-house. Each carried a long knife as well as the short, modern carbine. In the entrance they stopped, and their leader called imperiously in a strange tongue. The proprietor, who had come out at the shooting and now stood apprehensively a yard behind Robin's mat, said, 'I – I don't understand.'

They gabbled furiously at him. The merchant leaned towards Robin and muttered, 'They want kumiz – fermented mare's milk – lots of it, and meat. Kumiz, in the name of Allah, and we make fine wine and brandy here!'

The proprietor waved his hands helplessly, backing into the room as the others surged forward. Their leader bellowed cheerfully in vilely distorted Turki, 'Kumiz! Meat! Not care what meat. Horse, sheep, camel! Meat!' A thick smell of grease, horse, sweat-soaked wool, and old dirt made the air pungent in the room. The merchant whispered, 'We would be wise to leave now, I think.'

Robin muttered, 'They're like savages. Who are they?'

'Mongols. Allah knows what they are doing here. Are you coming?'

Robin shook his head. 'I'm waiting for my servant. God be with you.'

The Andijani rose, gracefully made his adieus, and strolled away up the street. Robin sipped his tea and listened to the guttural torrent of chatter over his shoulder. The proprietor scuttled forward with a goatskin full of kumiz, and the Mongols began to drink, passing the skin around, pouring the liquor down their throats and splashing it over their coats and yelling with laughter.

'More, more!' the leader shouted. He was shorter, wider, paler, dirtier, greasier, and more slant-eyed than any of his comrades. The street emptied slowly as the Andijanis, without loss of dignity, sauntered farther away. Nearby merchants quietly shuttered their shops, barricaded their doors and vanished.

The Mongol leader glanced around, met Robin's eye, and turned again to mutter something to his neighbour. A second later he leaped to his feet, came to Robin, and struck him a tremendous blow with his fist on the broad of the back. 'You, friend!' he bellowed. 'Where from?'

'Gharghara.'

225

'Where that?'

'Afghanistan.' Robin waved his hand to the south. 'A thousand miles.'

'Good. I – there!' The Mongol pointed to the north-east. '*Two* thousand miles. *Zavashay zdarovay!*'

'Good health!' It was a common Russian phrase, which Lenya Muralev had often used. The Mongol returned to Turki. 'Come. Drink.' He laid a thick hand on Robin's elbow and pulled. Robin allowed himself to be jerked to his feet.

As he sat in the rough circle among them they handed him the goatskin, and he tilted it and drank. The liquor was strong and musty and left him gasping. By now the Mongols had made up their minds that only horsemeat would do, and kept bawling, 'Meat, horse, meat, horse!' The proprietor yelped that he had no horse-meat to-day. The leader jumped to his feet, and a loud argument began among the group. At the end of it they all trooped out into the street, unsaddled one among their horses, slashed its throat, and together attacked the carcass with their knives. In an unbelievably short space of time they returned, carrying huge, bleeding chunks of meat. The disembowelled horse, slashed to ribbons, lay in the middle of the street. In the eating-house they threw the meat on the floor. The proprietor wailed, 'H-how shall I c-c-cook it?'

The leader shouted, 'Cook? Not cook! Beat!' He pounded one of the horse steaks with the butt of his carbine. 'Beat! Long time!'

They all drank together for another half hour. Upstairs the proprietor and his women and children beat frantically on the meat with clubs. The ceiling rattled, and the room was full of the nervous, quick thudding. When the meat came Robin had to eat his share. The Mongols drank some more and began to sing. The leader sang by himself, then the others joined in with a yell and a shout.

Without warning the whole mob leaped to their feet and ran for their horses, dragging Robin with them. He hung back, protesting that his pony was in the serai, but the leader swept him up with easy strength on to the front of his saddle. Another Mongol took up the fellow whose horse had been eaten. They galloped up the street, yelling, 'Women! Women!'

Before midnight every man was drunk. Robin was nagged by

a hazy sense that he ought to ask the Mongols some question or other. He said, suppressing a spasm of nausea, 'I never seen your country. You have good horses? I horse-trader.'

'Horses? Best in world. Go anywhere. Good to eat too.' The leader embraced him. Robin saw Jagbir's perplexed face in the entrance of another eating-house across the way, and burst out in a foolish giggle. Jagbir looked so disapproving; he knew that his lord Khussro wasn't just pretending to be drunk. He *was* drunk, drunk as a – as a Mongol horseman.

The Mongol leader whispered hoarsely in Robin's ear, 'Best horses world. Go anywhere, our horses. Know what? Go to India!'

'India?' Robin giggled again. 'Why go India? Hot. Full of Indians.'

'A-a-a-ah! Secret. Not go now. Later. What like India women? Big, little?' The Mongol measured imaginary spaces between his forefinger and thumb.

'But mountains to India, or deserts,' Robin said obstinately. 'You be tired. On way you rest my house, Gharghara, in Hazar-ajat, in Afghanistan.'

The leader threw back his head and laughed in high and bloodthirsty good humour. 'The First Horde not rest, ever! Eat, drink, gamble, kill, ride. Come see us. You my friend. No women. Mares all right. Russians not allow, but' – he spat on the floor – 'that for Russians! You come our camp. We hide.'

Robin dashed into the street and was sick. An opportunity had come to him because he had come to the right place at the right time. He was just sober enough to realize that. But in the next hour he saw the opportunity fading as his own drunkenness increased and the frenzy of the Mongols steadily mounted. He had to drink, because the leader challenged him to a competition. After that he could do nothing but stumble on foot in the wake of the others as their debauch rose to its finale. When they stripped a pair of whores and chased them down the street, he was not far behind. When they rode down a squad of foot police he arrived in time to see the end of the fray, with all the police-men but one running in flight, and the Mongol leader carving designs on that one's chest with his knife. After that he lost them. He ran on blindly for several minutes, cannoning from wall to wall of the narrow street. Then the wall on the left swung around and struck him a brick-like blow on the jaw, and he fell down senseless.

He awoke in half-light, inside a room, and recognized Jagbir before the vomit rose in his throat and a stunning pain in his head again cut out the light. There was a lamp near him next time, and it took him longer to be sick, and he managed afterwards to retain his senses. All night he lay on his mat. There was something he had to do. He would nearly catch it, then the walls swung, the lamp lurched horribly, and it was gone. After he had slept again, it was light. Light in the east. Dawn. He sat up. 'Those Mongols. Where are they? Did you follow them?'

'They went at this time yesterday. They got on their horses and rode away. The horses weren't drunk.'

'Which way?'

'West.'

With Jagbir's help he rose, dressed, and washed. The only words he could remember from the debauch were 'camp' and 'First Horde'. Jagbir said, 'They *were* soldiers, then? I noticed their carbines. They must have gone absent without leave from some camp, to get drunk.'

'We've got to find the camp. I wonder if other parties of Mongols have been into Andijan before, making merry. It seems extraordinary that the townspeople haven't mentioned it.'

'This is the first time. I asked some questions while you were asleep yesterday. The camp can't have been in existence long. Those people have no discipline. They'd be breaking out all the time.'

Robin considered as carefully as his shaky head would let him. If the camp lay to the west of Andijan it must be more than two days' riding away, because he and Jagbir had gone that far in making their inquiries about horses. It could therefore be somewhere in that area where the Hungry Steppe reached the banks of the Syr Darya, or it could be in the mountains, two hundred miles deep, which separated the Farghana in the south-east from Tashkent in the north-west. There must be several thousand men in a 'Horde'. Even in Central Asia such numbers could not live in a camp without word of their presence filtering out.

Robin and Jagbir set off the following morning and rode fast to the west. They asked wandering herdsmen on the edge of the

228

steppe; they asked tradesmen in little towns; they asked villagers in miserable hamlets where the houses were like the shelters of conies, half above and half below ground. Then, when so many shrugs and so many silent shakes of the head had assured them that no secret lay hidden there or in the steppe to the west, they turned north into the mountains.

Here they knew more exactly what they were looking for. It had to be a valley wide enough to graze, say, five thousand horses. It had to have reasonably good access to some town whence supplies could be sent up for the men in the camp. Certainly no supplies for any large number of men had passed northward through any of the Farghana towns. So they must come from the other side of the mountains, from Tashkent. Further, if the camp had been newly set up, it was probably meant to remain in existence through the winter – a broad grassy valley, therefore, with a good access both summer and winter from Tashkent, and at least fifty thousand gallons a day of waterflow that did not freeze up.

Deep in the mountains, the word of a chance-met shepherd sent them across staggering precipices into the next valley and thence north and east.

On a late afternoon they saw the camp in the distance. They climbed a hundred feet up the valley wall and looked again. What they saw bore no resemblance to a conventional military camp. Groups of the round black felt tents called yurts dotted the grass about a marsh-fringed lake – there would always be water under the ice. They could not make out men or horses as separate and identifiable objects, but Jagbir said, 'There are thousands of them, loose, all over the plain. The horses must be hobbled. We must get closer. What will we look for then? What more do we hope to see?'

'I don't know. But we must get closer.'

Standing side by side, they searched for a way to approach the camp – Robin still called it that, although, except for the great numbers, it looked more like the temporary meeting-place of a Kirghiz migration. Jagbir saw a way at last. The valley ran north and south, like a corridor, and seemed to be about twenty miles long and five miles wide. From where they stood at the southern end Robin estimated that the lake, under the eastern or right-hand wall of the corridor, was five miles distant. The mountain walls were split in several places on both flanks, where side-streams burst through into the main valley to trickle across the uneven flat into the lake. Jagbir pointed out one such break in the eastern ridge. 'There, lord – about two miles. If we can get in there we should be able to work farther north behind the wall. When we think we are opposite the camp, we climb up and look straight down on it. We can go now, I think. If there are any outposts short of the lake they're well hidden. These people have probably blocked only the other end of the valley, the Tashkent end.'

Robin nodded, and they mounted, walked the horses into the plain, and began to move steadily forward, hugging the foot of the eastern mountain wall. As darkness fell they entered the gap Jagbir had seen. At once the going became rough, and it was no use trying to get any farther. They halted where they were and lay down to sleep.

The next morning they worked northward, taking the first stream that entered the gorge from the left, and following it up. As they went on up the steep draw the horses began to scramble for foothold, frequently falling forward and scraping their knees. At last the draw widened, the hills drew back, and near ten o'clock they stood in a valley which was the miniature of the great one to the west. But this held no lake. Tethering the horses securely, they began to climb the ridge.

On the top Robin lay down carefully, got his breath, and stared in disbelief. The sun shimmered on the surface of the lake, the reeds waved in a light wind, the yellow-green grass of the plain rolled forward under the wind – but there were no tents, no men, no horses.

Jagbir touched his elbow. 'There!' Straining his eyes across the valley, Robin saw long columns of horses descending the opposite mountain, streaming down like ants into the plain. They watched in silence. Two hours later the black tents were up where they had been before, and thousands of hobbled horses wandered loose about the valley and cropped the grass. The men too must be eating – but no smoke rose from cooking-fires. There were none. Robin realized there was no fuel except perhaps dried horse dung, and hardly enough of that.

'Manœuvres over for the day,' Jagbir said shortly.

Robin thought of what he had seen. He said, 'To-night we

must climb down the face of the ridge and get closer still. I want to see how they carry those tents, what their equipment is, their formations. Do you see that they have no pack train, no commissariat?'

During the afternoon they scanned the hill below them, looking for a way down that would serve in darkness. They found the climb would not be difficult. Though the ridge was steep it was by no means a precipice; with some difficulty even horsemen could ascend or descend it. In the evening they returned to the ponies, watered them, ate, drank, and slept. At two in the morning they reclimbed the ridge, crossed over the crest, and scrambled carefully down towards the floor of the main valley.

When dawn came they saw that they had reached a point a hundred feet above the toe of the ridge. The lake lay less than a mile away, and the nearest black tent was much closer. Already the camp was astir. Men galloped about with shouts, driving the hobbled horses towards other men, as yet on foot, who ran up and caught them. With rising unwilling excitement Robin saw the men pull down the black tents, ten men to each tent. Each man took a strip of the felt, folded it, and placed it on his horse. Then they dragged out their light saddles and threw them on the ponies' backs over the felt. Then each man took one of the withy sticks that had made a framework to support the tent, and slung it across his back. Each man stowed away in the pockets of his sheepskin coat some of the leather thongs that had held the tent together. Soon the ponies were ready – carrying felt, saddle, bags of food, carbine in its bucket, and, at last, rider.

They gathered together, first in tens, then the tens into hundreds, the hundreds into thousands. All was performed on the move. No markers stood to indicate the line where the ranks should fall in, no trumpets sounded. The horsemen wheeled and swooped across the plain, and the dust rose at their horses' heels in the grey sunless air, and out of the changing pattern a troop of ten became a squadron of a hundred, loosely knit, in no known formation, cantering together, wheeling together.

Jagbir sucked in his breath, hissing through his teeth. 'They do have discipline. They're dangerous.'

Robin muttered, 'This is only the First Horde.'

As the sun came up one squadron broke away from the mass and trotted towards their ridge, heading straight for their hiding place. But at the foot of the slope, not two hundred yards away, the squadron bore half left and began to climb up the ridge, leaving Robin and Jagbir on its right. Another squadron shook out, trotted to the hill, and followed the first. Jagbir whispered, 'The first lot will be over the top soon. They'll see our ponies.'

Robin moved his shoulders uncomfortably. 'Depends which way they turn. Wasn't there a Russian with them?'

'Yes. There's one with each. Look, about half-way down the squadron.' Peering closely, Robin saw a taller man among the Mongols of the squadron nearest to him. He saw the glitter of a steel sword-scabbard. Otherwise the Russian wore the same dress and carried the same accoutrements as the Mongols.

As a third squadron faced the slope Jagbir said, 'Someone's coming up the valley from the south.'

Robin turned his head cautiously and watched the dust cloud approaching behind two isolated racing riders. They galloped between the squadrons and halted among a group of seven or eight horsemen who stood apart by the edge of the lake.

Jagbir said, 'One of those two was the woman.'

'The woman only? Not the man?'

'The woman only.'

It was no use doubting Jagbir's eyesight. Robin had expected Muralev, but Lenya had come – and she had come from the south, where Andijan lay. Therefore she would know that he and Jagbir had been through the Farghana. Therefore ...

A horseman shot out from the group by the lake and galloped to the next squadron as it circled into position for its climb. While he spoke with the squadron's Russian officer the squadron continued to circle, like a weight on the end of a string. Minutes later, as though the string had broken, the squadron moved off in a straight line down the valley, to the south. Another squadron followed. A third swung north, and another behind that. The messenger then put his horse at the hill, and the stones flew as it strove with all its strength to catch up the squadron climbing ahead of it.

Jagbir said, 'They're after us now. She's guessed we'll be somewhere on this hill.'

Robin thought. Two hundred men had gone south; they would find the gap he and Jagbir had used, and would follow it up. They would reach the tethered horses early in the afternoon.

Two hundred men had gone north – no need to worry about them.

Two or three hundred were already up the hill behind them. The messenger was on his way to tell that party to split up, some right, some left, until each met one of the other parties. There were still at least four thousand men in the main valley. Jagbir said, 'The officers by the lake have got their binoculars out. They're looking this way.'

Six fresh squadrons spread out in a long line and advanced slowly. Robin said, 'Come on! Don't waste time returning their fire. We ought to beat them up this slope.' They scrambled to their feet and began to climb. After a hundred yards, and two hundred feet up, the first bullets arrived. They dived into a steep gully and climbed faster. Sometimes they would be in full view for a minute, and then the bullets poured in, but always after a pause. Their clothes blended with the hill, and they made difficult targets as they appeared and disappeared on the mountain. Glancing over his shoulder Robin saw that a couple of Mongol squadrons were struggling up the hill on horseback behind them, but losing distance. The fire came from other soldiers shooting from horseback, halted, at the edge of the plain.

They stumbled over the crest, and Robin thought he could move no more. The muscles of his legs had bound together and would not obey his will. A quick look to the left, and he saw that the climbing squadrons could not have turned this way; there was no sign of them.

Jagbir said, 'As hard as you can go now, sahib,' and pushed him sharply in the back. Rhythmic pains stabbed his thighs, but he began to move. After twenty seconds he was going as fast as he could, already faster than he had ever before run down such a hill as this. But Jagbir – Robin counted the seconds wildly in his head as he ran, and at a hundred Jagbir reached the horses. He himself ran like an athlete used to the mountains, his eyes searching the slope below him for a place to put his flying feet, then another, then another – faster. Jagbir leaned forward over the drop and sprinted as though on the flat; Jagbir fell like a boulder, like a rifleman of the Gurkha Brigade.

When Robin reached the horses more than five minutes later, the Mongols still had not showed on the crestline. 'Which way?'

'Right. The way we came. Fewer of them about,' he gasped, scrambling into the saddle.

They slithered down the loose shale on the horses' rumps, sometimes a hundred feet at a time. The gorge walls closed in, and they had to pick their way down pace by pace. By now the two squadrons the woman had despatched southward down the valley would be at the gap where the stream came out. Certainly they would turn up it. There was a chance they'd miss the inflow of this draw – not much. They knew what they were looking for, they had a sense of ground as good as Jagbir's. They'd come on up the draw.

After three-quarters of an hour Robin could stand the strain no longer. At every second, at every forward step, around every rock and corner, he expected to see the leading Mongols. 'We've got to leave the ponies.' He reined in and slid shakily to the ground. 'Up the hill!' He pointed to the east, the side away from the main valley.

'The other side, sahib. They won't expect it.'

Robin did not argue. Trust to instinct, Jagbir's instinct. He remembered the ants' nest. They grabbed their food sacks off the saddles, turned the ponies' heads and beat them soundly on the quarter. In fright the ponies scrambled a few yards back up the draw, then stopped. 'They won't go any farther,' Jagbir snapped. 'Quickly, sahib!'

Jagbir led up the western ridge, which separated them from the main valley. Jagbir first heard the clash and clatter of the Mongol horsemen. He motioned sharply with his hand, and the two of them lay down like hares in form, pressing close against the hillside. The cavalcade passed up the draw two hundred feet below them. Robin counted – one squadron, a hundred men, withy sticks poking up like lances athwart their backs, carbines rattling in the buckets. Two squadrons had set out southward from the lake. The other must be waiting at the foot of the draw, near the gap.

As soon as the Mongols passed, Jagbir began to climb again. They had made another five hundred feet when they heard two shots fired in rapid succession from the draw, a pause, then another two. Jagbir threw over his shoulder, 'They've found our ponies. We've got to find a hole. That woman might have warned them – guessed what we'd do.'

Fifteen minutes later Robin pointed. 'How about that?' A low, cliff-like rock-face interrupted the uneven roll of the slope. A waste of shale fell away below it, and there were holes and small caves at its base.

'Too obvious, sahib. We must find a place in the open, the sort of place no one looks at. Down a bit. We're too near the top.'

Jagbir turned and hurried down across the face of the ridge. 'Here. Lie on your rifle. No reflection from metal.'

The hillside where he stopped and crouched was uneven, but no more. Higher up were the shale and the cliff and the caves and many tumbled boulders. Fifty feet above the cliff the irregular, notched skyline ran from north to south across their view. The sky was pale and clear, the light a filtered, flawless distillation of pearl. But on the slope immediately around them were only small, sharp pebbles. Robin lay down humbly; there was no cover here. Jagbir darted around on hands and knees, heaped the stones this way and that, sank to his stomach, and disappeared. Looking hard from fifteen feet off, Robin could make him out, but he knew that if he had been a searcher he would never have bothered to come this close. He'd have been sure he could see anyone on this slope from the top of the hill. Jagbir got up and fashioned another form for him, and he lay down in it. Jagbir's head faced north, Robin's south. Their feet were three yards apart. If the light was not too good when the Mongols came there was a chance. That depended whether they first searched this or the other side of the draw.

Soon they heard shouts on the opposite hillside, and Robin muttered, 'Listen! Can we move on?'

'No. Lie still. There's one squadron unaccounted for.'

Robin remembered then. That second hundred men might be on the crest above them, or working along the hill, or – worst of all – scattered around everywhere, silently watching and waiting.

The heat went out of the sun's rays. The sun sank, and immediately Robin heard the far tinkle of stones on their own hill. The sounds approached, moving down from the north. That was bad. It meant that the squadron to the south had not moved and was still blocking their escape in that direction. This was the first lot coming, having returned from the opposite hill – or another squadron altogether.

The Mongols shouted to one another. They were mounted still. Even on this steep slope they would not be separated from their horses. Robin buried his face in the gritty soil and tried to stop his breathing.

A horse's hoof slithered on the shale above him. A nasal shout rang over his head. They passed by, above and below.

Long after, still breathless, he heard them moving about to the north. Jagbir muttered in a penetrating whisper, 'More to the north – waiting, half a mile along the ridge.'

Robin heard the woman's clear, rich voice on the crest. She called to someone in Russian. Every minute the darkness crept up closer to them out of the gorge below. When it was quite dark Jagbir slithered around and put his head close. 'She might make them search it all again, if she can get them off their horses. But I think she's telling them to make a cordon.'

That was sense, from her point of view. At night the man who stays holds the advantage over the man who moves. But he and Jagbir had to move. To-morrow there'd be no hiding here from five thousand men. Sounds in the dark told that the squadrons were moving up, the cordon thickening.

Jagbir said, 'We've got to do it now.'

They crept up the hill; they lifted their feet carefully and placed them down carefully, but little stones fell away and trickled down the slope. A sentry showed in silhouette against the paler, star-powdered sky. The woman, very close, spat an angry word. They could not see her. The sentry grumbled, moved off the skyline towards them, and squatted down on his heels. The woman had ordered them all off their horses. Robin could just pick out the shape of the sentry who had moved, because he knew exactly where he was.

Jagbir rose and climbed diagonally up, to the right of the sentry. A minute, and Robin saw him against the skyline. In shape and clothes, except for the withy stick, he was a Mongol, and he stood where the sentry had been standing.

Jagbir's arm jerked. A stone clattered on the hill away to the left. The sentry started to his feet, and Jagbir's knife flashed. Robin ran up the hill. The woman's passionate contralto sprang out across the valleys, and Robin, as he ran, thought of their camp near the Karshi River and of the song she had sung.

Jagbir answered her, his voice taking on the exact guttural

pitch that Robin would remember, from the debauch in Andijan, to his last day. The words were half-swallowed Gurkhali, but the voice was Mongol. Robin thought of the little yapping dogs that had so upset Old Alma's horse outside Kabul, and struggled faster up the hill.

The woman spoke again, doubt in her tone. She must have been saying, 'What did you say? I can't understand,' but Jagbir kept moving, not running but moving fast. Robin joined him, and it was dark. As they crossed the crestline the woman yelled an urgent order. A flash of orange fire split the darkness, Jagbir muttered 'Missed the bitch!' and they began to run.

Jagbir yelled, '*Atlar?*'

A voice answered from below and to the right. They changed direction and in the darkness hurtled down on the voice. By the time Robin arrived the Mongol who had been left in charge of one of the groups of ten horses had died under the knife, the reins of two horses were cut, and Jagbir was in the saddle. Robin jumped up, and together they rode furiously down the slope. The hillside flashed into life around them. Rifle fire pinpointed the ridge, hundreds of men yelled, everywhere horses galloped and men ran.

In the plain they turned left and rode hard until the horses could run no more. They knew they were pursued, but the pursuit was far behind. They slowed to a trot and did not attempt to rush the valley's southern exit but turned west, crossed over, and climbed out where they had seen the horde exercising on the day before.

After that it was a hunt. They moved by side valleys and across forbidding, untrodden ridges. Twice they saw Mongols and twice avoided them. They dropped down at last over a high pass into the Farghana, feeling their way by night. There were men coming up in the dark who spoke to each other in a guttural tongue, and they knew whose mind had sent those men to this pass at this hour. The next night they crossed the Farghana plain, and the next climbed alone all night by the stars, and the next day rode all day under a hot sun across a dry plateau. The next day they slept, and in the night rode into China. Then they had to find food because their own food bags and the bags that had been on the horses were emptied, and they began to search for a Kirghiz encampment. Near the middle of the afternoon they saw three small yurts on the plain in the distance, and in the middle of the three a larger one such as were used by the tradesmen who went out to buy and sell among the Kirghiz.

They rode into the circle of yurts. The usual huge black dogs ran out at them to snap and snarl at their horses' heels. Robin opened his mouth to call a greeting. A man came out of the big yurt and walked slowly forward. Jagbir whipped up his rifle.

CHAPTER TWENTY-ONE

*

MURALEV was unarmed, and even as Jagbir's rifle flew to the aim Robin thought, *At last!* Jagbir tried to steady his sights while his pony danced and kicked at the dogs. Muralev stood still, the sun flashing from his spectacles. Two Kirghiz women ran out of one of the small yurts to shriek at the dogs, then paused and stared at the three men.

Robin put out his arm. 'No.'

Jagbir slowly brought the butt of the rifle to rest on his thigh, keeping his finger on the trigger and his eyes fixed hungrily on Muralev.

The time for pretence was past. Robin said in English, 'Muralev, if you try and harm us I won't be able to prevent Jagbir from killing you.' He could feel the surge of Jagbir's long-held, long-nourished hope.

Muralev said, 'I don't want to harm you. Don't you know that?' His English was slow but good. His shy smile broadened. He pulled at the lobe of his right ear and twisted his head. 'We might say, sir, that we are prisoners of each other.'

'You are unarmed.'

'Yes. The Kirghiz are my friends, though. You would not get far. Well, let us call ourselves each other's guests. Come in and rest.'

'No, thank you. We want provisions. Are there any?'

'Come in. There's no one.' He swept back the felt flap at the entrance of the big yurt. The women had re-entered their own yurt. Jagbir said, seeing Muralev's gesture, 'Don't go in, sahib. Let us get provisions, then make him walk five miles out with us, and there kill him.'

Muralev stood at the entrance to the big yurt, his hands behind his back, his feet enormous in the Kirghiz boots. He said, 'He is a good man. Greetings there, Jagbir – or Turfan – how are you?' He added the last words in the kind of Turki Jagbir had spoken when they last met. Jagbir's face remained implacable, and Muralev said to Robin, 'He's not really a Hazara, is he?'

'No.'

239

Jagbir broke in roughly. 'Food, grain. Where are they?'

Muralev waved at the yurt behind him. 'Help yourself.' Jagbir dismounted, leaving the pony standing, pushed his rifle forward, and entered the yurt. While he loaded the ponies with small sacks, Muralev raised his eyes, blinked twice, and said, 'May I come with you?'

Robin did not believe the other understood the meaning of the English words he had used. He said, 'What? Come with us?'

Muralev nodded, and Robin muttered, 'Where to? I don't understand. Your wife —?'

Muralev said, 'We have been married for ten years. We have been lovers – I suppose' – this last after a long pause. 'She will shortly be pursuing me with cavalry, if she has not already set out. I have left her and I have deserted the service of the Czar. She pursues me because she loves me. She is sure that I am only overwrought, that I need only rest and affection. She pursues me also as a servant of our government, whose secrets I hold.'

Robin said slowly, 'You've – deserted? You are coming over to us?' He did not want to believe it. It would solve so many problems – all except the greatest – but it would be wrong.

Muralev shook his head. Jagbir said harshly, 'Ready now, sahib. Shall I make him walk?'

'Wait.'

Muralev, with a glance at Jagbir, continued, 'I am deserting, but I am not joining you. That would be one degree worse than what I was doing before. I feel for my country as much as you do for yours. *You* understand why I'm going, don't you? I can't carry the loads they set on me. One morning in Andijan when a cold wind blew down from the pamir I knew I had to go. I told her.' He kicked the ground aimlessly with the toe of his boot, and Robin saw tears in his eyes. 'She cried and cajoled and swore. I might have given in. She could have broken me for good then, I was so weak. But word came that you had been there in Andijan and that you'd left. So it was her duty to go. She went. When she had gone, like a whirlwind of love and fear and anger, I went. She rode west, I east.'

Robin listened with growing recognition. Muralev loved his wife and his country, but he had to go. There had been a temporary, patched-up solution – Muralev's applying himself to this particular work – but it had not lasted.

Jagbir remounted his pony and sat with the rifle ready on his thigh. One of the dogs crept out and licked the backs of Muralev's boots. Muralev put his hand down absently to fondle its head. 'So you see, she is coming for both of us now. And I am going the same way as you, at least for a time – south and east.'

Robin said, 'We're going south-east. Your people control the country to the west. She can deploy big forces there to catch us, and use whatever telegraphs you've had built, but she daren't bring more than a dozen cavalrymen over on to the Chinese side.' It never crossed his mind to disbelieve Muralev. They had reached the level of truth, and all the words he heard from Muralev's lips were truth.

Muralev said, 'I am going to the Tsaidam first. And you to India?'

'India.' Robin thought of India, of Anne, of the babies, looked again at the pamir around him, and added, 'I suppose.'

Muralev walked away to catch a hobbled pony grazing close by. Robin told Jagbir that Muralev would be coming with them and explained why. Jagbir asked where Muralev was going and, when he was told, thought for a minute and said, 'He ought to stay with his wife and his raj. He's running away.'

Robin answered angrily, 'Perhaps. But he's coming with us.'

When the pony was loaded Muralev went into the black tent and came out with a thick leather wallet in his hand. The wallet had a small brass lock. He stowed it into his offside saddle bag. Jagbir whispered, 'See that?' Robin nodded. He saw it, but it was not important.

Muralev mounted. From horseback he spoke briefly with one of the women, who had come out to make butter in a crude churn. Then he shook the reins and walked over to Robin.

Robin took a deep breath. Happiness flooded in like draughts of ice-cold champagne. It was not a steadily mounting sense of well-being but a series of unaccountable lifts, each one more exhilarating than the last. The pamir rolled away in front and behind, to the right and to the left. A blue lake sparkled in the vivid distance. All deception had gone, truth reigned, his task was done. He had seen the horses in the north and the meadows where they fed. He had seen the men who would ride the horses and the men who would direct the course of the riders. He had seen the horses and the riders rehearsing for their assault on the mountains. When their day dawned the hordes would darken this pamir where his pony now plodded southward. They would force by thousands into the passes, leaving their dead, swirling on in thousands still. They were going to come over this northern route.

And it was axiomatic, first, that the Russian heavy forces could *not* use this route; and second, that the main and subsidiary efforts must be on adjoining routes. These had been his Notes Two and Three that long night of worry in Balkh. If the Mongol cavalry was going to use the northern route, therefore, the main attack must be going in on the central route; and the southern route was the level of deception.

He was happy because he understood all that Lenya Muralev had done from the beginning. She had led him and Jagbir south, every yard of the way. They had felt the leading reins but had not been able to believe in them because she was trying so hard to kill them. And she *was* trying – to the limit – trusting to his intuition and Jagbir's endurance that they would, in spite of everything, survive. The poison bottle had been a prop in a charade after all. She had thought they would live through it, and they had.

So the true, the last word was as clear as the sapphire lake in the east: The Russians would use two routes, their main weight centre, their Mongol hordes north. Up to the moment of assault they would lead their victims to believe that the main weight of attack was going south and might even be directed against the Turkish Empire. Such a deception, if successful, would catch the British and Indian forces up to a thousand miles out of place.

But would the commander-in-chief in India, who had never met Lenya Muralev, believe there existed a woman with the nerve, the skill, and the judgement to use a poisoned well as bait to catch men already dying of thirst?

He glanced sideways at Muralev's calm profile. Muralev had the written, irrefutable evidence in a wallet in that off-side saddle-bag. It would be wrong to demand to see it, though. That would soil the wind of truth that blew over the pamir and gave him this calm certainty. He would not do it.

Above all he was happy because he had found Muralev in the place where he ought to be and doing what he ought to do. Now they would have a chance to talk together. Perhaps, even, they would together find the home of the inaccessible bird. He might be able to persuade Muralev to come to India for a time. Once they were over the border there'd be no need for hurry. They'd have time to talk and think. He would be able to ask and learn, and in learning gather some of Muralev's hard-won peace.

Three days passed in rapid travelling. On the fourth morning Robin awoke two hours before the first light and awakened the others. At this time the wind was dark. Free-found it raced across the pamir and tugged at the mean lean-to shelter, two pieces of felt, which Muralev shared with them. Jagbir slept always with his rifle between his knees, embracing its cold wood and burning steel as a Dutch burgomaster embraces his Dutch wife. The season was far advanced, and their fingers often became solid so that they fumbled for minutes on end to fasten a single leather toggle. They ate ground barley mixed with curds in a bowl.

Muralev said, 'It will be a hard day. And remember, those Kirghiz told us the road's bad.'

Yesterday they had come upon four nomads who had told them that a thousand horsemen had moved into camp just over the Russian border. Muralev thought that three or four small parties of cavalry would already be on the Chinese side, looking for them. There were no boundary fences on the pamir, and an officer could easily say he had crossed over by mistake. One such party would surely be on the pass ahead. Muralev had agreed, therefore, that it wasn't safe to try the pass. Instead they must to-day find their own way over the spurs of Muztagh Ata. The pass was higher than sixteen thousand feet; their route would take them nearer nineteen thousand.

They mounted stiffly, and stiffly the ponies began to move. In the evening they had seen yurts in the plain five miles to the east, but no lights showed there now. In the fading stars, by the dawning rumours of day, Robin saw the two men ahead of him riding forward over the black nothingness of the ground. Here there were not even the bones of the preceding dead to guide them. After an hour he called out to Jagbir, '*Choro*, it sounds as though one of your food sacks is loose.'

Jagbir secured the thong, then turned his head with a smile. 'Thank you, sahib.'

The answering smile faded from Robin's lips. Jagbir's face was yellow under a spectral yellow wash evenly laid on, thin but bright over his dark skin. He glowed with an emanation like

243

that from decaying bodies or from jellyfish in eastern seas at night. His almond eyes contracted in amazement as he stared at something over Robin's shoulder. Robin turned.

Usually in the first light the world was pale and green as though lying under shallow coastal water. The pallor deadened all colours, so that a woman's scarlet sash would be seen as a lifeless, neutral slab. Now the light fanning out above the pamir, slanting up behind the distant serrations of the Alai, was yellow.

Muralev looked around and reined in his pony. The three came together and stared fearfully at the eastern horizon. Muralev said, 'It is the burhan – to-day of all days!'

Often in the caravanserais travellers talked of the burhan. Robin, watching the yellow light crawl up the face of Muztagh Ata, muttered, 'Shall we stay here until it's blown over?'

'We can't. The men in the yurts saw us. She'll know by now. To-morrow she'll be here.'

Robin said, 'It will be hard.'

Muralev answered, 'To-day you will see God.'

Jagbir said curtly, 'We're wasting time.'

The ground sloped up. An hour later the plateau broke into soaring ridges, and they entered a steep gorge. All the while the light brightened until the sky from end to end shone brilliant yellow, chrome yellow, unspeckled by cloud or shadow, possessing no centre because the sun was invisible. The wind died away, and in the new, fearful hush they struggled on. At the snowline no sound but the roaring blast of the horses' breath cracked the yellow ball of sky and snow imprisoning them.

The air began to move. A loud sound broke out, at once distant, close, unfocused, and oppressively loud, as though giants rolled rocks in the mountain under their feet and dwarfs rattled pebbles by their ears. The light flickered unsteadily, shading down from clear yellow to dull, to dark, to burnt ochre, to umber, the tones spreading across the horizon and racing up the sky. The blast hit them and threw them down, men and ponies, upon the shale and the snow.

Robin lay on his face, his fingers and nails pressed out and clawing into the shale to hold him. The wind boomed across the face of the ridge and dragged him with it. Pebbles and grit and snow lashed into his head and broke the skin, but the blood could not force out against the wind. The wind blew the breath back down his throat and he thought he would suffocate. The naked shingles of the world shifted under his fingers and tilted sideways.

Silence burst over the mountain, hurting his ears. He lay twenty yards from where he had stood when the blast came, and all the nails of his left hand were torn out by the roots. He began to bleed profusely. One pony lay kicking on its side, its back pressed against the rock whither the wind had blown it. A second screamed and struggled to its knees a hundred yards ahead. The third had vanished, leaving a broken rein in Jagbir's hand.

'Gone!' Muralev shrieked and pointed down the long buttress-slope, not steep, not shallow, on which they tremblingly stood. The wind had dropped to gale force, and they could think. 'Oh, hurry on! It'll come again, all day.'

'How often?'

'Every ten, fifteen minutes – less, more.'

They hurried upwards. When the burhan came the second time they saw it thundering down the mountain, jerking at the pyramid of Muztagh Ata. Then they flung themselves to the ground, each clutching with one hand at rocks, boulders, rifles, whatever was near, their ponies' reins looped around them. For the second time the burhan passed.

They stumbled upwards hour after hour through powder snow. This snow had been here since the beginning. The passing falls of the years were gone. The burhan took them and whipped them away across the roof of Asia. The light changed through the hours, minute by minute – yellow, green, yellow again, black suddenly, when they could see nothing, then yellow once more, and against it the needle-eyed notch in the snow wall ahead. The snow – green, yellow, with the light – hissed and crawled across the mountain. The burhan shouted to them that it came not from the earth but from under it.

Five hundred feet below the notch another thunderclap struck them. They clung together on a narrow rock shelf, the snow slope steep above them to their left and steeper yet below them to their right. Robin sheltered under an overhang, saw a hand close to his eyes. The fingers of the hand were dead white under the dark pigmentation of the skin. Then the snow drove at him, and he had to close his eyes. The fingers of Jagbir's left hand were frostbitten. Where were the gloves? Gone, blown off, lost.

The wind changed direction and blew his feet from under him. The lip of the slope came to him and he was looking down and moving down. The snow fell five thousand feet, not sheer but too steep to climb. He saw his pony tumbling head over heels down the slope, gathering speed in the centre of a cloud of racing, glittering, green snow. Perhaps the pony shrieked, but its shriek was lost in the wind. Then he was over, the wind swinging him around and forcing his body and feet over the edge. He dug in with his hands and hung on the lip, the wind turning him over on his wrists. He saw Jagbir's face a yard away. It was like a child's. Jagbir cried bitterly, his useless, frostbitten hands held out to Robin.

Muralev's hand gripped Robin's wrists. Jagbir sat down astride Muralev's back, and Muralev hauled slowly, jerked back, hauled again. The wind abated. Robin dragged snow-spray and air into his lungs and slowly came to the ledge. Muralev turned him over and began to rub snow into his face. Robin saw Jagbir, crouching back under the overhang, his mouth still open, and furious, helpless tears freezing on his cheeks.

Jagbir's faultless legs and cracked heart lifted them to the notch. Muralev's pony, too, Jagbir pushed up the mountain. Jagbir alone still had his rifle, strapped across his back. In windless silence, under a yellow sky, they crossed the notch.

By nightfall they had reached the snowline again. They tore up a strip of felt and made mittens for Jagbir's hands, and found juniper and stunted rhododendron on this southern face of the range, and lit a fire. The burhan passed away, and for a few hours they all slept, huddled together on the ground before the fire.

Robin awoke first and scrambled up to put more roots on the fire and blow it back into life. He glanced at the stars and knew it was about two o'clock. Muralev crept out to him, and for a while they crouched in silence by the fire.

Then Muralev said, 'Jagbir's left hand is bad. His right is much better.' Several days' growth of stubbly beard hid the outline of his face. Scratches and small holes pockmarked it where the burhan had blown stones and snow through the skin. His voice was harsher than ever, as though he had swallowed some of the flying gravel. When Robin nodded, he said, 'What sort of a name is that – Jagbir? I'd like to know, so that I can remember him better and can place him in the world.'

246

Robin said, 'He is a Gurkha, a Pun from Zilla Four Thousand Parbat in western Nepal. He is a rifleman of the Thirteenth Gurkhas.' The fire muttered sullenly, and a wandering shaft of moonlight flitted across the silent tower of Muztagh Ata.

Muralev said, 'He is the most loving man I ever knew. He is lucky.'

Robin nodded. He was tired, but with a pleasant lassitude, like a climber who has reached a summit, returned through the sleet, and come to his warm refuge. He said quietly, 'What are we going to do?'

Red lights from the fire glowed in the depths of Muralev's shadowed, bloodshot eyes. He had lost his spectacles in the burhan, and the eyes were puckered at the inner corners. He said, 'I don't know, Savage.'

Robin lay still. The moonlight went from Muztagh Ata, and Jagbir moaned in his sleep. Muralev said, 'The course of my life has shown me that I must go out and search. I think I may end in a monastery, but first – forty days in the wilderness. Or forty months. Or forty years.'

Robin said eagerly, 'Yes. But we ought to do good for people – not for any particular person, for all people. Perhaps we can find out things that are important but have been hidden or buried or forgotten.'

Jagbir had been moaning for some minutes. Now he got up, swaying unsteadily on his feet and blinking at the fire. They watched him, not speaking until he walked away into the darkness.

Robin rushed on. 'The people who act and work and love are good. People like us, who sit in deserts or are like Ishmael, people who try to get rid of all action, work, love – they are good too. God made all of us. Can we not find a bridge between the two kinds of people – buried in history, perhaps? In our minds, perhaps? We —'

He stopped short. Jagbir came towards them, heavy-footed and unsure, out of the darkness, and they rose together. After a long look into each other's eyes they turned to help the rifleman lie down. But Jagbir staggered on and stopped only at the end of the fire. His left arm ended in a lumpish tangle of bloody wool. Blood seeped through the wrappings and dripped sizzling into the fire. In his right hand he held Muralev's wallet. He was young and badly hurt. The wound showed in his eyes. Gently Robin took the bandaged stub in his hands. 'What have you done?'

'Cut off the fingers. Stopped most of the flow with barley meal – and the cold. I've got his wallet.' He stared at Muralev.

'You shouldn't have done it.' Robin began to unwrap the bloody strips of felt, but Muralev said, 'Leave it. We'll only start the flow again. There's nothing we can do.'

'*Chup!*' Jagbir silenced him with a threatening jerk of his right hand, which held the wallet. He returned to Robin. 'We must open this, sahib.'

Robin took it because Jagbir pressed it into his hands. The padlock hung broken from the hasp. Robin looked at it, then at Jagbir's hungry, hurt eyes. He did not want to open it. He did not need to. He knew the truth, and nothing in the wallet could make the truth truer.

Jagbir said, 'There will be papers in there. Proof. The Jangi Lāt Sahib will believe then.' It was true. It would be like the legend of Alexander. They'd want to see 'proof', and here it was.

Muralev said, 'Please don't open it.'

Robin murmured, 'Why not?' Of course he knew why not. Muralev had removed himself, once and for all, from the world of human struggles. Tacitly Robin had agreed to go with him, to travel with him at least until they could find their separate ways. But Jagbir's eyes flamed with fighting, jealous love, and his hand dripped blood, drop by drop. The pressure of Jagbir's love forced Robin's hand to the lock. It was wrong. The lock would burn him. This was what he had to leave behind. But he said again, his voice made harsh by guilt, 'Why not?'

'You know.'

Robin opened the wallet. There was a thin file of papers inside. Muralev tugged urgently at the lobe of his ear, and his long face wrinkled miserably as Robin brought the papers to the firelight and began to examine them. Jagbir stared angrily at Muralev – a long, still-hungry look.

There was a map of western Asia. A thick, blue-inked line sprang down from southern Russia, crossed western Persia, and swung east. The head of the arrow rested on the Bolan Pass. A second arrow curved down from the Farghana through Samarkand to Balkh and crossed the Hindu Kush, and the

head of that arrow rested on Peshawar. A few thin lines crept out
from the Farghana towards the Russian pamirs, but before they
reached the passes into India they swung back and rejoined the
second arrow at Balkh. There were figures inked in beside these
last lines.

'What do these figures indicate?' Robin asked tonelessly.

'The number of days ahead of the start of the main assault
that those forces are to begin their movements.'

'Sufficiently far ahead to give us time to commit our troops to
the northern passes?'

Muralev did not answer.

Robin held out another document, five pages of closely-
written manuscript pinned together at the top left-hand corner.
'And this?'

'The detailed plan to which the map relates.'

'And this?' Robin put his finger on an isolated group of letters
and figures in the top right-hand corner of the top sheet.

'The serial number of that copy. Number five. There are only
eleven in existence.'

Robin folded the papers back into the wallet. 'I'll carry it,'
Jagbir cut in, and held out his hand. 'Under my shirt.' Muralev
sat down by the fire and drummed his fingers on his knees.
Jagbir went back to the shelter.

Robin stood hunched and cold behind Muralev. Everything
that he had known to be truth was deception. The Russians were
going in centre and south – the main weight south, the Mongols
centre after a feint at the northern passes on their way from
Andijan to Balkh. So his visions were not visions but hallucina-
tions, his certainties the self-cozenings of a madman. And for
this he had committed a sin. Jagbir's love had driven him, and
his own love for his country. He had thought he would do
England this last service.

And there was Anne. Did he not see her face and eyes now?
Had he not hoped in the deep of his heart to do his task so well
that there would be recognition, medals perhaps, to make her
proud?

All these were kinds of love; so, once more, love had caused
sin. He was weak and foolish.

He said, 'I'm sorry. I've hurt – I've hurt myself and you, and
I'm – I'm sorry. What can I say?'

Muralev said, 'You haven't hurt me, my friend. Perhaps it is best that you did what you did. Perhaps I tried to stop you only because I did not want to be lonely. Really I know that you and I are not of one kind. I just hoped. But you do love, and I think you always will. I do not and never can. What are you thinking of?'

Robin caught quickly at the slow-passing images in his mind before the necessity to answer Muralev's question could jerk him back to here and the fire and this present reality. He said slowly, 'Anne – my wife. I was explaining why I had done it, opened the wallet. She was saying she didn't want me to do it for her sake – just if I thought it was right. We were in a shikara in Kashmir, and the lotus in bloom everywhere.'

'You see? You must go back. Jagbir is your charge and your load, because he will never understand. But I think your wife might. You must go back now and many times later, because also you must go away many times.'

'Yes, yes! When I am here I see her and the lake. When I am there, though I love her, I see this and the snow that no one sees and I keep wondering. What I'm looking for is always somewhere else.'

'Perhaps. But do not be unhappy about it. There is joy in the search if you know love. For me —' He hung his head, then got up slowly. 'I'll get wood and heat some gruel for Jagbir. Go over and keep him warm, friend, until I come.'

CHAPTER TWENTY-TWO

*

In the morning they got up and began to move. Robin walked with Muralev and ordered Jagbir to ride the one sick pony. Jagbir's face was stony with despair as he obeyed, because it was Muralev's horse, but he had no choice; for the first two days he was too weak to walk. His face was greeny-grey, and at night he shivered in a low fever, but the bandages smelled sweet and his hand was healing cleanly.

They pushed on south and came in four days to the next mountain wall. On the other side of it lay the Taghdumbash Pamir. Two passes, the Chichiklik and the Yangi, which were several miles apart, crossed the range. The travellers camped beside the trail until a party of Kirghiz came up, bound in the opposite direction. Muralev tried without success to buy two more ponies from them, but they sold him some food. Robin said 'Ask them what's happening on the Taghdumbash. Tell them we hear strange rumours.'

The leader of the Kirghiz beat his gloved hands together and spoke in short torrents of strange words. There was much activity over the border – he jerked his head towards Russian territory. The Chinese soldiers heard rumours and counter-rumours; they thought the Russians were going to attack them; they stayed inside their forts – the Kirghiz huddled dramatically into his coat and peered right and left – and they had no courage left even to pester travellers.

'Are there any soldiers on the pass here?' Muralev jerked his chin at the mountains ahead.

None on the Chichiklik – the Kirghiz had come over that. The Chinese never bothered to guard the Yangi. It was a difficult route and longer than the Chichiklik.

The party of Kirghiz rode on. Robin said, 'We'd better use the Yangi. Are you coming over with us?'

'Yes, if you'll let me.'

'Then?'

'The Tsaidam, by way of the Takla Makan. I told you.'

'Will you be there if I come looking for you later?'

'Perhaps.'

Jagbir interrupted them. 'It's time to go.'

Later Jagbir said to Robin, 'Is the woman, his wife, hunting us, sahib?' Robin nodded. Jagbir spoke in Gurkhali, which Muralev did not understand. Sometimes as he rode Jagbir would tap his chest where the wallet was concealed, and at night he always refused to sleep next to Muralev for fear it would be stolen back from him. He said now, 'Why should we not hunt her instead? She will expect us on the trail. She will be in ambush near it. Let us hunt her as if she were one of the big-horned sheep.'

'We don't know whether she'll be on the Yangi or the Chichiklik. She'll have men with her.'

'Her men will be on both passes. Not more than two or three on each, though. They'll find it hard to hide the horses up there.'

'What does he say?' Muralev asked.

Robin told him. Muralev said, 'She understands that and will be ready for it. She will welcome it. It is a game. But I cannot hunt her.'

'Of course not. None of us can hunt really. We're too weak.'

Late in the evening they camped on a long slope where thin grass bound the shale together and snow lay between all the stones. Jagbir moaned in his sleep during the early part of the night. The bitter wind sharpened before dawn, and then none of them slept. In the morning Muralev's pony lay dead in the lee of the shelter. Robin stood wordlessly over it, thinking of the road ahead and Jagbir's hand. As he stood, the rifleman came to him and said, 'It is better, sahib. Now we have to avoid the pass.'

'What do you mean?'

'I was going to say it yesterday but I was too tired. Now I am stronger. We have no hope of getting over the pass. She will be there. We must climb around it even if it takes us two days. A Pun's legs are better than any horse's.'

Robin told Muralev what Jagbir said, and Muralev pulled his ear doubtfully. At last, after scanning the mountains ahead, he said, 'He's right. If we have to go on foot, let us use the freedom of movement it gives us.'

They divided the food. Robin begged Jagbir to abandon his

rifle, but he would not. They faced the mountain carrying two days' food, the clothes they stood up in, the dead horse's saddle blanket, which Robin rolled and slung across his shoulders, and the rifle.

Five hours later they breasted the latest in a backbreaking series of ridges which had taken them up, in slow giant's steps, well above the level of the Yangi Pass. More ridges rose ahead, one behind the other, all running generally east and west across their front. The Yangi lay somewhere to their left front – perhaps at the foot of the next ridge ahead of them. A fresh wind blew from the east, and a cold, brilliant sun shone down out of a pale sky. As they paused to rest Jagbir pointed suddenly. 'There! On the next ridge.'

'What is it? What do you see?' The ground fell away two thousand feet from where they stood into a narrow gorge, then rose as steeply to the next ridge, which seemed a little higher than theirs.

'Something moved.' Jagbir shut his eyes, reopened them quickly, and after a second whispered, 'It is a big sheep, by the tablet rock jutting out of the snow. Right opposite. Right on the crest.'

Muralev peered and muttered, 'I'll never see it without my glasses.'

Robin said, 'I've got it. *Ovis poli*. The biggest horns I've ever seen. Well, we'd better get on.'

Jagbir said, 'The ram can see the other side of that ridge. The wind's blowing from left to right – to him from the Yangi. Something's happening down there. Look at him!'

'Which way is he looking?'

'The other way. Quickly but carefully, sahib – down!'

They hurried cautiously down the forward slope of their ridge. After a hundred feet a false crest had risen below the great ram's position to hide him from their sight. They stepped quickly then, and in less than forty minutes reached the bottom, struggled across a waste of boulders and through huge piles of drifted snow, bore right, and began to climb. After a thousand feet the angle of the slope eased, and fifteen minutes later Jagbir saw the ram. He was on the ridge crest still, a couple of hundred yards to their left, upwind. They intended to cross the ridge well downwind of him.

253

They climbed another hundred feet. Then Jagbir and Robin saw the ram throw up his head and stand alert, his right profile to them. They froze where they stood. The ram stared down the other side of the ridge, tossed his head twice, turned, and dropped below the crestline on their side. He had put himself out of sight of any enemy on the far side. He trotted along towards them. Robin thought: It might be an animal that has disturbed him. More likely a man – a man or men, men and a woman, coming up the other face of the ridge.

The snow lay in huge patches along the slope. The tablet rock where they had first seen the ram appeared to be the highest point within sight, certainly the highest point within rifle range. It was a great slab of black granite that stood up like a tombstone. Beyond, the ridge fell irregularly for a space and then dropped down out of sight to the Yangi Pass.

The ram slowed to a walk and moved back towards the crestline. Jagbir whispered, 'He can't get the scent properly this side. He'll go up until he does.'

Because they were below him the ram put himself athwart their skyline before he reached the actual crest of the ridge. He stood still, his head raised, his powerful neck and thick shoulders holding the weight of his gnarled horns. He stood a full minute, then tossed his head and again trotted fast towards them. Fifty yards off he saw them, changed direction with a convulsive jerk, and galloped full tilt down the slope.

Jagbir scrambled to his feet. 'They must've seen us a couple of hours ago. They're trying to get to the top first. Hurry!'

Robin grated his teeth as he climbed. He only wanted to slip past and go on his way. The woman was making him a hunter, a hound in the pack, following Jagbir. But he had no choice. They could not stay, they could not retreat, they could only get there first and shoot first.

Jagbir drove up the hill towards the tablet rock. Muralev stood still. Robin said, 'We've got to – I'm sorry. Jagbir's life depends —' Then he struggled after Jagbir. Muralev sat down slowly on the mountainside, his back to the crest, and stared out across the frozen sunlit ocean of rock and ice and snow.

Robin thrust with his right leg, lifted the left, thrust, lifted, thrust. The tablet rock loomed larger and blacker and more violently tilted above him. Stones flew out, clinking, from under his boots, then it was crunching snow, then rock, rock and snow.

'I – can – hear – them.'

Jagbir flung the words over his shoulder, poured all his force into his thighs, and sprang up and up. His rifle bounced on his right shoulder, his right hand holding it by the grip behind the trigger guard, his finger loosely alongside the trigger.

When Robin still had forty feet to go Jagbir burst over the skyline to the right of the tablet rock. The wind caught the skirts of his coat and blew them out, he brought his left arm up and his right hand down, the rifle barrel crashed to rest in the crook of his left elbow, his head dropped, his shoulder jerked. The shot boomed out over the tremendous chasms on either hand. He crouched against the tablet rock, reloaded, raised the rifle, and fired again.

Robin came slowly, dizzily, to the crest. A man in a long coat and high felt boots, a withy stick across his back, lay on his face in the snow a yard from Jagbir's feet. A second Mongol sat on the shale thirty yards lower down, holding his knee and groaning. A third man was running crazily down the mountain to the left, towards the Yangi Pass. Robin grabbed up the dead man's carbine, aimed at the ground in front of the running Mongol, fired, and shouted in Turki, 'Stop! Drop your rifle! Come here. We'll not harm you.' The man obeyed quickly.

The woman stood erect thirty feet down on the steep slope. She looked unwaveringly into the muzzle of Jagbir's rifle. In her right hand she held her own rifle. Her breath came in long, deep gasps, and dark rings circled her grey eyes. Jagbir said softly, 'Drop that rifle.'

She glanced then at Robin and let the rifle fall.

'Come here.'

She climbed up to Robin, a step at a time, and at his feet sank down in the snow. Her gloved fingers began to pick fumblingly at the wool of her coat. She said in English, 'It was hard luck.'

Robin turned and saw Muralev sitting on the hill where they had left him, looking steadily to the north. He waved his arm and shouted, 'Come on. It's all right.' Muralev turned around, and his sunburned face seemed white even against the snow. He rose to his feet and began to climb towards them.

The woman had not heard a word. The dead Mongol lay at her feet. She turned him over with her boot and said, 'The brain. A

255

kind shot. My husband, have you seen him? Have you heard word of him? He – he left me.' She beat her gloves on her thighs. 'He is ill, not well.'

Robin said, 'But didn't the Kirghiz tell your people he was with us? Weren't you waiting on the pass near Muztagh Ata?'

She mumbled, 'I heard nothing. Others went there. I came straight here for you. But my husband, he is not well. Did you say he was —?'

'He is.'

She heard the crunch of boots in the snow. His head appeared, rising steadily above the crest. He met her eyes, glanced from her to the dead man, and then around at the silent mountains. The wounded Mongol groaned intermittently on the patch of shale; the prisoner sat in gloomy immobility under Jagbir's rifle.

She rose slowly, colour flooding into her face. She spoke a jerky word in Russian, then a phrase, then a spate of sentences. Muralev answered her, a few quiet words after each outburst. When she fell on her knees Robin turned his head. He did not need to understand Russian to know what they were saying to each other. Perhaps he would have to face this. But Anne was not Lenya. He could only hope she would understand. He stared southward. The Mintaka lay there, under that growing bank of cloud.

When the woman's voice sharpened he turned again to watch them. She was on her feet. An image of hate filled and distorted her face but it was not real. It was a weapon she had forged to break Muralev's will and his desire, so that he would come back to her. When she had used it she would throw it away. She took hold of her husband's coat and shook him. Turning to Robin, she cried in English, 'He will betray you as he has betrayed us. He is just a – a weakling, traitor!'

Robin said, 'He is no traitor, ma'am.'

'So he says! Believe him? Why is he here then, with you?'

'He and I are going the same way. That is all.'

But the spurious, self-incited hate overcame her. She faced him furiously, screaming, 'Go on then, all of you! Get away! You've won. Tell your Viceroy that one weak traitor gave you the truth – the truth that was his own child, that he had thought, made, created.'

She ripped off her heavy sheepskin cap, so that the wind bit through the thick blonde hair into her skin. She lowered her voice. 'And make him see, if you can, the sight it would have been. He should have stood down there, your Viceroy, just down the ridge. He'd have seen the hordes pass, thousand on thousand, starving, freezing, eating the horses, driving on. Genghiz Khan's horsetail standards fly before them. The hordes pour over the Yangi, over Chichiklik, Mintaka, Baroghil, Karakoram, Muztagh, Babusar, Burzil, Zoji, Baralacha, Lachalang, Rohtang. We could have done it. We would have done it.'

Her eyes were half-closed. Robin listened, awed, as her passion fused the words into a double re-creation. This had been her life's work. This alone had held Muralev to the ground, where her arms could grasp him.

Then Robin saw the meaning of her words. He felt, like changing winds, the slow spread of confusion, doubt, and at last understanding, across his face. He saw her open her eyes and read his face, and then he saw the same emotions moving there, in the same order.

In the end she knew what she had done. Robin watched her, recognizing in every particular his own misery when Jagbir's love forced him to open the wallet. Like Muralev then, he stepped forward, meaning to give her comfort. But Jagbir was there first, patting her roughly on the shoulder and saying, 'Do not cry. It is all over.'

Robin said to him, 'Did you understand, then?'

Jagbir nodded, still patting her. 'I understand. I cannot read words, only people. Those papers were to deceive us – to deceive even their own generals until the last minute. The truth – nothing is written of it. It is in her head, and their Emperor's, and their Jangi Lāt's perhaps – and *his*. *He* would have let us go wrong, even though he pretends to be on our side.'

Robin turned away. Jagbir understood and did not understand. The woman's face was grey and old, her taut body unstrung so that the heavy coat seemed no more than a sheep's pelt flung carelessly on a scarecrow. Over and over again she muttered, '*I* told them, *I* told them.' Jagbir spoke to her, interrupting her, and she answered him, saying in Turki, 'It is finished. He will go. He will find no peace all his life. And that too I will have to think of all my life.'

Robin said, 'Jagbir, let us go. Muralev, are you coming down to the horses with us?' Muralev nodded.

'Wait, sahib.' Jagbir walked a few feet away and smashed the Mongols' carbines and the woman's rifle. He asked the unwounded prisoner, '*Atlar*, where?'

'On the pass.'

'Any more of your men there?'

'No. Horses picketed, behind black cliff.'

The three of them – Muralev, Jagbir, and Robin – went down the ridge together in silence. No one of them turned to look at the three Mongols of the Horde and the woman crying in the snow.

At the horses Muralev said, 'We shall meet again.' He mounted and rode away without looking over his shoulder.

Robin and Jagbir, leading a third horse, passed down in the direction of the Taghdumbash Pamir.

CHAPTER TWENTY-THREE

*

'HERE, haven't you forgotten this? Doesn't it go on under the coat?' Anne held out the canvas sword belt with its dangling straps of black leather.

'Oh, yes. Thank you.' He hoisted his jacket and fastened the belt around his waist underneath it. The two black straps, one short, one long, each ending in a strong steel clip, hung down his left thigh.

'Where's my sword?'

She looked inside the wardrobe but could not see the sword in its place. It usually hung on a nail inside the wardrobe door by one of the rings on its steel scabbard. She walked through the bathroom, opened the outer door, and called, 'Jagbir!'

Jagbir marched in, carrying the sword balanced flat on his left hand. She saw that the raw wounds where his fingers had been were well healed. He knelt, fastened the dangling clips through the scabbard rings and let the sword fall. The toe of the scabbard struck the stone floor with a clank, and the hilt fell forward until the short upper strap brought it up with a jerk. Jagbir eyed the angle at which it hung, muttered, '*Thik chha*' to himself, and got up.

Robin said, 'I see you've got your stripes up, *choro*. That'll cost you a lot of rum when you get back to Manali.'

Jagbir grinned. 'I don't mind. They have to drink it with me.' His round cap of brushed black fur was tilted forward and to the right on his head. His gleaming black chin-strap framed his face in an oval. The light glinted in the paler skin under the shaven stubble of his hair. At the back the long tuft, by which he hoped Krishna would pull him up to heaven when he died, was pushed out of sight under his cap.

Anne stood a little apart from the two men, listening to and half understanding their rapid Gurkhali. She watched the rifle-man bring a clean handkerchief out of his pocket and kneel again to wipe unnoticeable dust off her husband's boots. The little man was square and altogether tightly formed. He had a surprisingly strong face for one so young, and his lips were well curved.

It was the end of January, 1882. Three months ago the two had returned. By then the family group by the lake in Kashmir had long since broken up, so Robin had found her in Peshawar. He was supposed to be on leave still, but most days he worked with Major Hayling. Nothing much seemed to have changed, yet everything was different. Often she found herself holding wordless communion with Jagbir. Their mouths talked of boot polish, metal polish, and rifle oil – but silently, as they spoke, Jagbir standing at attention, she sitting in a chair, they sought each other's eyes and without words agreed that what must be, must be.

She left them and walked along the passage to the front veranda. They were in a little bungalow that the cantonment executive officer had given her when she came down from Kashmir. It stood on the western edge of cantonments, facing the Khyber Pass. When the wind rose it took the full blast, because it was unsheltered, and the windows rattled; but it was the only bungalow she could get.

She saw Major Hayling turn his horse into the short driveway. In his full dress he looked as distinguished, sinister, and sly as ever. He dismounted carefully, and his groom, who had been trotting behind him, came up to take the reins. The major walked up the steps on to the veranda and saluted her. 'Good afternoon, my dear. Is the hero getting dressed?'

'Heroes. They're dressing each other.'

'Ah, yes, I forgot Jagbir's decoration. When I see him I always think he's already got them all, somehow.'

'So do I. Rupert, I'd like to thank you for getting Robin this medal. Of course I used to think a D.S.O. would answer everything, solve everything. Then, when I saw him in Kashmir, I thought it would mean absolutely nothing. Now I'm not sure. Robin is really pleased, I think.'

Hayling's eyes wandered speculatively over her face. 'I'm glad to hear it, even if his pleasure is only on your behalf. Don't thank me. I told the chief about Robin's being considered a coward, and the chief swore he'd get him the D.S.O. for this work if he had to invent a battle in Afghanistan for him to win it in. Look, I just dropped in to talk with you for a minute, because

260

I've got to start packing as soon as the parade's over. You know, don't you? Simla. I wanted to ask if you know what Robin means to do next. You know what we think of him. Is he going to —?'

She felt the pain coming up in her chest and towards her eyes, but she had had plenty of practice now and could keep her voice steady. 'I doubt if he will return to your service, Rupert.'

He looked keenly at her. All the time he absently pushed the hilt of his sword up and down, making the toe of the scabbard clink on the tiles. He said suddenly, 'Well, anyway, our plan worked – for what you wanted it to at the time.'

She nodded. It had worked. Robin had won the Distinguished Service Order. But of course she had grown a thousand years older since McIain's drunken slap launched her on this course. She said, 'You know it was the wrong fight. You warned me then that it might be. Oh, Rupert, what do you think he'll do?'

He said abruptly, 'I don't think. I just believe that God helps men when their loads become greater than they can bear. Women too.' He saluted her again, went down the steps, remounted his charger, and rode away.

Half an hour later she drove with Robin and Jagbir in a carriage to the parade ground. Jagbir protested that he preferred to walk, but they overruled him, so he sat on the front seat, facing them. She watched his hand move around, checking the angle of his cap and the fastening of button and belt, touching the hilt of bayonet and kukri, searching anxiously for the rifle that was not there. When he remembered that his dress for the parade was Review Order, Sidearms Only, he sat still. None of them spoke, but it was friendly, and they smiled together as the carriage rolled along.

On the parade ground a battalion of infantry already stood in line. A small wind blew dust devils about and lifted the hems of the ladies' dresses where they stood behind a stretched rope which marked the edge of the parade ground. There was a table in front of the rope and a pair of black morocco cases on the table. Some staff officers in scarlet and drab were grouped around it, talking carelessly among themselves. There was a row of chairs to which the general's aide-de-camp led the commissioner's wife, the general's wife, and the wives of other notables as they arrived. The husbands stood behind the ladies' chairs or drifted off to talk with friends.

The A.D.C. came up, saluted, and led Anne to a chair in the centre of the row. She sat down slowly. Robin and Jagbir ducked under the rope and joined the staff officers near the table.

She greeted, and answered greetings, without knowing what she said or hearing what was said. Robin and Jagbir stood side by side now, apart, and no one looked at them or spoke to them. It might have been a conspiracy of all the others to pretend that they were about to be drummed out of the Army. Opposite, the low sun shone on steel and silver and the red splashes of the battalion's facings.

She sat in the same coma of waiting that she had been in since he left her in the Sind Valley. His return and their unspoken agreement to say nothing of what was closest to her heart had made no difference. Hayling was waiting, Jagbir was waiting; Colonel Rodney and Caroline – they were here, Caroline in the next chair, Colonel Rodney behind her. She spoke with them. The girls stood a little way off among young officers of the station, and she heard their low, excited laughs. Her own father and mother came. Her father had already begun to blow his nose violently into a huge khaki handkerchief.

But they all waited in a tension that they must conceal because they all had their lives to live. Sometimes, as at this moment, she expected Robin to break the tension by some violent blow, some detonation in the spirit, as an explosive bursts a dam. She thought: He will throw his medal in the general's face and run away, and we will all run after him, shouting, 'Come back! We love you.' She flushed. That was what they all had been doing, particularly she herself. She thought: He will turn around when the medal is on his chest and call me by name. I'll have to go out there. I'll hesitate and blush, but I'll have to go and stand beside him. Then he'll turn and shout in a loud voice, 'I love my wife and my bed and my home and my children, and —'

The general stepped forward, and everyone stood up. A gun boomed. The steel and silver and red shifted in focus and settled again as the soldiers stood at the Present. The clash of arms chimed across the parade ground. The dust devils rose, and she felt the light pressure of Colonel Rodney's hand on her shoulder.

She bowed her head.

They were all clapping and cheering and crowding around her. Robin stood there in front of her, the red and blue ribbon and the white enamel cross brilliant against the dark green of his tunic. Jagbir stood there, a bright red cordon around his neck and a bright silver medal flapping on the end of it as colonels and majors pumped his arm.

Everyone congratulated everyone else. The band played, the drums thudded, and the fifes wailed and the long files swung away. Suddenly she was among her own families, and Hayling and Jagbir were there. Robin stood opposite her, and everyone else had gone.

Each in his own idiom, they said a few words to Robin. She had long since given up trying to hold her face in a smile. She could keep it steady, but a smile was false. She stood, contained and serious, to one side of them all, watching and listening.

The girls touched his medal and flung their arms around his neck. Colonel Rodney's eyes burned like icy fire under his beetling eyebrows. He took his son's hand in both his own, but said nothing. Caroline did not touch him. She stood close to him and said, 'God be with you,' emphasizing the word 'God' as if no one else might be with him.

Anne's father seized Robin's right hand and shook it violently up and down, then dropped it to blow his nose. He cried, 'We'll see you a brevet major in no time, my boy, a general! There's no limit!' Her mother's voice scraped along. 'Wonderful, so pleased for your sake! How are the babies, the dear twins?'

Hayling put out his left hand, the palm twisted over so that it could meet another's right, but Robin had already put out his left, so their hands fumbled together for a second before meeting. Hayling said, 'You'll always know where to reach me.' Robin's set face relaxed quickly, and he smiled.

Hayling came over and took Anne's hand. '*Au revoir*. Let me know.' He walked away, and she watched his back until the groom helped him on to his horse.

In the carriage Robin and Jagbir talked in Gurkhali. After a minute Robin turned to her and said, 'Jagbir's going with Hayling as far as Amritsar. He'll have to sleep in Hayling's bungalow to-night.'

'He's got six months' leave, hasn't he?'

'Yes. Then he's rejoining the regiment. He couldn't be my orderly any more, anyway, now that he's a naik.'

Of course she had known that ever since Colonel Franklin

telegraphed that he was promoting Jagbir, but she had not faced the fact of it before this instant. At the bungalow she watched as they shook hands and spoke together for a minute. Then Jagbir turned away to the servants' quarters, and she waited by Robin's side at the head of the veranda steps until he reappeared with his kitbag slung over his shoulder. The gaudy cordon of the Indian Order of Merit no longer glowed around his neck. He must have stuffed it into his pocket. He marched down the drive, right, left, right, until in the road he turned and saluted. Robin raised his hand a few inches and let it drop. She stole a quick look at his face and saw that it had not changed. She waved her hand to Jagbir, and they waited on the veranda until he was out of sight.

Inside it was dark, and she called for the lamps to be lit and went to feed the babies. After she had begun Robin knocked and came in. He sat down in a chair opposite her and watched until they had finished. His eyes were deep, the lights in them deeper.

She said, 'My dearest, kiss me.' He kissed her, a long kiss, and she closed her eyes.

When ayah returned to soothe the babies she followed him to the dining-room. Alif served them dinner, and they talked about so many things that she could not afterwards recall the details – books, people, houses, horses, soldiers. He had not remembered to change, so he sat in full dress opposite her, the medal on his left breast. She never remembered him so calmly contented as this. Slowly she forced herself to admit that she knew the reason for it. He was going.

There, she had thought it. She waited but could not feel the terrifying sense of loss that she had expected. He was happy, and because she loved him she was happy. She felt his calm and his mysterious content invade her.

Before the end of the meal the wind got up. She told Alif to bolt the doors and windows. For this hour she would like to shut out the hiss of the wind, although she did not now regard it as her enemy. The whipping curtains hung still. She saw a light passing down the road and told Alif to draw the curtains and put more wood on the fire in the drawing-room.

When they moved there after dinner she took out a book and began to read, as had become her custom. The wind strengthened and rattled the window-panes. Something fell with a crash in the compound – a slate off the roof of the servants' quarters. She'd have to have it seen to to-morrow. She did not raise her eyes from the book but from that moment on she did not read. The pages turned steadily under her hand at the proper intervals of time, but she was not reading. The wind blew harder. Behind the wine-red curtains and beyond the shimmering glass panes of the window the night would be blue-black now, edged with the grey blades of the wind. Robin sat across from her, on the other side of the crackling fire, his eyes lightly closed.

She had fought the wrong fight and then discovered that the real, impalpable enemy was the wind and not to be gained against by any weapons within her reach. Now at last she knew that even the wind was not her enemy but her lover, who must come and go if he was to live.

She could say: We will be poor and lonely without you; the babies need a father; *why* do you have to go? Are you coming back?

Yes. But she could say also: I have grown as you have grown. I will be neither anchor nor rope to you. Because you must go, go, and I love you. When you come back again I will be here, and I love you.

Because he would go with her love and with all her true hopes that he would find what he sought, he would come back. Because the wind blew in him he could not stay, even when he returned, to become a furnishing of her life. She did not want that. The world would commiserate with her, but the wind would love her, and she was happy.

Robin got up silently from his chair. He looked down at his uniform and the medal and said, 'I've got to go and find something. It's for you and for Jagbir – for everybody. I must change.'

When he had gone she put down the book and waited again. Only a little more now, say half an hour. She knew suddenly that she was loved as few women had ever been. To this being, this Robin, God had given mysterious wings. She had shown Robin the rich prizes in the deep waters of human love and begged him to help her win them. He had thrown himself in and all but drowned. All the ways of men and women to each other were wonderful.

After half an hour she arose and walked easily along the passage. Their room was empty, the bathroom empty. His clothes lay neatly folded on the bed, his medal on top. His helmet was on its shelf and his sword-slings on their hook. The babies slept in their cribs in the alcove at the far end of the bedroom. She would have liked to know that he had kissed them, but she never would know. She stooped over and kissed them herself to be sure. When she got up she saw a small silver coin on her dressing-table. She recognized it and put it carefully away in a drawer. She would have a brooch made of it, not with the obverse uppermost to show the proud head of the young god, but the reverse, the indecipherable scrawl of a message in an ancient language.

It seemed stuffy in the room. She opened the long windows and looked out. The wind came though the night, over three thousand miles of desert, pamir, mountain, and steppe, and blew in her face. For a moment it whipped through the house, for that moment lending its nervous searching energy to the animate and the inanimate, so that the babies stretched out their hands in sleep and the curtains flew up in a curving dance.

If the lotus moved, it died. If the wind stayed, it died. She closed the window.

Some other Penguin books
are described on the
remaining pages

THE SELECTED TALES OF
EDGAR ALLAN POE

Edited by John Curtis

1109

Edgar Allan Poe (1809–1849) was brought up in England and later went to the United States. He was a journalist and poet, but is best known for his stories and for his invention of the detective story.

The aim of making this selection has been to include all Poe's best tales in one volume. The result is a collection full of variety and including several of the most famous stories in the world. Tales like *The Murders in the Rue Morgue*, *The Mystery of Marie Rogêt*, *The Purloined Letter* – three of the first detective stories ever written – and *The Gold Bug*, another story which became a prototype, have all held their own against the countless pieces of the same kind written since Poe's work first appeared well over a hundred years ago. Other tales in the book, like *Van Kempelen and his Discovery*, have a place at the start of an equally popular tradition, that of the currently fashionable 'science fiction'. Altogether, the selection contains tales representative of every kind written by Poe, ranging from macabre and horrifying stories like *The Black Cat* and *The Imp of the Perverse* to those which are humorous or purely descriptive pieces.

PASSAGES FROM ARABIA DESERTA

C. M. Doughty

1157

C. M. Doughty spent twenty months, from November 1876, in Northern Arabia wandering adventurously and making his penetrating observations on the life, character, and people of that land. His book presents a wonderfully detailed and human account of the country, but the style of his writing was perhaps even more important to him than its subject-matter. The English language was his constant study, and he attempted to rescue it from the decadence into which he considered it had fallen, and return to the tradition of Chaucer and Spenser. Consequently the creative and stimulating style of *Arabia Deserta* was a novelty when it was written, and Edward Garnett selected these passages for Jonathan Cape from Doughty's lengthy work to give the character and style of the original, which had a considerable influence on the work of T. E. Lawrence.

'Charles Montagu Doughty was one of the great men of our day, the author of a unique prose masterpiece. For many readers it is a book so majestic, so vital, of such incomparable beauty of thought, of observation, and of diction as to occupy a place apart among their most cherished literary possessions.' – *Observer*

'A book so faithful in its record and reproduction of the habits and customs of life and thought of a great race, that it might have been written in the golden age of English literature and achievement.' – *The Times*

ELEPHANT BILL

J. H. Williams

1120

'Elephant Bill' is the name by which Lt-Col. J. H. Williams was known throughout Burma, where he spent over twenty years in the jungle, living with elephants and their riders, working with them in the vast teak-forests. His life's work was the training, management, and well-being of elephants. He has stories to tell of elephants, in every aspect of their lives: of the wild herds and the lonely tuskers, of elephants in love and anger, of mother elephants and their calves, of rogue elephants, tigers and ghost-tigers, of elephants hauling great teak-trunks down from the mountains to the river.

The thrilling stories on almost every page are the more impressive for the quiet modesty of the writing, which is full of the author's humour and of the gentleness and charm which won him the confidence of the remarkable animals under his care.

During the war, when the Japanese overran Burma, Elephant Bill became 'Elephant Adviser' to the XIVth Army. In that capacity he organized the recruiting of elephants and their riders from behind the Japanese lines, and their employment in the jungle country on bridge-building and other military tasks. During the big Japanese advance on India he brought out as many elephants as possible by a new route over precipitous mountain-tracks and through pathless jungle. This fact surpassed Hannibal's crossing of the Alps, and is the climax of a book full of interest and excitement.

H. E. BATES

The Jacaranda Tree

When Japanese invading forces were nearing the Lower Irrawaddy, the remnants of an English colony in a small Burmese town were called together by the manager of the local rice-mill. A less determined man than Paterson might easily have failed in organizing this small evacuation, because his success was envied and the presence of his native mistress resented. (1034)

Colonel Julian

'He can set down an incident, and it has all the truth, the uniqueness, and also the melancholy of the senses; and his particular power has made him a short story writer unlike any other in this generation. ... In *Colonel Julian* they express the flesh and bone of this fine writer. They are the work of a most independent artist at the height of his gifts.' – C. P. Snow in the *Sunday Times* (1093)

The Purple Plain

'Splendid ... The people whether Burmese or British, are alive and convincing; the emotions are authentic; the countryside is presented with extraordinary vigour ... Mr Bates's writing has a quality rare enough in contemporary fiction.' – *Country Life* (1152)

Love for Lydia

'... a superbly written novel in which beauty and ugliness go side-by-side, and in which all the happiness and the sorrow of young people in love is put in its correct perspective by the maturity and skill of a born story-teller.' – Alan Melville in a B.B.C. broadcast. 'Bates at his best.' – Richard Church in *John O'London's Weekly* (1165)